Thirty-Two *and a* Half Complications

A ROSE GARDNER MYSTERY

Other books by Denise Grover Swank:

Rose Gardner Mysteries
(Humorous Southern mysteries)
TWENTY-EIGHT AND A HALF WISHES
TWENTY-NINE AND A HALF REASONS
THIRTY AND A HALF EXCUSES
FALLING TO PIECES (novella)
THIRTY-ONE AND A HALF REGRETS
THIRTY-TWO AND A HALF COMPLICATIONS
THIRTY-THREE AND A HALF SHENANIGANS
(November 4, 2014)

Chosen Series
(Urban fantasy)
CHOSEN
HUNTED
SACRIFICE
REDEMPTION

On the Otherside Series
(Young adult science fiction/romance)
HERE
THERE

Curse Keepers
(Adult urban fantasy)
THE CURSE KEEPERS
THE CURSE BREAKERS
THE CURSE DEFIERS

New Adult Contemporary Romance
AFTER MATH
REDESIGNED
BUSINESS AS USUAL

Thirty-Two *and a* Half Complications

A ROSE GARDNER MYSTERY

Denise Grover Swank

This book is a work of fiction. References to real people, events, establishments, organizations, or locations are intended only to provide a sense of authenticity, and are used fictitiously. All other characters, and all incidents and dialogue, are drawn from the author's imagination and are not to be construed as real.

Cover Design: Nathalia Suellen
Developmental Edit: Angela Polidoro
Copy Edit: Shannon Page

ISBN: 978-1495354250

Chapter One

Staring down the barrel of a gun was not how I wanted to start my day.

"Everyone put your hands on your heads and lay down on the floor!" the robber shouted, the ski mask over his face muffling his words. Without the gun, it would have been hard to take him seriously. His mask was plastered with pictures of SpongeBob SquarePants.

I started to get to my knees, clutching a deposit bag tight in my fist and cursing Violet under my breath. If I survived this, I was gonna kill my sister. I'd finished a job for a cranky elderly man the previous day, and he'd paid me in cash that still smelled of the dirt he'd buried it in. Nine thousand dollars. Little had I known that the hydrangeas I'd planted were less than six feet away from Henryetta's own version of Fort Knox, otherwise known as the metal box buried in Mr. O'Leary's backyard. Violet had agreed to drop the money off at the bank along with the day's proceeds, but she'd forgotten and left it at the store overnight. So it had fallen on me to make the deposit on my way to my landscaping job this morning.

Besides me, there were five other customers in the small lobby of the Henryetta Bank. Mr. Murphy, an older farmer who'd recently sold his property and moved to town, grumbled as he got down on the floor, his wife Miss Wilma following suit. A middle-aged man and a younger woman I didn't know were also lowering to the floor. But poor Miss Honeybelle, a member of the New Living Hope Revival Church, had recently had knee transplant surgery and was struggling to get to the ground.

"Faster!" Mr. SpongeBob shouted, waving the gun.

I hurried to the old woman's side and tucked my deposit bag under my arm as I grabbed her elbow.

The robber shoved my upper arm with his elbow and I cried out in pain and surprise as I stumbled backward several steps. "What do you think you're doing?" he grunted.

I knew I should have been more scared, but frankly, I was irritated as snot. Rubbing my arm, I glared at him. "She just had her knee replaced a month ago. She can't get to her knees!"

"She will if she wants to live." The cold tone in his voice told me he meant it.

Chills spread up my arms as I helped the shaking woman to the carpet. "It's okay, Miss Honeybelle," I whispered.

"No talking!" Mr. SpongeBob shouted, pointing his gun at me again. "Why are you still up?"

Seething, I lay down on the floor next to the now-crying elderly woman, making sure to put my bag beneath my stomach.

The robber's accomplice, who was wearing a Batman mask, approached the teller's window. His voice shook as he placed a plastic Piggly Wiggly bag on the counter. "Put all the cash in the bag."

The SpongeBob thief placed a foot on my side and gave me a half-hearted kick. "What are you looking at?"

Pain shot through my side but I knew I was lucky. He could have put a lot more force behind that kick. Nevertheless, these guys were starting to get me good and pissed.

I was surprised to see Samantha Jo Wheaton working behind the counter as a bank teller. Last I'd heard, she had a job at Wal-Mart. Her face turned red as she stuffed wads of cash into the plastic bag, her hands trembling. Out of the corner of my eye I tried to take in as many details about the two guys as I could. The Batman guy wore dingy white Nikes. His faded jeans had a worn spot on his left thigh, and he was wearing a gray zippered sweatshirt over a black T-shirt emblazoned with the Jack Daniel's logo. Wisps of dark blond hair poked out from underneath the bottom of his ski mask. The seam on the back of his head was off-center, then ran at a diagonal.

Mr. SpongeBob was wearing scuffed work boots with dried light red mud on the heels along with dark jeans, a light gray T-shirt, and a brown leather jacket. A chain connected to his belt was attached to the bulge in his back pocket.

Before I realized what was happening, he squatted next to me. "Do you know what happened to the curious cat?"

Crap. Bile rose in my throat.

He grabbed my arm and pulled me to my feet, leaving my bag on the floor. "Come on," he grunted as he pushed me toward the open safety deposit vault.

The Batman guy turned toward us, sliding the bag off the counter. "What are you doin', Mick?"

"Why the hell are you usin' my name?" The man next to me smelled of rust and something else I couldn't place. Standing as close to him as I was, it nearly made me gag. "I'm teachin' this one to mind her manners."

The faint sound of sirens filled the nearly silent room.

The Batman guy flinched. "We ain't got time for that. Come on!"

Mr. SpongeBob's grip on my arm tightened, his fingers digging deep. "If you know what's good for ya, you'll keep your mouth shut. Got it?"

Of course, it was at that exact moment when I felt a vision coming on. I'm powerless to stop them and can only let them run their course. They always follow the same pattern: I zone out for a few seconds and see something from the future of the person next to me. Then I return to the present moment and blurt out what I see. My visions are almost always inconvenient, and this proved to be no exception.

Everything turned black, and then I was in a rundown barn, standing next to an old gold-colored car. A man stood next to me, his face puckered into a frown. He looked to be in his early twenties and he had on the same outfit as the guy who was currently wearing the Batman mask. His hair was dark blond and shaggy, hanging slightly past his collar. "How much did we get, Mick?"

"Not enough, dammit." I took a drag from a cigarette, then tossed it on the dirt floor and stomped it with my worn boots. "That rat bastard didn't come through. We need more."

Then I was back in the bank, the robber still clutching my arm.

"You're not gonna get enough money," I gushed out.

"*What*?" he screeched. He dropped my arm and grabbed my face, pinching my cheeks as his angry brown eyes pierced mine. "What do you know that you're not saying?"

I shook my head, speechless.

"Mick! Let's go!" The other thief was already at the glass door, looking outside. The siren was getting closer.

Mr. SpongeBob shoved me to the floor and stomped toward my money bag, snatching it up.

"That's mine!" I shouted, sitting on my sore butt, my hands on the floor behind me.

The smug grin slid off Officer Ernie's face as he turned to look at the front door. "What?"

"That's what I was trying to tell you!" I shouted, getting up and walking over to poor Miss Honeybelle. "They were in the car you parked next to before running in here. A gold Charger with a dent on the front fender."

"*What*?" he screeched and ran outside.

Officer Sprout stood in place, his mouth gaping in shock. He pivoted to take in the room. With his round, freckled face, he looked like he should be in a high school chess club meeting, not investigating a bank robbery.

I pressed my lips together, trying to keep myself from saying something ugly. "I want to report a robbery," I said once I was feeling calmer.

That shook Officer Sprout out of his stupor. "Somebody *already* reported a robbery—or at least the bank's alarm system did. That's why we're here."

"Not just the bank money. They took my deposit bag. I want my money back."

Officer Sprout scowled, as if to rebuke me for making his life more difficult. "Well…I don't know how that works."

"What *do* you know?" Mr. Murphy asked, his contempt obvious.

Officer Ernie burst through the door. "I don't see anything."

I shook my head in disgust. "That's because they left already." I started for the front door, but Ernie blocked my path.

"And where do you think you're goin'?"

"I left my purse in the car, and I need to get my phone so I can call Mason."

He shook his head, his face breaking out in splotchy red marks. "Nobody's leaving this building until we get your statements and look for evidence."

"Aren't you going to go after them?" a man asked.

Everyone swiveled around to look behind the counter. I was surprised to see that Mr. Turner, the bank manager, was standing there with Samantha Jo. He'd been conspicuously absent during the robbery.

"When did you get here?" Mr. Murphy asked, pointing his cane at the middle-aged, balding banker.

He rested his folded hands on his paunch. "I was in the back…taking care of…something."

"You yellow-bellied, snake-eyed coward," Mr. Murphy growled. "You *hid*."

The banker's eyes widened. "I…"

"I need to call my husband," the younger woman said, wiping tears from her cheeks.

The middle-aged man turned to Mr. Murphy. "Why didn't you beat them off with that cane of yours?"

Pandemonium broke out, every one of us voicing our protests while Officer Sprout looked like he was about to take off running and Officer Ernie's ears turned bright red.

I edged over to an empty desk and picked up the phone. "Mason," I said when he answered his cell phone. "You're never gonna guess what happened."

"With you, there's no telling. Are you okay?"

"I'm fine. Mostly." I rubbed my bruised side. "But why are you asking? You don't even know why I'm calling."

"Rose, trouble finds you like a divining rod finds water." I heard the smile in his voice, but then he turned serious. "Where are you and what happened?"

"Do you think you could get away for a little bit?" I asked. "And meet me at the Henryetta Bank?"

"Are you having some kind of trouble at the bank?"

I took in the chaos around me. "You could say that."

Mr. Murphy's voice rose above the others. "I got all my money in this damned place. I better not have lost a penny!"

"Do I hear *shouting*?" Mason asked before switching to his official voice. "What's going on there, Rose?"

"I'll explain when you get here." I sighed as I hung up. Mason was right. This was just another day in the life of Rose Gardner.

Chapter Two

Mason walked through the bank's door fifteen minutes later. I had no doubt he'd have been there sooner if the brace on his leg hadn't slowed him down. He'd broken his leg a few weeks ago while we were evading Crocker and his men in the woods near Henryetta. The doctor had set it with pins and put him in a cast for two weeks, so the brace and the cane he was using with it were a graduation from crutches. Still, it slowed him down. And Mason Deveraux was a man who was always on the go.

His face was taut with worry until he saw me sitting on the metal desk, then it was replaced by relief. "Rose."

I hopped off the desk and met him halfway. He pulled me into a tight hug. "I called Detective Taylor on the way to find out what happened." He leaned back and examined me closely. "Are you really okay?"

Tilting my head to the side, I gave him a frustrated grimace. "I'm fine. Really. Just ticked off that the thieves took my deposit bag. I tried to report the theft to Officer Sprout, but he refused to listen to me…said he didn't know how to take my report."

He grinned. I loved how his smile was slightly lopsided, lifting up ever so slightly more on one side. Funny how I'd never noticed until we started seeing each other, right around the time Crocker broke out of jail. "Violet should have a record of all the checks, and the cash you take in at the shop is minimal. You can get customers to stop payment on the checks and issue you new ones."

Something in my stomach rolled around and tried to dive to the floor. "What about the cash?"

He shrugged. "It might be a total loss unless you recorded the bills' serial numbers. I doubt you'd hit your deductible anyway."

Suddenly, I felt hot and was having a hard time breathing.

Mason's eyes flew open in alarm. "Rose? What's wrong?"

I started to fan myself with my hand. "There was more than the usual amount of cash in the deposit bag, Mason. A lot more."

His voice hardened. "How much?"

"Nine thousand dollars." Feeling lightheaded, I stumbled backward.

Mason grabbed my arm and helped me sit down in the office chair in front of the desk I'd just hopped down from, taking the seat next to me. "What were you doing with that much cash?"

Tears welled in my eyes, but I refused to let them drop. "The big landscaping job Bruce Wayne and I just finished—"

"The retaining wall, trees, and shrubs for Mr. O'Leary?"

I nodded, feeling like I was gonna hyperventilate. "He paid me in cash."

He grabbed my face between his hands, his fingers gently rubbing my cheekbones. "Take a deep breath. It's going to be okay."

I nodded again. But nine thousand dollars was an awful lot of money. Money we needed. Violet had already allocated all the grant money we'd received from the Arkansas Small Business Administration and then some for our expansion into the empty lot next to our existing building. Unexpected expenses had popped up along the way, and we needed every penny we could get. We couldn't afford to lose nine thousand dollars.

"You have a copy of the receipt, right?"

"Yeah."

"Then you're fine."

"Except for the deductible. And our insurance rates will raise."

He frowned, then leaned in and gave me a gentle kiss. "You're forgetting that your bag was taken during a bank robbery. The bank's insurance should cover you one hundred percent. I know my own insurance predicament must have you worried, but I'll eventually get reimbursed, and *so will you.* Stop worrying."

I blinked in relief. Mason was right. He'd been fighting to get a settlement ever since Crocker burned his condo down weeks ago, and he was living with me until it was all sorted out. "Thank you. It's at times like these that I'm particularly glad I have you around."

He laughed. "Because of my legal expertise?"

I shook my head and grinned at him. "That comes in handy, but no." I leaned over the arm of my chair and looped my arms around his neck. "Because you're so calm, it makes me calm too."

His smile turned wicked. "You make me sound boring, but that wasn't the impression I got last night."

A blush rose to my cheeks.

He leaned closer, until his lips were practically brushing my ear. "There's a time for calm, and a time for…"

I lifted my eyebrows. "Not so calm?"

"I had a few other word choices in mind," he teased. "But you're right. I'm supposed to care about my reputation, and someone could hear us."

"I should say," said Miss Mildred, my old across-the-street neighbor, who seemed to have appeared out of thin air and was standing next to us. "I thought you were supposed to be a good example for the citizens of Fenton County, Mr. Deveraux. Not an example of lewd behavior. I can see that Rose's debauched nature has rubbed off on you."

Mason leaned back in his seat and smiled good-naturedly up at the elderly woman. Miss Mildred was eighty-three years old, but nothing slipped passed her. Which made her the perfect president of the neighborhood watch committee, also known as the Busybody Club. She was probably bored to tears since I was no longer in the neighborhood. Who was she spying on now?

"What are you doing here, Miss Mildred?" Mason asked. "How'd you get past the crime scene tape?"

"I'm here to see to it that my money's safe. The fool loan officer Mr. Sullivan's damn near given half the money in the bank away to the riffraff in this town." She shot me a glare, making sure I knew she included me in that category, before turning her annoyance on Mason. "And Officer Ernie wouldn't dare turn me away. I expected to find a crime scene, not your seedy display."

Who was she fooling? She was here to snoop.

"Not to worry, Miss Mildred. Your money's federally insured, so I can assure you that you haven't lost a penny." He chuckled. "And my girlfriend just had a brush with death. You can't fault a man for wanting to confirm she's okay...and that she knows he can't live without her."

Her frown froze, as if she couldn't think of any negative way to spin his statement...a first for her.

"What about your husband?" Mason asked. "I bet you two were inseparable when he came back from the war."

The elderly woman's cheeks turned pink.

Miss Mildred was actually blushing.

I almost gasped in surprise.

"He was a sailor, wasn't he? At the end of the Second World War?" Mason asked, wrapping an arm around my shoulder and pulling me closer as he spoke. The arm of the chair hit the spot on my ribs where I'd been kicked, so I shifted slightly. "I hear it's hard for a young girl to resist a man in those Navy whites." He grinned at me. "Maybe I should join the Navy."

"Don't you dare," I whispered.

Miss Mildred tugged at her sleeve, avoiding eye contact. "He had been gone a long time." Then, as though remembering who she was talking to, she stiffened. "Shouldn't you be investigating the robbery, Mr. Deveraux?"

He grinned and relaxed his grip on my shoulder. "Nope. The fine officers of the Henryetta PD have it under control. I'm here to make sure my girl's okay. I'll take over when they're done."

She gave her head a little shake, then pulled back her shoulders. "Fine officers, my foot." She cast a scowl at me. "They never did a blessed thing when I called them about *her*."

"I can assure you that they'd arrest her if they could find the evidence to warrant it," Mason said, grinning.

I pulled away from him. "Hey!"

Miss Mildred walked away, muttering under her breath about my wicked ways.

I turned sideways and glared at Mason. "The police would arrest me if they *could*? And why would you sound happy about that?"

His grin turned wicked again. "I like thinking about you in handcuffs."

My eyes flew open. "Mason!"

He laughed. "She's harmless, Rose. I don't know why you let her get you so worked up."

"You try living across the street from her for twenty-four years, and then we'll revisit the topic of how harmless she is."

"I'd rather spend every minute with you." He kissed me again, then pulled back with a sigh. "But the duties that accompany the never-ending job of an underpaid, underappreciated county attorney tend to interfere with that."

I smoothed out a wrinkle on his shirt with my thumb, wishing we could go back to the farm so I could take it off of him. "You love every minute of your job and you know it."

"Almost every minute." He gave me another peck on the lips and stood. "Except for the minutes it takes me away from you. I cleared my schedule for the next hour. Let's get out of here. I want to spend time with you, but not in this mess."

I looked around, taking in the sight of the still-chaotic bank lobby. "Don't I have to give my statement? I've got details about the robbers that I need to share."

"Not until Detective Taylor shows up. When I called him, he told me that there was something he needed to wrap up on another case before heading over here. I'll tell Ernie that I'm taking you into my personal custody in the meantime," he smirked. "And maybe we can borrow a pair of handcuffs for good measure. I'll be doing a public service by protecting the innocent citizens of Fenton County from a whirlwind of trouble."

"Very funny," I said sarcastically, but I couldn't hold back my laughter. I cast a glance at my second least favorite police officer—Detective Taylor being the winner in that category. Officer Ernie was trying to break up an argument between Mr. Murphy and the bank manager, reaching for the cane the older man was beating the younger one with. "Officer Ernie isn't going to like it."

Mason straightened his back, instantly looking more official. "Officer Ernie will have to deal with it."

As I'd expected, the Henryetta police officer frowned his disapproval, especially after an errant cane swing from Mr. Murphy hit his arm, but he didn't try to stop Mason. Most intelligent people with even half a brain wouldn't. After Mason took over the assistant DA position last spring, he quickly convinced most of the town he was someone to fear. Which is why I received applause when I told him off in front of a group of courthouse employees while I was serving on a jury. I was one of the few people with the gumption to stand up to him, and by the time the case I'd been a juror on was settled, Mason and I were friends.

Which had been a huge sore spot for my old boyfriend Joe. For more reasons than I'd understood at the time.

But just as we were slipping out the front doors of the bank, a black sedan pulled into the parking lot. Mason stopped in his tracks when Detective Taylor got out and started walking toward us.

My toast from breakfast turned into concrete in my stomach. "So much for escaping." A brisk November breeze lifted the hem of my jacket, and I reached down to flatten it against my jeans.

"I'm going to ask him to take your statement first. I want to be there when you give it."

I slipped my hand in his and squeezed in gratitude. He knew how nervous I got whenever the police questioned me. Especially after Henryetta's finest made me their number-one suspect after my mother was murdered months ago. They'd spent a good amount of time trying to find enough incriminating evidence to arrest me instead of looking for the real killer. But I also suspected he was impatient for more details about what had happened in the bank that morning.

He dropped my hand and left me by the doors, meeting the detective halfway down the sidewalk. They talked in voices too low for me to hear, and then Taylor shot me a scowl and headed my way, Mason by his side.

"*Ms. Gardner*," he began, and I had no delusions about why he was being so formal. It could be entirely attributed to the intimidating presence behind him. "Mr. Deveraux would like me to take your statement before he heads back to court." While his words were polite, there was an undercurrent of hostility in his tone, making me even more grateful for Mason's presence. "Let's go inside and see if there's somewhere to take your statement."

I followed him back into the chaos without saying anything. While Officer Ernie had successfully wrestled the cane from Mr. Murphy, his forehead now sported a red welt. Miss Wilma dabbed her eyes with a tissue, shouting protests of police brutality. Taylor walked past the commotion as if it were an everyday affair, stopping in front of the bank manager.

"Is there anywhere quiet—" he cast a quick glance toward the shouting match four feet away "—I can take this witness to interview her?"

Mr. Burns's face was red and he appeared pretty flustered as he looked around. "Uh… yeah… Norman Sullivan didn't come in this morning. You can use his office."

Taylor's eyes widened. "The loan officer? Did he call in sick?"

"No. He just didn't show up."

"Does he usually do that?" Mason asked.

Concern flickered in Mr. Burns's eyes. "No."

Detective Taylor pulled his notebook out of his pocket and flipped it open to jot something down. "I'm going to need Sullivan's address and phone number."

The bank manager nodded, then pointed to a small office to the side. "I'll get it for you. That's his office over there."

Mason led the way to the office and motioned for me to sit in a guest chair. Taylor, who pushed in past me, ignoring Mason's well-mannered gesture, circled the desk and sat in the loan officer's chair. My gaze swept the room as I sat down, and I noticed Mr. Sullivan's family photos were missing. I'd spent a good twenty minutes examining them several months ago when I'd been in this office applying for a small business loan.

Taylor shifted his chair and clicked his pen, narrowing his gaze on me. "And what was your purpose of bein' at the bank this morning?"

I looked at Mason for reassurance. He stood against the wall with his arms crossed. His face was expressionless, but he nodded his head. The last time I'd been questioned was after Jonah's mother had tried to kill me. While I'd been completely innocent in that case, Detective Taylor had made his extreme dislike for me crystal clear. "I was making a deposit for our business."

"The Gardner Sisters Nursery?"

I nodded. "Yeah."

"So tell me what happened at the bank."

"I was standing in line waiting to make my deposit when two men wearing ski masks—one decorated with SpongeBob, the other with Batman—burst in. They had guns and they pointed them at us. SpongeBob seemed to be in charge. He told all the customers in the lobby to get on the floor. But Miss Honeybelle had trouble getting down because of her knee replacement surgery last month."

He looked up. "So what happened?"

"I walked over to help her, but the guy didn't like that we were taking so long and he got grumpy."

Taylor started writing again, but Mason's jaw twitched.

"You need to tell him everything, Rose." Mason's voice was tight. "What did he do?"

I felt my cheeks redden. "He shoved me when I tried to help her, but I convinced him that she couldn't get down on her own, so he let me help her."

"Then what happened?" Taylor asked.

"The man with the Batman mask handed Samantha Jo Wheaton a plastic Piggly Wiggly bag and told her to fill it with cash."

Taylor scribbled his notes. "And how do you know Samantha Jo Wheaton?"

"She's a new bank teller here. But that's not how I originally know her. We went to school together. Plus everyone in Henryetta knows she burned her husband's fishing boat in their front yard last year. The married men were afraid to cheat on their wives for a spell, and the single men were afraid to date her after her divorce was finalized. She used to work at Wal-Mart."

"So are you friends or not?"

"No, more like acquaintances."

"Uh-huh," he grunted, writing his thoughts. "What else can you tell me?"

"I took note of what they were wearing while the Batman guy was getting the money. He had on jeans, a Jack Daniel's T-shirt, a gray fleece jacket, and worn Nikes." I looked over at Mason, who gave me an encouraging smile and a nod.

"And a Batman ski mask?"

"Yeah. Now that I think about it, I saw some of those Batman hats at the Piggly Wiggly last week when I was there. The SpongeBob one too."

Taylor looked up, suddenly more engaged in the conversation. "Now that's a bit of a coincidence, isn't it?"

I shrugged, uncomfortable with being on the receiving end of his cold, calculating attention. "I was there shopping. I thought about getting one for my nephew, but I didn't realize they were adult sizes until I picked one up and noticed the seams were off. The seam on the Batman hat the robber wore was catawampus. I'd bet my right arm it came from there."

"You don't say." He turned back to his notebook. "And the other guy?"

I rattled off my description, unnerved now, which probably made me seem guilty, although of what, I didn't know. I'd been at the wrong place at the wrong time. The only thing I could be accurately accused of was having extremely bad luck.

"What happened next?"

I squirmed. "I was purposely trying to take note of any identifying details about the robbers, and the guy in the SpongeBob mask didn't like it. He pulled me up off the floor and started to take me to the safety deposit box room. But we heard sirens and the other guy told him they had to go. He called him Mick."

"Mick? Anything else? Did he say a last name?" the detective asked.

"No."

"Anything else you remember about him?"

"When his sleeve got close to my face, I smelled rust."

"Was it a faint odor or a strong one?"

I thought about it for a moment, then cringed when I remembered him grabbing my face. "Pretty strong. He told me not to tell anyone else about what they looked like. Then he picked up my deposit bag off the floor and left. I watched them get into their getaway car right before the police showed up. It was an older Dodge Charger. Gold. Officers Ernie and Sprout ran right past them on their way into the bank. But when I tried to tell Ernie, he wouldn't listen. He pointed his gun at me and told me to get on the floor."

Mason's eyes widened. "So the police let them get away." It wasn't posed as a question.

I sighed. "By the time Mr. Murphy and I got a chance to tell them, the car was already gone."

"Did you get a license plate number?" Detective Taylor asked, his mouth puckered in irritation.

I shook my head. "No. I only saw the front of the car, and it didn't have a license plate."

Taylor looked up and quirked an eyebrow. "You have to admit that it looks suspicious that you've been dead center in a lot of illegal *occurrences* in Henryetta over the last few months."

Mason's crossed arms dropped to his sides. "Are you calling her a suspect?" he asked in his no-nonsense voice, the one that made people quake in their shoes.

Taylor cleared his throat. "No. I'm just saying it's an odd coincidence. You can't deny it, Deveraux."

Mason pressed his lips into a tight line and crossed his arms again.

Taylor gave me a sideways glance, the tiniest bit of a smirk in his eyes. "And how much money was in that bag of yours, Ms. Gardner?"

"About three hundred dollars in checks." I took a breath, feeling like I was gonna throw up. "And nine thousand in cash."

The detective's pen stopped mid-stroke and he looked up at me with narrowed eyes. "Why'd you have so much cash?"

"Mr. O'Leary paid me yesterday for a job we'd finished at his place."

"And he paid you in cash." His mouth twisted to the side. "That's an awful lot of cash."

I shrugged, uneasiness crawling up my back and burrowing in the base of my head. "It was a big job."

"Nine thousand exactly? Not a dollar more or less?"

Mason took a step forward, his voice deep and commanding. "What are you getting at, Taylor?"

"It just seems odd that it's such a round number." He shrugged. "It's an observation. No more."

Mason's jaw twitched again, but his face was expressionless. "You seem to be making a lot of unnecessary observations."

The police officer shrugged, nonplussed. "Just doing my job, Mr. ADA. You're griping all the time about us being sloppy and not asking enough questions." He flourished the notebook he'd been writing in at Mason. "This is me doing my job."

Mason's eyes darkened.

I shifted my weight, feeling the need to break the tension. "I had initially given him a higher quote, but Mr. O'Leary insisted he wouldn't give me the job if it was a penny more than nine thousand." I took a breath. "We weren't going to make much of a profit anyway, and we kept running into problems from start to finish. Now I'm gonna have a hard time paying Bruce Wayne's paycheck." All the more reason I needed to recover the cash.

"And do you routinely deal in cash?" Taylor asked.

Mason looked furious. "It's none of your damn business how Rose handles her money for the shop, Taylor."

The detective glanced at Mason with mock innocence. "I agree. I'm merely tryin' to gather all the facts is all."

We all knew that was a bald-faced lie, but there was no use protesting.

"And do you know anything else that might help us in this investigation?"

I *did*, but I couldn't tell anyone who didn't know about my ability…and I especially couldn't tell him. "No," I said, my tone making it clear that it was my final comment.

Taylor stuck his notebook inside his coat pocket. "Well, alrighty then. I'm gonna get the other statements. You're free to go, but if I have any other questions, I'll look you up." He cast a derisive look at Mason. "Looks like I know where to find you."

I frowned when I realized Mason had missed the detective's sneer. "Yeah."

Mason watched Taylor walk out of the office. "One of these days, the Henryetta Police Department is going to get cleaned out just like the sheriff's department was," he said. I could hear the lingering hurt in his voice. We'd helped uncover a leak in the sheriff's department after Crocker's escape, and unfortunately, it had been Mason's friend Chief Deputy Dimler.

I made a face. "Don't count on it. According to Aunt Bessie, they've been inept since before I was born." The lack of photos in the office unnerved me. "Don't you think it's strange Mr. Sullivan didn't come in today of all days?"

"It definitely seems like more than a coincidence."

I stood and moved around the side of the desk, examining the walls. "I was in his office this past summer when I applied for my business loan. He had photos of his wife and his son at the boy's high school graduation and another from his family trip to Cancun the year before. It seems odd that they're gone."

Mason turned to take in the room. "It most certainly does. I'll be sure to have Taylor follow up on it."

I stared out the window at the parking lot, my eyes finding the empty space where the getaway car had been parked. "Mason, there's something I couldn't tell Detective Taylor."

His head jerked toward me. "What?"

"I had a vision. While the guy with the SpongeBob mask was holding my face."

His eyes widened. "He was holding your face? Why didn't you tell Taylor that?"

I waved my hand. "That's not important. The vision is. The robber was in an old barn next to the getaway car, and he was talking to his accomplice. But the guy wasn't wearing the Batman mask anymore. I saw his face."

"You're kidding." He shook his head, dazed. "What did he look like?"

"He had long scraggly blond hair. He was pale-skinned and looked like he was in his late twenties, early thirties."

"What else did you see?"

"Nothing really, but the robber said they didn't get enough money. That the 'rat bastard'"—I used air quotes—"hadn't come through and they needed more."

Mason watched me for several seconds and then scooped me up in a hug, giving me a hard kiss. "You have no idea how helpful that is."

"How?" I asked, confused.

"First, if they didn't get enough money, they're probably going to rob somewhere else."

"Oh. *That* can't be good."

"No, but now we're on the alert."

"Yeah, I guess you're right."

"Second, I can have you look at mug shots to see if you can identify the guy. And third, now we know they either had an inside man or an accomplice who didn't come through. While I hate to jump to conclusions, Norman Sullivan is definitely suspect."

I found it hard to believe that the loan officer had anything to do with the bank robbery. He'd been so friendly and helpful in our meeting. But I had to admit that the circumstantial evidence was piling up. Still, circumstantial evidence had indicated Bruce Wayne and I were guilty of crimes we hadn't committed. In my eyes, Mr. Sullivan was innocent until proven guilty. "There's a problem, though," I said, sighing. "You can't use any of it. It's from a vision."

"Let me worry about that. Can you swing by my office for a bit and look at the mug shots?"

"Sure, but I need to go to the nursery first to break the news to Violet. And I suspect it's not going to go over well."

He lifted my chin and gave me a soft smile. "Hey, it wasn't your fault."

No, if it was anyone's fault, it was Violet's. But that had never stopped her from casting the blame on me, and I suspected this time would be no exception.

There was going to be hell to pay and Violet was gonna make me write a personal check.

Chapter Three

This was one time when I was sorry to be right.

"What do you mean they took all of our money?" my sister shouted, gripping the counter at the register of our nursery so hard I worried it would snap.

"While I know you've been working night and day on this Holiday Open House—" I gestured to the interior of our store, which looked like a Christmas bomb had exploded inside it "—I know you haven't lost your understanding of the English language." I took a step closer. "The robbers took the deposit bag. It's gone unless the police find the two guys who did this. And even if they do, we might be sunk since we didn't write down the serial numbers."

She looked down her perfect nose at me and tossed her perfect blond hair over her shoulder. "And you just gave it to them?"

My mouth dropped open in shock, then I closed it and shook my head. "Yes, Violet. That's *exactly* what I did. I said, 'Here Mr. Bank Robber, please take all nine thousand dollars that I worked my hiney off to raise.' Because the gun he was pointing at my face wasn't enough incentive."

Her face went ashen. "*Gun*?"

"It was a bank robbery, Violet. They typically involve guns."

"Rose, you could have been killed," she said, her voice quiet now, subdued.

"Well, thank you for finally figuring that out."

"Are you okay?"

I looked up at the ceiling and took a deep breath before leveling my gaze on her. "I'm fine," I said, my voice heavy with resignation. "No one was hurt." I subconsciously rubbed my side. "Well, other than where he kicked me."

She walked around the counter and wrapped her arms around me, her body shaking. "I'm sorry. I shouldn't have reacted that way. It's just…the money…"

Besides funding our paychecks, we'd been counting on using that money to pay for a shipment of Christmas trees. We'd gotten a special deal on them, but there was a catch—it was pay on delivery, and we were committed. The delivery was set for the Wednesday before Thanksgiving. Less than a week away and now we didn't have enough money. "I can make do if I have to go a couple of weeks without a paycheck, and we can cancel the Christmas tree order."

"We can't cancel." Her voice rose. "We're committed to it."

I stepped away and rubbed my temple. "We'll figure something out."

"There's nothing else to figure out. Given how much money we've invested in growing the business, we were barely able to scrape together enough for the trees and the Holiday Open House in the first place. There's nothing left for the paychecks and now it will be hard to pay for those trees too." Violet leaned her back against the counter. "What about Mason?"

I froze. "What about Mason?"

"He's living in your house, rent free—"

"No."

Her eyes widened as she continued to plead her case. "But I'm sure he'd be more than happy to help—"

"No!" I said firmly. "Like I said, I can go without a paycheck. I'm not asking Mason for help."

"Rose, be reasonable."

"I'm being perfectly reasonable. And I'm not asking him. This is *our* business. We've already asked him to go above and beyond by looking at our legal papers for the Small Business Administration grant and our agreement with the contractor." I knew I should just tell her that Mason didn't have the money to loan us, but since she already found him lacking because of his work schedule, I could only imagine what she'd say if she knew about his financial situation.

"Joe helped us a lot, and you had no problem with *that*." There was a hateful tone in her voice.

I put my hands on my hips, fighting tears. "I can't believe you brought him up."

Her face softened and she spanned the space between us, grabbing my arm. "I wouldn't ask you, but we're desperate, Rose. We're in worse shape than I thought. I haven't been totally honest with you. It's not just our salaries and the trees on the line..." She took a deep breath, guilt twisting her mouth. "This whole Holiday Open House has gotten out of hand."

I wasn't surprised. When Violet first mentioned the idea of having the open house, I gave her my full support. But when we got the several hundred thousand dollars in grant money, Violet's plans had grown proportionately. Too bad she hadn't read the fine print: the grant money was strictly allocated for the expansion of our store, and we would be in deep doodoo if we used it for anything else. She'd bought artificial trees of every variety and thousands of dollars in decorations. But by the time she realized the limitations of the loan, her plans for the open house scheduled for Black Friday were already well on their way, and the Christmas trees had been ordered. We were good and stuck.

In spite of the mess, I firmly believed the open house was still a good idea. She planned on having holiday refreshments and a violinist was coming to play Christmas music. Prizes would be awarded to random customers throughout the day, and I knew the Henryetta Garden Club had planned their November meeting around the event. The women in Henryetta loved Violet—which was one of the reasons she was in charge of the store while I handled the landscaping side of the business—and the event had even been written up in *Banner News*, the newspaper of neighboring Magnolia County. It was going to be *the* business holiday event of southern Arkansas, and I felt confident that it would firmly establish us as *the* nursery of Fenton and Lafayette counties—quite an accomplishment since we were only a few months old. But only if we could afford to pay for everything.

"We'll figure something out," I finally said. "Besides, the bank should eventually reimburse us."

Violet worried her lip between her teeth. "But you didn't make the deposit, right?"

"Well, no… But Mason thinks they will."

"I'm gonna call our insurance company to see what they say."

"Okay. I'd better get to the job site. Bruce Wayne probably thinks I've wandered off into the hills again." In all the excitement, I'd almost forgotten all about it, but we needed the money and I couldn't exactly afford to slack off.

Her head jerked up. "Don't even joke about that. You scared me half to death when I found out that you and Mason had been traipsing in the woods with a maniac after you."

"Well, we don't have to worry about *that* maniac anymore." Not after I'd shot and killed him in self-defense.

"Not that particular maniac, but there seem to be plenty more waiting to come after you."

I took a step toward the door. "And on that cheery note, I'm out of here."

"Rose. Wait."

I turned back to face her.

"I have a huge favor to ask you."

Violet had asked all kinds of favors from me lately. This had to be a doozy if she was calling it huge. "What is it?"

"I've been driving myself crazy with the preparations for this event and throw in the fact that I've moved back into Momma's tiny house with the kids…well, I was wondering if you'd consider hosting Thanksgiving dinner this year."

My eyes widened in surprise. "Oh."

"You're living in Dora's big farmhouse now, which means you have plenty of room. Even more room than I had in my house with Mike. And I can bring things too." She tilted her head to the side and gave me a pleading smile. "Please?"

Violet had hosted Thanksgiving for seven years, ever since she and Mike had gotten married. But they were separated now, and she'd had to give up the house she loved to move into Momma's house after I moved out of it. There was no reason to expect her to take the responsibility of hosting every year. It was long past time for me to step up. "Sure. Of course. I'd love to do it."

"Thank you." Her eyes turned glassy. "And I'm sorry about earlier. You know I love you, right?"

I gave her a sad smile. "Yeah, I know." Only it wasn't enough to make up for all the ugliness she'd shown me over the last few months. Still, she was my sister, and nothing could stand in the way of that. At least nothing that had happened yet. "I love you too."

After I'd climbed into my truck and pulled out of the parking lot, I called Mason. "Do I have to come in right away? I really need to go check on Bruce Wayne. We have a big job today, ripping out a bunch of bushes and a few small trees. I was planning to join him after depositing the money at the bank this morning, so I'm really late."

"I was about to call you. My boss can't be bothered to sit in on a deposition that he himself set up, so I have to go." His frustration was unmistakable. Mason was the assistant district attorney in title, but he did far more work than the actual DA, which was part of the reason he worked so many late nights. "Would you be able to meet me for a late lunch?"

"In your office again?"

"Yeah," he sighed. "I'm sorry."

"Mason, it's your job. I would never begrudge you that."

"I know, Rose. But the DA keeps shoving more and more responsibility on me, which is making it hard for me to spend as much time with you as I'd like." His voice lowered. "I've waited months to be with you, so *I* begrudge the fact my job is getting in the way." He paused. "I would consider quitting, but I'd have to leave Fenton County to find another job. I know you're committed to your business and the farm, and I'm not about to move away from you."

"Mason." My voice broke. "I don't want you to make yourself miserable because of me."

"I'm not miserable because of you. Don't think that." I heard his frustration again.

"It's okay," I assured him. "You know I understand your position, and I don't want you to move away from me either. Especially now. I'll bring you lunch and we'll eat in your office." I smiled to myself and said in a husky voice, "And we can shut your door."

"I like that thought," he said. "It's the only thing that's going to get me through this deposition."

I stopped at a stop sign and looked down at my faded jeans, worn long-sleeved T-shirt, and jacket. "Too bad I won't have time to change into something nicer before I come see you." Of course, he'd already seen me today, so it wouldn't exactly be a surprise.

"Rose, you could walk into my office wearing rags and you'd still be the most beautiful woman I've ever seen."

I laughed. "You're just trying to butter me up because you want me to bring you apple pie from Merilee's Café."

"How can you say that?" he asked in mock dismay. "You *know* I think you're beautiful. And if you don't, then I'm falling down on my job."

"So does this mean you don't want the apple pie?" I teased.

He laughed. "Now, don't get hasty."

Chuckling, I shook my head. "Any other requests?"

"Surprise me. The rest is superfluous as long as I have you."

My heart overflowed with emotion. I knew he meant every word. I suspected he'd go the rest of his life without another piece of pie if it meant being with me. "When should I come by? Does one work?"

"Can you make it one-thirty?"

"Done. I'll see you later, Mr. Assistant DA."

"Tell Bruce Wayne I said hi."

I hung up, already missing him, which was crazy since I'd woken up next to him in bed and then saw him again at the bank. Turned out I was a greedy woman. I wanted every moment I could get with Mason. I had half a mind to go kick the district attorney's behind myself.

When I pulled up in front of the Timberland house ten minutes later, Bruce Wayne was wrestling with an overgrown shrub. He'd already dug up two others without me. He stuck his shovel in the ground and looked up at me through his shaggy bangs. "Everything okay, Miss Rose?"

Bruce Wayne had to be ten years older than me, putting him in his mid-thirties, but he still insisted on calling me Miss.

We had first become acquainted when I was on the jury for his murder trial, which was incidentally when I'd first met Mason, who'd been the prosecutor for the case. I'd had a vision of the real murderer, but I couldn't tell anyone that, other than my then-boyfriend, Joe. A state police detective at the time, he'd encouraged me to trust the system. But I knew what it felt like to be suspected for a murder that I hadn't committed, so I'd done everything in my power to make sure Bruce Wayne didn't pay for someone else's crime.

And he never forgot that.

So when I was desperate for manual laborers to help with a big landscaping job at Jonah's New Living Hope Revival Church, Bruce Wayne had agreed to help. And the huge surprise to all of us was that he had a really good eye for landscaping…and he loved it. He had become a loyal and dedicated employee, but more importantly, a friend.

"I'm sorry I'm late, and I'm sorry I didn't call," I said. "This morning got a bit crazy." I gave him a goofy grin. "I was in a bank robbery."

Bruce Wayne took his hands off the shovel and stood up straighter—not straight, it was a rare day when he didn't hunch his shoulders—but still noticeably more erect. "Are you okay? What happened?"

"They took the deposit bag, Bruce Wayne." I grabbed the edge of my jacket and twisted it in my hand. "It was filled with all the O'Leary money."

"Oh, shit." He grimaced. "Excuse my language."

"No." I laughed even though my eyes were tearing up. "I think this warrants an 'oh, shit.'"

A goofy grin tipped up his mouth.

My own smile slid into a frown. "Violet has overextended us with the open house, so we're in trouble."

Bruce Wayne squirmed. "If you can't afford to give me my paycheck—"

"You stop right there, Bruce Wayne Decker," I said, my voice firm. "Paying you is at the tip-top of our list of priorities, and I won't hear another word about it. Understood?" I didn't know how I'd pay him, but I'd figure out a way.

He looked down at his feet. "Yes, ma'am."

I pushed out a huge breath. "Since David lost his job at the Piggly Wiggly last week, I'm sure you need every penny you can get. Especially with the holidays coming."

He shrugged. "So what are you gonna do?"

I grabbed the shovel Bruce Wayne had brought for me, wanting to take my frustration out on the roots of the shrub. "I don't know yet, but I need to come up with something fast. Ideally, I'd like to get my money back, but *that* seems unlikely. Unless…"

Bruce Wayne jerked his gaze up in surprise. "I don't like the look on your face, Miss Rose."

"If we can find out who robbed the bank, I might be able to get the money back."

"*We*?" he asked, grumbling. "You got a mouse in your pocket?"

"Very funny." I headed for the shrub next to the one Bruce Wayne was strong-arming and slammed the shovel into the ground with my foot. "You and I both know you still have some connections to shady characters in Fenton County."

He shook his head. "No, ma'am. I ain't gettin' involved. Half of Crocker's boys—the ones that are still hanging around—have it out for me."

"What about Scooter and Skeeter Malcolm?"

Bruce Wayne pressed his lips together.

"Can't you just ask around? See if anyone knows anything?"

He scowled. "I'll think about it, okay? No more pressuring."

I flashed him a grin. "Fair enough."

"How'd Violet overextend herself, if you don't mind me bein' nosy?"

"She's spread us out too thin by trying to grow the business too big, too fast, not leaving us with enough financial wiggle room in case something bad happened."

"Like gettin' your money stolen in a bank robbery."

"Yeah," I sighed.

"Sounds like my dad," he muttered.

It was my turn to jerk up in surprise. While I hadn't actually met Bruce Wayne's parents, I'd seen them in the courtroom during his trial. They'd seemed like nice enough people, although boring as milk toast. I still had a hard time accepting that they'd washed their hands of him. "Your father seems way too conservative for that."

He shook his head. "Russell isn't my birth father. I was just two when Momma married him, so she gave me his last name. My dad is at the Tucker Unit with the Arkansas Department of Corrections."

"*Oh.*" That explained so much.

"Yeah." Bruce Wayne pried up part of the shrub with his shovel. "My dad had too many pies and not enough fingers." He looked up at the roof. "Or was it too many fingers and not enough pies?"

I shrugged.

"In any case, this reminds me of when I was a kid and my dad was actually out of prison for a little while. In the weeks before he was arrested again—the one that put him away for good—he was juggling too many things and it caught up with him. He didn't have a backup plan. Yeah, that's it. Juggling, not pies." He paused. "Anyways, it sounds a bit like Miss Violet. No offense intended, of course."

"None taken." And besides, he had a point.

He looked me in the eye. "If you decide to start diggin' into this, be careful. You know you have a penchant for pissing off *shady characters*."

I nodded, since there was no use denying the truth.

We worked in silence for several minutes before Bruce Wayne cleared his throat. "My father used to lord it over me that my real dad was a good-for-nothing piece of white trash."

I waited for him to say something more. He rarely shared information about his personal life, let alone his past. I felt honored that he was comfortable enough with me to do so, but I also knew he wasn't a man to be rushed. Information came out in its own sweet time with Bruce Wayne.

"When I first got in trouble, he declared that the apple don't fall far from the tree." He jammed the shovel into the dirt with more force than he usually used. "He used a belt to drive home his point."

I kept shoveling and when he didn't say anything for nearly a minute, I decided it was safe to talk. Since he was giving me the gift of sharing his past, I felt safe sharing my own story with someone who would understand. "My momma wasn't my birth mother. Only I didn't find out until after she died. My daddy had left my momma with the intention of marrying a woman named Dora. That's my birth mother. She was pregnant with me when he walked out on my momma." I swallowed, trying to wet my dry mouth. I couldn't believe how nervous I was about telling him my story. "My momma *hated* me. After I found out about Dora, I found a photo of her holding me when I was a baby. Turns out that I kind of look like her, so I'm sure Momma didn't care for the reminder. My daddy only came back to her after Dora died, and he brought me with him. He did it for Violet. So I understand what it's like for a parent to hate you for no good reason other than who provided part of your DNA." I stopped and waited for Bruce Wayne to look up at me. "I understand."

He nodded and pressed his lips together. "I can see that you do."

We worked in silence for a bit longer, but I kept thinking about everything Bruce Wayne had told me. His family had deserted him shortly before his murder arrest, which they'd used as an excuse to completely seal the door on their relationship. The only person he had left was his best friend David. At least I still had Violet, even if she wasn't perfect. "Bruce Wayne, what are you doin' for Thanksgiving?"

"Uh...nothing. Probably going to Denny's in Magnolia with David."

"I want you to come to Thanksgiving dinner at my place."

"Uh..."

"Give me one good reason why you can't come."

He didn't answer.

"Then it's settled." I smiled, finally feeling happy about my first Thanksgiving dinner. "David's invited too."

"What about Mason?"

"Mason will love to have you there." And I had no doubt that it was true. He would welcome them both. That's one of the things I loved about Mason. While Joe looked down on Bruce Wayne as a man with a criminal record, Mason saw the same potential in him that I recognized. No, Mason wouldn't be an issue.

It was Violet who worried me.

Chapter Four

Several hours later I stood at the entrance to Mason's office, holding our lunch in two paper bags.

He was sitting hunched over a notepad on his desk, his pen in mid-stroke, when he sensed me in the doorway. A warm smile spread across his face. "I thought I smelled something good."

I walked over to him and set the bags on the one small empty spot on his desk. "I know you're smelling Merilee's pork chops and not me. I've been digging up shrubs."

He glanced up at me with a hungry look. "I thought you promised me a closed-door lunch."

My stomach quivered. I loved how he could set me aflutter with nothing more than a look and a few words. "I guess you're wanting me to shut the door then?" I teased.

"Yes."

I turned around and closed it, then whirled around to face him. "I'm hungry."

"So am I." His voice was low and sexy.

The fluttering in my stomach increased. "Mason, your secretary is right outside that door!"

"May I remind you that *you* were the one to suggest the closed door?" He stood and hobbled toward me, then pulled me into his arms, his mouth hovering a half-inch from mine. "We can be quiet." He kissed me and my knees went weak, which almost made me forget how hungry I was until my stomach growled loud enough for him to hear.

He lifted his head and laughed. "Your stomach has spoken. Let's eat. So you brought me pork chops?"

"It's your favorite, right?"

Mason gave me a quick peck on the mouth and took my hand. "You spoil me, Rose."

"Isn't that a girlfriend's job?"

"Well, you do it *exceptionally* well."

I grinned as we sat down and parceled out the food. "How'd the deposition go?"

He groaned. "I'd rather talk about your morning."

"I don't know that mine went much better." I handed him a napkin and plastic ware. "Violet didn't take the news about the money very well."

"Then Violet should have made the deposit last night like she was supposed to."

I glanced up at him in surprise.

"What?" he asked, stabbing the lettuce in the salad that went with his pork chops. "I pay attention to how you run the nursery. Violet handles the store and the books, including the deposits. You handle the landscaping jobs, deliveries, and collecting money from the job sites."

He *had* paid attention. "She asked me to host Thanksgiving dinner this year, and I said yes. I hope that's okay."

"That depends on whether you agreed because you *wanted* to host it or because she guilted you into it."

I lifted my club sandwich. "I wanted to do it. It's going to be our first Thanksgiving together." I offered him a soft smile. "I'd rather have it at the farm than at Momma's house."

"You know," he said, scooping up a spoonful of mashed potatoes. "It's telling how quickly you stopped calling it *your* home and started calling it your *momma's* house. You made the switch practically minutes after you decided to move to the farm."

I hadn't thought about it, but he was right.

He lifted his fork. "I'm just glad—for your sake—that you decided not to sell the farm."

Me too, even though we could have used the money for the nursery.

Mason grinned. "I love the idea of having Thanksgiving dinner at the farm, but you know I've existed on take-out for nearly a decade and can barely boil an egg. I'm not sure how much help I'll be."

"Violet's going to bring some dishes too."

He hesitated. "Would you mind if my mother came? This could be a good opportunity for her to visit. She's mentioned coming down to help me find a place to live once I get my settlement, and I think they're finally close to cutting a check. She can start screening places."

His words sobered me. After the Crocker mess died down, I'd suggested he move in with me until he found a new place. We'd never intended for it to be a permanent situation, but the thought of him moving out made me sad.

I forced a smile. "Of course. I love your mother." And I did. I'd met her twice now. The first time was before Mason and I started dating, when I was still with Joe. She'd been so kind to me, a sharp contrast to Joe's mother, whom I met the following night. The second time I met Mrs. Deveraux was when Mason was in the hospital after our final showdown with Daniel Crocker. She'd pulled me into a hug and thanked me for saving him, tears running down her cheeks. Mrs. Deveraux had already lost her husband and daughter. I couldn't stand the thought of her being home alone for the holiday. "Do you think she'd like to stay with us?"

He smiled. "I'm sure she'd love that. I'll ask her."

"I invited someone else too." I paused. "Well, two someones. Bruce Wayne and David."

Mason studied me for a moment. "Bruce Wayne is always welcome. Besides, it's your house, Rose, you don't need my permission."

"I know, but it involves you too."

"It sounds like it's turning into a party." He beamed at me, happiness radiating from him. "I like it."

"I guess you're right." I laughed. "And I like it too."

We finished our lunch, making small talk about my current landscaping job and which type of cranberries we preferred for Thanksgiving dinner. (Mason liked real berries and I liked cranberry Jello salad.) To my relief, he purposely avoided all mention of the bank robbery. The entire incident was catching up with me and my stomach was in knots.

I only ate half my sandwich and Mason—being the observant man he was—noticed. "Are you not feeling well? You were starving when you got here and you always have a healthy appetite after working at a job site."

I pulled his apple pie out of the bag and set it on the desk. "I'm fine. It's just nerves." Between the bank robbery and the financial mess Violet had gotten us into, it was a wonder I could choke down anything at all.

"I know things were tight, but how much trouble are you in without the money in that deposit bag?"

I knew in a heartbeat that Mason would whip out a check and write it for any amount I needed—if he had the money. But he didn't. There was no sense making both of us miserable. "Not to worry. We'll figure it out. We'll come up with some creative juggling."

"Maybe you should take the afternoon off and go home and lie down. You've had a rough morning."

"I'll be fine. Eat your pie."

"I don't feel right eating in front of you."

"Please," I laughed, leaning back in the chair. "I thought you had sworn to uphold the truth, Mr. Prosecutor, and that's an outright lie. You ate half a batch of cookies in front of me just last Sunday."

"And you know full good and well why I did."

I lifted my eyebrows in mock reprimand.

"It's a well-known fact that every batch that comes out of the oven has to be sampled. I was merely performing my civic duty, as any good ADA would."

"So you were motivated by pure selflessness?" I teased.

He leaned over and pulled me out of the chair and onto his lap. Before I even knew what he had in mind, he was kissing me senseless.

"And what was that?" I asked when he finally lifted his head.

"With all the hours I've been puttin' in these last two weeks, I've left you sorely neglected."

I rubbed his shoulder with my fingertips, then lifted them to his face, staring into his warm hazel eyes. It was easy to get lost in them. "You're not neglecting me, Mason. We're makin' it work. Surely this won't last forever."

"The DA is up for re-election next fall. Hopefully, he'll get replaced and we'll have a more fair judicial system in Fenton County."

"Dare to dream." As far as I could tell, Mason was the only cog in the Fenton County wheel of justice that gave two figs about being fair. "Say, you haven't had a chance to re-open Dora's case, have you?"

Guilt flooded his eyes. "No, I'm sorry. I've been working on all the charges associated with the fiasco in the sheriff's department, as well as a special project that's taken precedence." He sighed. "In fact, I suspect that the DA has caught wind of my project, and all the extra work he's thrown my way is his attempt to create a roadblock."

I sucked in my breath. "Can you tell me about it?"

He placed a gentle kiss on my lips. "I'd rather not for now. You've got enough to worry about. But I'll let you know when I've made some headway. Okay?"

I knew I could trust him. Mason didn't keep secrets from me, a refreshing change from Joe, whose entire existence was clouded in secrecy and half-truths. "Okay."

"Which brings me to another potential issue," he said, closing the lid on his partially eaten slice of pie. It had to be serious for him to not finish his pie.

"And that is?"

"We're going to have a problem with the mug shots."

I blinked. "Why?"

"Because I can't get them on my own. I'll need to use the police department to pull them. They already second-guess everything I request, and they're going to be extra suspicious if I request mug shots for an unfiled case, hours after my girlfriend was involved in a bank robbery."

"So what does that mean? We give up?"

"No, there's another way." He hesitated. "The sheriff's office has access. We can get someone there to pull them." His gaze settled on my face, watching for my reaction. "One deputy in particular."

My stomach dropped. "Joe."

He nodded, but he didn't look happy about it. "Since this isn't official, I wanted your permission before contacting him." He sighed, worry filling his eyes. "We both know he wants you back. It's the only reason he took the chief deputy position. Hell, he just lost a state senate race and his father is

J.R. Simmons. He could fly a hell of a lot higher than the Fenton County Sheriff Department."

I wasn't so sure about that, but I had no desire to contradict him. When Joe was working for the state police in Little Rock, he'd applied to get a regular deputy job so he could be with me in Henryetta. The long distance, along with a host of other issues, had been hard on our relationship. But pure happiness had leaked out of Joe when he told me about applying for the position. Something had told me that he truly wanted the job and wasn't just doing it for me. But then I'd believed a lot of things about Joe that had turned out not to be true. I gave myself a mental shake. Joe's happiness or unhappiness in his current career was no longer my concern.

Mason shifted me on his lap. "I can send him a list of parameters based on the description you gave me and ask for him to send me the mug shots, but he'll want to know why I'm calling *him*. He won't cooperate unless I tell him…and I won't lie, Rose."

The unfinished *like him* hung in the air. I had no intention of asking Mason to jeopardize his integrity. "And if we find the guy in the mug shots, what will we do? It's not like we have any definitive proof. Are we wasting our time?"

"Unless the money they took from you changed your vision, they didn't get enough loot for whatever purpose they have. Like I told you, they're probably going to rob something else. Another bank. A store." He took my hand in his. "They had guns, Rose. One of the guys got physical with you, and I suspect you haven't told me everything that happened. What if he really hurts someone next time?" Worry filled his eyes. "Not to mention that you said he threatened you if you told anyone about them. What if they figure out who you are? They have your deposit bag. I bet there was a deposit slip in there with the name of your business, right?"

My already queasy stomach started to churn. I hadn't even thought of that. "Yeah."

"So no, we're not wasting our time. We need to ID this guy as soon as we can. And once we find him, Joe will help figure out a reason to make the arrest. We just need to piece things together before they strike again. And maybe hurt someone this time." He hesitated.

"Go ahead and say it."

"I'm worried that they might come looking for you. In fact, I'm thinking about asking the sheriff's department to send out a patrol to check on your house when I'm not there."

"Don't do that. You know who will volunteer for the job."

"Your safety comes first, Rose."

I groaned. What a mess. "I really don't want to see him."

"I don't want you to *have* to see him, but you know he'll insist on it, patrol or no patrol. Once he realizes I'm pulling those mug shots for *you*, he won't send them to me. He'll insist you come to him."

I felt like I was going to throw up. "You're sure there's not another way?"

"None that I can think of. Believe me, I'd rather keep him out of this too, but I don't think we have much of a choice."

I swallowed and nodded, turning to look out the window.

"Talk to me, Rose."

"You're right. I don't want to see him, but I need you to know that it's not because I still want him..." I turned back to face him.

"I do know that."

"I just felt like everything was finally settling down." I gave him a grim smile. "But I can be a grownup. I can do this."

"Do you want to be with me when I call him?"

I shook my head. "No. Just tell me when and where I'm supposed to go after you talk to him." I stood, pulling free from his grasp. "I need to get back to work."

"Rose." He reached out and grabbed my hand again. "Don't be upset with me."

"I'm not upset with you. I promise." I leaned over and kissed him. "How late do you think you'll be at work tonight? I can fix us something to eat."

"I'm not sure yet. I want to work on that case I was telling you about, but I can do that in the office at the farmhouse. Don't go to any trouble with dinner."

"Call me when you know something."

"Okay."

I left Mason's office and took the staircase down to the first floor of the courthouse, heading for the personal property department. My best friend Neely Kate was sitting at her desk behind the counter, her usually long, fluffy blond hair pulled back in a ponytail. Her face was practically bare of makeup—very unlike her—and she was eating a saltine. Her coworker was noticeably absent, and I was happy we were alone.

Her eyes widened when she saw me come through the door. "Hey, Rose. You here seeing Mason?" she asked.

Her question made me feel guilty. I used to come to the courthouse to see her. Now she was a secondary reason. "I wanted to see you too. Sorry that I've been busy."

"Please." Her nails were painted in light teal and white stripes. "You have no idea how happy I am that you two are together. But I will admit to missin' you."

"How about lunch tomorrow? If you're up to it, that is. How's the morning sickness?"

She put a hand on her stomach. "Not so great. But I can handle lunch. Wild horses couldn't keep me away from spending time with you."

"I guess Violet was lucky. She never had much morning sickness."

Neely Kate's eyebrows lifted. "If that was some lame attempt to make me feel better—or make me feel worse—keep it to yourself." She released a low chuckle. "I had no idea that the minute you announce that you're pregnant, every woman in a two-block radius feels the need to share each excruciating—" her eyes pierced mine "—and I do mean *excruciating,* details about her pregnancy." She shook her head and quirked her brow at me. "I'm tellin' you, the Eastern Fenton County High School had their abstinence program all wrong. What they should have done was bring in a few of the women I've encountered to tell their stories to the student body. Then we'd have a *negative* population growth."

Whenever I got pregnant, I was going to keep it to myself until they wheeled me into the delivery room. "I'm sorry you're feeling so bad."

She patted my hand. "Not to worry. She says I'm gonna have a healthy boy. Now tell me about that bank robbery. I had to hear it second-hand, and I was worried sick."

I cringed. "I'm sorry."

"Well the least you can do is tell me what happened. Do you have any idea who the robbers were?"

I moved closer. "Officially? No. They wore ski masks. But unofficially, I saw one of their faces in a vision."

Neely Kate got excited. "Oh! You had a vision on purpose to help solve a mystery? *Finally*!"

"No!" I squirmed. "And I've had visions on purpose before."

"But not enough of them."

I frowned. "Well, this one just popped into my head right before the robbers ran off." I paused, my stomach twisting again. "Mason's going to have me look at some mug shots."

She narrowed her gaze. "Why do I hear a but in there?"

"We can't tell the Henryetta police why I need to look at mug shots, so Mason is going to call the one person we know in county law enforcement who will understand my need for secrecy."

Comprehension washed over her face. "Joe."

"Yeah."

"I know you've been worried about seeing him since he moved back to town, but you can face him, Rose. You already have. Multiple times…and you've put him in his place too."

I lowered my voice to a whisper. "Neely Kate. He moved here for me."

She studied me for several seconds, and my face heated under her scrutiny. "Does that have any impact on your decision to be with Mason?"

"No!" I hissed. "Not one day has gone by that I've regretted being with Mason. I just feel guilty. I never gave Joe any indication that I'd change my mind, but he uprooted everything to move here anyway."

"Rose Anne Gardner, you have *nothing* to feel guilty about. You have no control over where that man chooses to live. If he moved here to get you back—well, that's all on him. Not you."

I reached over the counter and pulled her into an awkward hug. "That's why I love you, Neely Kate. You're my voice of reason."

A smug smile spread across her face. "Tell me something I *don't* know."

"Okay." I tilted my head. "How about this: did you know that Samantha Jo Wheaton is working at the Henryetta Bank and Trust?" Even though Neely Kate wasn't much of a gossip, she somehow knew just about everything about everyone. I was hoping I'd scooped her on this one.

"*Please.*" She rolled her eyes. "She started working there three weeks ago. It was quite the promotion for her after working behind the electronics counter at Wal-Mart for six months. She only got the job because she's the second cousin of the bank manager. It ain't gonna help her though."

"What do you mean?"

"Her scumbag ex racked up a ton of credit card bills with her name on them. She's about to declare bankruptcy. So while she's bound to be making more money at the bank, it's too little too late. She's already lost her house."

"Oh."

"When are you going to figure out that I know everything?"

"Not quite everything," I gloated. "I found out what happened in Little Rock to force Mason to leave his DA job there and come to Fenton County."

She shrugged, trying to play it off. "Everyone has an off day now and then."

"Okay, how about this?" I asked, giving her an ornery look. "Norman Sullivan, the loan officer at the bank, didn't come in to work today, and all his family pictures were missing from his desk."

She lifted her eyebrows and gave me a mock bored look. "His wife left him last month."

"Oh."

She sat on the desk-height counter and scooted closer to me. "She started seeing a guy from El Dorado who owns a chain of Waffle Houses. Now she lives with her new boyfriend." Neely Kate waved her hand in a sweeping arc. "She said she was looking for a man who would allow her to live the life she was meant to lead."

"So Mr. Sullivan might have robbed the bank to get his wife back."

"If he did, that was pretty stupid. He's gotta be suspect number one. Even the Henryetta Police couldn't miss that one."

"Mason said they were going to check it out."

She nodded, but I could tell I was losing her attention. She looked a little green around the gills. "Are you doin' okay, Neely Kate?"

"My cousin had a bunch of miscarriages and the doctor told her that morning sickness is actually a *good* sign. It means all your hormones are strong and protecting the baby. So I'm happy—mostly—I'm feeling sick. Besides, Grandma read my tea leaves." She sat back, her face taking on an even greener tone. "Speakin' of which…" She hopped off the counter and dashed around the counter without another word.

"Bye," I called after her as I followed her into the hall, but she'd already ducked into the bathroom.

Bruce Wayne was still working when I got back to the job site, but the wind had picked up, bringing a cold bite with it. We'd removed all but a few bushes, so we spent the next hour digging the rest out so that we'd have empty beds to get started on the next day. Just as we were packing up our tools, Violet called me. I hesitated before answering, but I knew she'd hound me until I did.

"Rose, I need a favor," she said as soon as I picked up.

Another favor, but she sounded frantic. "What's wrong?"

"Mike was supposed to pick up the kids, and his parents can't do it because they went to Arizona. Can you get them?"

I glanced at the time on my phone. "Ashley got out of school ten minutes ago. Is she still there?"

Violet started to cry. "They're holding her in the office. I didn't want to call you, but I can't close early because I have a customer picking up a big order this afternoon. I know I keep asking for favors."

"Vi, it's okay. Calm down." I gave Bruce Wayne a reassuring smile in response to his worried glance. "I love Ashley and Mikey, and Bruce Wayne and I were just packing up. I'll go get them now."

"Thank you," but her words were muffled with her tears. "Just take them to the house if you don't mind. Mike said he'd pick them up by five-thirty. It's his night to get them."

"Okay," I said, but suddenly my stomach flopped like a fish out of water.

It was the logical place to take them, but it meant I'd risk seeing Violet's new next-door neighbor.

Joe.

Chapter Five

Violet and I were more worked up about picking the kids up late than they were. They were excited to see me, especially when I told them we were going to head out to the farm to get my little dog Muffy before heading back to the house on Meadow Street.

When we parked in the circular drive in front of my two-story white Victorian house, I told the kids they could get out and wander around while I let Muffy take care of her business. They'd only been out to the farm once before and both had been fascinated with the barn and adjacent pasture.

Although Ashley had started kindergarten only a couple of months ago, she now acted like five going on thirteen. But instead of developing the usual tween attitude, she seemed to have cultivated an increased sense of responsibility. She unbuckled her twenty-month-old brother Mikey from his car seat before I could get around to the other side, and helped him down from my pickup truck.

I hurried up the steps to the covered porch and unlocked the front door while Muffy barked her fool head off inside. When I flung the door open, my little brown mutt burst through the open doorway and immediately jumped up on my legs. I leaned over to pet her. "I missed you too, girl, and I'm sorry I didn't bring you with me. But it's getting cold outside and I didn't want you to get sick from being outside all day." I knew I was an overprotective pet owner. Heavens only knew what kind of helicopter parent I'd be one day.

Ashley stood at the bottom of the porch steps, holding her little brother's hand. "Why do you talk to her like she's a real person, Aunt Rose?"

I shrugged. "Well, I guess because I think of her as a person."

"But she doesn't talk back."

"She does in her own way."

Having sufficiently greeted me, Muffy released a deadly wave of noxious gastrointestinal fumes and ran down the steps toward my niece and nephew. Mikey pulled himself loose from Ashley and clapped his hands. "Muppy."

My little dog covered him with licks, and he tumbled onto his backside. Mikey squealed with excitement when she climbed onto his lap.

"See?" I said. "Muffy's talking right now even if she isn't using words. She's giving Mikey kisses to say she missed him and she loves him."

"Just like when you and Joe used to kiss."

My stomach twisted. "Uh…yeah." The kids had gotten used to seeing Joe on the weekends and he'd always taken time to play with my niece and nephew. They missed him after our breakup, and given that her own parents were in the process of splitting up, Ashley hadn't taken it well. "But I'm not with Joe anymore. Remember?"

"I know," she sighed. "You're with Mason, but we still play with Joe sometimes."

I'd been climbing down the steps to join them, but froze in my tracks. "You do?"

"Yeah." Her head bobbed enthusiastically. "Sometimes he comes over and watches us when Mommy has to go to the store."

"Huh." Part of me wasn't surprised. The kids had known Joe for months, after all, and he was once again living in the little house next door to my old house. The same one he'd lived in when he was undercover and going by the name Joe McAllister. But I *was* surprised Violet hadn't told me. And I had to admit that I didn't like it one bit. A couple of weeks ago she'd made it pretty clear she didn't approve of Mason. Funny how she hadn't approved of Joe either until after our breakup.

Muffy took off running toward the barn and we followed behind. Mikey struggled to keep up, so I picked him up and settled him on my hip.

"Are you gonna get horses, Aunt Rose?" Ashley asked as she watched Muffy duck under the wooden fence surrounding the horse pen. "Momma says she thinks Miss Dora had horses."

"I don't know. Horses are a lot of work and I can hardly take care of Muffy."

Ashley giggled.

I let the kids play for another ten minutes before I said, "Come on. I need to get you guys back home." I didn't relish facing Joe, so a part of me wanted to ask Mike to pick the kids up from the farm. But I knew I'd have to see Joe at some point, especially if he agreed to Mason's request about the mug shots.

The kids reluctantly climbed back into the truck, but I assured them they'd be out at the farm for Thanksgiving and promised we could take a walk down the road next to the fields if it wasn't raining.

"What about the woods, Aunt Rose?" my niece asked, her voice high-pitched with excitement. "Can we go out in the woods?"

"No. Not the woods." It was going to take a while before I was ready to walk in the woods again.

I drove through the short patch of trees lining the driveway and stopped at the edge of the highway that led to Henryetta. A shiny black pickup with a long scratch along the side drove past us, but just as I was getting ready to pull out, it did a U-turn and headed back the other direction.

"That truck's not bein' safe, Aunt Rose," Ashley said in her mini-grownup voice.

"No. It's not," I agreed as I pulled out behind it. We followed it for half a mile before it turned left onto a narrow private drive. As erratic as the driver was behaving, I wasn't sorry to see it go, but I had to stop and wonder if there was some truth to Mason's observation—trouble seemed to surround me like a whirling dervish.

Ashley talked about school and how one of the boys in her class had cut another little girl's hair with scissors. I listened absently, my mind combing through all my current dilemmas. The most pressing problem was our money situation, so I racked my brain trying to come up with a way to raise nine thousand dollars in case the insurance company didn't reimburse us. No obvious solution jumped out at me.

But thinking about it helped get my mind off my second biggest dilemma, which I found sitting on my old front porch in a rocking chair, holding a bottle of beer.

"Joe!" Ashley and Mikey squealed while Muffy barked with excitement.

Traitors.

My niece threw open her door, abandoning her brother as she bolted for my ex-boyfriend, Muffy fast on her heels. Joe set his bottle on the table and stood to greet her. Ashley leaped for him, and he scooped her up into a hug, spinning her around.

"How's my little Asherella?"

She giggled. "It's not *Asher*ella, Joe. It's *Cinder*ella."

"Ashes. Cinders. Same thing." He walked down the steps to the front yard and set her down. His huge grin faded as he watched me free Mikey from his car seat and deposit him on the ground.

"Joe!" Mikey shouted and ran for him.

Joe knelt and hugged the little boy a moment longer than I would have expected, then stood and took a step toward me. "Hi, Rose," he finally said.

He was wearing jeans and a tan jacket. The brown thermal shirt he wore underneath made the natural copper highlights in his dark brown hair stand out. When we were together, the sight of him had always stolen my breath away. Today was no exception, but the reasons were much different than they'd been before.

I'd last seen Joe almost two weeks ago, when he'd pulled into the driveway of this house to tell me that he was moving back to Henryetta and taking the sheriff's job. I'd handled that just fine. And the last time I'd seen him before that was four weeks ago in the woods after he'd shown up to save Mason and me from Daniel Crocker. But seeing him with the kids was my undoing. A lump burned in my throat as memories of all our dreams rushed into my head. We'd talked about a future that had included children, but it had all come crashing down when the time came for Joe to pay the piper—his father, who had gotten him out of jam after jam. Joe's parents demanded that he cut all ties with me unless I gave up all the important, but socially unacceptable, people in my life so Joe could run for the state senate. In the end, we both knew I couldn't do it, no matter how much we loved each other. And Joe couldn't have told his father he wouldn't cooperate because J.R. Simmons had trumped up some false charges against me, Violet, and Mike, and had threatened to make them public unless Joe played his game.

So Joe left me behind broken-hearted and had run off on the campaign trail with his long-time ex-girlfriend Hilary at his side. And in his bed. I could understand why he'd agree to a pretend engagement—Joe had told me that a single man had little chance of getting elected in our neck of the woods—but I couldn't accept that he'd let Hilary snare him into a real relationship. Again. He'd fallen back into his toxic entanglement with her time and time again over the past ten years. In fact, Mason's sister had paid the price with her life.

No, Joe McAllister—the man with whom I'd fallen in love—was not the man in front of me right now. He never had been. It had just taken me a while to figure it out.

I swallowed the lump. "What are you doing on my front porch?"

His mouth twisted into an ornery grin, but it was obvious his heart wasn't in it. "If I remember correctly, this is no longer your front porch. Did you move back in?"

"No."

Ashley tugged on his jacket. "Joe, can we play hide-and-seek?"

He looked down at her, his face softening. "Not right now. I need to talk to Rose for a minute and your daddy is coming to get you. Why don't you make sure you have Mr. Snuffles in your bag?"

"All right," she muttered in disappointment.

"And could you take your brother and Muffy with you? The DVD Mikey likes is ready for him to watch. Just press play."

"Okay, Joe," she said, taking Mikey's hand and leading him inside, Muffy following obediently behind as if she'd understood Joe's words.

How much time did he spend with my niece and nephew anyway? "You still have a key to my house?" It occurred to me that I'd never gotten it back.

"Yeah, Violet told me to keep it."

"What are you doing here, Joe?" I asked with a firmer tone.

"I talked to Mason this afternoon."

"So? You could have called me."

"Would you have taken the call?"

Before this afternoon, probably not.

"See?" he said when I didn't answer. "Look, Rose. I know you're still angry with me, and you have every right to be, but I'd never let my feelings for you get in the way of protecting you or preventing a crime. Surely you won't let your animosity for me get in the way of either of those things."

I knew he was right, but the way he'd wormed his way back into Ashley and Mikey's life pissed me off. And I was about to throttle Violet for letting him. When Joe realized I was never going back to him, he'd probably leave Henryetta and Fenton County the first chance he got, crushing their little hearts a second time.

But what did I expect? Joe Simmons left broken hearts everywhere he went. Sometimes literally.

I turned away and stared at the house where he was living again. It looked so much quieter now that my friend Heidi Joy and her brood of kids had moved out. But I had to admit that his car looked like it belonged in the gravel driveway.

My hair was still pulled back in a ponytail, but several strands had worked loose. The breeze swept them into my face, so I reached up and tucked them behind my ears before I turned back to him. "So Mason told you about the bank robbery?"

Anger filled his eyes and his hands clenched into fists. "What were you thinking by studying them like that, Rose? I called Taylor after I talked to Mason and he said one of the guys was about to take you in the back and kill you!"

"No, he wasn't, Joe. He was taking me in the back to—"

His voice softened. "To hurt you, Rose. He was worried you could identify him. You're at risk…again."

I shook my head in dismay. "What would you have had me do, Joe? Bury my head into the floor?"

He closed the distance between us and grabbed my upper arms. "Yes. That's exactly what you should have done. When will you learn to be more careful?"

I looked up at him, my eyes narrowing. "And is that what you would have done? Ignored them?"

Irritation flickered across his face. "No. Of course not. But I'm a law enforcement officer."

"You don't carry your gun everywhere you go. At least you didn't when you were with me. What if you'd been in that bank with no gun? Would you have buried your head into the floor then?"

"No."

I jerked my arms out of his grasp. "Then don't ask me to do something you wouldn't."

He spun away, cursing under his breath, then turned back to me. "Well, here we are again. *You* stumbling into danger and getting your life threatened. How many times do we have to go through this same song and dance, Rose?"

I gasped and crossed my arms over my chest. "How *dare* you? *You* don't have to go through *anything*. What happens to me has nothing to do with you because we are no longer together!"

"I still love you, Rose! Of course this affects me."

Rage billowed in my chest. "*You love me?* You slept with Hilary! How many times did you sleep with her, Joe?" The words coming out of my mouth were black and ugly. And totally unlike me.

Joe's eyes widened before he recovered. "We were split up, Rose. I thought you were with Jonah."

And the fact that he'd actually believed I was sleeping with my friend Jonah was an insult. But I'd heard it all before…we were just rehashing the conversation we'd had when he visited the nursery for a campaign stop several weeks ago. Tears blurred my eyes and I shook my head. Pushing past him, I marched up the steps to the front porch. "I can't do this right now. I have too much else on my plate."

"You can't walk away from me, Rose," he called after me. "Your life is in danger."

I spun around, my hands on my hips. "Then why didn't you send the mug shots to Mason like he asked? If you really cared about me, you would have already done it."

"It's not just the mug shots. You're out on that farm all alone—"

"I'm not alone! I have Mason."

His face twisted into an ugly sneer. "You blast me for sleeping with someone else, when I thought there was no hope for us—"

"Not just someone. *Hilary*!"

"—but you didn't waste any time setting up house with the assistant district attorney."

"I didn't start seeing Mason until after you confirmed you were sleeping with her. Besides, his condo was burned down by Daniel Crocker. He had no other place to stay."

"*Really*?" he sneered. "He had no other place to stay?"

I looked up at the ceiling of the porch and took a deep breath before leveling my gaze on him. "What do you *want,*

Joe?" My voice was calmer, making my words sound cold. "You're standing here insulting me when you claim to want me back. *What do you want?*"

He bolted up the porch steps, not stopping until he was standing directly in front of me. "I want *you.*"

I bit my lip and shook my head. "*That* is a non-issue, so if you're standing here hoping to plead your case, then turn around, pack up your car, and drive back to El Dorado."

His face hardened, but he didn't budge.

"So other than that, why are you here right now?"

"I want to protect you."

"Then send Mason the mug shots."

"No." His voice was firm. "I'll show you the mug shots, and then we'll set up some type of protective detail with the sheriff's department for when you're out on the farm."

I released a sarcastic laugh. "Yeah, because that worked out so well last time."

"Things are different. Several deputies were corrupt and in league with Crocker, but the department has been cleaned out now, and anyone watching you would really protect you this time."

While Mason had suggested the same thing, I was still nervous about trusting the sheriff's office. "Just let me look at the mug shots. Hopefully, I'll find the guy on the first try and you can go arrest him. Then we'll talk about the detail."

He took several breaths before answering. "Fine. We'll go with that plan for now."

"So when are we going to look at the mug shots?"

"I haven't pulled them yet, but I can do that now and come out to the farm tonight."

I shook my head. "No. I'll come to your office."

"Everyone in the sheriff's department knows you're dating Mason. And they also know that you and I used to date.

How's it going to look if you come to my office and we close the door?"

I closed my eyes. I knew Joe didn't give a rat's ass how it looked. But he knew that I wouldn't want to hurt Mason's reputation and he was using that fact in his favor. "Fine. Come out tonight."

"I'll cook you dinner if you'd like. I know you love my chicken parmesan."

"No. This is *not* a date. You bring the mug shots, I'll look through them, and then you leave."

"You have to eat, Rose."

"Stop it, Joe, or I won't let you come at all."

"Fine, no need to get worked up." He grinned, making me instantly regret my agreement. "I can bring them out to you at around seven."

"Okay." I turned around and grabbed the doorknob.

"Rose."

I paused and looked over my shoulder.

"It's good to see you again. I've missed you." Then he turned around and walked down the steps.

I went inside and closed the door, pressing my back to the wood. What had I just gotten myself into?

Chapter Six

I dug out my phone and called Mason, grateful that he answered on the first ring. "You were right about Joe."

He paused. "So he called you?"

"No. I had to pick up Violet's kids and bring them to her house because Mike got tied up. Joe was waiting on Violet's front porch. Waiting for *me*."

"How'd he know you would be there?"

"Violet. I'm sure she told him."

"Why?"

"I don't know. Maybe he told her why he wanted to talk to me." But it was just about more than I could take. She could have at least warned me. I'd never felt more betrayed by her in my life, and that was saying something.

"How'd it go? Are you okay?"

"It was ugly. But I'm fine."

"I called him right after you left, but he didn't say much. He just told me that he'd think about it and get back to me. I'm sorry, Rose. I should have warned you."

"It's not your fault." I tried to stuff down my frustration. "He says he'll bring the mug shots out to the farm tonight."

"The farm?"

"He says it will look bad if I show up at his office and he shuts the door."

Mason was quiet for several seconds before he exploded. "*Goddamn* him. I knew he'd take advantage of the situation, but I should have realized he'd go above and beyond my expectations. That self-centered, egotistical, entitled bastard."

I wasn't sure what to say.

"Did he say what time he's coming?"

"Seven."

He groaned. "I have a meeting at seven. With the sheriff." He cursed again. "But then he knew that. He did this on purpose."

"I'll cancel."

"You can't. We need you to ID the guy so they can catch him."

"Just hurry home when you can, okay?"

"I will. Call me if you need me."

I hung up and spent the next half hour with the kids before Mike knocked on the front door. Ashley ran to it and threw it open.

"Daddy!"

I was sitting on the sofa with Mikey on my lap, so I stood and set the little boy down. "Hi, Mike." It was hard to believe that I hadn't seen him since Halloween. "How are things going with you and Violet?"

He grimaced. "She hasn't kept you informed of our progress?"

"No. We don't talk too much outside of work lately."

His smile fell. "Things really *have* changed between you two."

"Yeah."

"Well, we're still going to a counselor, but it's rocky." He lowered his voice so the kids couldn't hear. "I think she might be seeing Brody again. Ashley mentions that Mommy goes to the store a lot but doesn't come home with any bags." He took a deep breath. "For now, I think it's best if we don't spend much time together outside of therapy." He bent down and picked up Mikey. "I'm still trying to forgive her. And if she's seeing Brody again—especially since he's back with his wife—I'm not sure I'll *ever* forgive her."

I gave him a kiss on the cheek. It hadn't occurred to me that Violet might be seeing the mayor again, but I wasn't exactly surprised. "I'm sorry you're going through this, Mike, but I'm always here for you. You deserve better." I pulled Ashley into a hug. "I have to go, but I'll see you later."

"Bye, Aunt Rose."

Although we were almost out of food, I skipped going to the store and headed straight home with Muffy. Mason had his meeting, which meant he'd probably order something from Merilee's, and my stomach was too worked up for me to consider eating. Instead, I grabbed a package of crackers out of the pantry and considered reading one of the business books on my nightstand, but something else was pulling me. I dug my birth mother's diary out of the dresser in Dora's old bedroom, where I'd originally found it. Muffy had chosen this bedroom for me when we first stayed on the farm, and it was the room Mason and I now shared.

When Mason and I were under protective custody, I'd taken the opportunity to explore my birth mother's house while we waited for Crocker to be apprehended. It was the first time I'd ever been there. My uncle, who had been the executer of my estate until I discovered the truth about my birth mother, had kept everything almost exactly the way it had been when Dora left for work the day of her car accident. When I was less than two months old.

I'd found the diary and a box of photos and, most shocking of all, the nursery Dora had made for me. I'd read a few of her diary entries and examined some of the photos, but most of her private things were still untouched. I'd been busy after our nightmare with Crocker came to a close, so I hadn't had time to properly explore these remnants. But now, as I waited for Joe to come and attempt to disrupt my life once again, I wanted to read the entries in which my birth mother grappled with the biggest decisions of her life.

Muffy hopped up on the canopy bed that had been Dora's and curled into a ball in the middle of the queen-sized mattress. I'd kept most of the furniture in the house, only replacing the living room set. My sofa and chair were only a few months old and Dora's had been uncomfortable. But now the bed looked enticing. It wasn't even six yet, but I was exhausted after my crazy day. I lay down and rolled onto my side, opening the diary to the first page.

Dora had started journaling in high school. The first entries said the journal was a project for her junior English class. But she wrote in it sporadically through the rest of high school and even after she graduated.

Her first entry was general, but enlightening. Dora was an only child and her parents had died in a car accident when she was five. She barely remembered them, which bothered her more than she let on to most people. She'd moved in with her grandparents here on the family farm, but her grandfather had died her freshman year of high school. Her biggest fear was her grandmother dying and leaving her alone. Her greatest joy was her horses.

My eyelids were heavy, so I closed the cover and rested my eyes. When I woke up, the room was dark. I heard banging on the back kitchen door, followed by the sound of breaking glass.

I sat upright in bed, my chest tightening. Where was my phone? Fear shot through me when I realized I'd left it downstairs in the kitchen. I was on my own.

Muffy hunkered down on the bed and released a low growl.

I rested my hand on the back of her head and rubbed lightly. "Easy, girl." If Muffy had been a bigger dog, I might have let her loose to try and scare off my intruder, but it would be too easy for someone to overpower my eight-pound dog. I couldn't risk letting her get hurt.

When Mason and I had first checked out the house, we'd both walked right by the converted sunroom that was attached to the master bedroom. If Muffy and I hid there, we might go undetected.

I slid off the bed and was reaching for my dog when I heard my name shouted.

"*Rose!*"

I froze, recognizing the voice. "Joe?" I called out.

Joe had broken into my house.

I turned on the bedside lamp, then headed into the upstairs hallway.

"Rose? *Where are you?*"

The last thing I wanted was for him to come upstairs. "I'm heading down."

A light flicked on in the living room, illuminating Joe, who was standing at the base of the stairs with a pistol in his hand.

"Did you break my back window, Joe McAllister?" I asked in disbelief.

He gave me an exasperated look as he shoved his gun in its holster. "Why didn't you answer? I knocked and tried calling. I knew you were here because your truck's out front. With the bank robbers on the loose, I was worried something might have happened."

It was hard to be mad at him when he'd broken into the house with the best of intentions, but now one of my windows needed to be replaced. With money I didn't have. "I fell asleep."

Worry replaced his irritation. "Are you not feeling well?"

My stomach had been a mess of nerves most of the day, but I wasn't about to tell him that. "I'm fine, just tired. Bruce Wayne and I had a big demo job today," I said as I descended the staircase, Muffy bolting ahead to greet Joe.

He bent down to rub her head. "What do you mean, demo job?"

"You know how I hired Bruce Wayne and David to help me with the landscaping job at Jonah's church?" Of course he did. He'd never approved of the decision. "Well, turns out that Bruce Wayne and I both love it. So we started a landscaping side for the nursery and we've had plenty of business. We ripped out a bunch of shrubs and bushes today and I got worn out."

"You shouldn't work so hard, Rose. I know you like the planting, so why don't you hire someone else to help Bruce Wayne with the hard labor?"

I stopped at the bottom of the stairs and looked up at him, shaking my head. "Stop."

His mouth parted as I walked past him and into the kitchen to examine the damage.

The kitchen door had nine rectangular windows on the top. The one directly over the doorknob had been knocked in, and shards of glass littered the wood floor.

Muffy must have sensed the tension in the room because she headed straight for her dog bed underneath the windows on the back wall, burrowing into it.

I grabbed the broom and dustpan from the pantry, but when I headed for the mess, Joe blocked my path. "You don't have any shoes on. You're going to get cut."

I looked down at my feet, forgetting I'd taken my shoes and socks off.

"I see that you go barefoot even in the winter," he said, his voice lowering. "I always wondered what it would be like to sleep with you in the winter. Whether you'd put your cold feet on my legs."

My back stiffened with anger. "Let's get one thing straight right now." I glared and pointed my finger at his shocked face. "You are here for a *professional* matter, *Deputy Simmons*. You are here to show me mug shots so that I can point out the man I saw in my vision. If, God willing, I find him, you will figure out how to arrest the man. But let me be *perfectly* clear: *You and I* are no longer together. *You* walked out of my house two months ago. That was the end of us, whether you changed your mind or not. So I will not tolerate your continued intrusion into my personal life and matters. Is that clear?"

To my surprise, he grinned. "Yes, ma'am."

I shoved the broom and dustpan at him. "You broke the window, so you can clean it up."

He took them from me, actually chuckling now.

That was not how I'd expected him to react. With my hands on my hips, I scanned the room. "Where are the mug shots? I'll look at them while you clean."

"Shouldn't the chief deputy sheriff be the one issuing the orders around here?" he teased.

"Shut up and give me the mug shots."

"I left them in the car. When I saw that the lights were off but your truck was here, I worried something had happened to you."

That curbed my anger right quick. "Thanks."

"Just doin' my job, ma'am." He rested the broom against the kitchen counter. "I'll get the photos. Leave the mess for me to clean up while you look."

"Okay."

He headed to the living room and out the front door while I grabbed the tea kettle from the cabinet. After I filled it with water and set it on the stove, I pulled out two cups, tea bags, and a jar of honey, setting them on the counter.

"Are you actually making me a cup of tea, *Ms. Gardner?*" Joe asked when he re-entered the kitchen. "Doesn't that cross the boundaries you established mere moments ago?"

I lifted my eyebrows. "Do you want a cup of tea or not?"

"Yes, ma'am. I do."

I scowled. Joe was definitely up to something.

He pulled a folder out from under his arm and set it on the kitchen table. "Just look through these and let me know if any of the guys look familiar." Then he pulled the chair out, waiting for me to sit.

I narrowed my eyes.

"*Ms. Gardner,* my mother, bitch or not, taught me to be a gentleman, just like any other well-bred Southern man. We may be treating this as a professional situation, but I will treat you with the same respect I would give any other woman. I open doors. I pull out chairs. Deal with it."

"Fine," I grumbled as I sat down and opened the folder.

Grinning, he grabbed the broom and started to sweep up the glass while I started to look through the huge pile of photos. Several minutes later, the tea kettle began to whistle, but he waved me back down when I made a move to get it. "You keep at it. I'll make the tea. I know how you like it."

I looked through more sheets of photos of a wide array of men with an even wider array of expressions. Most of them looked like they'd slit your throat without thinking twice, but a fair number of the men had bewildered expressions and terror in their eyes. Had they been arrested for something they didn't do, like Bruce Wayne? Or were they just sorry to have gotten caught with both hands in the cookie jar?

"You're concentrating pretty hard," Joe said as he set my tea next to me.

"It's a heavy responsibility," I said, flipping a page. "If I accuse the wrong man, I could ruin his life forever."

"Rose, these men you're looking at were already arrested for committing crimes. It's not like you'd be pulling an innocent man off the street."

I looked up at him, my stomach cramping. "You said the exact same thing about Bruce Wayne when I worried about him going to jail for a crime he didn't commit."

A sadness filled his eyes. "I know this is a burden for you, but all you can do is your best. You're human just like the rest of us. We make mistakes."

While his words sounded preachy, I knew his intent was good. I also wondered if he might be talking about himself. "Okay."

"Just relax and do the best you can. That's all you can do. I'm going to go drink my tea in the other room so you can be alone."

I blew out a breath. "Okay."

He offered me a soft smile before he rounded the corner to the living room.

By the time I finished flipping through the stack—twice—my half-full cup of tea was cold. I hadn't found the bank robber, and Joe still hadn't returned.

I stood and rolled my head around, trying to ease the tension in my shoulders as I walked into the empty living room. "Joe?"

"Up here." His voice floated down from upstairs.

What was he doing upstairs? Livid, I stormed up the staircase. "Where are you?"

"In the bathroom."

The hall bathroom door stood ajar. What was he doing in there?

I hesitated in the doorway before peering in and found him lying on his back on the floor, his legs sticking out from the bathroom cabinet. "What on earth are you doing down there?"

"I had to use the bathroom, and you were concentrating so hard I didn't want to disturb you by using the one off the kitchen," he answered, his voice muffled. "I figured there was one by the bedrooms, so I came upstairs and found it. But when I flushed the toilet, I realized the water in the tank keeps running unless the handle's jiggled, so I fixed it. Then I noticed the sink was clogged up, so I'm fixing that too."

"Why?"

He grunted, then slid out and sat up. "Because it needed to be done. These old houses require lots of work and you know I like tinkering with things."

"Joe—"

"Yeah, I know. I'm here for a professional matter, but I found some tools under the sink and it gave me something to do while I waited on you." He picked up the wrench and got to his feet. "Did you finish going through the photos?"

"Yeah, twice. I didn't find him. Are you sure you brought all the ones that fit the parameters Mason gave you?"

He sighed. "Unfortunately, yes. It means the guy's probably never been arrested before."

"So what happens now?"

"I can arrange for you to meet with a sketch artist, but it's pricey and you told Taylor you only saw the guys with their masks on. There's bound to be questions we won't be able to answer."

"So that's it?"

"No. The guy threatened you. We have that on record, so I'll have a sheriff's car sit in front outside your house all night while you sleep."

"Are you sure it's necessary?"

Pinning his gaze on the faucet, he turned the handles on and off. "Why don't we look at your history? We'll start with the latest. Crocker. He escaped from prison and came after you. Before that, Jonah's mother stalked and kidnapped you. If someone had been watching you, you wouldn't have been kidnapped. You wouldn't have almost gotten killed."

I didn't respond. I noticed he didn't mention that Mason had been the one to save me.

"Before that, there was the killer who should have been on trial instead of Bruce Wayne. If a deputy had been tailing you, you wouldn't have been attacked in your home and you wouldn't have been kidnapped at gunpoint later." He pushed past me through the bathroom door and moved down the hall toward the staircase. "And then there was me."

"You?" I asked, following him down the stairs.

"I was working for Daniel Crocker undercover, Rose, and yet you trusted me."

"Newsflash. I didn't trust you, but my visions kept telling me that I was going to die in a few days anyway. I figured I had nothing to lose."

"You needed protection. I practically blew my cover to protect you."

"Does all this have a point?"

"Yes, that you have a penchant for trouble. Having a protection detail watch your house is a logical decision." He gestured toward the front door. "I fixed the lock in the doorknob. I noticed that it was hard to turn so I oiled the mechanism." He looked back at me in disbelief. "Honestly, I can't believe Mason hasn't done these things for you."

"He hasn't had time. After he got out of the hospital, he's been putting in long hours at the DA's office to try and catch up, not to mention the fact that his boss keeps throwing all this extra work at him. I'm sure the last thing he wants to do is fix things in a house that's not even his."

He looked unimpressed. "Hmm."

I put my hands on my hips. "What on earth does *that* mean?"

"It means that I did plenty of things around your house and your nursery and *they* weren't mine."

I closed my eyes and leaned the back of my head against the wall. "Stop. If you care one iota about me, then *stop.*"

He moved closer and pressed his body against mine. "Rose, I know I've hurt you and I'm handling everything wrong. *I know it,*" he whispered, staring into my face. "But when I found out that you were a hostage in that bank robbery…that your life had been threatened, I nearly went crazy." His hand slid up my neck, burying in my hair and tilting my face up so he could search my eyes. "The thought of losing the chance to win you back made me desperate. I want you to know how special you are to me. How irreplaceable. I could search the ends of the earth and *never* find another woman like you." His other hand held my other cheek. "I need you, Rose. I am nothing without you. Do you want me to beg?" His eyes were wild with desperation. "Do you want me to get down on my knees? Because I'll do it. I'll do anything."

I shook my head, tears burning my eyes. "No." My voice cracked. "Stop. You have to stop. We're over. I've moved on. I'm sorry you're hurting, and I'm sorry you haven't let me go, but you have to *stop.*"

His hands dropped to his sides, and he took a step away from me.

"I still care about you Joe. I do. But we can only be friends."

He laughed. At first I thought it was a bitter sound, but after several seconds, I realized it was genuine.

"What's so funny?"

He put his hand on his stomach and caught his breath. "You just friend-zoned me."

I shook my head. "And why is that funny?"

He gave me a wicked grin. "It's the exact same position Mason Deveraux was in three months ago." He studied me for several seconds, and I could tell he was calculating something in his head. "Do you mean it? About being friends?"

Good heavens. What can of worms had I just opened? "Yes."

"Then I accept," he said with an air of confidence. "I want to be your friend."

"Okay." How was Mason going to take this? How was *I* going to take this? While I'd only thrown out the offer as a way to get him to back off, I had to admit there were parts of Joe I missed. Still, this was probably a disastrous idea. "But you have to stop putting the moves on me every chance you get. If you persist, we can't be friends anymore."

He pushed his bottom lip out in a smirk. "Okay."

This was never going to work. But then I suspected Joe was counting on that.

Chapter Seven

"I like your new house, Rose," Joe said, wandering over to the office off the living room. Mason's paperwork was stacked into piles on the desk. "It really suits you, although I have to confess that I was surprised to find out you were living here. The entire time we were together you never once expressed an interest in even seeing the place, let alone living in it."

"I *didn't*. I was about to sell it to help pay for the nursery expansion, but Jonah suggested that I see it first." I stood in the doorway, leaning against the doorjamb. "But when Mason and I used it as our safe house, I was surprised by how much I felt I belonged here. Plus, Mason thought it would be a good idea for me to live outside of the Henryetta city limits. He suggested that the sheriff's department might be more receptive to my 911 calls."

"Mason was right about *that*," he said, checking out the bookshelves. I couldn't help but wonder if he was referring to himself and his own willingness to help me.

Mason's voice interrupted him. "Glad to know you think that I'm right about something," he said good-naturedly from behind me. But there was a slight edge to his voice. Something most people wouldn't catch.

I spun around in surprise since I hadn't heard him come in. Joe must have oiled the hinges on the front door too. "Mason. You're home," I said, happy to see him.

He rested his cane against the wall and smiled down at me. He wrapped an arm around my waist and pulled me in for a soft kiss. "Finally. The sheriff can be quite chatty when he wants to be." He glanced up, leveling his gaze on Joe. "But then Chief Deputy Simmons must know that, don't you?"

"I've only been with the department for a couple of weeks. I suspect you know him better than I do, Deveraux."

Mason ignored him and turned his attention back to me. "Did you have any luck with the mug shots?"

I shook my head. "I went through them twice without seeing him."

"What about a sketch artist?" Mason asked, dropping one arm, but keeping the other around my waist.

"I'm going to see what I can do." Joe stared at us for a moment before leaning his arms on the back of the office chair. "The problem is that Rose never officially saw his face. So if we bring in a sketch artist, we'll be asking for trouble. I'm going to see if there's a way around it."

"Keep me informed," Mason said. There was no mistaking the fact that it wasn't a request but an authoritative demand.

"I will." Joe nodded, then gave me a smile. "Thanks for the tea, Rose. I'm going to go collect the photos and head home." He walked past us as he left the room and headed into the kitchen.

Mason's face lowered toward my ear. "Are you okay?"

I smiled up at him. "I'm fine. I think we've come to an agreement. At least for the time being."

"And what's that?" he asked in surprise.

"We're going to be friends."

Mason's expression froze for several seconds before he asked, "Do you really think that's possible?"

"I don't know," I answered honestly. "But it's bound to be better than his full-on alpha dog behavior."

Mason tensed, his eyes hardening. "What did he do?"

I patted his chest. "Not what you're thinking. Just a few digs at you. He's trying to reinsert himself into my life while making his intentions toward me perfectly clear. If he's gonna be around, it would be better to keep things positive between us. Hopefully being friends will do that. Maybe he'll see how happy you and I are and decide to leave me alone."

"I think you're deluding yourself, but if that's what you want…"

Joe emerged from the kitchen, clutching his folder. "Let me know if you have any problems with the toilet or faucet, and I'll be more than happy to come out and look at them again for you."

And there was the expected—but delayed—dig at Mason. "Thanks," I muttered as Mason stiffened slightly.

Joe started to open the door, then stopped. "I'm sending a deputy over to watch the house tonight."

"The entire night?" Mason asked, sounding surprised. "Not a drive-by? When I asked the sheriff about it, he said he'd get back to me."

"Yeah, all night. I pulled a few strings after making a case about Rose's prior incidents. I doubt these guys will try to find her, but I'd rather have the peace of mind."

"Thanks. So would I."

Joe nodded. "We should have someone out here within the hour. Rose, do you want me to take Muffy out before I go? I'd rather you not go out alone at night."

"Thank you, Chief Deputy Simmons," Mason said dryly. "I can manage it myself."

Joe shot him a smart-assed grin before heading out the front door.

After the door shut behind him, Mason shook his head and grabbed his cane. "This is never going to work, Rose. He sees it as a challenge."

"With any luck at all, I'll rarely see him, and it will be a moot point."

"He's going to find any and every possible reason to see you. This case just gave him ample opportunity, and I handed it to him on a silver platter."

I pressed a kiss to his lips. "I want *you,* Mason."

"He's trying to wear you down. He's like a pit bull that won't let go of a bone."

"Gee, that's every girl's dream—being compared to a dog's chew toy." I grinned, cocking an eyebrow. "I don't know if you've noticed, but I'm a bit stubborn. I don't wear down easy."

His face darkened. "You're a grown woman capable of taking care of yourself, so I've refrained from interfering lest I insult you. But I can't guarantee how much longer I can keep my opinion to myself. I might have to say my piece."

Changing the subject seemed the best course of action. "I'm glad you're home," I said. "Are you hungry?"

"Nah. I had something from Merilee's delivered. What about you? Don't tell me you had canned soup again."

I grimaced. "I had some crackers and tea. All this fuss has been messing with my stomach."

Worry filled his eyes. "Are you feeling all right?" He lifted the back of his hand to my forehead.

I pulled his hand down and kissed his palm. "I'm fine. Just too much excitement."

"This excitement seems pretty tame for you." He gave me a wry smile. "Do you feel like eating something now? You didn't eat much lunch either."

"Maybe I'll make a sandwich."

"I'll come with you."

"You need to prop up your foot. You've done a lot of standing and walking today. The doctor's liable to make you use crutches again."

"God forbid," he grumbled. "How about I sit with you and put my foot up on a chair? I've missed you, Rose. I want to be with you."

"Okay," I smiled, heading for the kitchen.

He hobbled behind me and froze in the doorway. "What happened to the window?"

I explained while Mason sat down, casting a glance at the gallon-size plastic bag that covered the opening with duct tape. "Maybe you should get an alarm system," he said, scowling. "You were lucky it was Joe this time. Next time…"

"There won't be a next time." I pulled out a jar of peanut butter and a knife. "Besides, I can't afford an alarm system right now."

"Then let me pay for it. I'm living here right now too, Rose. You wouldn't let me help pay for your moving costs. Let me help with something."

"You can help pay for the food for Thanksgiving."

"*Rose.*"

I pulled a plate out of the cabinet and put everything I'd need for my sandwich on the kitchen table next to Mason. "I'll think about it, okay?" I had no problem letting him help with the utilities and food, but I didn't feel comfortable letting him pay for something so permanent, not when he was planning to move out. "Did you find out anything about Mr. Sullivan?"

He gave me an ornery grin. "Now you know that's official business that I shouldn't comment on."

I stopped opening the peanut butter jar, my hand still on the lid, and lifted my eyebrows. "But…?"

"But there was no sign of him at his home and his car's missing. It looks like he left his house in a hurry. Drawers open and clothes strewn around. He pretty much cleared out his bank account."

"You think he left town?"

"Sure looks that way."

"Do you think he took my money with him?"

"Honestly, Rose, I have no idea, but he was known for his foot-loose and fancy-free attitude toward loans over the last few months. The bank manager now suspects he was embezzling money."

I sighed. *I'd* gotten a loan from Mr. Sullivan. Did that mean more trouble for my business? "I won't be able to eat lunch with you tomorrow. I'm meeting Neely Kate."

"Why don't you see if she has any info on the bank robbery suspects," he teased. "I swear the Henryetta police would close more cases if they kept her on retainer."

"Better yet," I grinned and licked the peanut butter off my knife, "maybe she and I should form our own investigation agency."

"If you did, you'd put them out of business in a week."

As much as I distrusted them, I had to admit it was tempting.

***

The next afternoon, I arrived at Merilee's at noon to meet Neely Kate. Whenever we made plans for lunch, she usually arrived first, eager to leave the office she hated. But today she was conspicuously absent. I glanced at my phone to check the time and make sure she hadn't called or texted to cancel, but there was nothing. So I got a table and waited several minutes until she came through the door, looking paler and thinner than I was used to seeing her. Just how bad was her morning sickness?

I stood as she slid toward me down the narrow aisle between the tables. "Neely Kate, have you been to the doctor lately?"

Her mouth puckered with disapproval at my question, but she sat down without commenting.

I took my seat again and leaned across the table, lowering my voice. "How much weight have you lost?"

She studied me for several seconds. "Eight pounds. I thought you were supposed to gain weight when you had a baby," she said, forcing a laugh.

"Neely Kate, I'm worried about you."

"I'm fine. I'm telling you that morning sickness is a good sign. Even the doctor says so."

Guilt washed over me. I hadn't noticed the extent of her sickness because I'd been a terrible friend lately. Neely Kate and I used to have lunch several times a week before Mason and I got together, but lately I'd been eating lunch with him nearly every day since he worked so late at night. Without meaning to, I'd neglected my best friend.

A waitress checked on us and Neely Kate ordered a bowl of chicken noodle soup while I ordered two salads—one for me and one to go.

"For Mason?" Neely Kate asked.

"He gets so busy he forgets to eat lunch if I don't bring it to him. It's a wonder he didn't starve to death before we started seeing each other."

"Nah," she laughed. "He was too busy eating lunch here hoping to run into you."

I blushed. I suspected she was right.

She winked. "Besides, all the waitresses here have a crush on him. They would have brought him food just to get a chance to flirt with him."

I knew that had to be true too. I was thankful they didn't seem to harbor a grudge against me.

"How are your sessions with Jonah going?"

"Great. In fact, I have one with him later this afternoon."

"I bet you have a lot to tell him about the bank robbery. What's going on with the case?" she asked, playing with a strand of her hair.

"It's looking pretty likely that Mr. Sullivan had a part in it. He appears to have left town."

"But he wasn't one of the robbers?"

"No, I'm sure of it."

"So that means there's two guys still out there besides the loan officer."

"Guess so." I told her about Joe's shenanigans, and how it had caught me off guard to realize how much time he'd been spending with Violet and the kids.

"I don't trust him," she said, taking a sip of the soup the waitress had brought out.

"I don't either, but I'm not sure what to do. I've done a great job of avoiding him for the past couple of weeks since he came back to Henryetta. Besides, I agreed to be friends with him."

Her mouth gaped open. "Why on earth would you do such a thing?"

"Because he's being persistent in his attempts to win me back and this way he'll at least back off."

She shook her head, her mouth puckering with disapproval. "That's never gonna work."

"That's what Mason said, but he told me he was gonna leave it up to me." I sighed. "It's the best way to handle it. I'm stuck with him until they catch the bank robbers."

"So why wait for someone else to do it? Let's catch them ourselves."

I laughed. "I suggested to Mason that you and I should form our own detective agency and he said we'd put the HPD out of business in a week."

"Then let's do it." She looked halfway serious.

I choked on a bite of my salad. "I didn't know pregnancy made expectant mothers delusional."

Neely Kate rolled her eyes.

"How on earth would you propose we do *that?*"

"Your visions, of course." She shook her head and lifted her spoon. "You know that you don't use them *nearly* enough."

"Who do you propose I have a vision *of*? Should I wander up and down the street with a sign asking people if I can touch them to see if they know the robbers? Or maybe I should just hang out at the Trading Post bar out on Highway 84 and have visions of their patrons?"

"Of course not." She waved her hand. "The sign part would be way too conspicuous and I suspect you'd probably better stay away from the Trading Post for good. Maybe Skeeter Malcolm's pool hall."

I dropped my fork into the bowl with a clang. "You're serious."

"Well, not about the *sign* part, but us finding them? Yeah, I am." She set down her spoon. "Then once this case is closed, you can go back to making goo-goo eyes at Mason without Joe getting in the way." She tilted her head to the side and added, "Besides, look how many cases you've solved without hardly trying. Imagine what we could do if you put your mind to it."

She did have a point. "Do you think we can get my money back?"

She lifted her eyebrows, an excited gleam in her eye. "If I say yes, will you try to find out who they are?"

"Maybe." I really needed that cash back.

"The guy in your vision said they didn't have enough money. They're probably saving it up for something. As long as they haven't robbed any other places yet, I bet they still have it."

"But I wouldn't even know where to start looking for these guys."

"The best place to start is with that gold Charger. Too bad you don't still work at the DMV. Do you have any friends left there?"

I exhaled my disappointment. "No. Not really."

"Joe could look it up, but then I suspect he already has if Mason told him about the car."

"Asking Joe for help is not an option." I shook my head adamantly. "First, I don't want to talk to him and two, he wouldn't want me to get involved. He got irate because I *looked* at the bank robbers to get their description." My stomach churned, so I grabbed the package of crackers that had come with my salad. "He'd have a coronary if he knew I was digging into any of this."

"So we're back where we started," she said. "You need to try to have some visions."

My eyes widened with an epiphany. "Wait, Neely Kate. I have another idea... Bruce Wayne used to work at Crocker's mechanics shop. Even though the shop served as a front for his pot business and the stolen car parts ring, the mechanic shop was legit. If these robbers are part of the less-than-savory life of Fenton County, I bet they would have gotten parts for the Charger there at some point."

"But I thought Bruce Wayne pissed them all off when he turned his back on Crocker to save you."

"He pissed some of them off," I admitted. "But Crocker was so crazy at the end that plenty of the guys wanted to ship him back to prison themselves."

"So do you think that Bruce Wayne can look into that for us?"

"I'm not sure," I said, trying to eat another bite of my salad.

"Well, it's a place to start, right? And you won't know unless you ask him."

"True." I pushed the plate to the side and took a drink of my water.

Her eyes narrowed. "Why aren't you eating? You usually have the appetite of a wild boar."

"My stomach's been a mess the last week," I said. "I don't know what's wrong. It must be all the excitement."

Neely Kate gave me an ornery grin. "If you weren't on the pill, I'd think you were pregnant too."

My chest tightened and I struggled to find the breath to talk. "I'm not on the pill right now. I didn't have my pill pack with me during the whole Crocker mess. I went for so many days without them that the doctor told me to restart them after my next period."

Her smile fell. "And you haven't started your period yet?"

"Well…no."

"Did you and Mason…*you know*…while you were hiding out at the farm?"

My face turned red. "Well…yeah…"

"And you didn't use any other protection?"

The sick feeling in my stomach got worse. "Not until I got back home."

"Rose, that was weeks ago."

"Oh, crappy doodles." My head felt faint. "I was supposed to start at the beginning of the week."

"It's only Friday. That's just a few days."

"But I'm *never* late."

"You're pale as a ghost and look like you're about to pass out. Lay your head down on the table."

I shook my head, forcing myself to take slow, steady breaths. "Oh, God."

She reached across the table and grabbed my hand. "Rose, calm down. It's probably nothing."

I nodded. She was right. It was probably nothing.

But what if it was *something?*

Chapter Eight

Neely Kate grabbed her wallet out of her purse and laid several bills on the table before standing and pulling me to my feet. "Come on."

I stared at her, still in shock. "What about Mason's salad?"

"We'll get it later," she said, dragging me to the front door, only stopping for a moment to holler at the waitress that we'd back in a bit for our order. She didn't drop her hold on me until she'd tugged me across the street to the park bench next to the courthouse. After pushing me down on the seat, she sat down next to me. "I understand why you're shocked, but I need to know why this is freaking you out so much."

"Everything. Mason and I…we're so new…"

"Do you want kids?"

I flinched in surprise. "Of course I want kids! I've wanted kids since I was practically a kid myself. Joe and I had even started dreaming about a family…" My voice choked off as tears slid down my cheeks.

Neely Kate wrapped her arm around me and pulled my head onto her shoulder. "It's gonna be okay. You're probably not even pregnant. Maybe you're late because of all the excitement, not to mention that the pill sometimes screws with your hormones."

"Yeah." I nodded. "That's probably it."

"But if you *are* pregnant—" she wiped my tears and gave me a warm smile "—I can guarantee you that Mason Deveraux would be a wonderful father."

I grinned through my tears. "Yeah, he would."

"He'll stand with you in this, no matter how it turns out. But the first thing you need to do is take a pregnancy test."

I nodded. She was right, but I wasn't sure I was ready to know yet. If I found out I was pregnant, I'd need to tell Mason right away. Selfishly, I wanted the two of us to have more time alone together without planning for a baby. I hardly saw him as it was. But even more than that, I'd always thought about pregnancy as a positive, happy thing. When I found out I was having a baby—either now or in the future—I wanted my tears to be from happiness, not worry and sorrow. I'd spent my entire life knowing I wasn't wanted by one of my parents, so it was important to me that any child of mine be loved and cherished from the very moment I knew for sure about his or her existence. I needed some time to wrap my head around the possibility first.

"In the meantime, it might be a good idea to start taking prenatal vitamins."

"*Oh, crappy doodles.*" I felt like I was about to hyperventilate. In a matter of minutes, this was getting too real.

"I can give you some of mine in a bag so that Mason won't ask you any questions until you're ready to talk about it."

"Okay," I said, nodding my head like a fool. "Good idea."

"It's probably nothing. You've been careful since you got home, right?"

"Yeah." I teared up again.

Neely Kate pulled me into a hug. "Don't worry. It's going to be okay, either way."

"*What's* going to be okay?" Joe asked, sounding worried.

I jumped, bumping my head on Neely Kate's. We'd been too wound up in our conversation to notice his approach. He was standing right in front of us, dressed in a Fenton County Sheriff's Department uniform of a khaki button-down shirt, a black tie, and pants. His badge was pinned on his left chest. I'd never seen him in a uniform before, not even when he was with the state police. I had to admit that it caught me off guard. Joe looked good in a uniform. Really good.

"Nothing," Neely Kate answered, glaring up at him. "It's none of your business, Joe Simmons."

Joe's face hardened with determination; he was obviously not about to be deterred by my bulldog friend. "You're wrong there, Neely Kate. I care about Rose, so whatever concerns her *is* my business."

She hopped off the bench faster than I would have thought possible for a pregnant woman with grievous morning sickness. She put her hands on her hips and glared at him. "Don't you dare try to tell me you care about her, you boll weevil!"

His eyes flew open in surprise. "Neely Kate. I thought we were friends."

"We *were* friends until you told Rose she had to dump all the people closest to her because they weren't good enough for you and your family."

He groaned. "That wasn't me, Neely Kate. That was my father. You have to know I didn't agree with him."

She shook her head. "Be that as it may, I know you'd prefer for Bruce Wayne to be out of her life, and I won't even get started on Jonah."

Joe had the good sense to blush a little.

"And you can blame your daddy all you want, but we all know he didn't do a darn thing to force you to play slip-and-slide in the sheets with that red-headed witch."

His face turned a dark shade of scarlet.

"And it sure was *you* lettin' your family treat Rose like she was a leper." When his eyes widened, she jabbed a sharp-nailed finger into his chest. "Oh, yeah. She told me all about it, you two-timing, hypocritical, high-falutin' snob."

He held his hands up in surrender. "You're right."

Her finger stopped mid-jab and the anger fell off her face. "What?"

His hands lowered to his sides. "I said that you're right. About all of it. Rose and I may have been broken up, but I still betrayed her by sleeping with Hilary, and I will regret that until the day I die. You have to believe that."

Neely Kate snapped back to attention. "Don't you dare think you can get off that easy by batting those puppy-dog eyes at me and telling me I'm right."

Joe chuckled. "Do you want me to tell you that you're wrong?"

She squinted at him, anger rolling off her like heat off pavement in August. "Don't you play those games with me, you fast-talkin' scumbag. You hurt Rose, one of the sweetest, most loving women I've ever met. You do *not* get to do that, and then expect everything will be okay because you've had the sense to apologize."

His smile fell, replaced by a more serious expression. "At the risk of aggravating you more, I have to say you're right again. I love her, despite what you think, despite how I've behaved. *I love her.*"

"If you love her, you'll leave her alone and let her be happy."

"Is she really happy?" He waved to me. "She's sitting on this bench crying."

"Did you ever stop and think that she might be crying over *you* screwin' up her life, you moron?"

I finally stood. "Both of you stop." I took a deep breath. "Is there something you need, Joe?" I was aggravated with myself for having waited so long to intervene, but I'd been too shocked by their show to do a plum thing about it.

He scowled. "Yeah, I need to know that you're okay, and before you tell me it's none of my business, let me remind you that we're friends, per your new rules."

"I'm fine and I've got to get back to work," I said gruffly. I grabbed my best friend into a hug and whispered in her ear, "Thank you."

She pulled back and looked into my eyes. "Call me later. I mean it."

"Okay."

I was about to start walking across the street, but Joe called after me, "Rose!"

I turned around to face him. "What do you want?"

He took several steps closer until we were no more than a few feet apart. "I wanted to tell you that I might have a way around the sketch artist situation."

I blinked. "Oh. What is it?"

"I don't feel comfortable saying yet, but I wanted to let you know I'm working on it."

I smelled a trumped-up excuse to talk to me, but I was too eager to get away from him to call him on it. "Great," I said, turning around. "Let me know when you have something you can share."

I hurried across the street, thankful that Joe didn't follow. I picked up Mason's salad and hurried up to his office on the second floor of the courthouse, hoping he wouldn't notice I'd been crying. And hoping I didn't run into Joe again.

Mason was on the phone, shouting at someone about following the proper procedure, when I walked into the office. He glanced up at me, surprise washing over his face, followed by just about the brightest smile I'd ever seen. "I've got to go," he said. "No, I'll think about it over the weekend, and we'll discuss it on Monday." There was no mistaking the command in his voice. He hung up and grinned at me. "Rose. I thought you were eating with Neely Kate today."

"I did, but I was worried you wouldn't eat," I said, walking behind his desk.

Gratitude flooded his eyes as he stood and grabbed my arms, tugging me to him for a gentle kiss. "You're the best thing that ever happened to me. Thank you."

I gave him a saucy look. "If that's the response a salad gets, I wonder what a piece of lemon crème pie would get me?"

He laughed, a rich, pure sound that filled the room. "Maybe you should bring me one and find out."

Something warm and overwhelming bubbled up inside me. Was this love? It was hard to compare it to what I'd had with Joe. But while that relationship had been built on a stack of lies and half-truths, I knew I'd loved him. And if Mason and I were possibly going to have a baby together, I needed to be sure I loved him. Did I? I was sure Mason loved me even if he hadn't told me yet. In fact, I suspected he had loved me before we even started dating. Back when I was with Joe.

"Rose?" Mason asked, his eyes narrowed. "You look tired. In fact, you've been more tired than usual lately. Are you sure you're feeling okay?"

I realized I'd spent several moments staring at him. "I'm fine. I just love lookin' at you."

He smiled again, warming my insides like a sunny summer day. "And I love looking at you too. Let's spend the entire weekend just looking at each other."

"While that sounds wonderful, I have to work at the store tomorrow."

He groaned, but I knew he wasn't upset. He knew my work schedule and respected it just like I respected his.

"But only in the morning. You know that I don't spend much time at the store. Bad for business and all." I winked. "Have you ever stopped to consider that associatin' with me could potentially tarnish your sterling reputation?"

A playful look filled his eyes. "I'm counting on it, sweetheart." Then he kissed me senseless right in front of the open door of his office.

"Mason," I sighed when he finally lifted his head. "That's a good way to mess up that reputation."

"Go out to dinner with me tonight."

"We eat dinner together every night you can get out on time."

"No." He shook his head. "A date. At a restaurant with us dressed up."

"You're always dressed up." I tugged on his tie.

"Well, then with you dressed up too. We can go to Jasper's." His face froze. "If you want to, that is. Maybe you'd rather stay home."

I shook my head. "Nope. I'd rather go out with you. I'll even wear a dress." I used to wear them all the time before I started my landscaping business, and I realized I missed it.

"I was hoping you'd say that," he murmured in my ear, his hand resting on my hip and sliding down to cup my bottom. "I love looking at your bare legs." His voice was husky and it sent flutters through my chest, warming my lower parts.

"Then I really need to wear dresses more often."

"I like the sound of that."

I gave him another kiss and realized I was still carrying the bag with his salad in my hand. "You've been complaining about not getting to exercise with your broken leg and worrying about that nonexistent pouch on your belly," I teased, putting the bag on his desk. "So do not take the salad in this bag as a criticism of your physique because I definitely have *no* complaints."

He kissed me again. "Maybe we should skip dinner," he murmured, moving his mouth to my ear and gently biting my earlobe.

Shivers ran down my spine and I wished we were at home. But we were in his office and anyone could walk in through the door. Mason might claim he didn't care about his reputation, but I knew better. I broke free of his hold. "Nope. We're goin' out. You want to see me in a dress and I aim to please."

His eyes were hooded with desire. "I hope you continue aiming to please when we get home."

My face burned and I was amazed he could still make me blush after everything we'd done together. "I better go. I'm hoping Bruce Wayne and I can finish that wall before my appointment with Jonah."

"Okay, but if you see a truck parked in front of the house when you get home, don't get worried. I hired a guy to replace the window in the backdoor."

"Mason!"

He grinned. "I knew you'd tell me no, so I hired him this morning, hoping to have it done before you got home, but he called and said he's running late."

I threw my arms around his neck and kissed him. "Well, thank you."

His smiled brightened. "You're welcome."

When I got back to the job site, Bruce Wayne was laying out the landscaping stones for the low wall we were putting on the side of the house.

"Did you even take your thirty minutes for lunch, Bruce Wayne?" I asked as I surveyed the progress he'd made. "You know you can even take a little longer than that if you'd like. We both know that I do."

"I eat my lunch in my car, Miss Rose. You know that." He shrugged as he leaned over and picked up a landscaping stone. "Plus, you also know I love doin' this work."

It still didn't feel right. I'd have to invite him to lunch with me and Neely Kate one day next week.

We worked in a comfortable silence for several minutes before I decided to blurt out my question. No use skirting around it. "Bruce Wayne, do you still have any connections to Weston's Garage that you can use? Or did you give it all up after Crocker tried to use you to find me? I know you said half the guys have it out for you, but what about the other half?"

His jaw stretched and his mouth worked before he answered. "Why are you askin'?"

"I'm curious."

His eyes lifted to mine. "What are you *really* up to?"

I gasped. "Who says I'm up to something?"

He chuckled and set a stone on the wall.

I sat back on my heels. "If I tell you the truth, will you be more likely to answer?"

He continued to study me, making me squirm. "Yes," he finally said.

I turned my gaze on the stones. "I didn't tell you that I saw the face of one of the robbers."

"I thought they were wearing ski masks." For a one-time stoner who usually missed a lot of social cues, Bruce Wayne wasn't letting anything get by him today.

"They were." I hedged. "It was an inadvertent sighting."

"So what does that have to do with you asking if I still have anything to do with the garage?"

"As you know, Joe's working for the sheriff's department. He finagled his way into showing me some mug shots, but I couldn't find the guy and the robbers still have all my money." I looked up at him. "I figured if I could find them—"

"No."

"You don't even know what I'm asking!"

"You're not messing with those people, Miss Rose."

"Which ones?"

His eyes widened in exasperation. "Any of them." He turned away from me. "Daniel Crocker wanted to kill you, and there's still guys at that garage who are ticked about what happened."

"So I'm supposed to let those robbers take my money?"

"I thought insurance was gonna pay for it."

"Violet's working on it, but Mason's insurance company is still giving him fits about his condo burning down and his claim is indisputable. We need the money by next Wednesday for that big Christmas tree delivery." Not to mention his paycheck, but I wasn't about to tell him that.

"What does Mr. Deveraux say?"

"He doesn't know."

His mouth dropped open. "Why haven't you told him?"

I grimaced. "Because he'll want to help me financially, and he doesn't have any money right now. You know Mason, it will kill him. The less he knows about the direness of the situation, the better."

"He's a pretty smart guy. He might be able to figure something out. You should tell him."

The world was spinning on its head if Bruce Wayne was giving me advice…not to mention advice that made so much sense. But I still couldn't bring myself to follow it. Not yet anyway.

We wrapped things up at three-thirty and I was on my way to Jonah's church for our weekly counseling session when Violet called.

"Thanks for helping with the kids," she said, sounding nervous. I wondered if she was about to ask me to pick them up again today.

"You know I love them." I suspected it wasn't the response she was looking for, but it was all I could give. "Joe was on your front porch yesterday when I brought them home. It was like he was expecting me."

"He probably was. He called to ask if you were at the store. I told him no, but that you were picking up the kids and taking them to my house. What's the big deal?"

"The big deal is that he's my ex-boyfriend, Violet. We broke up. You should have at least warned me."

"He said it was official business, Rose. About the robbery. It never occurred to me to tell him no. He's the chief deputy sheriff now."

"And is the fact that he's been spending so much time with the kids lately due to *official business?*" I knew my tone was hateful, but I didn't care.

"No! It's called being neighborly. It seems to me that you got pretty neighborly when he lived next door to *you.*"

I gasped, then demanded, "Just how *neighborly* are you two getting?"

"That is none of your business. Besides, like you said, you two broke up. He asked you to come back and you turned him down. Why would you care if he's seeing someone else?"

"Not *someone* else, Violet. You. My own sister!"

"Since when did you care about my personal life?" she asked, her words dripping with contempt. "The minute Momma died, you became totally absorbed in your own little adventures and stopped caring about what was going on with my life. You don't give a flipping wink about my feelings or what makes me happy."

"That is *not* true!" I was parked at a stop sign and I shouted so loudly, the woman standing at the street corner walking her dog stared at me. "I started this nursery with you! It was all your idea! I couldn't stand how unhappy you were when you separated from Mike, so I took my trust money from Dora and sank it into our business. *All because you wanted to start the nursery.*"

Deadly silence was her only answer for several long moments. "You said you wanted to be part of this too, Rose."

"I did…but some days I don't think we're going to work out."

"You and I aren't going to work out?" she asked, her voice under tight control. "Or you and I working in the *nursery* together aren't going to work out?"

"Honestly, Vi. Some days both."

She released a short, bitter laugh. "Well, you just might get your wish."

An oily feeling coated my gut. "What does that mean?"

"It means both insurance companies—our business's and the bank's—claim they aren't required to pay the claim. Which means we're out nine thousand dollars."

"*What*?"

"Not that they'd cut a check in time to cover our losses anyway. They wouldn't pay until Christmas at the earliest. Do you have any more jobs lined up after you wrap up at the Timberland's place next week?"

I pulled into the church parking lot, my stomach tumbling like a washer at the Suds for Duds. "None of that will make up the difference after we pay for materials and Bruce Wayne's labor."

She was silent for a moment, and when she spoke, her words were soaked with guilt. "There's something else you need to know."

"What?"

"I've been doing a little...creative bookkeeping."

My breath caught in my throat. "What does *that* mean?"

"It means we've been strapped for cash, and with all our plans for the expansion and the open house... I haven't been making all the loans payments to the bank."

I parked in the nearly empty church lot and shoved the gear shift into park. "What?" I asked in a daze.

"It's not as bad as it sounds...or at least it wasn't until a few days ago. I talked to Mr. Sullivan about it, and he told me not to worry. He said the Gardner Sisters Nursery was a great addition to the town and I could make a balloon payment after the open house."

"The loan was in my name, Violet. How could you do something like that? Did you forge my signature?"

"No." She cleared her throat. "It wasn't anything official. Mr. Sullivan said my word was good enough."

Comprehension washed through me. "But now Mr. Sullivan has disappeared."

"That's the problem." Her voice sounded thin. "A little while back, I received notice that we had thirty days to pay or else, but when I talked to Mr. Sullivan, he told me it was a formality and not to worry about it. But yesterday, Mr. Burns, the bank manager, told me that we have to pay all the missed payments by next Friday or he'll lock us out of the building."

"Can he do that?"

"The bank owns the property and has the loan. And we received official notice." Her voice broke. "I don't know. Maybe."

We held on in silence for several seconds before my shock gave way to my anger. "How many payments have we missed?"

"Three."

"Three?" A quick calculation told me that three payments were just shy of five thousand dollars. We were worse off than I thought. "And you didn't think to tell me? The loan's in my name, Violet! It's my credit you're ruining!"

She choked on her words. "I'm sorry."

"*That's not good enough!*"

"It's all I have right now!" she shouted back. "Instead of assigning blame, we need to figure out how to fix this mess."

I wanted to cry, but if I gave into my tears, I worried that I wouldn't be able to stop. "*Is* there a way to fix this mess? Or have you killed our business before it even had a chance to get off the ground? You couldn't be happy with taking it slow. You had to expand immediately. You insisted on not only having a Holiday Open House, but one Fenton and all its neighboring counties would talk about for months to come. It just kept growing bigger and bigger."

Her temper flared. "You were on board with all of this, every step of the way, so don't you pretend to play innocent now."

"That's because you told me we could afford it!"

"And until Mr. Sullivan disappeared and those crooks took our money, we could! I can't help it if the man decided to play Jesse James!"

I closed my eyes and leaned my head back against the truck seat. What on earth were we gonna do?

"Rose." Her voice was harsh. "You need to stop being so mule-headed stubborn and ask Mason to help out."

"No."

"*Rose!*"

"No! That's your solution to everything! Ask someone else to bail you out. You got us into this mess, so we need to bail *ourselves* out, Violet! We need to stand on our own two feet."

"Is that a thinly veiled insult about my personal life?"

"It wasn't intended that way, but if you want to take it that way, go right ahead. You have to admit there's a buttload of truth in it. You left Mike to have an affair with Brody MacIntosh, *the mayor*. Then, when you figured out that Joe's daddy had photographic evidence of your misdeeds and planned to use it to destroy you and Brody's future political career, you ditched him and tried to get back with Mike. You're scared of being alone. You like to have someone else around to solve all your problems."

I could hear her sharp intake of air.

"Not to mention you needed me to help open your nursery."

"*Our* nursery."

"Honestly, Violet, what was the last thing you ever did on your own? Good heavens, you've even roped Joe into helping you with the kids. And don't fool yourself—he's only interested in you and the kids as a way of getting back with me."

"Oh! Because there's not a chance he's interested in me?"

"No, Violet. There's not a snowball's chance in hell that he's interested in you."

She was quiet for several frosty seconds. "Don't bother coming into the store to work tomorrow," she finally said. "I'll get someone to cover for you."

"Is there even a store to go into?" I asked snidely.

"There's no reason to take that hateful tone with me, Rose Anne Gardner! The bank manager has given us until next Friday to pay it off so we can at least enjoy Thanksgiving."

"Enjoy Thanksgiving knowing the bank is about to foreclose on us? *Are you kidding me?*"

Violet hung up on me and I turned off the engine, staring out the windshield as I tried to figure out what had happened. In the course of less than a minute, I had lost my business and my sister.

Thank God I was on my way to a counseling session.

Chapter Nine

Okay, slow down," Reverend Jonah Pruitt said. We were sitting next to each other in the chairs in front of his office desk. He was sporting a new hairdo, including a full set of highlights and a liberal use of gel. He was the vainest man I'd ever met, but then again, he was the only man I knew who spent a good deal of time in front of TV cameras. And the viewership of his weekly Sunday morning church service broadcasts was growing by leaps and bounds. Soon he'd be so big he wouldn't have time for someone as lowly as me. But that wasn't true. Despite Jonah's TV show appearance, he had a heart of gold and would do anything for his friends. I was lucky to be included in the group.

"Okay." I sniffled.

He handed me a tissue to dry my eyes. "Why don't you start from the beginning?"

So I did. I told him about the bank robbery, Joe's intrusion into my life, and my possible pregnancy—which felt weird discussing with a man of the cloth even if it *was* Jonah—ending with an account of my blowout argument with Violet and the possible demise of our business.

"Wow," he said, sitting back in his seat. "You've had quite a week. Even for you."

"Yeah, I know." I wiped my nose.

"What's upsetting you the most right now?"

"I don't know. It's so hard to choose. The fact that I might be on the verge of losing all my money and destroying my credit? Or that my ex-boyfriend doesn't understand that I'm no longer interested in him? That my sister has completely and utterly betrayed me? Or that I could be pregnant with the baby of the man I think I love but have been seeing for less than a month?"

He chuckled. "The fact that you still have your sense of humor is a good sign."

"Is it? Or does it mean I've officially lost my mind?"

"No, you haven't lost your mind, although you do seem to have more than your fair share of complications. What makes you different from most of my parishioners is that you don't seem to bring any of it on yourself. It just finds you."

"Maybe I'm cursed."

"Do you believe in such things?" he asked, watching me carefully.

"Well, I never used to, but one has to wonder. Maybe getting rid of curses is on Neely Kate's list of newly acquired pseudo-supernatural abilities."

Jonah chuckled. "Seeing how I'm your pastor, I shouldn't be saying this, but maybe you should consider it. Fair warning: I suspect chicken bones might be involved."

"So what am I going to do, Jonah?"

He gave me a gentle smile. "Out of the entire list of complications you've just told me about, which is the most important?

I leaned my elbow on the armchair and rested my chin on my hand. "I don't know."

"I'm sure you do, Rose. If you could only fix one of your problems, which would it be?"

"Whether I'm pregnant or not doesn't change anything in the short term. I'm sure Mason will stand with me either way."

"I agree, but the not knowing is probably making it more stressful. Besides, you've learned not to hide from your troubles, so it's important for you not to return to old habits."

"You're right, but I'm not hiding from it, I promise. It's just that once the possibility is confirmed, I won't be able to keep it from Mason. And I can't deal with *that* and everything else at the same time. Just give me a week or so. If it's still an issue, I'll take the test." I told him about how I wanted the baby to be loved and wanted from the moment I found out for sure.

"Rose, plenty of babies have led wonderful childhoods after being accidently conceived. The baby surely won't know the difference."

"I know," I said, twisting the hem of my shirt. "But I want to want it when I find out." I looked up at him. "Is that so wrong?"

"No." He smiled softly. "It sounds very much like you. Besides, a week or so won't make a difference in the scheme of things. So which problem is most pressing?"

"What's going on between Violet and me has been brewing for some time. I'm not gonna fix that in a few days. If at all."

"I agree you won't be able to resolve it that quickly, but where there's love, there's always hope. And despite it all, you still love each other."

It was hard to admit at that moment, especially if she'd set a course to singlehandedly financially destroy me, but I did love her. "So what's left is the money. That seems so wrong."

"No, Rose, it's not the money. It's your business. Your heart and soul. You didn't just start the nursery for Violet, but even if that was your primary motivation, you love it now. It gives you a purpose that's all your own, separate from Joe and Mason and even Violet, despite the fact that she shares it with you. You love landscaping and you're good at it. And let's not forget Bruce Wayne."

I closed my eyes. "He can find another job if need be. Mason will give him a recommendation to go along with my own. The assistant DA standing up for a man with a criminal record should help, right?"

"Working with you isn't just a job for Bruce Wayne, Rose. It gives him a purpose too. For the first time in his life, he feels like he belongs somewhere. Just like you do." His hand covered my upper arm. "The money is just part of the bigger picture. You're fighting to give all three of you a purpose."

I shifted my gaze to him. "Three?"

"Violet. She needs this too, even if you don't want to hear that right now."

He was right. But what Violet needed was the last thing I wanted to think about. I'd much rather focus on helping Bruce Wayne and me. "Okay."

"You know Mason loves you even if he hasn't said it yet. He'd do anything to help you. Perhaps you should shelve your pride and ask him for help."

"You're right about my pride—it would kill me to ask him for help, but even if I conquered that, asking him wouldn't do any good."

Jonah tipped his head back. "You're not insinuating he wouldn't help you, are you?"

"No, not at all. I'm saying he *can't* help me." I sighed. "Between paying off his student loans and his legal troubles over what happened with his sister's murderer—not to mention the fact that he paid for her funeral expenses—he doesn't have anything to help me *with.* He doesn't even have the money to move out of my farmhouse until his insurance company cuts him a check." I put my hand on Jonah's arm. "But he's a proud man, so please don't tell him I told you."

"Of course not." Jonah gave me a soft smile. "You know what we talk about is confidential."

"Before Savannah's murder he was financially stable—*better* than stable—and I could tell how hard it was for him to admit the extent of the situation to me. He'd hate for anyone else to know. Which is something I can't explain to Violet, of course."

"Not to worry. He'll never know you told me. But he loves you and he'll want to know what's going on. At least tell him you're in trouble."

I shifted in my seat, my stomach cramping. "I can't. Not yet. Once he figures out what's going on, it will devastate him to know he can't help me. You *know* him."

Jonah tapped his finger on the chair arm for several seconds. "I'll let the subject drop for now, but at least think about how he's going to feel when he finds out that you kept this from him."

"I'm not going to keep it from him indefinitely. Besides, we might figure something out."

Jonah's silence was answer enough.

There was a knock on the door and Jonah said, "Come in."

A pretty blond poked her head in the doorway and her smile widened as her starry-eyed gaze landed on the minister. "Jonah, your next appointment showed up early. What would you like me to do?"

"Tell Mr. Smeller I'll be right with him, Jessica," Jonah said. "We'll be done here in a few moments."

When she shut the door, I grinned. "Why don't you just ask her out already?"

Jonah looked like an opossum caught by a flashlight in the backyard. "What are you talking about?"

My mouth gaped. "You seriously don't know that poor girl has a crush on you?"

His face turned pink. "She does?"

"All those cookies and muffins she makes for you weren't clue enough?"

He gave a half-hearted shrug. "I just thought she liked to bake."

I laughed and stood, picking up my jacket. "For someone so smart, you are entirely clueless about women. Jessica likes you. She used to glare at me every time I came to visit you before she realized I was dating Mason. I think she saw me as a threat since we spend so much time together behind a closed door."

"I…I had no idea." He stood and moved behind his desk, pointing his finger at me. "And nice attempt at deflecting this conversation from you."

"Jessica really *does* like you."

"Maybe so," he conceded. "But we haven't necessarily finished dealing with your issues."

I slipped my arms into my jacket sleeves and shrugged my coat on. "Honestly, Jonah, I'm not sure there's much left to discuss. Besides, I need to let Muffy out. She's been home alone all day." I walked around the desk and gave my friend a hug. "I know you're a busy man, Reverend Jonah Pruitt, and gettin' busier every day with that TV show of yours. You have no idea how much I love our chats, but if you ever find you don't have enough time for me—"

He grabbed my shoulders and pulled me back. "You stop right there, Rose. I'm your friend, just like I was before I became your counselor. You stood by me when no one else would. I'll always have time for you."

I smiled, feeling sappy. "Same for you, Jonah."

He kissed my forehead, then dropped his hold. "You better scoot along. But call me if you need me for anything. I mean it."

"I will."

I headed home, already feeling guilty that I'd only be with Muffy for a couple of hours before leaving to meet Mason for dinner. When I opened the front door, I expected my little dog to run up and greet me. Instead I heard a muffled snarl from the back of the house.

"Muffy?"

I found her in the middle of the kitchen. She was attacking something that looked like a sleeve as a low rumble issued from her throat.

"Muffy, what on earth…?"

She stopped and glanced up at me with an "oh, crappy doodles" look, the tan fabric still in her mouth.

I gaped at her in shock when I realized it was part of my lightweight work jacket. She had never destroyed anything in all the months I'd had her, but now my coat was ripped to shreds and strewn across the floor.

Muffy came to her senses and dropped the sleeve before running under the table.

Sighing, I dropped to my knees. It was obvious she missed me and this was her way of telling me. "Muffy, come on out. I'm sorry I've been leavin' you so much."

She stayed under the table, but I about fell over from the poisonous gas floating out through the chair legs.

"Muffy," I groaned, waving my hand in front of my face. "I said I was sorry!"

Her belly to the floor, she scooted out under a chair, her leash in her mouth. She must have found it and dragged it into the kitchen.

I couldn't help but laugh as I took the leash from her. "I know. I've neglected you. I can't take you for a walk today, but I'll take you on a real long one tomorrow, okay?"

My answer seemed to appease her because she hopped up on my lap and covered my face with licks. I squeezed her tight, rubbing her head. "I love you too, girl. Come on, let's go outside."

We went out the backdoor, and I noticed the pane had been fixed. Mason was right—I would have told him no if he had offered to pay for it, but it gave me a warm feeling to know he'd taken care of it anyway.

Muffy ran up to the barn and romped in the horse pen. Watching her made me think about bringing Ashley and Mikey out here the day before. Would Violet try to cut me out of their lives now? I couldn't bear the thought. Violet and I had had our share of spats since Momma's death, but none this serious. I'd said some ugly, hurtful things I wished I could take back. I knew I should apologize, but I couldn't bring myself to do it.

When we went back inside, I noticed the house was colder than usual and the thermostat read sixty-four instead of its usual seventy. Frustrated, I headed down to the basement to check out the ancient furnace. We'd had problems with the pilot light going out a couple of times over the past few weeks, and sure enough, it was out again. Crouched on my hands and knees, I stared at the old furnace, wondering when I would catch a break.

"Rose!" Joe's voice called out from upstairs.

I groaned. Obviously, I wasn't catching one yet. "Why do you insist on continually breaking into my house, Deputy Simmons?" I shouted toward the staircase.

Several seconds later I heard footsteps on the creaky wooden steps. "I'm not breaking in this time. You left the front door unlocked."

I was on my knees, which robbed me of a fair amount of dignity, but I still put my hands on my hips and narrowed my eyes at him. "I didn't expect someone to barge right in. And I sure didn't expect a break-in last night."

He stood several feet in front of me, still wearing his uniform, and gave me an ornery grin. "No one ever *thinks* their house is going to be broken into."

"I don't think that's altogether true," I teased, despite myself. "I expected a couple of the break-ins that happened at my old house."

"Well, you always have been different than everyone else." His voice turned husky. "And in a very good way."

"Joe," I warned, turning my attention back to the furnace.

"In any case, you need to be more careful and lock your doors during the day. You have a better-than-average chance of an intruder while those bank robbers are on the loose."

I scowled at him. "What are you doing here, Joe?"

"Just performing my duty as a public servant."

"More like hoping to catch me alone while Mason's at work."

"No…" he protested half-heartedly. "I was patrolling in the area and decided to make sure there hadn't been any break-in attempts and that Muffy was okay."

"Muffy is just fine." The traitor jumped on his leg as if on command, begging for his attention. "And I didn't realize high-ranking sheriff's deputies were asked to do patrols. Sounds like you need to renegotiate your contract."

He laughed. "What are you doing down here?"

"The pilot light keeps going out. I was about to relight it."

"That shouldn't be happening. Why don't you let me look?"

I wasn't sure that was a good idea, but I couldn't afford to have a repair man make a service call. Maybe he could give me a preliminary diagnosis so I'd have some idea what I was facing. When I started to get to my feet, Joe offered me his hand, but I ignored it and stepped back to give him room, brushing my hands off on my jeans.

He took off the front panel and poked around for several minutes. "This thing is ancient. I can't believe it's still running, but I think I've figured out your problem."

I groaned. That didn't sound good. "How bad is it?"

"Honestly, you need a new furnace, but the immediate problem is there's a scale buildup around your pilot light. If we scrape it off, you can make it limp along a little while longer."

"And how much would a new furnace cost?"

"Several thousand dollars."

"I don't have that kind of money," I said before I thought to stop myself.

He turned around to face me, shock in his eyes. "What about your inheritance?"

"I don't get access to all of it at once, remember? And I've used up what's available to me until I turn thirty. That's why I considered selling the farm last month. To pay for the expansion of the nursery. But then we got the SBA grant." I scowled. "But you know all about *that.*"

He looked exhausted. "Rose, I swear to you I didn't know anything about my father setting up the campaign stop at the nursery or the strings attached to the SBA grant until it was too late."

Joe's father had arranged the whole thing just to ensure I knew Joe and Hilary were back together…as well as to give Joe a not-so-veiled threat that something bad could and would happen to me if he didn't stay in line. While I'd seen glimpses of the real Joe before, that day he'd shown up with the veil completely thrown off. I had seen Joe in all his non-glory.

Not that it mattered. What was done was done. "The SBA grant can only be used toward the expansion at the store and, like I said, the rest of my inheritance is off limits to me for years. The money has to come from somewhere else."

"Rose, you know I can help—"

"Stop right there. You'll do *nothing*."

Strangely enough, he kept silent.

I waved toward the furnace. "So I can scrape the scales off? If I do, how much longer will it last?"

"A few weeks? Another year? It's hard to say." He reached for the gas valve. "I thought I saw a screwdriver over by the washing machine. Can you bring it to me?"

I knew I should tell him to step away from my furnace and leave, but he was about to save me a huge repair bill. When I handed him the screwdriver, he took it without comment, then bent over and poked around inside the bottom of the giant tank. Within several minutes, he had the pilot light reignited. "That should fix it for now, but like I said, this thing's old." He replaced the cover at the bottom and turned to face me, looking serious. "You should ask Mason to help pay for it if he's living with you. It seems reasonable."

"No. Our living situation isn't permanent. He's just helping with utilities and food until he finds a new place." Why had I told him that?

"How long has he been living here? Is he even looking for another place? You can bet I wouldn't be if I were in his shoes. I'd be stalling just like he is."

"And thank you for that confirming character assessment."

"Hey." He held his hands out at his sides. "When a man knows what he wants, he goes for it. Full throttle."

"And maybe that's the problem." I shook my head. I didn't want to discuss *us* anymore. "For the record, he's been waiting on his insurance check, but it should be arriving soon, so his mother is coming next week to help him look."

Joe laughed. "His mother?"

"Shut up." I rolled my eyes, heading for the stairs. "You're one to talk, Mr. I-Let-My-Daddy-Run-My-Life."

"That was different," he mumbled.

"Yeah, Mason's *sweet* mother is coming to help him out, while your father's like Attila the Hun—determined to conquer and destroy everything in his path. Sounds pretty different to me."

"If Mason's so wonderful, why's he moving out? Why'd he move here in the first place?" Joe asked, stomping up the stairs behind me.

"Not that it's any of your business, but Mason's house was burned down by Crocker because of me. Then he broke his leg." When I got to the kitchen, I turned around. "He had no place to go and I'd just decided to move out to the farm. It seemed like a good short-term solution."

"But not long-term? You don't see this thing between you two going anywhere?"

I released a loud groan. "That's not what I meant and you know it." I grabbed my tea kettle and filled it with water. "What do you want Joe, other than the obvious?"

"The obvious isn't what you're insinuating, Rose. You and I are friends, remember?"

"Oh, I remember. I wish to high heaven I could forget. What do you want?"

"I tried to get the status of Henryetta's progress on the robbery investigation, but not surprisingly, Taylor's not being very forthcoming."

"I'm shocked," I said in mock surprise as I put the kettle on the stove and turned on the burner.

"I also wanted to tell you that I don't think I'm going to be able to get that sketch artist after all. It's going to draw too many questions. But there haven't been any more robberies, so we might be safe."

I sat down at the kitchen table and Joe claimed the chair next to mine. "Do you think they still have my money, then? My nine thousand?"

"I don't know." He ran a hand over his head. "I guess so."

"So if you catch them, I'll get my money back?"

"Eventually. But it would be taken as evidence."

"What? It's my money!"

"That's the way the law works, Rose."

"Well, the law sucks." I shook my head. I'd been holding out hope that the police would make headway on the case, but apparently it wouldn't matter. We still wouldn't get the money in time to save the business. "Wouldn't your time be better served if you were out there trying to catch them instead of here bothering me? Or maybe Violet and her kids were busy so you didn't have anything else to do."

His eyes widened in surprise. "What's that supposed to mean?"

"Why are you spending so much time with them?" I held his gaze while I said it.

"Violet needs help. And you know that I love Ashley and Mikey."

"Is Violet interested in you?" I regretted the question the moment it left my mouth.

"What? She's supposedly getting back together with Mike, although that seems to have hit a snag. I think she's still pursuing the mayor."

"Why would you think that?'

Joe shrugged. "Violet has asked me several times to watch the kids for an hour or two so she could meet 'someone'. Ashley and Mikey were caught in the middle, so what was I supposed to do?"

Joe was the second person to volunteer their suspicions about Violet and Brody. I definitely needed to ask Neely Kate about this one. "How is it that my ex-boyfriend knows more about my sister's relationship status than I do?"

"Maybe it's because you keep pigeon-holing us."

"What's that supposed to mean?" I glanced at the clock and saw that it was almost six o'clock, then stood. "Never mind. We'll have to discuss this later. I have to get ready to go, so you have to leave."

"Go where?" he asked, sounding surprised.

"That's none of your business, Deputy Simmons. Now go."

"I could argue that my friend status gives me the right to ask, but instead I'll go with the official explanation: I need to know so I can make sure my deputy doesn't sit out there all night with nothing to watch."

"I'm going to Jasper's for dinner, and I don't know when I'll be back."

"Are you going with Mason?"

I put my hand on my hip. "Good night, Deputy. Thanks for the bad news all the way around."

He had the presence of mind to cringe. "I wish I had something good to tell you."

"Then tell me that you've convinced your father to destroy all the blackmail material he had against us."

He swallowed. "I wish I could, but I can't." He moved closer to me. "But I'm not running for office now. We can be together, Rose. I'll protect you."

"You haven't changed one bit." I choked on the lump in my throat. "You've spent your entire life doing what *you* want and hoping everything works out, not giving two thoughts to what happens to the people around you if it doesn't. You leave a trail of suffering behind you, while your daddy rushes in to save you from it." I took a breath, anger boiling up inside me. "Your daddy owns you, Joe, and you've handed yourself over a piece at a time with every screw-up. And instead of waking up to that fact, you keep doing the very same thing again and again." I shook my head, forcing the tears in my eyes to dry.

"Rose." The pain in his voice was almost too much to bear.

"Sure, you're willing to take the risk with me because you've got nothing to lose, not really. So you get me short-term until J.R. decides it's time to pull you out of political retirement. Then if you don't toe the line, I'm the one who will get destroyed."

He didn't say anything, but his expression was shell-shocked.

I charged toward the front door and opened it. "Get out."

His face hardened. "No."

"*No?*" I shouted. "This is *my* house, Chief Deputy Simmons! You have no reason to be here, which means you're trespassing. *Get. Out.*"

He moved in front of me. "This isn't over, Rose. *We* aren't over."

"You're deluded, Joe. I'm with Mason. I'm exactly where I want to be." I was shocked at the chill in my voice. "If you continue to harass me, I'll have Mason file a restraining order against you."

"No." He shook his head. "You're wrong. I love you and I won't let you destroy that."

"I don't have to because you've already done that. *Now get out.*"

He stomped out of the door and I closed it behind him, locking it with a shaky hand. I grabbed my phone out of my purse and called Neely Kate as I heard his car start and take off toward the highway.

"Rose? Is everything okay?" she said when she answered. I never called around six because I knew she liked to fix dinner for herself and her husband Ronnie most nights.

"No. *Nothing* is okay."

"What happened?"

I told her about my fight with Violet and my impending financial ruin along with what had happened with Joe. "I'm destroying relationships right and left," I joked.

"You stop that right now," she said, but her voice was warm. "Both of those relationships were already in ruins."

"The worst part of it is that Joe told me even if the police get my bank deposit back, it will be held as evidence for weeks. That'll be way too late, Neely Kate. We need that money by Friday or I'm gonna lose it all."

"Then *we* are gonna have to find it. Between your visions and my insider information, we'll easily outwit the Henryetta PD. Seeing the look on Officer Ernie's face will be well worth the effort."

"I'm not sure it'll be that easy." I released a heavy breath. "Besides, I have another problem…"

"Too bad problems aren't worth money…you'd be rich."

"Very funny. I'm going out to dinner with Mason tonight and it now occurs to me that he's going to order wine. How am I going to explain why I don't want to drink any?"

"Hey, I know. Tell him you might be pregnant."

"Ha ha. I can't do that yet. I'm not ready, plus I'd like to fix all this other stuff first."

"If you're waiting for your relationship with Violet to get patched up, you might want to reconsider. Your baby will be graduating from high school before that'll ever happen."

"Very funny."

She was silent for a moment. "I have an idea."

"What?" I asked, skeptical after her other suggestions.

"How about if Ronnie and I show up at the restaurant and the four of us eat together? You can pass on the wine by saying you're skipping it out of solidarity."

"Oh!" I said, perking up. "I think that might just work. Now how do we make it happen?"

"That's the easy part. How about we accidently run into each other there around seven-thirty?"

"That should work. I still need to get ready and Mason should be home long before then. Thank you, Neely Kate. I owe you!"

"What are friends for?"

I only wished two other people in my life would figure out what real friendship was.

Chapter Ten

My stomach felt like it had a baker's dozen of hummingbirds flapping around inside it. I hoped this scheme worked.

Mason and I were waiting for a table in the foyer of Jasper's, but Neely Kate and Ronnie were nowhere to be seen. In hindsight, I should have just told Mason I'd invited my friends. He wouldn't have minded. That's one of the things I loved about him—he was so accepting of my friends, even the ones who were rough around the edges. But he'd made a big deal about this being a date night, and it might have hurt his feelings if he thought it was more important to him than it was to me.

His arm was around my waist and he slid his hand down, letting his fingers curl around my hip. "I almost regret suggesting we go out tonight," he whispered in my ear. "Do you have any idea how sexy you look in that red dress and those stiletto heels?"

I gave him a suggestive grin. Neely Kate had convinced me to buy it the week before. I'd protested it was too clingy, but now I was glad I'd listened to her. "Patience, Mason Deveraux."

"I spent months being patient. In fact, I continued to exert patience after you decided you were ready to start a relationship with me. Now that the door is open, patience has flown out the window."

And therein lay the key difference between the two men who wanted me. One was willing to wait and the other was like a steamroller, trying to convince me I was wrong. "At least no one is gossiping about you being gay anymore."

He laughed, a rich, throaty sound that warmed my insides, then leaned down and kissed me. "And just imagine. I'm only getting warmed up."

"Warmed up to what?" Neely Kate asked.

I pushed out a sigh of relief. "Neely Kate!" I said, trying to act surprised. "Imagine running into you here!"

"Ronnie and I haven't been out in ages!" She bounced her long blond curls as she spoke. "And I was in the mood for steak, so Jasper's seemed the logical choice."

"I don't know why we're wasting our money on good steak," Ronnie grumbled, but he cast an ornery grin at his pretty wife. "It ain't gonna stick around in your stomach long enough for us to get a good return on our investment."

"Ronnie!" Neely Kate gasped.

Mason kept his left arm around me, but held his right hand out to Ronnie. "You must be Ronnie. I'm Mason. I've heard wonderful things about you from your wife. It's nice to finally meet you."

Ronnie shook his hand, looking nervous at first—a common reaction for those who knew that Mason was the ADA—but more at ease as Mason spoke. "Nice to meet you too."

"Do you have reservations? If not, you two are more than welcome to join Rose and me. Our table should be ready any time now."

Neely Kate beamed. "We'd love to."

Seconds later, the hostess called Mason's name and after he told her that our party had grown by two, he waved for our friends to precede us. He leaned down to whisper in my ear,

"If you wanted to have a double date with Neely Kate and her husband, you could have just told me."

I leaned back, my eyes wide as I searched his face. "I…"

"But then you already knew that, which tells me that you're up to something. I plan to take my time interrogating you later." His voice was deep and full of innuendo. "So think about *that* while we're at dinner."

I flushed with anticipation.

A grin spread across his face. "Now let's go eat with your friends."

"You really don't mind?"

"Why would I? After Jeff…" His voice trailed off. "Let's just say I could use more friends in Henryetta."

We sat in a booth and looked at the menus. Mason mentioned ordering a bottle of wine, then glanced at Neely Kate. "I'd almost forgotten you can't drink in your glowing state."

"I'm going to have to remember to call it that," Ronnie joked, winking at Mason. "When she's hanging over the toilet for the tenth time for the day."

Mason's smile fell slightly. "Rose had said you were having a hard time of it, but I didn't realize it was that bad."

Neely Kate waved her hand. "It's nothing I can't handle. Although I do confess I miss wine."

Mason lifted his water glass. "To a healthy baby and a bearable pregnancy."

We all lifted our water glasses and clicked them together while Neely Kate shot me a glance.

Hopefully, that toast wasn't applicable to *me.*

"I'll skip wine tonight too, Neely Kate," I said. "I don't want to tempt you with mine."

Mason shot me a glance, but he didn't seem overly curious. Despite my worries about tonight, we weren't big drinkers.

The waitress came and took our orders, calling Mason "Mr. Deveraux" in a flirty tone, but he ignored it, focusing his attention on me and our guests. We were halfway through dinner—Neely Kate having eaten half of her steak—when a perplexed look crossed her face and she set down her fork and steak knife.

"Rose, I need to go to the bathroom. Do you want to come with me?"

It would take a dead person not to realize she wanted me to come for some reason. "Sure."

Ronnie turned to his wife, worry in his eyes. "Are you feeling okay? Do you need to go home?"

She gave him a smile, but it was forced. "I'm fine. We'll be right back."

Neely Kate and I were both sitting against the wall, so the men had to slide out of the booth to let us out. When we were in the hall, and out of their hearing, she grabbed my arm. "We're not really goin' to the little girls' room," she said, her voice giddy with excitement. "You'll never guess who's here!"

"Who?"

"Samantha Jo Wheaton's ex."

My eyes bugged out and I glanced around. "Where?"

Her fingers dug deeper into my forearm. "Sitting at the bar. I saw him walk through the dining room toward the bathroom. He might be able to give us some answers about whether she needed money."

I cast a wistful look toward the bar. "I know they had an inside person, and Mr. Sullivan's lookin' pretty guilty, but I hate pinning it all on him with nothing but circumstantial evidence." I was worried about Mason's reaction if he found out what we were doing, but I wanted to investigate all angles. It was worth the risk. "We need to talk to him."

"I. Know." Her eyes widened and she enunciated the two words as though I was a small child. "Which is why I came up with an excuse for us to leave the table."

"Is he still in the bathroom?"

"Nope," she said smugly. "He's back at the bar. Come on." She led the way through the back entrance to the bar so the guys wouldn't see where we were going. I wouldn't know Samantha's ex from any other men in the room, but Neely Kate headed straight over to one of the guys at the bar. He was trying to talk to a woman who clearly wasn't interested. "Let me handle this one," Neely Kate whispered when we were several feet away.

"Okay."

Neely Kate slid into the empty barstool next to the guy. Now that we were closer, I had a better look at him. His longish dark blond hair was slightly greasy and his face was covered in dark stubble. The dark circles under his eyes hinted that he'd been drinking since the beginning of happy hour, not that Jasper's had one. In fact, Jasper's seemed much too upscale for him with his Alan Jackson concert T-shirt, dirty jeans, and cowboy boots.

"Hey there, stranger," Neely Kate practically purred, leaning close to him. "You look like you'd be more at home at the Trading Post." Obviously, we were on the same wavelength.

"Neely Kate!" he said, sounding happy to see her. "I'm just waitin' for a friend." He leaned back on his barstool and almost fell backward. Lucky for him, the body of the woman he'd just been trying to pick up stopped his downward momentum.

The woman spun around, her long, dark hair whipping him in the face, some of it landing in his open mouth. He coughed and sputtered, his tongue thrusting out of his mouth as he batted her hair away with both hands.

She jerked away and shot him a glare. "What the hell do you think you're *doin'*?"

"What?" he asked, holding out his hands and appearing genuinely confused.

Yep, it looked like he'd downed plenty of beers while waiting for his friend.

He shuddered, then turned to Neely Kate. "Long time no see." He eyed her up and down, or at least I thought he did. His eyes were unfocused, and they were doing wonky things. "I haven't seen you in ages."

Her mouth twisted into a condescending smirk. "Not since your wedding to Samantha Jo a few years back."

"Two-timing bitch," he snarled, picking up a beer mug and taking a swig. When he drained it, he slammed it on the bar with more force than necessary, shouting at the bartender to get him another. He reached for his wallet in his back pocket, nearly falling off his stool again in the process. "Can I get you *loverly* ladies a drink?" His gaze shifted to me, as though seeing me for the first time. "Neely Kate, you didn't introduce me to your friend."

"Rose, this is Toby Wheaton. Toby, Rose. But she's very taken, so hands off." His grimy hand was reaching toward me, but she smacked it with her manicured fingers as if he were a misbehaving school boy.

Toby snatched his hand back. "Oww."

I couldn't help but compare his dirty fingernails and stained knuckles to her pristine ones. I'd seen hands like those before. When Joe was undercover as a mechanic.

Neely Kate plastered a cheesy smile on her face and returned to her interrogation. "That's not how I heard it, Toby. The way I heard it, *you* were the cheater."

His mouth puckered in disapproval. "Well, she cheated first. And even if I was unfaithful, she didn't have to set my fishing boat on fire. Who does that?"

"Crazy bitches," Neely Kate muttered. "Do you talk to Samantha Jo much since you two split? I heard she was working at the bank."

"Why do I give a damn where she works? I still have to pay the bitch alimony." He leaned forward, his face inches from Neely Kate's. "Can you believe *that*?"

Neely Kate waved her hand in front of her nose, her face turning pale as she swallowed. His alcohol fumes seemed to be setting off her upchuck reflex.

Oh, crappy doodles.

Ever the trouper, Neely Kate pressed on. "Rumor has it that you haven't been paying your alimony and Samantha Jo is hurtin', especially after you racked up charges on all her credit cards before you did the naked shimmy with Lyla Dumont."

His mouth opened like a fish's and he started to say something, but nothing came out.

"I heard she's pretty desperate, movin' in with her cousin even. I've heard she's lookin' for part-time employment." She winked. "If you know what I mean."

He shook his head, frowning as he handed the bartender several bills in exchange for his refill. "Ain't nobody in this town making *part-time* money since Crocker met up with the grim reaper."

"I heard Skeeter Malcolm was taking over Crocker's pot business."

It was my turn to look surprised. She hadn't told me that.

"Maybe. Maybe not." He shrugged, trying to look disinterested even though the smug look in his eyes proved otherwise.

I wondered what it all meant.

"So if Samantha Jo needed money and couldn't find part-time employment, do you think she'd be capable of robbing the Henryetta Bank?"

Toby busted out laughing, guffawing and slapping his leg. "*Samantha Jo?*" he asked when he finally settled down. "She's dumber than a cat drowning in a puddle. There ain't no way she could plan a bank robbery."

"But she's really pretty," I interjected.

Neely Kate cast me a curious glance.

"I bet she had dreams of bein' an actress," I added.

"Hey." His eyes lit up. "How'd you know that?"

"I saw her in the Henryetta outdoor theater production of *Romeo and Juliet* two summers ago." Momma had pitched a fit when I left her to go see the play with Violet. It had been a disaster from beginning to end. The sets looked like they'd been painted by preschoolers, and the acting was even worse, Samantha Jo's included. But she seemed to take her part very seriously, oblivious to her lack of talent. Of course I'd paid my dues with Momma afterward, enduring her temper for two days for my disobedience—never mind the fact that I was a twenty-two-year-old.

"We were still together then." A wistful, faraway look filled his eyes and he grabbed his beer and downed a good portion of it. "She would practice her lines with me. She kept telling me it was her big break. That she was going to be discovered and taken off to Hollywood."

Judging from her performance as Juliet, Hollywood would have barricaded the doors before she showed up. Samantha Jo had a better chance of starting a new reality series, *Trashy Housewives of Henryetta.* "Do you think she'd take an acting job on the side?"

"What do ya mean?" His body weaved on the stool and his words were slurred.

"If someone offered her a part, say to play a prank on someone, would she take it?"

He grinned, nodding. "Yeah, she sure would."

"Even if it was illegal?"

His eyes narrowed as he tried to study me. "Like sex stuff?"

"No, more like robbery."

He nodded so vigorously he almost fell off his stool. "Yeah, if they paid her enough."

Neely Kate's face had a green tinge to it. "Thanks." She stood, looking a little frantic. "I've got to be goin'. Good seein' you, Toby."

"Wait," I said, hoping to get more answers. "Toby, are you a mechanic?"

"Yeah, at Ted's Auto Service, close to Pickle Junction."

"And have you seen any gold Chargers there lately?"

Surprise covered his face with worry quickly behind it. "Why are you asking?"

"Rose, I have to go *now.*"

My head tingled and everything faded to black with a vision. I found myself in a jail cell, hanging over a metal toilet. "Why didn't that bastard show up?" I said in Toby's voice.

Just as quickly, I was back in the bar, staring into Toby's drunken face. "You're gonna get arrested," I blurted.

Toby's head jutted back and his body swayed from the sudden movement. "*What?*"

"It was nice seeing you again," Neely Kate said as she started to back up, but Toby grabbed for her and pulled her into a bear hug, burying her face in his greasy hair.

"It was good to see you too, Neely Kate. Don't be such a stranger."

She pushed on his shoulders, but he didn't take the hint—he continued to hold on tight as he spoke, his words slurred. "We need to keep better track of our—"

I smelled it before I heard it. Neely Kate vomited down Toby's back, some of it landing on the woman behind him. Toby dropped his hold and spun around to see what had struck him from behind.

The woman screamed as she peered over her shoulder and down her back, looking at the chunks of Neely Kate's dinner mixed in with the pink and white polka dots of her dress. Then Toby lost it, adding his own apparently meager dinner to the mix.

Neely Kate had stumbled toward me after being sick, and I grabbed her arm as we both watched the horror we'd wrought unfold.

The aggrieved woman screamed again, shoving Toby off his stool. He landed on his behind hollering as she screamed, "I'm going kill you!" It was clear she blamed him for the whole mess, not thinking to accuse the two well-dressed women who were dashing to the bathroom.

We shut and locked the door to the single-stall room behind us, both of us silent as Neely Kate turned on the faucet. She rinsed her mouth out before glancing up at my reflection in the mirror, her eyes wide with horror. "I'm so sorry."

"Remind me to invite you out to dinner again. You're very entertaining."

She held back a giggle. "The look on that poor woman's face!"

I shook my head, trying not to grin. "She never suspected it was you, particularly not when he lost it seconds after you did."

"Oh, my!" she murmured, trying not to smile. "We are terrible people."

"Especially for letting Toby take the blame."

We stared at each other, equally horrified and amused.

She took a deep breath. "Don't you dare tell Ronnie he was right about wasting all that money on steak!"

"I wouldn't dream of it."

"We need to get back to our table. You know as soon as Ronnie and Mason hear the ruckus they're gonna suspect our involvement."

My mirth fell away. "You're right." Mason already suspected I was hiding something from him...what would he think now?

After a quick check to make sure Neely Kate had escaped any splatter, we hurried back to the table. Ronnie looked worried, but Mason had an ornery expression as he slipped out of the booth to let me in. "Did you girls have to dig your own latrine?"

"Very funny." I tried to sound serious, but a small giggle slipped out.

"You know how it is," Neely Kate said, arching her eyebrows. "Us girls have to primp for our men."

"Rose doesn't need to primp," Mason said, giving me a grin that suggested he didn't believe a word of our flimsy cover story. "She's perfect the way she is."

Neely Kate clasped a hand over her heart. "Awww...that is the sweetest thing I've ever heard. Why don't you say things like that to me, Ronnie?"

"Maybe because you don't let me get a word in edgewise," Ronnie protested, and the two of them bantered good-naturedly while Mason's hand took hold of my knee under the table, his fingers sliding several inches up the inside of my thigh. He leaned in to my ear, his breath and touch sending shivers down my back. "I know you're up to something. I expect full disclosure when we get home."

I turned to face him, about to say something seductive, but my heart jolted when I noticed the good-looking couple standing at the end of our table.

"Well, hello, Rose. Mason," Joe said. "Fancy seeing you two here." His eyes twinkled with mischief, but there was definitely an air of challenge there as well.

He'd changed out of his uniform into a gray suit and an ice blue tie, but the biggest shock of all was the woman standing next to him.

"Violet. I see you're being *neighborly,*" I said in a saccharine-sweet voice.

She looped her arm over his, having the audacity to give me a condescending smile while wearing *my* peach-colored dress and matching heels that I'd loaned her several weeks ago.

Neely Kate decided to ignore Southern etiquette, the kind that says every insult must be layered beneath several *bless your heart*s. I suppose you could get away with that when you'd just barfed your expensive steak dinner down someone's back. "Violet Beauregard. What in the Sam Hill are you *doin'?*"

Violet lifted her delicate eyebrows with a haughty glare. "What's it look like? I'm on a date."

Joe gasped and started coughing while Violet shot him a glare.

"With your sister's ex-boyfriend?" Neely Kate practically shouted. "Have you no *shame?*"

"Neely Kate," Ronnie muttered, grabbing her arm. "Stay out of it."

"Is there something we can help you with, Deputy Simmons?" Mason asked, using his official voice. His body was as rigid as a steel rod.

Mason had officially had enough.

Oh, crap.

Joe got ahold of himself and grinned, beaming over the fire he was stoking. "Nope. Since Mike has the kids tonight and I was alone, I asked Violet if she wanted to go out to dinner since we have something important to discuss."

"You're out with *my* old boyfriend, Violet? Are you here discussing *me*?"

She narrowed her eyes. "Contrary to what you think, Rose, the sun does not rise and set on your world. Not everything has to do with *you.*"

Joe pulled his arm out of her death-grip.

If Mason hadn't been blocking me in, I would have jumped out of my seat to throttle her.

"Thanks for dropping by to say hello," Mason said, his voice tight. "But we don't want to keep you from your dinner any longer."

Joe started to lead Violet away, but then he turned back, his eyes lighting up. "What were you doing in the bar a few minutes ago, Rose?"

My stomach seized. "What are you talking about?"

"There was quite a commotion in the bar when we first came in. As soon as I saw you here, I knew you must have had something to do with it." He winked, leaning closer. "Taking care of you is a full-time job. I'm more than happy to take back the position."

Mason clenched his hands into fists so tight his knuckles turned white. "Is there a point to this, *Deputy*?"

Mason's controlled anger only encouraged Joe. It also made him act like an idiot.

"I just know how Rose likes to get into trouble." His grin widened as he straightened. "In *all* kinds of ways."

It was a vague innuendo, but it was enough. Mason burst out of his seat, leaving his cane behind as he lunged for Joe, swinging his fist at the same time.

From the look of surprise on Joe's face, he was caught off guard. He stumbled backward when Mason's knuckles connected with his cheek.

"Mason!" I shouted, scrambling out of the booth and grabbing his arm when it looked like he was about to hit him again.

Joe hunched over, his hands on his knees, and looked up at Mason with murderous eyes. "I could press charges for this, Deveraux. Assistant DA or not."

I stepped in between the two men, my pulse pounding in my head. "If you even consider it, Joseph Simmons, I swear on my mother's grave that I will never speak to you again. *Do I make myself clear?*"

Joe looked like he was about to lunge past me, but I stood my ground, staring him down.

"Do I make myself clear?" I repeated.

Joe shook his head, his cheek already bruising. "You're taking his side over mine? He swung first and peace-loving Rose Gardner is taking his side?" He turned away. "*Unbelievable.*"

"Yes. I'll choose his side every time, Joe. I'm with Mason now. You have to get that through your head." My voice was calmer than I would have expected given the fact that my nerves were strung like an over-tightened fiddle string.

Every patron in the restaurant had their eyes glued on us in various expressions of disbelief and shock. I wanted to crawl under a rock and live there. But that wasn't an option.

I turned to face Mason, whose expression bounced between rage and horror. "Mason, let's go home."

He nodded, obviously dazed.

The manager, who seemed completely shocked that Mason would be involved in this kind of drama, walked over to our booth. "Is everything all right, Mr. Deveraux?"

"Yes. We've straightened everything out. But we'll need our check," he said, regaining his composure as he spoke.

"We'll be more than happy to comp your meal to make up for the inconvenience." The manager obviously hadn't seen what had happened.

"No," Mason said forcefully. "No. I'll pay."

The manager turned to Joe, his face scrunching with disapproval. "Sir, we're going to have to ask you to leave."

Joe laughed, but it was an ugly sound. "Fine, I'll leave." He turned his attention to Mason. "You may have fooled Rose and the rest of this town into believing you're someone you're not, Deveraux, but you haven't fooled me. You can bet your ass I'll be watching you."

"Joe," I warned, my side plastered against Mason's chest, pushing him back when he tried to lunge for my ex-boyfriend again.

"Sir." The manager grabbed Joe's arm. "You need to leave before we call the authorities."

Violet, who had been standing behind Joe in horrified silence, jumped into action. "Do you have any idea who he is?"

Joe kept his gaze trained on me. "Violet, enough. We'll leave."

"But, Joe!"

"We'll leave." His voice was serious, but it lacked the usual air of authority he laced with it. He put his arm around Violet's back and led her to the foyer.

"Oh, my stars and garters," Neely Kate said, waving a hand in front of her face. "I'm feeling a little dizzy from all that excitement."

Then she fell over in a faint.

Chapter Eleven

We got Neely Kate revived and Ronnie took her home. He promised me he'd call the doctor when they got home even though Neely Kate insisted it was just part of being pregnant.

Mason insisted on paying for their meal as well as ours, but he was so startlingly quiet and reserved, he frightened me. As soon as we got out to the parking lot and next to his car, I pulled him into a hug.

He stiffened in my arms. "How can you want to hug me after what I just did?" His voice broke as he pulled away.

"He goaded you into it, Mason. This is *not* your fault."

"Of course it's my fault! I'm a grown man. In control of my own actions. For God's sake, I prosecute people for doing what I just did in there." He shook his head and ran his hand through his hair. "I should be in prison right now. But I'm *here.* Doing it all over again."

Oh, God. He was talking about the beating he'd given Savannah's killer. I grabbed his cheeks in my hands. "No. This was different."

He looked into my face, his eyes full of fear. "Was it? I didn't want to stop hitting him, Rose. I probably would have beat Joe senseless if you hadn't stopped me. What kind of monster am I?"

"No, Mason. Don't say that." Tears burned my eyes. His reaction was scaring me. "You're not a monster. I know your heart. You're an amazingly good person. If anyone's to blame it's me. He goaded you to get back at me for telling him off earlier today."

His eyes widened slightly. "When did you see him earlier?"

"He stopped by the house before you came home with some trumped-up reason to see me. I suspect he knew you wouldn't be home." His body tensed. "But I told him if he didn't stop harassing me, I'd get you to file a restraining order. He wasn't happy when he left. And I'm sure it wasn't an accident that he showed up tonight. I told him he had to leave so I could get ready to go out for dinner. I let it slip that we'd be here. I'm sure he brought Violet because of my argument with her earlier. This is all my fault. I'm so sorry."

He shook his head, bringing his forehead down to mine. "You have nothing to be sorry about, Rose. You didn't do anything wrong."

I stood on tiptoes and pressed my lips to his, wrapping my arms around his neck.

He groaned and placed his palm on my back, tugging me firmly against his chest and kissing me with abandon. "Let's go home," he grunted.

"Yes," I sighed against his lips.

The fifteen-minute drive home felt longer than usual, but when he pulled up in front of the house, he got out of the car faster than usual with his brace and his cane. I met him at the front of the car and he grabbed my hand, leading me to the porch.

He opened the door, and we let Muffy out to wander around the yard while we stood on the porch making out like we were teenagers and he'd brought me home from a date. But just as we were about to go inside, headlights appeared in the drive.

"Muffy!" Mason called out.

She'd been sniffing something in the yard, but her head jerked up and she came running to the front porch. She sat next to my leg and issued a low growl.

"Rose, take Muffy inside."

"Mason, we don't even know who it is." But as the car got closer, I could see there was a light bar on the top. It was a sheriff's car.

"*Rose*."

"Okay," but I only went inside because I was sure it wasn't Joe. The only reason he would have shown up in a sheriff's car would be to arrest Mason. But if he'd had any intention to follow through on his earlier threat, I was certain he would have arrested him in front of the diners in the restaurant to add to Mason's embarrassment. Still, I couldn't help but wonder what kind of fallout Mason would face for punching the chief deputy sheriff. He'd apprehended one. Hit another. Things weren't looking so good for his relationship with the Fenton County Sheriff's department.

We'd left on a lamp in the living room. After all my previous break-ins, I hated walking into a dark house. But tonight I wished it were dark so I could spy out the window without being obvious. I parted the curtain anyway. Mason knew me well enough to know I would be watching, and I didn't care what the deputy thought. Mason was leaning in the window of the patrol car, but after a moment he straightened and hobbled to the porch.

Several seconds later, Mason came inside and closed and locked the door behind him.

"Everything okay?" I asked. "Why is the car here?"

"Everything's fine. It's the patrolman Joe sent to watch over you." He reached a hand out to me and I walked into his arms, then he kissed me.

"While I love standing here kissing you, I think we need to get you off your feet."

He grinned at me, but he was more reserved than usual. "I hope that you and I have the same thing in mind."

"Come upstairs and find out," I said as I started up the steps.

"That's not fair," he called after me. "You're a lot faster than me."

Rather than answering, I headed to our room and lit several candles. When he walked in, I was standing at the foot of the four-poster canopy bed, waiting for him. Though I'd kicked off my shoes, I was still wearing my red dress.

I could tell he'd walked too much today because he moved more slowly than he had earlier in the day, not to mention his antics with Joe couldn't have helped matters. When he reached the edge of the bed, I pushed him down onto it and took off his leg brace, tossing it under the bed so neither of us tripped on it. Then my fingers started on his tie, slowly unknotting it and sliding it from around his neck. Staring into his face, I unbuttoned his shirt, taking my time until I reached the bottom, then unfastened his belt and pants.

When I was done, he stood up, balancing on one foot while resting a lot of his weight against the edge of the bed. He was still studying my face, his expression a mixture of lust and something softer…adoration? Love?

The silence was unlike us. I liked that we talked during sex—sometimes fun teasing, other times hot sexy talk that I had been surprised to discover how much I liked—but tonight was different, *deeper*, and neither of us seemed ready to break the moment.

I tugged off his shirt, then his pants and underwear, and pushed him back down on the bed, worried he'd accidently put weight on his leg if he kept standing.

I stood between his legs and he reached for my face, pulling my mouth to his before his tongue began to explore, making me impatient with need. Mason slid an arm around my back and tugged down the zipper of my dress, his mouth still teasing mine, then tugged the fabric off my shoulders. The garment fell to the floor, leaving me in just my black bra and panties. He leaned back to look at me, sucking in a breath. His gaze rose to my face, his expression pure lust as he lay back on the bed, pulling me with him.

I straddled his hips and his hands found my waist, gliding up and around to unhook my bra. He tugged it off in seconds. I climbed off the bed to strip off my panties while he scooted around until his head was on his pillow. He watched me crawl toward him and grabbed me and pulled me to him when I wasn't fast enough. He kissed me again, his hands roaming my body until I was panting with need.

Sitting up, he rolled over to grab a condom from the nightstand, but I pushed myself up and grabbed his hand as he was about to put it on.

No more secrets. Not about this.

"I'm not sure if we need one," I whispered.

Confusion flickered in his eyes. "I thought you had to wait to take the pill again."

"I did."

He shook his head. "Then what changed?" An instant later, his eyes widened and he glanced down to my stomach. "Are you?"

Tears filled my eyes. "I don't know. Maybe."

His palm cupped my cheek. "Why do you look so scared? Were you worried about my reaction?"

I nodded, a tear falling down my cheek.

"Rose, I love you. No matter what. Baby or not. I'm yours forever."

I kissed him as more tears fell down my cheeks. He pulled me back, worry in his eyes. "Why are you crying?"

"Because I love you too." And in that moment I knew it was true.

My words released a possessiveness in him I hadn't expected, and he kissed me with a passion that made me desperate for more. He finished putting on the condom before I straddled him and began to move, my mouth returning to his as his hands found my hips. I climbed to dizzying heights, then exploded with an intensity that amazed me, Mason close behind.

We stared into each other's eyes, both of us still catching our breath.

"Say it again," I whispered.

"I love you, Rose."

I smiled, new tears burning my eyes. "I love you too, Mason."

He grinned. "Are you going to cry every time I tell you I love you? Because I plan on telling you a lot and that might put a damper on things."

"I'm sorry you have to deal with Joe and his obsession with getting me back."

He raised a gentle hand to the side of my face. "Hey. You are not responsible for Joe Simmons's behavior."

"But you hit him tonight, not that I blame you, and then you were so upset—"

"Not at you, Rose. I was upset at myself. I swore I'd never hit anyone again, but he was standing there, insulting you…and I couldn't take it. I'm sorry."

I shook my head. "No more sorries. We're full up of them." I glanced down without thinking, but Mason tipped my chin up until our eyes met.

"Do you really think you're pregnant?"

"I'm not sure. Maybe. I'm late and I'm never late."

"And if we are pregnant," he said, his eyes imploring. "How do you feel about it?"

I hesitated. "How do *you* feel about it?"

"Honestly?"

"Yes."

"Obviously it's not ideal. I hoped we'd have more time alone together. But—" he added when I tensed "—I know beyond a shadow of a doubt that I want children with you one day. So if it happens sooner rather than later, I'd still consider it a blessing."

I kissed him, filled with gratitude. I wasn't sure what I'd ever done to deserve him, but I thanked my lucky stars he was mine.

He pulled back and studied my face. "Now you tell me, Rose. How do *you* feel?"

"I've wanted kids for as long as I can remember. And I still do…"

His thumb rubbed my cheek bone. "But?"

"But not yet. And no one is more surprised I feel that way than I am. I want more time alone with you too. I don't want the beginning of our relationship to be focused on me barfing and sleeping all the time and picking out nursery bedding." I paused. "Does that make me a bad person?"

He smiled. "It makes you perfectly normal. And since we're being entirely honest, I'm profoundly ashamed to admit that I'm happy to hear you want me to yourself too."

I shook my head, grinning. "But what if I *am?*"

"Then I will love you and our baby and all the other babies to come after him until my dying breath."

"Him?" I teased.

"Or her." He shrugged, then leaned down and kissed me until I was senseless. "You looked gorgeous in that sexy red dress tonight. Do you have any idea how hard it was for me to not kiss you like this at dinner? I'm sure I deserve sainthood for that."

I snuggled into him. "Saint Mason." I laughed. "I prefer Wicked Mason."

He chuckled and kissed the top of my head. "Now tell me about your fight with Violet."

"You remember that?" I asked in surprise.

"Of course I do."

I filled him in on our phone conversation but left out the part about her missing the loan payments.

"That helps put what she did tonight in context. Joe probably brought her along to spy on you, but she wanted to sink her claws into him to prove to you that she could." He grimaced. "I thought Neely Kate was going to rip her throat out. She's definitely a good friend."

"Yeah, I'm lucky to have her."

"So Violet went out with him to piss you off and he went out with her to spy on you and perhaps make you jealous?" He paused. "Sounds like a match made in heaven."

But I couldn't ignore the fact that it *had* made me jealous to see the two of them together. That was a conversation I needed to have with Jonah. And soon.

"Would you mind if I asked Jonah to join us for Thanksgiving?" I blurted out.

His eyebrows rose. "Um... That seems out of nowhere, but yes. Of course."

I lifted my head to kiss him. "Thank you."

"This is your house. You can invite whomever you want."

"But it's your Thanksgiving too," I said, suddenly worried.

"Hey. I didn't mean that how it sounded. Your friends are my friends. The more the merrier, truly, Rose."

I closed my eyes, suddenly overwhelmed with sleepiness. Mason pulled me close and tugged the covers over us.

"Do you really have tomorrow off?" Mason murmured before I drifted off to sleep.

"Yep. We can stay in bed all day long."

"You have no idea how much I like the sound of that."

I smiled to myself as sleep overtook me. Actually, I did. After all the storms that had been blustering around me and inside me, I needed a moment of calm.

Chapter Twelve

I woke up to the sound of Mason groaning, and was instantly alert in the pitch-black room.

"Mason?"

"No!" he shouted, still lying next to me.

I breathed a sigh of relief. He was dreaming. "Mason." I touched his arm and he jolted, his hand grabbing my arm roughly as he pushed me down on the bed.

"Mason!" I shouted, terrified.

He dropped his hand and bolted upright. "Oh, my God. Rose."

I tried to catch my breath as he turned on the light, his eyes filled with terror.

"Did I hurt you?" His hands roamed my arms, looking for nonexistent bruises.

I put my hand over his. "I'm fine. Don't worry."

He lay back down next to me and scooped me into his arms. "I'm so sorry."

"Did you have a bad dream?"

"Yes."

"Do you remember what it was about?"

He hesitated. "Yes."

When he didn't say anything else, I rolled over so our chests were touching. "What was it about?"

"Him. Savannah's killer."

I gasped. "Oh."

He scrunched his eyes closed. "I used to get nightmares right after it happened. More like night terrors. But they went away. I haven't had one for months."

Until he hit Joe.

"What made them go away before?"

"I don't know." He sounded short. "Everything in my life changed when I moved here. The dreams just went away."

I reached my hand up to his scalp and played with a strand of his wavy dark blond hair. "Mason, it's okay."

"No, it's not, Rose. I see the proof of it on your arm."

I glanced down at the red marks on my bicep from his fingers. "I'm fine. It's nothing."

"This time. What if it happens again? What if I hurt you worse?"

"That's a lot of what-ifs."

He started to get up, but I pulled him back down. "Where do you think you're going?"

"I'm going to sleep in the other room."

My hold tightened. "No. You're not. You're going to sleep right here next to me."

"Just hours ago I swore to you that I wouldn't hurt you and look what I did."

"Mason, you were sleeping. It was one dream."

I finally convinced him to sleep with me, but when we woke up in the morning, he was quieter than usual.

He studied my face, gently brushing the hair off my cheek.

"When did you first know you loved me?" I asked. "You said it for the first time last night, but I've suspected for a while. Was it when you were in the hospital after the Crocker ordeal?"

A smile lifted the corners of his mouth. "Longer than that."

"When you came over in September and told me about Savannah?"

His smile fell, making me instantly sorry to have brought up his sister. "Longer."

I refused to lose our moment. "Then tell me."

He laughed. "If I tell you, you're going to think I'm lame. I don't want you to kick me out of your bed."

"Now you *have* to tell me."

"Fine." His grin grew. "Sometime between when I found you drunk and about to make out with Skeeter Malcolm in the pool hall—"

"I was not about to make out with Skeeter Malcolm!"

"—and when you showed up outside the courtroom and asked me to help set up a meeting with Bruce Wayne's attorney."

"Mason," I said, flabbergasted. "That was in July."

He cringed. "I told you it was lame."

"I think it's sweet."

"When did you know you loved me?"

It was my turn to cringe. "I've been thinking about it for days, but I wasn't certain until last night. I felt like I had to tell you or I'd burst."

He smiled. "I know exactly what you mean." His hand covered my stomach. "When are we going to find out about this?"

"We could just wait nine months?" I teased.

"I've heard there are better ways to find out," he said dryly, but he was still grinning. "They have these newfangled things called pregnancy tests."

I cocked an eyebrow. "You don't say?"

"You seem reluctant."

"I'm reluctant for the same reason I was reluctant to tell you about the possibility in the first place. If the test is positive, it will become a sure thing. Right now there's just you and me, and if we find out I am pregnant, there'll be three of us. Let's just give ourselves a little more time before we know…okay?"

"Sure, but how long do you want to wait? Don't you need to go to the doctor?"

"As long as I don't drink or take any medication, I'll be fine. Neely Kate suggested I take prenatal vitamins to be on the safe side."

"Neely Kate? How long has she known?"

"Since yesterday afternoon. She actually raised the possibility before I did."

"Of course she did." He laughed. "But seriously, how long do you want to wait?"

"A week or two, tops."

"Okay."

"Thanks for being so wonderful about all of this."

"I love you, Rose. I'm not doing anything extraordinary other than that."

"I love you too."

We got up and took a shower, and by the time we got out, Muffy was pacing the bathroom floor.

I headed downstairs to let her out and started a pot of coffee. While I waited for Mason to come down, I mixed pancake batter and fried bacon. I was used to having Sunday mornings off from work, but Mason and I had started going to Jonah's church together. This was the first morning I'd had completely free in ages.

After Mason came down and we sat together at the kitchen table for breakfast, I watched Muffy pace the length of the kitchen.

"Do you have any work to do this morning?" I asked him, stabbing my fork into my pancake.

His face scrunched. "I do. I thought you'd be working at the nursery."

"I'm not asking to make you feel guilty, Mason. I told you that I'd never begrudge you your work. I'm only asking because *I* feel guilty."

"You? About what?"

"It's a beautiful day and Muffy's been cooped up all week. I want to take her for a walk."

He sucked in a breath and slowly released it. "I don't know, Rose. Don't get me wrong, I have no issue with you going on a walk. In fact, if I didn't have this bum leg, I'd ask to go with you. But the bank robbers are still on the loose. And while I may fault Joe Simmons for a lot of things, there's no doubt he wants to keep you safe. I can't help thinking he might be right in this."

"Mason. There has been no sign of them. At. All. Don't you think they would have turned up by now if they had some issue with me? No one's heard hide nor hair of them. They're probably long gone." I smiled sweetly. "Besides, it's broad daylight."

He groaned. "All right. But bring your phone. And promise you'll call me at the first sign of trouble."

"I will."

We cleaned up the kitchen together after he insisted he could stand on his leg for long enough to help. When we finished, I gave him a long kiss. "Get your work done so we can take a nap together later."

He grinned. "Why are we taking a nap?"

I grabbed Muffy's leash and walked with him to the door. "Because I plan to get you good and worn out first." I started to walk away, but he grabbed my hand and pulled me in for a kiss. It was almost enough to make me reconsider going on a walk, but Muffy had seen the leash and was whining at my feet.

"Duty calls," Mason murmured against my lips. "Be careful."

"It's a walk," I said, descending the porch steps. "What could happen?"

"*You* should never ask that. Just be careful, okay?"

"Okay."

As soon as we got outside, Muffy started running in excited circles at my feet. I stooped to put on her leash, then stopped mid-action. For the most part, my little dog minded me well and she was happier roaming free, not that I blamed her. I figured I'd let her have her way.

We'd been on a few walks since moving to the farm and we'd always gone north, toward the acres and acres of fields I owned. Today I wanted to go south. I knew I owned a few acres of grassland scattered with trees in that direction and a neighboring farm jutted up against my property. I wanted to check the area out.

We found a natural path close to the woods, and I tried to ignore the unease that crawled up my back. I couldn't avoid the woods forever. Maybe once things died down I could take Muffy on a walk through them, create some new memories.

Muffy bounced down the path, thrilled to be roaming outside. I needed to make more time for her. I supposed I'd have the opportunity if the nursery folded.

The knowledge slammed through me: Unless something changed, I was about to lose my business.

White-hot fury burned in my gut when I thought about Violet destroying our business and my credit. I couldn't sit idly by and let it all fall apart, but I didn't see any way to pay off the loan, let alone finance our other bills. Finding the robbers and getting back my cash from the O'Leary job was starting to seem like the only solution.

A world with me and Neely Kate playing amateur sleuths was a world turned on its head. But since the world had already gone crazy, maybe the only thing we could do was follow suit. We just needed to figure out what—or who—to investigate next.

Still, money aside, part of me wondered if closing the doors to the nursery wouldn't be for the best. Violet and I were definitely at odds and I couldn't imagine us working together peacefully any time soon. But if the nursery closed, I was out hundreds of thousands of dollars. And if I was really pregnant, I couldn't afford to lose all that money. Mason and I would have another person to take care of. The thought was sobering.

Jonah was right—one problem at a time.

Then it hit me. Maybe I was going the wrong direction. Perhaps we should concentrate our efforts on finding Mr. Sullivan. Then maybe he could tell Mr. Burns he'd given Violet an extension, buying us more time to get my money back. That is, after I beat him with a shovel until he told me who'd robbed the bank.

Muffy ran up to a dilapidated wooden fence and I realized that this area had to have been a horse or cow pasture at one point. It was just missing a few sections of fence, which had most likely fallen down. A wooden gate hung on one hinge, leaving a gap big enough to walk through, which Muffy took as an invitation.

"Muffy," I called after her as she slipped through the opening.

She stopped and turned to look at me, tilting her head to the side and giving me a sad look.

"Oh, okay," I groaned. The way that gate hung open told me that the field couldn't possibly be in active use, so I didn't have to worry we'd be trampled by cows. I knew there was a farmhouse on this property. Maybe I could I introduce myself to my neighbor.

When I didn't continue to protest her movements, Muffy took off running in the overgrown grass, finding a narrow dirt path. I traipsed through the grass after her as she bolted toward a gravel road. By the time I caught up, Muffy was waiting at the edge of the road. There was a field of miniature goats in an enclosed pen on the other side, and the animals were totally captivating her attention.

As soon as she saw me, she ran straight across the gravel street toward the barbed wire pen and started barking at the animals. Without warning, all but one of the ten goats fell to their sides, their legs sticking straight out from their bodies. I released a shriek. "Muffy, you killed them!" Then the last standing goat fell over.

Muffy had already lost interest in the goats by then. She'd trotted over to the ditch between the penned area and the road and started whining at something inside it.

I hurried over, panicked by the possibility that we'd somehow killed a field of goats. How had it happened and how in the world would I be able to reimburse the farmer who owned them? As I walked toward my little dog, one goat began to revive, thank God, and several were climbing to their feet by the time I'd made it across the road. Muffy almost immediately released a loud, smelly fart. I waved a hand in front of my face, as I peered into the ditch.

"What are you looking at?" I moved her slightly to the side, the blood rushing from my head when I saw what had grabbed her attention.

The good news was that finding Mr. Sullivan had been easier than expected.

The bad news was that he wouldn't be of much use, seeing how he was dead.

His pale, bloated face stared up at me with vacant eyes, and I screamed even louder than I had the first time.

The goats bleated, then fell over like they were frozen solid.

"Again?" I shouted, my hands shaking as I dug my cell phone out of my pocket and dialed 911. "I found a body next to a field of goats that keep fallin' over," I said as soon as the operator answered.

"*Excuse me?*"

"I'm next to a field full of goats that keep tipping over on their sides and my dog just found a man in a ditch. I'm pretty sure he's dead."

"And where is this body located?" The bored tone in her voice suggested she wasn't too impressed. How many dead bodies turned up in Fenton County?

"I'm at the farm just south of 27078 County Road 24."

"Okay, ma'am," she said in that same flat tone. "Now, are you sure he's dead? Perhaps he just needs medical attention."

I inched closer to Mr. Sullivan, as though he might reach out and grab me. He wore black dress pants with black loafers and a black wool coat. His open, blank stare was the only confirmation I needed. Along with his pale-blue skin. "No. I'm pretty sure he's dead."

"I already have a deputy on the way, ma'am,"

"Thank you," I mumbled. To my surprise, I could already hear faint sirens.

A sheriff's car turned down the road and stopped several feet before reaching me. I was relieved to recognize the deputy who climbed out of the car door.

"Deputy Miller!" I said. He'd been the officer who had watched over us the most at the farm during the Crocker mess.

When Crocker's men showed up at my property, Deputy Miller had pretended to be one of them. But it turned out that he'd been working with the state police as an informant the whole time. In fact, he'd been the one to keep Muffy safe until Mason and me were found. Muffy loved him and she was an excellent judge of character.

"Rose!" the dark-haired man called out as he approached. Muffy ran up to him and Deputy Miller squatted down to pet her. "Hey, girl! How you doin'? Did you miss me?"

Muffy answered by licking his hand and filling the air with a stench that would make paint peel. Deputy Miller stood, scrunching his nose and waving his hand in front of his face. "Muffy, we need to make you a police dog and send you into tense situations in lieu of tear gas."

I was usually offended when someone insulted my little dog, but Deputy Miller was one of only a handful of people besides me who appreciated her scrappy appearance and thought she was cute. And besides, he had a point.

"I had a strange call reporting that someone had found a dead body here in a field full of dead goats."

"That's only half right." I grimaced.

He stopped in his tracks. "There's a small herd of goats eatin' grass over there, so I'm guessing that's the part that's wrong."

I pointed to the ditch behind me. "The goats came back to life, but the guy in the ditch still looks pretty dead. I'm pretty sure it's Mr. Sullivan from the bank."

He made a less-than-eager face. "Okay, let's check this out."

Muffy got excited and started to bark and run circles around the deputy.

Just then, the goats bleated and fell to the ground, the thuds filling the air.

"*Again*?" I shouted, turning to Deputy Miller while pointing to the field. "They keep tipping over!"

"They're supposed to do that. They're fainting goats."

Why in tarnation would someone want a field full of fainting goats? "Well, they certainly live up to their name."

He stood and inched closer to the ditch, leaning over the man's body while I hung back on the road. "Yep, he's dead all right. And you think it's Mr. Sullivan? Do you know him?"

"Only from dealing with him at the bank."

"How'd you find him?"

"*Muffy* found him. We were on a walk."

He squatted next to the ditch, still examining the body. "I wonder how he got here. Do you think he knows your neighbor?"

"I don't know. I haven't met my neighbor yet."

I expected some sort of rebuke, but the deputy seemed indifferent. "I'm gonna have to call a detective and the coroner." His gazed lifted to mine. "And the chief deputy sheriff."

I cringed. "Are you sure you have to call *him*?"

"He gave us very strict instructions to notify him in case you were involved in any messy situations."

I put my hands on my hips. "You're kidding me!"

"He was very adamant."

"I'm *sure* he was."

The deputy walked back to the patrol car and squatted to rub Muffy's head while he made his calls. I held my own phone in my hand, racked with indecision. Everything in me wanted to call Mason, but after last night's debacle in Jasper's, I didn't want to risk some sort of confrontation between him and Joe. I could handle Joe on my own, and didn't want Mason to be any more upset than he'd been last night.

About ten minutes later, a car I didn't recognize turned down the gravel road while I rested my backside on the hood of Deputy Miller's cruiser talking with the officer.

I didn't recognize the detective who got out of the car. A middle-aged man with thinning hair parted to the side, he walked up to Deputy Miller and me with a scowl on his face that looked somewhat permanent based on the deep grooves carved into his jowls.

"Where is it?" he barked.

Muffy hunkered down near my feet and released a low growl.

The detective didn't look amused.

Deputy Miller bent down and gave Muffy another rub on the head, then stood and pointed to the ditch. "Ms. Gardner was out walking with her dog Muffy—"

The detective's head jerked back to me. "Wait. *Rose* Gardner?"

I hesitated. "Yeah…"

His scowl deepened and he shook his head in disgust before returning his attention to the body.

I raised my eyebrows at Deputy Miller in dismay and whispered, "What did I do?"

"You helped get Chief Deputy Dimler arrested."

"But he was on the take from Crocker!" I protested. "And he almost got the new chief deputy killed."

Deputy Miller shrugged.

The detective hovered over the body. "Miller, are you planning to chit-chat all day or are you going to tell me about this case?" His booming voice burst through the stillness.

Most of the goats squealed and fainted, their bodies dropping like flies.

"*What the Sam Hill…?*" the detective shouted as he jumped several feet backward, tripping and very nearly falling on his butt. The goats that were still upright tumbled to their sides.

"Fainting goats, sir," Miller said. When the detective shot him an odd look, he added, "My uncle has some."

The detective scowled again and took notes as the deputy filled him in on what little information he had. Another car turned down the lane and I looked over my shoulder, my stomach dropping when I recognized it. It must have been Joe's day off since he wasn't driving his sheriff's car. I was glad for the warning, but no amount of preparation would make me ready to face him after the disaster of the previous evening.

But Joe ignored me when he got out of his car, sporting a bruised cheek, and sauntered over to the detective. Muffy wasn't having any of it. She yipped with excitement and jumped up on his legs, eager for acknowledgment. He knelt down and grabbed her face in his hands. "Not right now, Muff. I'll play with you in a little bit, okay? Go back to your momma."

Muffy's head drooped and Joe rubbed behind her ears. "It's okay, girl, I'll come see you. I promise."

She walked back to me, her tail between her legs. I picked her up and petted her, unnerved by her reaction to Joe. Poor Muffy. She didn't understand how much had changed in a couple months. She only knew she missed Joe.

Damn him.

After he spent several minutes talking about the cause of death with the officers—probably multiple gunshot wounds to the chest—he finally meandered over to me, his face expressionless. He reminded me of the Joe McAllister I'd met the night of Momma's murder, aloof and detached. It was better this way, so why did his chilly attitude bother me?

"Rose, why don't we take a little walk?"

I set Muffy down on the gravel. "Okay."

He led the way at least twenty feet down the road, out of earshot of the other two men. Muffy trotted along beside him, her tongue hanging out.

"Is it all right with you if I pet your dog?" he asked dryly.

"You know she loves you. It would hurt her if you didn't. She doesn't understand what's wrong."

He squatted and picked Muffy up, cradling her and rubbing her head. "You mean like how Ashley and Mikey wouldn't understand why Joe lives next door and refused to play with them any more like he used to?"

I groaned. What a mess.

"How is it you stumbled upon the first dead body discovered in this area in the last five years?"

I twisted my mouth to the side. "That bad luck of mine?"

His eyes narrowed as he studied me. "Have you been doing some investigating of your own for the bank robbery case?"

Sure, Neely Kate had interrogated Toby Wheaton and I'd asked him a question too, but that didn't mean we were actively investigating. Yet. Besides, that had nothing to do with how I'd discovered this body. I put my hand on my hips, trying to make my outrage believable. "I can't believe you asked me that."

His eyebrow lifted, but there was no hint of teasing. "And you still didn't answer the question."

"No, I'm not investigating. Happy now?" I made a face.

"Then how is it that you found a body? *You.* Out of all twenty-four thousand residents in Fenton County."

"I don't know, Joe," I said getting irritated. "I haven't been taking Muffy to job sites over the last week or two and she's been cooped up. It's a beautiful day, so I decided to take her on a long walk. Muffy led the way and I followed her."

"And you just happened to stumble across a dead body? The body of the missing loan officer?"

"Good heavens. Will you let that go already?"

"No. I *won't* let it go already. You have a penchant for trouble and what do you know?" He waved his hand back toward the body. "Here you are."

"I don't know what you want me to say, Joe. I took Muffy for a walk and this is where she went. Maybe you should interrogate her."

Joe set Muffy on the ground, then took a step closer to me. We stood several feet apart, closer than was comfortable, but I wasn't about to back down. Especially from him. "Rose, you've gotten lucky so far with your crazy antics—"

"Crazy antics!" I shouted, drawing the attention of the other two men.

"You are going to get yourself killed." Joe's voice broke and he swallowed, glancing at the country road before turning back to me. "I understand that you seem to stumble into these things, but just because you step in a dog pile doesn't mean you have to roll around in it."

My anger singed my ears. "Do you have a point, Chief Deputy Simmons? Because I've made it crystal clear that I had nothing to do with this."

"What does Mason say about this?" He continued to study me, the bruise on his cheek a painful reminder that Mason was involved in all of this too.

"What do you care what he thinks?" I spat out.

He leaned closer, hatred in his eyes. "I don't give a flying flip about Mason Deveraux, but I do give a flip that he's putting your life in danger. Does he even try to stop you?"

I put my hands on my hips. "Unlike you, Mason sees me as a grown woman, perfectly capable of making my own decisions."

"So he encourages you in your foolishness?"

I threw my hands up in the air. "What the hell are you talking about, Joe? I was minding my own business when the bank was robbed, just like I was minding my own business when Muffy found that poor man's body. How in the world does that constitute Mason encouraging me to put myself in danger?"

His jaw locked. "Don't you stand there and lie to me, Rose Anne Gardner. You're the one who's always busted my ass for keeping secrets and telling lies and you're doing the exact same thing to me now."

"*What are you talking about?*"

"I know you talked to Toby Wheaton in the bar last night."

The blood in my face rushed to my toes.

His eyebrows lifted and a grin tipped up his mouth, but he didn't look all that amused. "That's right. I actually saw you and Neely Kate talking to him. Did you do it because I'd questioned him earlier in the day? What were you asking him?"

My outrage exploded in my chest. "You were spying on me?"

"Call it what you like. Someone has to keep track of you, and Mason's obviously not doing the job. He was sitting on his ass in the next room."

"How dare you!" I shouted, not caring that we now had the undivided attention of the two other law enforcement officials. "I don't need a keeper, Joe McAllister! I need a man who's going to love me for who I am without belittling my every move. Who's going to respect my decisions and judgment and not make me feel like an idiot because I'm not doing things his way."

"You are putting your life in *danger*. I don't know how to get that fact into your thick head!" His voice rose, echoing around us. I hoped to high heaven Mason hadn't heard him at the farm, half a mile away.

"Do you have any other questions, Deputy? Because I'm done discussing my personal life with you."

"Goddammit!" He grunted, then he took a deep breath. "Get in my car now."

My eyes widened. "Why?"

"I'm taking you in for questioning."

My chest tightened and I had to force my words. "For what?"

"Whatever I feel like, *now get in the damn car*."

I took a step backward. "No."

His eyes hardened and he glanced at the two men who were standing twenty feet down the road, now openly gaping at us. "Don't make me pull out my handcuffs."

"You can't handcuff me for no reason. You told me that yourself when Momma died."

His jaw clenched and he forced out through his clenched teeth, "Try me."

I was close to panicking. I'd obviously pushed Joe over an edge I hadn't noticed and I had no doubt he'd arrest me just to prove he could. But I was also enraged. He was clearly using his power to pursue his own personal vendetta. He had no grounds for arresting me. Even if he thought I was investigating the robbery. But most of all, I was terrified of Mason's reaction if Joe actually brought me in to the station. He'd be on Joe's turf and I'd be locked up and unable to help him.

Tears filled my eyes. "What do you want, Joe?" My voice broke as I fought to keep from crying.

My tears softened him. He took a step closer and reached an arm around my back, but I shrugged him off. "You do *not* get to threaten to arrest me and then put your arms around me."

He lowered his arm but stayed close, tenderness on his face. "Rose, I know you don't want to hear this, but I still love you. Would you be able to just stand back and watch someone you love do something you knew would get them into trouble?"

I didn't answer, pressing my knuckles to my mouth.

"I'm not going to arrest you." He slowly reached a hand to my arm and rubbed lightly when I didn't pull away. "I'm only trying to get you to listen. You're so stinking stubborn, sometimes words don't get through to you."

"I want to go home."

"Okay, let me wrap things up and I'll take you."

I lifted my gaze to his, my back stiffening. "I walked here with Muffy and I'll walk back."

A hard look filled his eyes. "I'll drive you." His tone made it clear he wasn't going to back down.

"Fine," I grunted.

"But I can't go yet. It'll be five to ten more minutes." He looked up at the cloud-darkened sky. "Are you cold? Do you want to sit in the car?" His voice softened and he sounded more like the Joe I had known over the summer. The one who would come see me for the weekend, sweeping me up in his arms and spending every possible moment with me before he had to leave again on Monday morning. We'd been our happiest then, and it made me sad to remember those days. It occurred to me there were so many versions of him. Which was the real one?

I wondered if Joe even knew.

Chapter Thirteen

I waited outside if for no other reason than I didn't want to spend any more time in his car than necessary. There were too many painful reminders.

Muffy stuck with Joe, making me feel even worse. I'd adopted her during the time when Joe had entered my life. It had been obvious he loved her and she him, and they clearly missed each other. Why had I never considered that before today?

When Joe finished his business, he walked over to me, looking cautious. He knew he'd gone too far and I supposed he was wondering if I was going to make him pay for it. "We can go now." He opened the passenger door. "Hop in, Muffy."

She jumped into the backseat, obviously happy to be there, while I slid into the front seat, a familiar place that was no longer mine. Nostalgia washed over me, hot and bittersweet. Joe was my first love. Our breakup had nearly destroyed me. I suspected it had done the same to him. But nothing had changed for Joe. He was still a slave to his father. I was still a slave to his father's false accusations. Joe was still on Hilary's hook, whether he liked it or not.

I was a different person from the one who'd fallen in love with him.

I wasn't the naïve young woman who'd never gone on a picnic or flown a kite. I'd drunk beer and danced in the rain. I'd kissed a man and *done more* with a man. It was on the night Joe and I met that I created a list of the twenty-eight things I wanted to do before the vision of my death came true—my wish list. And I'd done them all. Some on my own. Some with the man climbing into the car next to me now.

But it was time to make a new list—one that didn't include him.

To Joe, I was still a damsel in distress who needed help becoming a woman capable of navigating the world. To Mason, I already *was* that woman.

Joe closed his car door and started the engine. "Is Mason at your farm?"

"Yes."

"I need to talk to you, Rose, and your farm doesn't seem like the best place if he's there."

I shook my head, refusing to look at him. "There's nothing left to say."

"Yes. There is. We can't keep going on like this."

"Then leave me alone."

He pulled up to the stop sign and sighed, draping his arm over the steering wheel and staring out the windshield. "You know I can't. Not if I'm a sheriff's deputy and you keep finding trouble."

He was right. We were going to keep butting heads. We needed to form some sort of truce.

"Fine."

He turned left. Away from the farm.

My stomach tightened. "Where are we going, Joe?"

"Somewhere private to talk."

"I don't think that's a good idea."

"Why?" He turned to me and lifted an eyebrow, shooting me a sarcastic leer. "Don't you trust yourself?"

"No. I don't trust you."

Joe pulled the car to the side of the road and threw it into park. "Of all the things you've ever said to me, you've never hurt me as much as you did just now. What the hell do you think I'm going to do? When have I ever insinuated that I'd hurt a hair on your head?"

I started to cry.

"Rose. What do you think I'm going to *do*?" he asked, insistent. And angry.

"I don't know." I wiped my tears and looked out the window. "I just want to go home."

He was quiet for several seconds before he finally said, "To him."

I didn't respond.

"Do you really think I'd hurt you?"

"Not intentionally. But you keep doing it anyway. Please. Just take me home."

A car whizzed past us.

"No," he said, his voice rising again. "We'll do this on the side of the road if we have to, but we're *going* to talk. How am I hurting you?"

My head swung toward him. "You won't leave me alone!"

Exasperation spread over his face. "How can I leave you alone when *I love you?* We belong together, Rose. I'm trying to make you see that."

"You can't *force* me to be with you just because *you* think we belong together." My anger was rising again. "You think you can dictate the way things should be and you expect me to just follow along. I'm a *grown woman*, Joe. I have a mind and I have opinions of my own." I turned to him, leaning into the console. "Mason respects me. He values my opinion. He listens to what I have to say. He—"

Before I knew what he was doing, Joe grabbed the back of my head and pulled my mouth to his. His kiss wasn't tender like the first time he'd kissed me on my front porch, months ago. That kiss had been full of wonder and playfulness. This was wild and desperate—his mouth claimed mine while his arm reached around my back and pinned my lower abdomen to the console, his upper chest pressed against mine.

I strained against him and tried to push him away, but my arms were caught at my sides. Fear bubbled up in my gut, not because I thought he would hurt me, but because I felt myself weakening.

My body was reacting to his.

He groaned when my lips parted in response to him, and I sank into his chest. He moved his hand up to my head and buried his hand in my hair, holding me in place as his mouth devoured mine. I kissed him back with abandon.

His other hand slid to my waist, slipping under the edge of my jacket to tug up my shirt.

His cold hand on my bare skin brought me back to my senses. He'd freed my arms, so I lifted my hands to his chest and pushed hard, breaking his hold. "No!"

Joe sat back in his seat, stunned, his eyes still hooded with lust. "Rose."

I shook my head in horror, scooting away from him until my back hit the car door. "How could you? I'm with Mason!"

He ran a hand through his hair, his eyes pleading. "If you really wanted him, would you kiss me like that?"

"It's called chemistry! I never once claimed we didn't have chemistry!" I took a deep breath and choked back a sob. "Take me home."

"No!" Anger burned in his eyes and he reached for me, but I shrunk away. "I was trying to prove a point!"

"And you did, just not the one you intended. Did you even listen to a word I said?"

He shook his head. "That you want to be with him? I heard the words, Rose, but the evidence proves otherwise."

"This—" I waved my hand between us "—proves *nothing*." My words were hateful, but at that moment I truly hated him. I hated that he was trying to steal the happiness I had with Mason. "All you did was prove the point I was making before you kissed me." My voice turned cold. "I was telling you that Mason respects me. He values my opinions. He doesn't shove his agenda at me and expect me to obey." I swallowed the lump in my throat. "Mason's loved me for months. Don't you think he wanted to kiss me ages ago? To prove there was something between us? Because there is, Joe, there's something *wonderful* between us. But he didn't because I was with you. He knew me well enough to know that forcing himself on me when I was with someone else would *devastate me*."

His mouth opened and closed as he started to say something and stopped.

"He knew that kissing me might prove we had chemistry, but I couldn't handle the fallout. That right there is just one of the many differences between you. He loves me enough that he'd rather live without me than rip my heart to shreds. He loves me unconditionally, Joe. That means putting the other person's feelings before your own, a concept you clearly don't understand."

"Rose…"

"Take me home," I said, trying to keep myself from falling apart.

"You and I still have something, Rose. You can't deny that."

"We did once. But you killed it. You stomped on it and destroyed it and destroyed me too. Now I have to walk into that house and face the man I love knowing I just cheated on him." A sob broke loose. What had I done?

"You didn't cheat." A mixture of regret and frustration filled his words. "We only kissed."

I released a bitter laugh. "After hearing your definition of *not cheating*, I'm even more glad we're not together."

He shoved the car into gear and whipped it around in a U-turn. Thankfully he was silent the rest of the way home. When he parked in front of my house, I reached for the door, but he said, "Rose, I'm sorry if I hurt you."

"*If* you hurt me?"

He released a breath. "Okay, I'm sorry that I hurt you."

I started to get out, but then turned back to face him. "And don't hold out hope that Mason will see the guilt on my face and break up with me. If that man walks out of my life because of what just happened, I will *never* forgive you."

"Rose." He grabbed my wrist. "He's only interested in you because of me. Think about it. He blames me for Savannah's death. It's the perfect way to get back at me. He thinks I stole his sister from him, so he's decided to steal the most precious thing in the world to me: you. He has you now, but when it serves his purposes, he'll crush you. You can't trust him, Rose. Even if you don't take me back, don't let him hurt you."

My mouth sagged open. "How can you sink so low? He's been interested in me for months. And that's not just him saying so. Everyone noticed but me."

His eyes narrowed. "*I* noticed, Rose. I noticed the day on the courthouse steps after Jimmy DeWade was arrested."

"If that's true, you're suggesting that he's been planning this for months." I tried to jerk away, but he held my arm tight.

"When Mason was in Little Rock, he was known for his patience in the courtroom. He lulled the opponent into a false sense of security before going in for the kill."

"I can't believe you! Is this your slimy way of making me feel better about that kiss?" I scrambled out. "Come on, Muffy."

"Rose, you have to listen to me," Joe pleaded.

Muffy looked torn but finally hopped out of the car, and I slammed the door shut. I stood in front of my house and looked up at the porch as Joe drove off, realizing the main reason this place felt like home to me was because of Mason.

And there was a very good chance I was about to lose him.

The front door opened and he stood on the threshold, leaning on his cane. "Rose?" His gaze lifted to the parting car and his face hardened. "Was that Joe?"

I started to cry and Muffy whined at my feet.

Mason hobbled toward me, but I ran up the steps and flung myself at his chest, throwing him off balance.

He caught himself and his free arm wrapped around my back, squeezing me tight. "What happened? Are you hurt?" He sounded panicked, not that I could blame him. I was a sobbing mess.

I shook my head, trying to catch my breath. "No." At least not physically.

"Rose, you're scaring me. What happened?"

"We found a dead body."

His body tensed. "Where? And who's we?"

"Muffy and me. On our walk. We found Mr. Sullivan from the bank in the ditch next to the gravel drive on the next farm."

His hand gripped my bicep and he pulled me back to look into my face, obviously trying to understand why I was so upset. "Did you see it happen?"

"His murder? No. We just stumbled upon the body."

Irritation flickered in his eyes. "I told you to call me if you ran into trouble. Why didn't you?"

"I was going to. But Deputy Miller showed up as soon as I got off the call with the 911 operator, and he told me that Joe was coming."

"You didn't call me because you didn't want Joe and me to be together in such close proximity."

I nodded.

The left corner of his mouth tipped up slightly as he tried to piece everything together. "It stands to reason he'd be there. Contrary to your track record, there aren't many murders in Fenton County."

"That's not the only reason he was there."

His face went slack. "You."

"Deputy Miller said he's told all the deputies to call him if I'm involved in anything."

His jaw hardened. "Okay. So what happened?"

I cringed. "We had a huge argument. He accused me of finding the body on purpose, which is ridiculous. Muffy found him. Along with a field of fainting goats. In any case, he thinks I'm investigating the bank robbery."

"Are you?" he asked dryly.

My heart lurched. "Why do you ask?"

"As we've already established, I'm an intelligent man. You and Neely Kate disappeared for a prolonged length of time last night. Then there was a commotion in the bar and you two reappeared just minutes later. Seeing as how I can't come up with a reasonable explanation for one pregnant woman and another possibly pregnant woman to visit a bar, I can only presume you were up to something."

I smiled at him through my tears. "I love you."

"Rose, why are you crying?" The muscles in his chest tightened. "What did Joe do?"

I was torn with indecision. I didn't want to lie to him. I *refused* to lie to him, but to tell him the truth could drive him away or push him to do something he'd regret.

"I want you to tell me everything."

"Okay." I nodded. "But let's sit down first. You shouldn't be on your leg."

He hesitated, but then grabbed my hand and laced our fingers together, pulling me into the house. We sat on the sofa and I started from the beginning—stumbling upon the body, the deputies showing up, then Joe's arrival and our argument.

"He threatened to arrest you?" His voice rose as his face reddened. "That is a blatant abuse of power. I could file charges against him."

"Mason," I begged. "Please don't."

He pulled his hand from mine. "There's more," he said quietly, watching my face. "I can tell there's more."

"I'm not going to keep anything from you. I promise. I just haven't gotten there yet."

"Go on." His eyes darkened.

"He wanted to go somewhere to talk. I initially agreed, thinking I could convince him to leave me alone."

"Did you really think that was possible?" There was a hard edge in his voice I wasn't used to hearing. At least not directed at me.

I twisted my hands in my lap. "I started to panic about everything, so he pulled over to the side of the road. I told him that he had to leave me alone. That I belonged with you. I started to tell him why—that you respect me and value my opinion and then…he kissed me."

The fury in Mason's eyes sucked my breath away. "Did he force himself on you?"

I could see where he was going with this. His mind was already racing to figure out what charges to file against Joe. "At first."

"At first," he repeated without emotion. "What exactly does that mean?"

I turned away, unable to look at him. "He caught me by surprise, and I started to kiss him back before I came to my senses and pushed him away."

"Did you do anything else?" His voice was cold, as though he was questioning a witness. I supposed he was.

"No." The word was cut off by a sob. "No. The kiss lasted ten seconds or less."

"You kissed him back."

"Yes, I refuse to lie to you."

"But you didn't *refuse* to kiss him."

How did I get here? How did I let this happen?

Frustrated, I started to stand, but he pulled me back down. "No, you don't get to walk away from this."

"It's not what you're thinking, Mason. I swear. He caught me by surprise and pinned me to him. I couldn't get away at first."

His eye twitched but his face remained expressionless. "Did you really want to get away?"

Shock washed through me. "How can you say that?"

"You admitted that you kissed him back." His voice was still cold.

"I don't know why I did it. Like I said, he caught me off guard. It was a momentary reaction, and then I shoved him away. I told him that I want *you*."

"And *do* you want me, Rose?" His voice was still dark as he tipped up my chin, forcing me to look at him. Anger and power oozed from him.

My breath caught in my throat at the sexual tension that erupted between us.

His hand slid behind my head, his fingers threading through my hair, and he pulled my face inches from his. "I love you, Rose, but I will not share you. I let you have your time and space to make a decision. I finally told you that I love you after months of wanting you, but those three words aren't trivial to me."

His breath was hot on my face and I ached to touch him, but I wasn't sure that was what he wanted from me. "They're not trivial to me either."

"But you kissed him back." It was a low rumble in his chest.

"I wish to God I could undo it, but I can't. It didn't mean anything to me, Mason."

"I want to believe you, Rose, I swear that I do, but all I can think of is him kissing you." His hand tightened in my hair. "And I have plenty of visuals from when you two were together to fill in the footage."

I pressed my lips to his unresponsive mouth. I had to make this better. I couldn't lose him. Not now. Not ever. "I love you, Mason. *You*."

He hadn't pushed me away, which I took as a good sign. I reached for the hem of his thermal shirt, but his free hand covered mine. "Stop." He pulled my head back and stared into my eyes. A fire burned behind his gaze, a potent mixture of anger and passion. "I want you, Rose, more than the air I breathe. But I need to know that you want to be with *me*. I need to know you're not going to change your mind and go back to him. *Especially* him."

I shook my head. "I'm yours, Mason. Yours. I don't want him. I want you."

His mouth covered mine, and he kissed me like a drowning man hanging on for dear life. Grabbing my coat, he jerked it off and tossed it to the floor. I pulled his shirt over his head, taking in the sight of his naked chest. He kissed me again, and suddenly his hand was on my jeans, unbuttoning them with a frenzy he didn't usually possess. I fumbled blindly for the edge of his sweat pants, but he moved my hand away. When he pulled down the zipper to my jeans, he pushed me onto my back on the sofa and tugged my pants over my hips, my panties right behind them. I stared up at him as he pulled his sweat pants and underwear down, but they caught on his brace and he growled in frustration.

A passion I'd never seen before filled his eyes as he took in the sight of me lying there, naked from the waist down.

I reached my hands up to unbutton my blouse, but he pushed them away, then grabbed the top of my shirt and jerked it open, ripping the buttonholes and sending the buttons flying. My chest heaved as my body ached for him with an intensity stronger than I'd ever felt.

His hands covered my breasts, his thumbs brushing the sensitive skin under my thin bra. "Which one of us do you want?"

"I want you, Mason."

He moved a hand between my legs, watching my face as my back arched and my breath came in short pants.

"Who's driving you wild right now?" he asked, his voice low, his eyes dark.

"You are."

I was close and he knew it, so he slowed down the pace of his strokes. When I whimpered, he released a low guttural laugh. "Who do you belong with, Rose?"

"You. I belong with you, Mason."

His hands began to move again. "Do you want me?"

"Yes," I panted in agony of want. "I want you. I *need* you."

He spread my legs and entered me in one deep plunge. I cried out, lifting up to him, but he couldn't find the traction he needed with his leg.

Slipping an arm around my back, he pushed me into a sitting position. I straddled my legs around him and wrapped my arms around his neck, kissing him wildly as he grabbed my hips and began to guide my movements.

Within minutes, I was close again and he stilled me, pulling my body up and off of him so his mouth could find my breast. I squirmed, desperate, and tried to guide him back in, but he held me in place and turned his attention to my other breast.

"No," was his gruff answer.

"Mason," I begged. "Please."

"Not yet," he growled, his hand finding the spot between my legs that sent me climbing again. He tortured me until I cried for release. He looked in my face, his eyes dark with need. "Who do you choose, Rose?"

"I'm yours, Mason," I whimpered. "I'm yours."

He pulled me on top of him and proved it was true, taking me higher than I'd ever been before. I cried out when I reached my peak, Mason right behind me as he grunted into my neck. I collapsed against him, exhausted.

He leaned my head back to look into my eyes while he gently stroked my cheek. "I love you, Rose. I need you so much it frightens me."

"I love you too, Mason," I said through my tears. "I was terrified I'd lost you."

His gaze was serious. "I'm giving you my heart, Rose Gardner. Please don't destroy it."

"I won't. I don't want to lose you."

"As long as you love me, I'm yours."

Then he pulled me down on the sofa and I fell asleep, cradled in his arms.

Chapter Fourteen

Mason was more reserved the rest of the afternoon, but at least he wasn't avoiding me, not that I would have blamed him. I'd cheated on him. Joe could deny it all he wanted, but it was true. I'd betrayed Mason's trust and he was handling it far better than I deserved.

While Mason worked in the office, I spent the afternoon going through more of Dora's photos and papers, but my heart wasn't in it. I was too worried about the future to think about my past. I put the things in a box in the closet and was about to head downstairs and cook dinner when the door to the sunroom caught my eye.

The bedroom windows were covered with sheers that blocked out the view of my old nursery, making it easy to ignore the room. But I'd spent the afternoon fighting nausea and I couldn't pretend I might not need to use this room in nine months. I opened the door and leaned inside, taking in the contents.

The décor was startlingly pink, which would work well for a girl, but we'd have to come up with something else if we had a boy. I put my hand on my stomach, wondering what it would be like to have a baby growing inside me.

I heard Mason's cane thump on the floor behind me, but I didn't turn around to face him, still too ashamed after my earlier confession.

He pressed his chest against my back and wrapped his arm around me, placing his hand over mine. "Are you staying with me because we might be having a baby together?" he asked, no accusation in his voice.

I shook my head and pressed my other hand on top of his. "No. I would never do that to you. You have to believe me."

His body relaxed into mine. "I do, but I needed to hear it."

"Maybe we should move somewhere else," I said, resting the back of my head against his chest, needing to be as physically close to him as possible. "Far away from Henryetta. Then we can get away from him."

"What about your business? You love it."

"I might not be working there much longer anyway," I sighed.

"I know you and Violet had a terrible fight, but you own more of the business than she does. In fact, she has no capital in the business at all other than sweat equity. I'd have to brush up on my business law, but I'm nearly one hundred percent positive that doesn't give her any ownership unless you two are married." There was a teasing tone in his voice. "You're not, are you?"

I laughed and closed my eyes, grateful that things between us were getting back to normal. "No. This may be Arkansas, but I believe two sisters marrying—even half-sisters—is still illegal."

"Good thing for me." He spun me around and gave me a kiss. "I know we're in a rocky spot right now, but we'll get through it."

I nodded, hoping it was true. "There's something else I need to tell you about the Gardner Sisters Nursery." It was time to tell him everything else too.

His eyebrows lifted. "What?"

"It has to do with that money that was stolen in the robbery."

The chorus of Laura Bell Bundy's *Giddy On Up* filled the room—Neely Kate's ringtone on my cell. Mason gave me a half-hearted grin. "I believe your culprit in crime is calling. Answer your phone." He gave me a squeeze and headed for the doorway. "I can interrogate you later about what you two are doing."

I answered the phone just before it went to voice mail. I had so much to tell her. "Hey, Neely Kate."

"Why didn't you tell me that you found Mr. Sullivan's body this morning?" she asked, her voice thick with irritation. "I had to find out from my cousin. I'm sure you can imagine how *embarassin'* it was for me to not know *anything* about my best friend finding the loan officer lyin' dead in a ditch. I have reputation to uphold, after all."

I cringed. "I'm so sorry, Neely Kate. But Joe showed up at the crime scene and…" My voice cracked. I wandered into the baby's room and sat in the rocking chair.

"Why do I get the feeling something really bad happened?"

"I suspect because you know me so well." I took a breath. "Muffy and I went for a walk and wandered over to the farm to the south. Muffy found him in the ditch next to the gravel drive. I called 911 and Joe showed up." I gave her a very condensed version of what happened before we got in the car.

"Do you think he was really goin' to arrest you?"

"Honestly, Neely Kate, I wouldn't have put it past him. Especially after the stunt he pulled when he was taking me home."

"What did he do?"

I hesitated, suddenly unsure of sharing my secret shame with my best friend. What if she thought I was a horrible person? But one thing I'd learned about Neely Kate was that she was loyal. She loved me and would stand by me no matter what. "He kissed me."

"You're kidding me."

"I wish I was, but the worst part is that I kissed him back."

"Oh, Rose..." She hesitated. "Did you change your mind about Mason?"

I shook my head even though she couldn't see me, my voice breaking. "No! I love Mason. It was an in-the-moment thing. I was caught off guard is all."

"What are you gonna do if Mason finds out? You know Joe will be sure to tell him just to rile him up, although you think he'd know better after last night."

"I already told Mason." I took a breath. "I had to. No secrets."

"Oh, mercy. How did he take it?"

"It's a bit rocky right now, but I think we'll be okay." I hoped. "He seems to have forgiven me, even if he hasn't forgotten." Not that I expected him to. If I'd found out that Joe had kissed Hilary while we were still together, I would have needed a *lot* more time to get over it.

"I guess I can let it go that you didn't call me about Mr. Sullivan. You obviously had bigger issues to deal with. Besides, I have news of my own." She paused dramatically. "My second cousin knows a woman whose uncle works in Ted's Garage with Toby. He said Toby's worked on a gold Charger multiple times. Which explains his weird reaction when you asked him about it last night."

"You noticed?" I teased. "I thought you were completely focused on finding the restroom."

"Very funny." But she didn't sound amused. "Yes, I noticed, which is why I did some digging. And I found out something else: the car belongs to a guy who worked at the Henryetta Bank."

"*Mr. Sullivan*? But he wasn't one of the bank robbers. I'm sure of it."

"I don't know. My cousin didn't know his name. Mr. Sullivan would have been stupid to let them use his car if he was involved, but I doubt he drove that Charger around town. I never saw it in the bank parking lot before. Did you?"

"I can't say I paid much attention."

"Which is why I know so much more than you," she gloated. "I bet no one even knew he owned it. My cousin said it was one of those collector cars, so he probably kept it tucked away in a garage. Maybe we should go snoop at his house."

"Do you really think that's a good idea?"

"Have you got a better one?" she asked.

"Don't you think the police or sheriff's deputies are all over his house, especially since they just found his body?"

"Oh, yeah," she grumbled. "I suppose you're right. But we have all kinds of questions we need answered. Why was Mr. Sullivan killed and who killed him? Why was his body dumped at the farm next to yours? Who were his accomplices?" She paused. "You didn't have a chance to go through his pockets, did you?"

"No!" I practically shouted, but after a second I added, "A sheriff's deputy showed up before I got the chance."

"I wonder if we could sneak into the morgue." She sighed. "Probably not, and I suspect the police have already confiscated all the good stuff anyway."

We were silent for a few moments. "So does this mean Samantha Jo is innocent?" I pondered out loud.

"I don't know. Maybe it's just a coincidence that she's desperate for money and happened to be working at the bank three weeks before its first robbery in *fifty years*."

Maybe, but I didn't think so, and obviously Neely Kate didn't either. Something stank worse than a three-day old herring.

"Since we can't go through Mr. Sullivan's house or things, I think we need to corner Samantha Jo," Neely Kate said.

"And I suppose you already have a plan for that?"

"I do, but as much as I hate to admit it, it's gonna have to wait until tomorrow. I promised Grandma I'd bring Ronnie over and spend the day with her and all my aunts and uncles and cousins."

"Well, let's hope it's less eventful than your dinner last night," I said dryly.

She laughed. "Oh, I don't know. I kinda like the excitement you bring with you."

"If I remember correctly, you brought some of your own excitement."

"True…"

I heard yelling in the background.

"I'm comin', Granny!" Neely Kate shouted. "I gotta go," she said to me in a lower voice. "I'm supposed to help Granny make a batch of pickled pigs' feet. My cousins are all taking bets on how long I'll last without barfing."

I cringed. "Good luck."

"Thanks, I need it. I've placed my own bet for fifteen seconds."

I heard more yelling on the other end of the phone.

"Oh, Lordy. I gotta go. My cousin Witt has Ronnie in a headlock. Can you get away tomorrow afternoon? I think I know where we can find Samantha Jo."

I glanced back toward the bedroom. "Yeah, I don't think it will be a problem."

"Great. Let's go after church." Then her voice rose before she hung up. "Witt! You put my husband down, right now!"

When I went back downstairs, Mason was on his laptop in his office, so I went into the kitchen to figure out dinner. I started a pot of chili, then sat out on the front porch with a cup of tea while Muffy played in the front yard.

The front door opened after I'd been outside a bit. I glanced up to see Mason staring out into the yard. "Something smells good in the kitchen."

"I've got a pot of chili cooking."

Mason sat in the chair next to mine. "She seems happy romping around," he said, gesturing to Muffy.

"I figured this was a good alternative since our walk got cut short." I turned to him. "Did you get all your work done?"

He sighed and stretched his legs out in front of him. "No." There was an awkward pause before he asked, "How's Neely Kate?"

"Good…" I almost cringed, waiting for his interrogation.

"Does she think less of me after what happened last night?"

That wasn't the question I'd expected. "No, Mason. I'm sure she thinks he deserved it. She's been pretty aggravated with him herself. The only one feeling badly about you right now is you. Well…" I added with a little laugh. "And maybe Joe's cheek bone."

Mason kept his gaze on Muffy. "Did my behavior last night influence your behavior with Joe this morning?"

"What?" I asked in shock. "No. I promise you it didn't."

"I love you, Rose, and I forgive you, but I keep seeing it in my head. It's going to take a little while for it to go away."

I closed my eyes to keep from crying. "I'm so sorry, Mason. You're the best thing that ever happened to me and I hurt you. *I'm sorry.*"

I stood to go inside, but he grabbed my hand and pulled me back. "Stay with me for a bit. It's beautiful out here. And I miss you."

"Okay."

He stood, tugging me over to the edge of the porch and sat down, his leg extending over the steps. I sat next to him and he snaked an arm around my back. I snuggled into his side, grateful he was still with me. His cheek rested on the top of my head and we sat in silence for several minutes before he finally spoke.

"So what did Neely Kate call about?"

"She was irritated she had to hear from her second cousin that I found Mr. Sullivan's body this morning."

He chuckled, the sound warming my insides. "I can see how that would upset her."

"She also said she found information indicating he owned a gold Charger."

"She's correct."

I jerked my head up to look at him. "You knew? How?"

"I'm the ADA, Rose. There was a murder of a bank employee who owned a car similar to the getaway car. They're going to tell me."

"Why didn't you tell *me*?" I asked in disbelief.

"You didn't ask."

"Mason!"

His hand on my waist tightened, tugging me against him again. "I just found out about forty-five minutes ago. Sullivan's been missing since the morning of the robbery, which is highly suspicious. And seeing how there wasn't much money taken, besides yours, of course, we were sure he wasn't off sipping Mai Tais in the Cayman Islands. Other than his disappearance and his boss suggesting uncorroborated embezzling, finding out he owned the make and model of the getaway car has been our first strong lead."

"So you really think he was in on it?" I still had a hard time believing it.

"Official opinion or personal?"

"Both."

"Officially, we have nothing beyond circumstantial evidence to tie him to this crime. But your vision leads me to believe there was an inside man, and he fits the bill. But of course, there's nothing I can do about that."

"Are the Henryetta police doing anything?"

"Chasing their tails, like they usually do. But the fact that the body was found outside of city limits means the sheriff's department can officially come on board. At least for the murder. And then with any luck at all, they'll find evidence to tie it in to the robbery."

"Do you still think I'm in danger?"

His arm tensed. "No. If the robbers were going to come after you, I think they would have done so already. And with your permission, I'd like to call the sheriff's department and cancel their watch."

I squeezed his waist. "Sounds good to me."

"It sucks that Joe's the chief deputy sheriff and has a whole department at his beck and call. But he's an outsider brought in to replace a guy most of the deputies loved. They hate me for busting Chief Deputy Dimler, but they also resent Joe for taking his place. They may be accepting his arbitrary orders about you at the moment, but they'll grow tired of it before too long." He shifted his leg. "What were you and Neely Kate doing in the bar last night?"

"The truth?"

His grip tightened. "Always."

"Neely Kate saw Toby Wheaton in the bar and decided we should go interrogate him."

"Should his name be significant?"

"His ex-wife, Samantha Jo, was the bank teller during the robbery. We thought she might have been the robbers' informant. Joe told me he'd questioned him earlier that day. I don't suppose he told you."

"No." Mason's hold loosened and he shifted to look at me. "But why would you think she might be an informant?"

I gaped at him. He really wanted my opinion. "Well, she was divorced from Toby. Neely Kate heard she was hurting for money after he racked up debt on all her credit cards before their divorce, and she's only worked at the bank for a couple of weeks."

"Huh," he said. "Anything else?"

"Yeah." I sat up straighter, starting to get excited. "Samantha Jo always wanted to go to Hollywood. She was in all the school plays, and she did some summer theater stuff after graduation. She thought she was destined for greatness. It occurred to me that she might have agreed to help them by playing the part of the frightened bank teller."

Mason's eyes bore into me, deep in concentration. "And how was her performance?"

"I only caught a glimpse of her. When I looked up at the counter, she did look genuinely scared. Her face was red and blotchy."

"And what did you find out from her ex-husband?"

I shook my head. "You *really* want to know?"

"Of course I do. Look at all the people you've helped apprehend."

I scrunched my nose. "I'm not sure those count. A lot of it was accidental."

"Accidental or not, you've played a major role in the apprehension of multiple criminals. I'd be a fool not to listen to you."

I leaned over and gave him a kiss on the lips.

A slow grin lit up his face, although I sensed he was still holding part of himself back with me. "What was that for?"

"For believing in me."

His mouth parted as though he was about to say something, but then he stopped himself. "What did you find out?" he said instead.

"Toby says she's not smart enough to plan a bank robbery, but in his opinion she'd be willing to play a part in it for money."

"So we need to talk to Samantha Jo and find out if she knows anything."

I snorted.

He looked confused. "What was that for?"

"You really think Samantha Jo is going to talk to the Henryetta police or the sheriff's department?"

He looked taken aback. "If it's handled properly."

I laughed. "You obviously don't know Samantha Jo."

"And you do?"

I cocked an eyebrow. "Not personally, but I know enough to know she won't talk to the police or the sheriff. She was in my grade at school. Samantha Jo lived in the trailer park outside of town. Her brother Dickie was a year older than her, and he sold pot and moonshine to the kids in high school. He got busted plenty of times as a minor. But then they busted him the day after his eighteenth birthday. Rumor had it that the sheriff's department set up a sting especially for Dickie. They knew he was heading out hunting, and they arranged for a kid to meet him on a country road to buy some pot and alcohol.

Dickie got busted and of course they found loaded weapons in his truck."

"Damn." Mason looked disgusted. "And they threw the book at him."

"Yeah. He'd been selling to help support the family. Their daddy had run off and their momma had health problems. He got fifteen years. Samantha Jo's momma died soon after. Some of the women at church said she died of a broken heart because her son had brought her so much shame. The kids at school said it was because she couldn't afford her medication. Samantha Jo moved in with her aunt and uncle after her momma's passing, and she started showing up at school with bruises. Needless to say, Samantha Jo hates the sheriff and the police. She blames them for taking away her family and ruining her life."

Mason ran a hand over his head, looking like he was about to be sick. "Yeah, I can see why she wouldn't talk to any law enforcement officials." He lowered his hand slowly. "So will you tell me what she says after you talk to her?"

My eyes flew open so wide they felt like they were going to pop out. "What?"

"I know you're going to talk to her, and I'm giving you my blessing. Find out if she was in on it or if she knows anything."

I shook my head, sure I'd heard him wrong. "Are you *serious*?"

"Yes, totally. If she's involved, she probably played a minor role. Does she seem dangerous to you?"

"Samantha Jo? No."

"Then there's little risk of you getting hurt, though if you feel threatened in any way, I want you to get out of there right away. Of course, none of the information you get will be admissible, but it might give us a few leads."

I stared at him in disbelief. "I can't believe you're encouraging this. Joe would just as soon lock me in the bathroom." I instantly regretted bringing up his name.

Mason's eyes darkened. "Unlike Joe, I consider you to be an intelligent woman. Besides, something tells me that Samantha Jo needs a friend…and who better than you?"

"Me?"

"People down on their luck are drawn to you, Rose. Bruce Wayne, Jonah." He squeezed my hand and gave me a soft smile. "And me. I was in a bad place when I first came to Henryetta and you were like a ray of sunshine. I tried to tell you that once in the courthouse elevator last July, with disastrous results, but it's as true now as it was then."

I gave him a kiss. "That's one of the sweetest things anyone has ever said to me."

"I'm only speaking the truth." He sat back. "Now when do you plan on talking to Samantha Jo?"

"Neely Kate and I are going to see her after church tomorrow."

He smiled. "Great. Now tell me what caused all that commotion at the bar?"

I grimaced. "I don't think you really want to know."

He pierced me with his penetrating gaze. "Try me."

I scrunched my face to the side. "Well…Toby was drunk and his bad breath was more than Neely Kate could take. She ended up barfing all down his back and on the woman next to him."

"Remind me to never take Neely Kate into a bar." He chuckled, then said, "She's having a rough time of it, huh?"

"Yeah, she's even lost weight."

He took my hand again. "You haven't been throwing up, have you?"

"No, but I have been feeling sick to my stomach a lot. Violet was lucky. She only had mild nausea off and on. I hope I'm like her…when the time comes."

"I hope so too."

So much would change if it turned out that I was pregnant. Mason and I weren't even married. I could only imagine how scandalized Momma would have been. But then my birth mother hadn't been married to Daddy when I was born. In fact, Daddy had still been married to Momma at the time. That was even more scandalous than my situation, and untraditional families were much more common now. Still, the nursery could suffer with the good Christian folk of Henryetta. If there was a nursery left to save. Horror washed over me as I realized it would be that much worse for Mason…it could kill his career.

If I was pregnant. This was all speculation at the moment.

I looked up into Mason's face and found him watching me, like he knew I was working on a problem and he was waiting me out to see if I solved it. He deserved a better woman than someone with as much baggage as I had, but I was too selfish to give him up.

Maybe I was more like Joe than I thought.

Chapter Fifteen

Mason woke me up again that night. The room was dark except for the moonlight shining through the sheer curtains on the windows. This time he was thrashing around, a few words mingled in with his grunts.

"You son of a bitch…you think you can…"

Steeling my back, I placed my hand on his shoulder and gently called his name. "Mason."

He bolted upright and threw me backward onto the bed. I lay on my back and watched him come to his senses. He spun at the waist and looked down at me, his face twisted with dismay. "Did I hurt you?"

I sat up and tried to give him a hug, but he scooted away from me.

"Answer me, Rose, did I hurt you?"

"No."

"I want the truth, *dammit*."

I cringed. "It's the truth. I promise."

He reached for me then, tugging me to his chest. "I'm sorry."

"You didn't do anything wrong. It's a nightmare, Mason. You can't help that."

"They'll just keep getting worse. They did before."

"Your dreams…they're about the man who killed Savannah?"

He swallowed. "Yes."

"Are you dreaming about…" my voice trailed off, unable to finish the thought.

"About beating him?" His words were harsh. "Yes."

I picked up his hand and kissed his knuckles, still bruised from hitting Joe. He tried to pull away, but I turned his hand over and kissed his palm. "I'm not afraid of you, Mason. But I'm afraid *for* you. I want you to talk to Jonah. He's helped me more than you know. I think he can help you too."

He sat still for several seconds. "Okay."

"Thank you," I whispered. "Now let's go back to sleep."

I tried to pull him down, but he resisted. "I'm going to sleep in the other room."

He started to get off the bed, but I held on tight. "Mason, no."

"They *will* get worse and I *will* hurt you. I couldn't live with myself if I did." When I still wouldn't let him go, his hand covered mine. "Rose, please."

"I like having you with me. I'll be lonely in bed without you."

He cupped my cheek and gave me a gentle kiss. "Sweetheart, it's not just you we need to think about. What if you *are* pregnant? What if I accidentally hurt you and the baby while coming out of a dream? It's safer to me to sleep in the other room."

Not wanting to make him more agitated, I let him go without saying another word.

I tossed and turned after he left, missing him, which was just silly. When Joe and I were together, we'd only spent about three nights a week in the same bed. This was just further proof of how much I needed Mason.

I woke up to sunshine and Muffy snoring at the foot of the bed. I reached for Mason and found only an empty pillow. I sat up and noticed the door to the sunroom was open, which I was sure had been closed the night before. I slid out of bed and padded across the cold wood floor, stopping in the threshold. What I saw inside made my breath stick in my throat.

Mason sat in the rocking chair, staring at the crib against the wall. A baby blanket lay across his leg and there was a tiny onesie in his hand. Sensing my presence, he turned his head toward me and held up the pink-footed onesie, giving me a half-hearted smile. "It's hard to believe you were this tiny."

Sometimes it was hard for me to register that this room had been mine for the first month and a half of my life. It had been left pretty much exactly as Dora had left it that fateful day of her car accident, like a time capsule of the life I was supposed to have had.

"I know." I took several steps inside, feeling like an intruder. "What are you doin' in here?"

"Trying to wrap my head around the possibility of having a baby." He definitely didn't sound too happy about the prospect.

My breath caught and I felt like I was going to throw up. What if he changed his mind about doing this with me?

"I'm going to let Muffy out, then take a shower and get ready to go to church."

His gaze returned to the crib. "I think I'll skip today. I need to work on my case."

"The one you won't tell me about?" When he didn't answer, I pressed on. "Does it have to do with the shakeup in the sheriff's department?" I knew he'd spent months searching reports trying to figure out who was responsible for the leak.

"No."

I held back a groan of frustration. But he'd promised to tell me when he was ready. Besides, it was probably official business he wasn't supposed to talk about. I had to accept that Mason's job was cloaked in a lot more secrecy than mine.

I texted Neely Kate once I was ready, asking her if I could sit with her at church since I'd be alone. She texted back to tell me that she'd pick me up at the farm, which was on her way into town. Ronnie was going fishing, so she'd be alone too.

Mason was in the office, fully engrossed in his work, when Neely Kate pulled up the drive. He'd been acting distant and I was worried. He was either concerned about his nightmares, me kissing Joe, him *hitting* Joe, or all of the above. None of it was good. I stood in the doorway, sucking my bottom lip between my teeth as I watched him type on his laptop. Several seconds later, he glanced up and saw me in the doorway.

I must have had a pitiful look because he spun his chair around and reached for me. "Come here."

I went to him and he pulled me onto his lap, giving me a gentle kiss. "I'm sorry I'm not coming with you, but this is important."

"I know."

His mouth lifted into a soft smile, but his eyes were filled with regret. "I don't want you to think I'm not going because I'm angry with you."

I didn't say anything.

"I won't lie. I'm still upset over what happened between you and Joe. But right now I'm more upset with myself. I have some things to sort out."

"Okay." It wasn't, but there wasn't anything I could do about it.

Giddy On Up blared in the silence of the room and I grimaced as I pulled my phone out of my purse and turned it off.

"Sounds like Neely Kate is waiting for you. You better go."

I stood up and turned to leave, but Mason caught my wrist and pulled me back. "I love you, Rose."

I swallowed the lump in my throat. "I love you too."

Neely Kate knew something was wrong the moment I slid into the passenger seat.

"What happened?"

I filled her in on everything that had happened since our phone call.

"I can't believe Mason *wants* you to talk to Samantha Jo."

"I think he figures I'm gonna talk to her anyway, so I might as well get helpful information out of it."

"Still…"

"He wouldn't willingly let me do anything dangerous," I said, suddenly feeling defensive.

"Good heavens, Rose. I know that. It's just I'm so used to you sneaking around, it feels weird being so up front about it."

I couldn't argue with that. "So our original plan of finding her after church works out great. Mason's working and Ronnie's fishing."

A smile spread across her face. "A girl's day out!"

"I'm pretty sure whoever came up with that term wasn't talking about interrogating suspects in a bank robbery."

"For heaven's sake," she said in mock annoyance. "We're simply planning to make a Sunday afternoon call on poor Samantha Jo."

The church was mostly packed when we entered the sanctuary, but we found seats about halfway down the aisle in the center of a pew.

"Rose." Neely Kate tugged on my sleeve, then pointed to the other side of the aisle. "Look who's here."

Two rows ahead of us, divided by the aisle, was Samantha Jo Wheaton with a big tattooed guy who looked like he'd rather be chewing on glass than sitting in the New Living Hope Revival Church.

"What's she doing here?" I asked. "I've never seen hide nor hair of her in church."

"Guilt makes people look for atonement." My best friend gave me a smug grin.

Of course, the explanation could be simpler than that: Jonah's church was the hot new Sunday morning entertainment. For a town used to hymns sung to organ music and shouted sermons about fire and brimstone, the citizens of Henryetta were flocking to Jonah's church, which boasted a live band and songs that sounded like they could be on the radio. The fact that the service was televised didn't hurt. But I didn't see the point of telling Neely Kate that.

The band took the stage, the musicians wearing jeans and T-shirts. Momma surely must have been rolling in her grave two miles away. Just as they started to play, someone caught my eye.

Violet. She was walking down the aisle, wearing her favorite plum-colored dress and her Coach purse, which she only pulled out for special occasions.

And then I saw what her occasion was.

She wasn't alone.

I realized Neely Kate must have seen them too, because she reached for my arm, her nails digging into the flesh. "*How could she*?"

Several people around us turned toward Neely Kate, but she didn't even notice. She was too busy staring at Violet, who was slipping into the pew, Joe following behind holding Ashley's hand. Violet must have put Mikey in the nursery.

Neely Kate was livid. "Didn't he just kiss you yesterday morning?" she stage-whispered.

More people turned around, their eyes widening when they realized that she was addressing me. Mason was well liked in the congregation, and everyone knew we were a couple. Several gave me disapproving frowns.

"Neely Kate," I hissed into her ear. "People can hear you!"

"I don't care. Who does he think—?"

"Neely Kate!" I said, more insistent. "Think about Mason and me."

She pressed her lips together, refusing to sing the first song because she was so busy shooting a laser-like glare in Joe and Violet's direction. I stole glances of my own, barely able to focus on Jonah's sermon as I tried to figure out why I cared so much about them spending time together. Joe and I weren't together, so he could date whomever he wanted. But my sister? Though I was far from convinced there was anything going on between them, it felt wrong on so many levels to see them together.

And Violet. She was the one who really made me mad. She was jumping from man to man, taking the one who had the most to offer. Joe was currently the flavor of the week, it seemed. Maybe her attempts to reconnect with the mayor had hit a snag. Or maybe she was just trying to prove me wrong about Joe not wanting her.

Neely Kate was still seething when the service ended, and I suspected what she had in mind as she started to push me out of the pew.

"Neely Kate! Stop!" I turned and blocked her path. "I can't face him. Not after yesterday... I need to stay as far away from him as possible."

Some of the fire left her eyes.

I grabbed her arm. "We need to find Samantha Jo. I need to get my money back so I can at least save *my* portion of the nursery. I love my landscaping business, Neely Kate. And Bruce Wayne likes it too. I don't want to lose it. I need to put all this other nonsense to the side and focus on getting my money back."

"Okay."

"But once all the debts are paid, the Gardner Sisters Nursery will no longer exist in its present form."

She gasped. "You're going to split it up?"

I expected to feel more anger, but instead a heavy weight pressed on my chest. "I can't work with her anymore. Not after this."

"Well—" she looped her arm through mine "—let's focus on getting your money back or there won't be anything left *to* split up. Let's go find Samantha Jo."

We headed out the aisle, and I was surprised to see that Violet, Joe and Ashley had already left their pew. Since Violet was making such a show of her presence, I figured she'd spend more time making sure that everyone knew she was here with Joe Simmons, Fenton County Chief Deputy Sheriff, former candidate for the Arkansas State Senate and son of J.R. Simmons, the most powerful man in southern Arkansas.

And her younger sister's ex-boyfriend.

Part of me felt relieved to have dodged that bullet, but the rest of me was a mess, including my guts. I reminded myself of the fact that I'd only just gotten finished convincing Neely Kate we needed to talk to Samantha Jo—*not* Violet—only she was gone too.

"Where is she, Neely Kate?"

"There," Neely Kate pointed to the exit. "She's headed for the foyer." She started pushing her way through the crowd. "Out of the way! Pregnant woman! I'm gonna be sick! Let me through!"

The crowd parted like the Red Sea, giving her plenty of room to pass.

I followed on her heels, trying to ignore the glares some of the bystanders were throwing my way. "I'm with her," I said in my defense, giving them a weak smile. "I hold her hair."

But then the visual of Neely Kate hanging over a toilet bowl and retching filled my head and I started to gag.

Neely Kate heard me and turned around. "Are you okay?"

"No." I pushed past her and ran to the bathroom, bursting through the swinging door. I found the first empty stall and ran in, barely getting the door shut before my meager breakfast of toast and coffee came up. When I finally stopped heaving, I waited another minute to make sure I was done.

Neely Kate was standing outside the stall when I opened the door, her eyes filled with worry. I rinsed out my mouth and stared at her reflection in the mirror.

"You still haven't taken the test yet, have you?"

I shook my head, tears blurring her image.

"Rose, just find out one way or the other. Put an end to your misery."

Tears started to stream down my cheeks and Neely Kate made a pouty face and pulled me into a hug, stroking the back of my head as I cried.

"It's not just my worry about being pregnant. It's Mason. I've screwed up something wonderful, Neely Kate. How could I let that happen?"

"Oh, sweetie. You kissed Joe for a few seconds before coming to your senses and pushing him away. Did you want to jump his bones when you were sitting in the car with him?"

"Of course not!"

A loud thud came from the end stall followed by the clatter of something hitting the tile floor. I swung my attention to the corner in time to see a plate of dentures skitter across the floor and land at my feet.

I screeched and jumped backward, dragging Neely Kate with me until we bumped into the counter. We gasped at the same time when we saw who was inside the stall.

Chapter Sixteen

The stall door had flown open and Miss Mildred stood in the opening, her dress hiked up and tucked into her panty hose on one side in the back. Her face was so red I worried she'd have a stroke. She pointed her finger at me. "Jezebel!" she said, her voice heavy with judgment. Only without the top portion of her teeth, it came out muffled.

"Miss Mildred," I muttered, backing up more even though there was nowhere else to go. "I didn't know you were in here." I shot Neely Kate a glare and her eyes widened as she mouthed, *I'm sorry. I didn't see her*.

"Fat's obious," she mumbled out, looking around until she spotted her dentures on the floor at my feet.

Scrunching her nose in disgust, Neely Kate bent over and picked up the fake teeth. She rinsed them off in the sink—looking like she was about to lose her own breakfast—and then handed them to the elderly woman. Miss Mildred snatched them and popped them into her mouth, wiggling her mouth around to settle them into place.

Neely Kate, already pale, covered her mouth with her hands and bolted into a stall. The sound of retching soon followed.

But that didn't distract Miss Mildred, whose face had settled back into a sour grimace now that her teeth had been restored. "After you helped find Dorothy's killer, I thought maybe you had seen the light. And I was willing to overlook how you're tainting the district attorney's reputation, living with him out there on that farm doin' God knows what. And now *this*." She pointed to my stomach. "While fornicating with another man? It's inexcusable."

"She wasn't fornicating," Neely Kate piped up, her voice muffled inside the stall. "She was only kissing him."

I froze in shock. My secrets were out in the open, and the president of the Busybody Club knew all of them. "Miss Mildred… I…."

She advanced toward me. "How can your heathen soul stand to be in the sanctuary of our Lord?"

I swallowed and lifted my chin, fighting a new wave of nausea as I listened to Neely Kate start another round of vomiting not six feet away from me. "Jesus welcomed the sinners into his fold, Miss Mildred. And so does Jonah."

"That boy's a fool."

"*Jesus*?" Neely Kate called out from behind the closed door.

"Of course not *Jesus*! Blasphemy!" Miss Mildred shuddered, then recovered enough to continue, "*Reverend* Jonah. Lettin' all them heathens in the door." She leaned forward, squinting her eyes. "Tattooed ladies and men with earrings. Have you *ever* seen such a sight?"

"Jesus ate with the tax collectors, Miss Mildred."

"Well, then Reverend Jonah can go out to lunch with Dennis Pontel at the Golden Corral buffet. Dennis works for the IRS."

"He works for H&R Block," Neely Kate called out.

"Same thing." Miss Mildred waved her hand in annoyance. "The point is that this is a place for holy people, Rose Anne Gardner. You don't belong here."

My anger rose up. I was tired of this woman belittling me at every step. "Last I checked, Miss Mildred," I took a step forward, feeling bolder, "we're in a restroom, which is where crap belongs." I lifted an eyebrow and gave her a snotty look. "I guess that explains why *you're* here spoutin' off." Then I stomped out of the bathroom, leaving Miss Mildred frozen in shock by the sinks and poor Neely Kate still barfing.

I took a second to steady myself, which is when I saw Samantha Jo and her tattooed date talking to a couple of guys who looked like they belonged to the church's Onward and Upward support group. The majority of the group's members worked—or had worked—at Weston's Garage. When Jonah started his church, one of the first things he did was found a support group for men in need of rehabilitation, which included a number of members who had worked for Daniel Crocker. I glanced back at the bathroom door. I would have preferred to wait for Neely Kate before talking to Samantha Jo, but she was doing the telltale tug on her boyfriend's arm.

That settled it.

I made my way through the crowded foyer, approaching her and the group of four men. When I was less than three feet away, I felt my peripheral sight fading as a vision descended.

I was in a dark room, lit only by the pale light beaming in through a curtainless paned window. One of the panes had a diagonal crack in it, shaped like an upside-down Y.

"You didn't have to kill him," a man grunted as he came into my view, the red glow of the tip of his cigarette lighting up his face. His face was covered in heavy stubble and his cheeks hollowed in as he took a long drag. "You said no one would get hurt."

"He wanted out and he never would have kept quiet. It was too risky," said a guy in the shadows. I couldn't make out any defining features, but I recognized his voice. "Have you picked out where we're going next?"

"It ain't that easy, Mick. That nine thousand in the cash bag helps, but we need another ten K. This is Henryetta. Where in Sam Hill are we gonna find that much money?"

Mick laughed, but the sound came out garbled. "I know just the place."

The church foyer came back into view and I blurted out. "You're gonna rob another place."

The heads of all four men turned toward me, their eyes burning with hostility.

Oh, crappy doodles.

Even though I'd recognized Mick's voice, none of the men's faces matched the guy with the cigarette or the Batman robber whose face I'd seen in my previous vision. I realized in that split second that the person I'd been in the vision had never said a word or given me any other clue of his or her identity. It could have been any of the four men or even Samantha Jo. That meant there were at least four of them, five if I included Mr. Sullivan.

One of the men in the group stomped over to me, clearly angry. "What did you just say?"

I put the back of my hand to my forehead and took a step back. "I'm sorry, I don't remember what I said. I'm not feeling well, and I've been blurting out odd things right and left. Must be delirious."

I took another step back. He took one forward.

Fear cramped my already delicate stomach, but the rational part of my brain screamed that we were in church. What could happen?

The contorted face of the man in front of me made me reconsider that question.

"Hello, gentleman," Joe said from behind me, moving to my side and putting a hand on the small of my back. "I'm not sure I've had the pleasure of meeting you." He extended his right hand, keeping his left at my back. "I'm the new chief deputy sheriff. Joe Simmons." A bright smile lifted his mouth, but his eyes were hard.

His hand hung in the air for a long moment before the man finally gave it a short shake and then dropped it like it was covered with maggots. "Welcome to town, *Sheriff*."

Joe gave him a cocky grin. "Oh, I'm not the sheriff." Then he winked and cast me a quick glance. "But you just never know what the future may hold."

I wanted to shake him off, but I couldn't deny Joe had intervened in something that was about to get ugly. To try banishing him now would be foolish.

The man looked from me to Joe, narrowing his eyes. "Is there anything I can do for you, *chief deputy*?" He grinned. "Sorry we haven't had a chance to drop off a plate of cookies to welcome you to town."

The men behind him laughed.

"Oh, that's not necessary," Joe drawled, rolling back his shoulders. "There's plenty of time for all of us to get acquainted. And I have a feeling we will."

The man staring down Joe grumbled, then turned away, heading out the doors with his friends. And Samantha Jo.

"What the hell were you doing, Rose?" Joe's angry voice barked as soon as they were out of earshot.

"I'm in *church*, Joe." I shrugged off his hand and stepped away. "Surely you can't object to that."

"That's not what I'm objecting to, and you know it." He moved closer. "Why were you talking to those guys? Did this have anything to do with you talking to Toby Wheaton at Jasper's?"

"Why do you always assume the worst of me? I was heading over there to talk to Samantha Jo. We went to school together and she was in the bank robbery too. I was going to check on her and see how she was handling it." It wasn't a total lie.

Joe's anger visibly faded. He seemed to be buying my story.

"You can check the police report to verify that she was at the bank that day," I volunteered. "And ask your *date* if I went to school with her."

His mouth dropped in shock. "Date? Who said we were on a *date*? Violet asked me to help her get the kids to church."

"Why on earth would you agree to that?" I scoffed. "You can't stand Violet and you never once went to church the entire time we were together."

His grin turned wicked. "Maybe that's because when I was with you I had better things to do in the morning before I got out of bed."

A blush rose to my cheeks, but thankfully Neely Kate appeared beside me.

"Well look at you, Detective Simmons," she said, looping her arm through mine and pulling me back a step. "I didn't know you were a church-goer."

"Seeing as I'm no longer with the state police, detective is no longer necessary," he said, tilting his head good-naturedly, but I knew him well enough to read the challenge in his eyes. "It's Chief Deputy Simmons now."

This was all for show. Joe was well aware that my best friend knew about his current employment. So what was he trying to prove?

"Do you know what's so strange?" she asked. "You always hated this town. Yet here you are, living in it by choice."

He shrugged one shoulder and gave her a smug grin. "Well, that's the beauty of being in the sheriff's department. I don't have to live in town. I only have to live in the county."

He turned his attention to me and winked. "Are any of the places by your farm available for rent or sale, Rose?"

"Leave her alone, Joe Simmons," Neely Kate spat out.

Joe's smile fell, and a mask of authority settled over his features. "If you just wanted to talk to Samantha Jo," he asked me, "what caused all that ruckus?"

I shrugged. "I don't know. Maybe they recognize me because of Crocker."

It was obvious he didn't believe me, but he wasn't sure what to do about it. "You better not be trying to investigate this case, Rose."

Neely Kate's eyebrows lifted in surprise. "What case?"

He grinned, but it wasn't friendly. "Don't encourage her, Neely Kate. Tell her to leave this one to the authorities. Next time I might not be around to save her."

"I'll tell her to keep that in mind."

I snorted. "Or you two could pretend that I'm actually here."

Neely Kate looked past Joe and smirked. "Someone's not happy, Joe," she singsonged.

Sure enough, Violet walked up with Mikey on her hip. Ashley was with a group of little girls on the other side of the foyer. Violet put her hand on Joe's upper arm, her face tight with anger. "Joe, I wondered where you had gotten off to."

"I had some official business to take care of, and lo and behold, I ran into Rose." He waved a hand toward me as though he was presenting a prize.

Violet gave me a withering look. "Imagine that."

"I'm surprised you're not here with Brody MacIntosh," Neely Kate sneered.

Violet tried to look affronted, but instead she looked like she'd been caught red-handed. "What a silly thing to say,

Neely Kate. Everyone knows that Brody got back together with his wife."

Neely Kate glared at my sister. "As if that would stop you."

Rage flooded Violet's face. She glanced around, but I knew it was all for show. "Where's Mason?"

"Working."

"On a Sunday morning?" she gloated. She'd warned me before that she thought he was a workaholic.

"He's working on a big case."

"Oh, really." Joe shifted his weight. "Which one?"

I straightened my back and crossed my arms. "Seeing as it's official county business, how do you suppose I'd know, Chief Deputy?"

Violet put her hand on Joe's arm. "Sundays are sacred. And how you choose to spend them says a lot about your character."

"Yeah, it sure does," I said dryly, arching my brow at her pointedly. "And in Mason's case, it says he's a dedicated, hard-working, conscientious man who works long hours to ensure that the citizens of Fenton County get justice."

Violet grabbed Joe's hand and interlaced their fingers. "No, Rose. It shows where his priorities lie. And that's clearly not with you."

I expected Joe to gloat, but his expression was rigid as he jerked his hand away.

"Go enjoy my castoff boyfriend while living in my castoff house, Violet. I hope you're very happy being second best."

I spun around and started for the door, Neely Kate right behind me, when I heard Jonah call my name. I groaned, not because I didn't want to see him, but because I needed to escape from Violet.

But Jonah was an observant man—part of the reason he was a great therapist—and he followed me out the door and onto the white concrete steps. "Hey," he said when he caught up with me. "Got a minute?"

I nodded, afraid to say anything. Neely Kate and I followed him to the end of the wide steps, where we would have a little more privacy.

"I saw what happened in there. I'm sorry."

"You mean with Violet?"

He leaned closer, lowering his voice. "All of it. You need to be careful with those guys, Rose. They may go to church, but they mostly do it to prove they're rehabilitating."

Neely Kate put her hands on her hips and shot him a glare. "Then why do you let them into your church?"

"I don't consider them dangerous to most of the parishioners, Neely Kate. Otherwise they wouldn't be here. But Rose is a special case…" He looked into my eyes. "You had a vision of one of them, didn't you?"

I gasped. "How did you know?"

"I know you by now. I know they only last a second or two, but your face gets an odd expression, as if you've gone on a trip and left your body behind."

Neely Kate's eyes brightened. "Yeah! You're right, Jonah. I hadn't thought about it." She lifted an eyebrow at me. "Although you don't look like that when you close your eyes and have one on purpose. Only when a vision catches you off guard and your eyes are staring off at nothing."

"Okay…"

"So did you have a vision?" he asked.

"Yeah, only I don't know whose head I was in. I didn't say or do anything in the vision. I just saw two guys in a dark room. One of them was Mick, the bank robber in the SpongeBob mask."

"Did you see his face?" Neely Kate asked, excited.

"No, but I saw the other guy's face." I took a deep breath. "They need ten thousand dollars more and they figured out a place to rob. But my vision ended before they said where." I sobered. "And Mick was the one who killed Mr. Sullivan…I'm sure of it. He said Mr. Sullivan knew too much and was going to give them away."

"You have to tell the police," Jonah insisted, a worried look in his eyes. "What did you say after you had your vision?"

"That they were going to rob someplace else. All of them heard me."

Jonah's mouth pressed tight. "You're not safe, Rose. I know you can't report your visions to the police department, but you should tell Joe."

My shoulders tensed. "I can't."

"Why not? I know it's an awkward situation, but he knows about your visions. He'll believe you."

Neely Kate shook her head. "There are a few things you don't know about."

He looked around. "I noticed Mason's not here. Did you talk to him about…you know…?"

I gave him a soft smile. I knew what he was asking. "Yes, and while he admits the timing stinks, he would welcome it. And Neely Kate knows all about it."

"So what do I not know?"

Neely Kate filled him in on everything, but stopped after saying that Joe had insisted on driving me home after I found poor Mr. Sullivan's body. I took over from there and told him the hard part.

Jonah was just as understanding as I'd known he would be. "And how did Mason react when you told him about the kiss?" he asked.

I sucked in a deep breath and waited for the burning in my eyes to fade. "Not well. But he forgave me and we made up. Kind of…It's just going to take some time." I paused. "But he needs to talk to you, Jonah. Can you call him and set something up? *Soon*?" I leaned into his ear and whispered, "Hitting Joe unlocked his guilt over what happened in Little Rock. He's having violent nightmares. I'm scared for him." I swallowed the lump in my throat. "He told me he's open to talking to you."

Jonah gave me a hug. "I'll call him this afternoon."

"Thank you." I kissed his cheek and leaned back. "Now tell me who those guys are."

"Rose…" he groaned.

"Now you know why I can't ask Joe for help. But if you tell *me* their names, I can give them to Mason. He'll figure out a way to unravel this mess."

He grimaced and looked out into the now-emptying parking lot. "I'm not sure this is a good idea."

"Jonah, at least one of those men was involved in Mr. Sullivan's murder. What if they kill someone else?" It was a low blow and I knew it, but I was desperate to save my business.

Jonah cocked his head. "And you'll tell Mason all the information I give you rather than trying to solve this on your own?"

"I'll tell him. I promise," I said, leaving out the fact that I fully intended to continue pursuing the matter with Neely Kate. I felt more than a little guilty about making a lie of omission to a man of the cloth, but desperate times called for desperate measures.

He released an exaggerated sigh. "Okay…the big guy with the tattoos and the earrings—he was standing next to the pretty girl—is Moose Mahoney. He works out at Weston's

Garage. The skinny guy next to him is T. J. Majors. He works with Moose. The other guy, the redhead, is Eric Davidson. He's got a job as a manager at the Burger Shack. And then Lars Jenkins is the one who came up to you after your vision."

"And where does Lars work?"

"He's currently unemployed."

My attention perked up. "So he'd need money?"

"*Rose*."

"This is all information for Mason."

"Maybe I should just talk to him myself."

"No." I shook my head. "He stayed home because he said he's working on some big case he can't tell me about. He's anxious about this one, but he won't tell me anything about it." I gave him a smile. "He worked in the office at the farm all day yesterday, and then he was back at it this morning."

Jonah's smile twisted slightly. "Mason needs to find more balance between work and a personal life. I was hoping he'd find that with you."

A band squeezed my heart.

"Oh, Rose," Jonah exclaimed when he saw my face. "I didn't mean that the way it sounded. It's not a sign that he doesn't care about you…it's just his personality."

"It's okay." I shook myself. I needed to stop worrying about my relationship with Mason. I'd done everything I could to make things right. And the perfect way to keep my mind off my relationship troubles was to focus on recovering my money. "So what did Lars used to do?"

Jonah gave me a look that told me he'd taken note of the change of subject, but he answered anyway. "Lars has an interesting past. He used to be a ranch hand in Texas."

"So what brought him here?"

"A job. A farmer in northern Fenton County was starting a big cattle farm. He hired Lars to oversee it."

"So what happened?"

"Lars has a temper, and one day he cracked and beat up his boss. He served some time, but then he returned to Fenton County."

"So he doesn't have a job now?"

"No, he's currently living with a woman out at the Lazy Dazy trailer park."

That was more information than I'd hoped to get. "Thanks, Jonah. You've helped more than you know."

"From the look on your face, I think I've helped you too much. *Tell Mason*."

"I will." I grabbed Neely Kate's arm and dragged her down the steps. Neither one of us said anything until we got into her car.

She hung her hands on the steering wheel, tapping the plastic with a pink nail painted with white polka dots. "Well, *that* was quite a morning."

"I don't even know where to start."

She turned to face me. "I don't know about you, but I have a hankering for the Golden Corral."

I broke into laughter. "Miss Mildred might be there, and seeing us would sure send her teeth flying across the buffet."

"Oh, my stars and garters!" she laughed. "I couldn't believe my eyes when that happened!"

I stopped laughing. "She heard us, Neely Kate. She heard I might be pregnant *and* that I kissed Joe."

Neely Kate released a huff and her mouth twisted to the side. "How bad could it be?"

"I don't care about *me*, Neely Kate. I'm thinking about Mason. What if I destroy his reputation?"

"Mason will be just fine. And women like Miss Mildred only have power over us because we let them."

I knew she was right, but I was still worried.

"I'm hungry," she said, turning on the car. "What do you say we skip the flying teeth at the Golden Corral and get ourselves over to Big Bill's Barbeque?"

My mouth dropped open. "Hot wings? Are you serious?"

She shrugged and started to pull out of the parking lot. "Ronnie Junior likes 'em."

"Ronnie Junior?"

She shrugged again. "If it's a boy. Maybe."

If I were pregnant, Mason and I would have to discuss things like that too. It was an overwhelming thought, so I pushed it away, moving on to something over which I had more control. "We need to talk about my vision and try to figure out which one of those people was attached to it."

"Let's do it over lunch. Do you need to go home to Mason to check in before we visit Samantha Jo?"

The flutter in my stomach at the words *home to Mason* made my lips tip up, but the smile fell just as quickly. Part of me wanted to kill Joe for doing this to me, but the tension between Mason and me was partly my own fault.

"No, he's busy with that case I mentioned. But I'll call to let him know." I pulled my phone out of my purse but the call went to voice mail after several rings. "Hey, Mason. I'm going out to lunch with Neely Kate before we go see Samantha Jo." I paused. "I miss you and love you. I'll see you when I get home." I hung up, feeling sad.

"He didn't answer."

"No, and that's not like him." I frowned. "Maybe he decided to start the housing search before his momma gets here."

"That was the plan all along anyway, right?" she asked. "For him to move out?"

"Yeah, but I like having him there. I'll miss him too much if he leaves, especially with his busy schedule. I don't want him to move out."

"So tell him you want him to stay."

"Yeah…" Although I'd felt this way before Joe and the baby, I still worried that asking him to stay would come across to him as reactive.

Neely Kate pulled into the gravel parking lot of a ramshackle old house that looked like it was about to cave in. It had once been painted white, but what little paint hadn't flaked off was now a drab gray. A lopsided sign hung on the roof boasted the faded words *Big Bill's Barbeque*. I'd driven by Big Bill's plenty of times, and one of my male coworkers used to bring their hot wings for potlucks when I worked at the DMV, but I'd never actually been there. Now I was having second thoughts.

Neely Kate laughed. "I know it looks scary, but it's worth riskin' your life for, I promise."

"Maybe I should force a vision and make sure we'll survive our lunch," I joked.

Her eyes lit up. "That's a good idea."

I shook my head. "If you're really that concerned about your stomach, maybe we should skip this…"

"Not for that, silly. For the case." She turned to me, her eyes narrowing. "I've said it before—you don't use your gift nearly enough. Think of all the things you could figure out. *We* could figure out."

"And *blurt* out. Don't forget that part. That's what got me into trouble with those guys."

"Well, let's get our wings and figure out which guy was the object of your vision while we eat."

After our bathroom encounter at the church, I wasn't sure wings were the best choice, but I wasn't about to contradict Neely Kate.

We walked into the main room, which was crowded with about fifteen mismatched tables covered in red-and-white-checkered plastic tablecloths. Almost all of them were occupied. The baseboards were coated in grime, and greasy spots coated the tops of the walls. The entire restaurant looked like it needed a good scrubbing, but from the way the ceiling sagged slightly in the middle, I had to wonder if dirt was the only thing holding the place together.

"You *do* know this place violates a ton of health codes, don't you?" I whispered into Neely Kate's ear. "How do they not get shut down?"

"They pay off the inspector, of course." She waved a hand. "Not to worry. Whatever germs came in here have no chance of surviving contact with the hot sauce Bill puts on his wings."

"That's not all that reassuring."

She shook her head like I was simple-minded. "Don't be such a worrywart. My grandma's been eatin' these things for years and it hasn't killed her yet."

"Not for lack of tryin'," I said, eyeing the menu board. "How many times has your grandma been to the emergency room after eatin' Bill's wings?"

Neely Kate waved off my statement. "That doesn't count. She's got an ulcer."

"And she still eats here?"

"Some things are worth the pain."

Before I could give her statement more thought, the person in front of us moved forward and it was our turn to order. I put in a large order of mixed wings, planning on taking most of them home to Mason. After I placed my order, I pulled out my wallet and handed my debit card to the older man at the cash register.

He handed it back, curling his lip in disgust. "We don't take that here."

Who didn't take Visa? "But I don't have a MasterCard."

His eyes narrowed into a glare. "Cash only."

Grumbling, I dug through my purse to find enough loose change to pay. After Neely Kate placed her order, we stood to the side with a good twenty other people waiting for their food.

"I can't believe this place doesn't take debit cards. You'd think they'd lose business by being cash only."

She shrugged. "They've always done it this way. It's what people expect. And look at this place." She waved at the crowded dining room and the line that was steadily swelling. "They're definitely not hurting."

The temperature was in the fifties and the sun was out, so we went outside and sat on a wooden picnic table. Plus, despite Neely Kate's protestations to the contrary, I expected the ceiling to cave in at any moment.

I ate two mild wings before closing the container to save the rest for Mason. I leaned my head back and sucked in several deep breaths, trying to get my stomach to settle. "I should have just stuck with Texas toast."

"Why don't you just take the test already?" she asked.

I shook my head, not wanting to explain myself. Propping my chin on my hand, I said, "Now let's try and figure out whose vision I experienced."

"Okay." She watched me for a moment. "Where were you?"

"It was nighttime and I was in a dark room. There was a window divided into panes and the bottom one was cracked in an upside-down Y. There was a light shining in the window, but I'm not sure what the source could have been."

"Okay, what else? Did you smell anything distinctive?"

I hadn't actually thought about it much, so I searched my memory for the answer. "Yes," I said after a moment, "the room was stuffy and smelled… kind of like rust and something earthy." A strange feeling of déjà vu tickled the back of my head, and then it hit me like an anvil. "Wait. Mick—the robber—he smelled of rust and dirt. And he was in the room in my vision."

"So it was his smell."

"No." I grabbed her hand, excited. "It was the room's… It's a clue!"

Based on the way Neely Kate scrunched her face, she was less hopeful about the lead—or maybe it was just the hot wings. "What else do you remember?" she asked.

"The room was too dark for me to see much, but the one guy was smoking and I could see part of his face. He hadn't shaved in a couple of days. Mick was angry. He said he killed the guy because he knew too much."

"And what about you?" she asked. "What were you doin'?"

"I didn't pay much attention—I was too busy trying to absorb as many details as I could. I think I was standing."

"Anything else?"

"Just that they need ten thousand more on top of my nine thousand." I tilted my head.

"Plus the four thousand they got from the bank."

I wanted to ask her how she knew how much had been stolen, but thought better of it. "So they have thirteen thousand and they need ten more. Twenty-three thousand. What in tarnation do they need it for?"

"A car? A boat?"

Maybe, but I didn't think so. "I think there were at least five of them—Mick, the scruffy guy from this vision, the guy with the Batman mask, and the guy at the church."

"And poor Mr. Sullivan."

"Yeah. Poor Mr. Sullivan." I tried not to think about how bloated his face was when I found him in the ditch. "So they'd have to share the money or whatever it was they were buyin'. Of course they might already have some money and be adding to it."

"True."

"Let's go talk to Samantha Jo. You said you know where to find her?"

"She's livin' with her cousin at the Lazy Dazy trailer park."

I whipped my head around to look at her. "That's where Lars lives with his girlfriend." Could the coincidences pile up any higher? "It sounds like we're headed in the right direction."

We drove back through town, but Neely Kate pulled into the parking lot of the pharmacy.

"What are we doing here?"

"Those wings are burning a hole in my stomach, so I'm gonna get an antacid. You can wait here if you'd like."

I nodded. "I want to try calling Mason again."

"I'll be right back."

I pulled out my phone and dialed Mason. This time it went straight to voice mail without even ringing. Part of me was cataloguing a whole host of terrible and dreadful reasons why he might not have answered—from being kidnapped by Crocker's friends to him leaving me—but I knew the most likely explanation was that he'd forgotten to charge his phone and it had died.

Neely Kate came out a few minutes later and set a bag next to me. "I got you a couple of presents," she said as she started the car.

"Me?" I sat up. "What are they?"

"Open it and find out."

I picked up the bag and peered inside. There was a bottle of pills and several differently sized rectangular boxes. I pulled out the pills first and shook my head. "Prenatal vitamins." My stomach knotted.

"You don't take any vitamins at all now, so you need *something*. Just in case. And they won't hurt you if you aren't."

I pulled out one of the boxes next, my breath sticking in my chest when I realized what it was. My nausea roared back to life. "A pregnancy test."

"You don't have to take it now, but at least you'll have it when you decide you're ready. I got you several different brands. Just so you have lots of options if you don't like the results of one. And you didn't get seen buying it, so you don't have to worry about gossip…or at least not any more gossip than is already brewing about you."

I hadn't even thought of that part. "Thanks, Neely Kate."

"What are best friends for?"

I put the bottle and the boxes in my purse. I was going to have to face the truth sooner or later. Neely Kate was right. The uncertainty was killing me and I was starting to get used to the idea. If I found out we were having a baby, I wouldn't be devastated like I would have been a few days ago. But I still wasn't ready.

I took a deep breath. "Let's go pay Samantha Jo a visit."

The Lazy Dazy trailer park had seen better days, although it was hard to tell in its current state. A giant sign stood in the front advertising the name of the park in faded yellow letters.

A painted daisy was in the corner, only someone had added their own creative touch, giving the flower a phallic look.

"Heavens to Betsy, I bet you ten bucks Miss Mildred hasn't seen that. She'd bring a ladder out here and paint right over it."

Neely Kate laughed. "I wouldn't put it past her."

We turned down the gravel road, and I sighed when I saw the state of most of the trailers. The sides were dented and covered in rust. Most driveways were lined with rundown cars and there were a few scattered motorcycles. It was hard to believe anyone lived this way.

I checked my phone for a missed call from Mason, although I had no doubt I would have heard his ring. There was nothing other than a text from Joe.

I saw you talking to Jonah after church. Investigating a crime on your own while the sheriff is conducting an investigation is a felony punishable by law. Think about that before you do something to get you into trouble.

I read the text out loud and glanced at Neely Kate. "Is that true?"

She rolled her eyes. "He's callin' your bluff. I've seen plenty of TV shows where the main character investigated a crime while the police were doing the same…and it always went just fine."

"That was TV, Neely Kate. This is real life."

"Seriously. It's Joe. Do you really think he's going to arrest us? And even if he does, there's no way Mason will prosecute us."

While Neely Kate had a point, I wouldn't put it past Joe to do it just to prove he could and Mason…well, he wasn't answering my calls. What did it mean?

Neely Kate pulled up next to a trailer with a stained white toilet stuck in the middle of the tiny yard. The pot was filled with dead plants. She shook her head, tsking. "At least they made an effort, sad as it is."

"It might look cute with live flowers," I said, for some reason feeling the need to defend the owner. Maybe it was because I saw the clay pots scattered around the yard, all filled with more dead plants.

"Samantha Jo is staying here, but the trailer belongs to her cousin, Carla. She was one grade ahead of me, so I know her. Let me do the talking." Neely Kate tilted the rearview mirror down and reapplied her lipstick.

"Gladly." After seeing Neely Kate in action in the bar on Friday night, it was apparent she had a knack for questioning.

We got out of the car and walked up to the front door.

Neely Kate climbed the rickety steps to the front door while I stayed put in the yard. The steps were too narrow for the both of us, never mind that they might not hold our combined weight.

The front door opened and I gasped.

Standing in the threshold, squinting down at us, was none other than David, Bruce Wayne's best friend.

This mess was getting stranger and stranger.

Chapter Seventeen

"What on earth are you doin' here, Miss Rose?" he asked.

"I could ask you the same thing."

His face contorted into an annoyed grimace. "I'm visiting my girlfriend."

"*Samantha Jo*?" While she wasn't the sharpest crayon in the box, I was sure she wouldn't resort to seeing a pothead with no job…or at least not a pothead with scraggly hair and a scrawny body. He was nothing like the hard-edged guy she'd been with at church.

"No." He laughed. "Carla."

It was Neely Kate's turn to gasp. "You're dating *Carla*?"

He jutted his head back. "Why do you sound so surprised?"

"It's just—"

A cute redheaded woman with freckles dotting her face appeared behind David. "Neely Kate? Is that you?" she squealed, pushing past her boyfriend to nearly tackle Neely Kate with a hug.

"Carla!"

Carla pulled back, her eyes wide with excitement. "I heard you got hitched. Lemme see the ring!"

Neely Kate lifted her hand in a dramatic fashion, waving her fingers to show off her sparkly quarter-carat diamond.

"O.M.G.!" Carla squealed again, dancing in place. "It's gorrrr-geous!"

"Ronnie got it at the pawn shop. He got quite a deal, which is why it's so big. And it's not cubic zirconia either."

Carla shook her head, looking at Neely Kate with undisguised good-natured envy. "You are one lucky girl, Neely Kate."

The brightest smile broke out across my friend's face. "I know, right?" She patted her belly, tears in her eyes. "And I'm havin' a baby."

They squealed some more before Carla glanced at me, smiling. "And who's this?"

Neely Kate reached an arm around my shoulders and pulled me close, squeezing. "This here is my best friend Rose Gardner. Rose, this is Carla Mansfield."

I smiled. "Nice to meet you."

"Any friend of Neely Kate's is a friend of mine." Then Carla grabbed Neely Kate's arm and started to tug her up the steps. "What are we all doin' out here? Come on in and have some lemonade."

Neely Kate glanced over her shoulder and I nodded as Carla dragged her though the door.

I followed them into the dark mobile home, which was filled with furniture that looked like it had been new when the trailer was…about half a century ago. The once cream and avocado tweed sofa was stained and the cushions sagged. Carla waved for us to sit as she went into the tiny kitchen and opened the refrigerator door. "So what're y'all doin' here, Neely Kate?"

David sat on the chair across from me and I stole a glance at him. David had a girlfriend? I still couldn't get over it. David didn't seem like the boyfriend type. I couldn't help wondering why Bruce Wayne hadn't mentioned it.

Neely Kate crossed her legs. "We saw Samantha Jo at church this morning and thought we'd stop by and say hello to both of y'all. I heard she's been staying with you."

"She was at church? That girl doesn't go to church."

"Well, she was there today."

Carla grimaced and shook her head. "That girl's a hot mess."

"How so?"

Carla pulled an ice tray out of the freezer and put cubes into glasses. "She's plum broke, for one thing. Lord only knows what that girl does with her salary from the bank." She looked up at Neely Kate, an annoyed look on her face. "Paying me rent sure ain't one of 'em."

"But the bank has to pay better than Wal-Mart!"

"Not as much as you'd think, but still…" She walked into the living room and handed Neely Kate and me glasses of lemonade. "That girl doesn't have any bills or expenses. I ain't got any idea where she spends it all."

Neely Kate looked at David out of the corner of her eye, then back to Carla. "What about recreational drugs?"

Carla's eyebrows lifted and she shook her head. "Oh, no. She hangs out with guys who use drugs, but she says she's keepin' her body pure by avoiding anything that could defile it."

Neely Kate snorted. "I saw her grabbing a Big Boy bacon cheeseburger at the Burger Shack last week. Last time I checked, the EPA was looking into using the fat from those burgers as an alternative energy source. She can't be trying *that* hard to keep her body pure." She snuck a grin at me and whispered, "Especially with the company she keeps."

Carla shrugged. "That's why she has a boyfriend." She gave David a wink. "To help keep her supplied. Although she's more into alcohol."

I tried to hide my surprise. Without a job, I wasn't sure how David could afford to get his own pot, let alone Carla's.

Neely Kate took a sip of her lemonade. "I heard about the bank robbery last week. How is Samantha Jo handling it?"

Carla shrugged her shoulders and took a sip. "Honestly, watchin' her, you'd never know it had happened."

Leaning over her knee, Neely Kate asked, "She was held at gunpoint and she seems just fine?"

Carla's forehead furrowed. "Gee, now that you mention it, that is kind of odd."

"Has she been spending more money lately?"

"Huh... She did buy a bunch of new clothes when she got sent home from the bank that day. Said she was finally planning her trip to L.A.to make it big in Hollywood. I figured I'd let it go since she'd been through such a shock."

The timing seemed significant and then some.

"Carla," I said. "Do you think Samantha Jo might have had something to do with the bank robbery?"

"How so?" Carla asked, clearly confused.

"Do you think she helped the bank robbers?"

"I guess you could say so since she handed over the money." Carla's face scrunched up again, as though she was in pain from thinking too hard.

"Well, I would too if some guy in a dang SpongeBob ski mask was pointing a gun at my head," Neely Kate said.

"The guy holding the gun on her had on a Batman mask," I said. "The other guy wore a SpongeBob mask."

David burst out laughing and Neely Kate and I turned to him in shock.

"What's got you in stitches?" Neely Kate asked.

"We had some of them masks at the Piggly Wiggly. That's what got me fired. I wonder how them robbers got them since we never sold any."

I cocked my head to the side. “How did they get you fired? Did you steal them all?”

“I took’em, but it wasn’t stealin’.” He shrugged. “I thought Bruce Wayne and I could wear them when we were playing paintball with the guys. You know, so we could be undercover.”

Carla made a lovey-pouty face. “Awww… Daveypoo. I didn’t know you played paintball.”

He leaned back, propping his foot on the opposite knee. “What can I say? I’m a complex guy. A man of mysterious ways. Just like last night.” Then he waggled his eyebrows at her.

My nausea roared to life and I tried not to gag.

Neely Kate seemed nonplussed. “So *you* stole the ski caps from the Piggly Wiggly? Why in the world would you do *that*?”

“I didn’t steal them. I swear. I set them out in a display bin in the morning, but the next day a customer pointed out how screwed up the seams were. The assistant manager, Merrill, that is, was madder than hell and wanted to keep sellin’ ’em, but the manager said we couldn’t. So I pulled all of ’em. The company that sent them didn’t want them back and Merrill told me to throw them away. I figured that was a waste, so I took them home. When Merrill found out, he fired me.”

“How could he fire you for that?” I asked, outraged.

David shrugged. “He said they was property of the store.”

“Did you fight him on it?”

He snorted. “That would have been a waste of time. He’s hated me ever since he took the assistant manager job a month ago.”

“Why?”

He shrugged. “We used to be friends ten or so years ago. Then he got married and moved away to be closer to his wife’s family. They had a couple of rugrats and then they split. I told him not to get hitched, particularly not to her, but he didn't listen. Instead, he wasted all them years, and now look at him." He spread his arms on the arms of his chair, a lazy grin spreading across his face. "I think he's jealous of me." He looked like a king surveying his kingdom.

I took in the dingy paneling, the matted carpet, and the musty smell that was making me gag. It was apparent his standards were pretty low.

Neely Kate choked on her lemonade.

Carla reached over and patted her leg. "Are you okay?"

She nodded, trying to hold back a laugh. "I'm fine."

"So if you took them all, how did the bank robbers get them?" I asked. "What did you do with them?"

"I brought some here to Carla's. She was having a party and a bunch of people took them."

"Like who?" Neely Kate asked.

He shrugged. "I dunno, I was kind of out of it that night." He gave me a wobbly smile.

"Moose took a bunch," Carla piped up. "He said he could use them out at the ranch."

"I didn't think he was working at the ranch," I said.

Carla shrugged.

"Speakin' of Moose," I said, taking a sip of lemonade. "I saw Samantha Jo at church with him today. He looks like quite the catch. How long have they been dating?"

She looked lost in thought for several seconds. "I don't know—she's been dating Moose two, maybe three weeks."

"So about the same time she started working for the bank?"

"Yeah, I guess so."

"How'd she meet him?"

"Who knows how Samantha Jo meets her guys. It's a wonder guys still go out with her after what happened with Toby's boat. They stick around until she goes all psycho, and then they dump her like a hot potato." She grinned. "Now that I think about it, I'm kind of surprised Moose is still puttin' up with her. She's flipped her shit more than a couple of times with him." She rolled her eyes in disgust. "From what I've heard she's not *that* good in bed."

"Good to know," I murmured.

Neely Kate looked pale and a few drops of sweat dotted her forehead. "I don't think those wings are agreeing with me now."

"We better get going." I stood. I couldn't think of any more questions to ask and I was eager to get home and check on Mason.

Carla stood when Neely Kate did and pulled her into a hug. "Don't be such a stranger, little miss!"

"You too, Carla. We should get together and have lunch someday—when I can keep it down."

"Yeah, sounds good." She opened the front door to let us out. As we were descending the steps—Carla and David following us out the front door—an old car slowed to a stop and Samantha Jo hopped out of it, moving faster than a toad on hot pavement. Moose climbed out of the driver's side a second later.

"I can't believe you!" Samantha Jo screamed. "I was right *there*, you pus-covered boil!"

"I swear to *God* I wasn't lookin' at her!"

"I saw it with my own eyes, Moose! You wanted to screw that bitch."

"You have to believe me, baby. You're the only bitch I want to screw!"

Neely Kate and I stared at them in disbelief.

Samantha Jo started to stomp right past us when she stopped next to me. "Hey, I've seen you before."

"Samantha Jo," Carla said, "this is Rose Gardner."

"We went to school together," she murmured, looking down her nose at me. "But you weren't cute then and you were definitely weird."

Neely Kate's hands tightened into fists. "Well, at least she's not incredibly rude, which can't be said for you."

I grabbed Neely Kate's arm and pulled her back. "Neely Kate, it's okay. She's right."

Neely Kate's face reddened and she looked like she wanted to hit someone, preferably the woman in front of me. But we needed information from her, and Neely Kate punching her wouldn't help our cause.

"Samantha Jo, I was at the bank last week. During the robbery."

Her eyes widened with a fear that quickly faded. "Oh, yeah. That's why I remembered you. You don't look anything like you used to back in school."

"I was actually hoping to ask you a couple of questions about the robbery."

She blinked. "Why?"

I hadn't been prepared for that, but it made sense that she wouldn't want to talk about it if she was in any way involved. "Because I thought you might like to talk with someone who was there and understands what you went through."

She looked at Moose, then shook her head. "Well, you're wrong. I *don't* want to talk about it. Especially with you."

She turned to leave. We hadn't gotten any information from her, so I decided if I was actually going to try Neely Kate's crazy idea about forcing visions to solve the case, it was now or never.

I stretched out my hand and grabbed her arm, closing my eyes to concentrate.

"What the hell?" Samantha Jo shrieked, trying to jerk her arm free.

"Rose?" Neely Kate asked, but she must have figured out what I was doing because I felt her move closer. "She's trying to comfort you through prayer, Samantha Jo. Just give her a moment."

Samantha Jo didn't seem to appreciate my comfort and jerked on her arm again. The distractions were making it hard to concentrate, so I tightened my grip. Finally, the darkness behind my eyelids gave way to a stained ceiling.

Moose stood naked at the bottom of the bed. "I know how you like it, baby."

"You know it, tiger," I said.

He lowered to the mattress and it sank in the middle as he started crawling on his hands and knees toward me.

Pure panic rushed through me as I realized what was about to happen, and I fought the vision, trying to escape. But escaping a spontaneous vision never worked and it turned out it didn't work for voluntary ones either. Seconds later, just before Moose was about to make the big plunge, I was finally freed, my eyes flying open as I blurted out, "You and Moose are gonna have sex." My hand dropped her arm like it was on fire.

"*What?*" Samantha Jo asked. "What are you? Some kind of *pervert*?" She stomped toward the trailer.

I stumbled backward and turned to Neely Kate, who was staring at me with wide eyes. She'd clearly cottoned to what had happened.

Carla glanced from Neely Kate to me as Moose ran after his girlfriend. "Well, anybody with any sense in their head knows they're gonna have sex later." She shrugged, unconcerned. "It's what they do."

The buffalo wings in my stomach started a protest.

"It's no surprise she didn't take to your comfort. She hasn't been herself lately," Carla said. "She's been meaner than a one-eyed snake."

"Lately," David snorted, then choked, leaning forward and coughing.

Neely Kate rolled her eyes. "And with *that* we'll be goin'…"

She had started walking back to the car, dragging me with her, as Moose stormed back to his vehicle, his phone in his hand. I overheard him as he got into his car. "If I stay with this bitch much longer, I'm gonna kill her and that ain't no lie." He door slammed shut, muffling his voice.

When I got into Neely Kate's car, she was clutching the steering wheel, shaking. "Did what I think just happened actually happen?" she whispered.

"If it's that I just forced a vision of Samantha Jo and she and Moose were about to have sex, then *yes*, that's *exactly* what happened." Unable to contain my nausea any longer, I opened the car door, leaned out, and vomited on the dead grass.

I sat back up and shut the door. "I'm never doin' that again."

Neely Kate had the sense to be quiet for a moment. "So…that didn't go exactly according to plan…"

"*You think?*"

"Okay, calm down. It could have been worse."

"How could it have been worse? Did *you* see Moose naked?"

"But they didn't actually *have* sex?"

"No, thank God, but it was really close."

"So I can't ask if he was any good."

"Neely Kate!"

"Moose has really big feet, and I've heard guys with big feet have big—"

"*Drive*."

She turned to look toward the trailer, her eyes narrowing. "She was really rude to you. I feel like going in there and snatchin' her bald."

"Neely Kate, *go*."

"At least tell me if she was wearing one of them fake leather bustiers from Frederick's of Hollywood."

"*Neely Kate!*"

"Fine! Jeez, Louise," she grumbled as she turned the key and started the engine. "You never tell me the good stuff."

Neely Kate didn't say anything else until she was heading out of the trailer park. "I think she did it."

"You're only saying that because she was mean to me. She didn't do it, but she may very well have been a part of it. Moose started dating her around the time she started to work at the bank and she didn't want to talk about the robbery."

"Although that part may have been because she didn't like you."

"Well…that's true." I twisted my mouth to the side. "And what about her shopping trip the day the bank was robbed?"

"As much as I hate to defend her," Neely Kate grumbled, "she may have been stress shopping."

"True. But Moose was groveling with her to her face, then threatening to kill her out of earshot."

"Yeah. So was Moose the guy you had the vision of? It seems logical." She turned to me and grinned. "Too bad he wasn't naked in the vision this morning. You know, so you could compare."

"Shut up, Neely Kate," I grumbled, but then I couldn't help laughing.

Neely Kate's hand twisted back and forth on the steering wheel. "So David took the hats from the Piggly Wiggly and Moose took some of them. Is there any chance Moose and Mick are the same person?"

I shook my head. "No. I'm certain of that, but he could have been the guy from church whose head I was in."

"So Moose gets the caps, takes them to his buddies, they rob the bank, but what do they need the money for?"

I shrugged. "I don't know."

"I think we need to take a think break." She pushed out a huff. "Plus I'm hungry. Let's get ice cream."

I laughed. "Is that what I have to look forward to if I'm pregnant? Alternating between barfing and eating?"

"Yeah. Pretty much."

"I just threw up less than five minutes ago," I protested.

She turned to me and playfully lifted an eyebrow. "So…ice cream?"

I checked my phone for any messages from Mason, and was disappointed when I saw none. While I was eager to get home, if Mason wasn't there, I'd go stir-crazy wondering where he was. I'd rather hang out with Neely Kate. And at least we seemed to be making some progress. "Sure."

She drove to the Burger Shack, which was in better structural shape than Big Bill's Barbeque. The paint job was worse, if that was possible. The Sunday afternoon crowd had thinned since it was two o'clock, so we walked right up to the counter.

No one was at the register, but one of the four guys from church—Eric—stood in the opening to the kitchen, talking on the phone.

"You came here because of *him*," I whispered.

She shrugged. "We need to check them all out and he seemed the easiest to talk to next."

"How'd you know he'd be here?"

"Jonah said he worked here and I really *was* hungry for ice cream, so what did we have to lose? I took a chance."

Eric seemed to be alone other than a guy at the grill, and he was oblivious to our entrance. "No, I can't get away right now. You'll have to do it without me," Eric hissed into the phone. He looked up and noticed he had customers and confusion flickered in his eyes. "I gotta go," he said as he hung up and approached us, looking around. "Austin!" he shouted toward the back, but no one came out. Eric stepped up to the counter, close enough that I could read the name tag on his striped shirt: *Eric, Assistant Manager*. "You can't find good help these days. I'm pretty sure he's makin' out with his girlfriend behind the vegetable oil can by the Dumpsters."

The thought made my stomach cramp.

"So…" Eric said. "What can I get you?"

Neely Kate leaned her hand on the counter. "I want a banana split and a hot fudge sundae." She looked back at me. "What do you want, Rose?"

"Um…a small Sprite." Ice cream didn't seem like the best idea right now.

Eric filled our order and I struggled with how to get answers from him. Neely Kate, on the other hand, seemed to be a pro. Maybe this was why she knew so much about everything.

"Eric, you look so familiar. Didn't you go to Eastern Fenton County High School? You graduated four years ago?"

He shook his head. "I'm from Magnolia. I moved here a couple of years ago."

"You're really good at your job. No wonder they pulled you down here to work."

He laughed. "Oh, no. I came down to work in the garage north of town. Then they laid off a bunch of mechanics and I was stuck."

"That must be where I saw you!" she squealed. "When I took my car out to Weston's Garage. My car never ran better than after you worked on it."

He beamed.

"So what are you doing *here*?"

He smile fell. "There aren't many mechanic's jobs around here."

"Why not move back to Magnolia and work there?" Neely Kate leaned closer. "Only be sure to let me know what garage you end up at so I can be sure to bring my car to ya."

He shrugged. "I've got a girl here. We're getting married, and she doesn't want to move away." He spread out his hands. "So I'll just keep being the assistant manager of the Burger Shack until I can find something else. But not to worry, I've got something promising on the horizon."

We took Neely Kate's ice cream and my drink to a table by the window and Neely Kate scooped out a huge bite from her banana split. "What do you think?" she asked.

"I don't know. He obviously needs the money, but does he really seem like the bank robber type?"

"No, Moose fits the bill more than he does."

"Agreed."

We sat in silence for several minutes until I saw a car streak by.

"My word, Neely Kate! Did you see that car? It's the gold Charger!"

She was out of her seat faster than I'd expected, throwing out what was left of her banana split but keeping her sundae.

Though I'd barely put a dent in my drink, mostly because of my stomach, I threw mine away too and ran out the door behind her. As soon as I had my door shut, she was peeling out of the parking lot and heading in the direction in which the car had disappeared.

"Neely Kate, what are we going to do if we catch up to it?"

"Let's just find it first and then decide."

My stomach seized when we saw the brake lights of the car at a stop sign. Neely Kate pulled up behind it and I tried to peer through the back window.

"I can't see who's in there."

"Should I pull up alongside the car so we can look in?"

"No! What if one of the bank robbers is in there and he recognizes me?"

"So what do we do?" she asked as the car started to pull away.

"Get the license plate number. Follow it but not close."

We had to wait for two cars to go through the stop sign before we could get through the intersection. The road forked a half mile down the road. The right fork went into town but the left fork headed to an abandoned plant. We saw the car disappear down the road to the left.

"It's the old fertilizer plant," Neely Kate said. "What are they doing *here*?" She pulled to the side of the road and we watched the Charger pull around the side of the building.

"I don't know, but we can't go back there. They'll see us."

"But if we—"

"*No.*" I sounded harsher than I'd intended, but it scared me how tempted I was to let her follow them, no matter how great the danger. "Neely Kate, they killed Mr. Sullivan and obviously stole his car. It's not just us we need to think about. You're pregnant. You have to consider your baby."

She gripped the steering wheel and nodded.

"Let's park across the street at the gas station and wait for them to leave so we can get their license plate number. Then I'll give it to Mason."

She groaned. "Since when did you become the voice of reason? That's my job."

I rolled my eyes and squeezed her arm. "Maybe you're rubbing off on me…and I'm rubbing off on you."

Laughing, she made a U-turn and parked in the gas station parking lot, the car's windshield facing the road. We stood watch for several minutes before Neely Kate released a groan. "I need to find the bathroom."

I looked down at the melting sundae in the cup holder in the console. "Now?"

"I can't wait. You sit in the driver's seat so you can follow them and get their plate number if they leave."

"I can't leave—"

She bolted out of the car before I could finish my sentence. I got out and walked around to the driver's side, then pulled out my phone and checked it for a message from Mason. Instead I found a text from Joe.

I WILL arrest you for obstruction of justice if I find you investigating this case.

Watching for a car to get its license plate wasn't investigating, was it? I was just being a good citizen. Once I got the number, I was definitely going to give it to Mason.

Neely Kate took longer than usual. She walked toward the car, her face pale, a hand on her stomach. She slid into the passenger seat and groaned. "Next time I decide to mix hot wings and ice cream, smack me upside the head."

I chuckled. "Deal."

Moments later, we saw movement by the empty plant. Dust filled the air and the Charger zoomed past us.

"I'm going to follow it for just long enough to get the plate number," I said, starting the engine.

"Okay." Neely Kate started to dig a pen out of her purse.

The Charger stopped at the end of the road, then turned toward town. I was about to follow it when two more vehicles emerged from the plant. A black pickup turned in the opposite direction from the Charger, and I recognized the long scratch down its side.

"Neely Kate! I've seen that truck before! It turned down the road toward the farm where I found the body. I saw it the day after the robbery."

"Are you serious?"

"Which one do I follow?"

"I don't know. Uh…the Charger. Best that we don't follow the murderers. We'll just stick to car thieves."

And bank robbers, but that one seemed a given at this point. "Okay." I turned right and went after it, but it sped up to beat an oncoming train, crossing the tracks only seconds before the bars went down.

I pulled the car to a stop. "Please tell me you got the license number."

"No. Sorry."

"Why was it speeding? Do you think they knew we were following them?" I hated to think of what they might do if they did.

"I don't know." She sounded worried. "Maybe they're just thrill seekers."

"Maybe." But now we had nothing to show for our stakeout. Or did we? "I'm going back to that plant."

She sat up straighter. "What?"

"Maybe we can see what they were up to. It should be safe. We saw them leave."

"Okay. Let's do it."

I released a nervous laugh. "Weren't you supposed to be the voice of reason?"

"I barfed on a guy in a bar. I think we're long past that."

I made a U-turn and steered Neely Kate's car down the cracked asphalt road to the dilapidated fertilizer plant. It was comprised of several buildings connected with large metal pipes that stretched a good fifteen feet over the road between the structures. Several smaller buildings were scattered around the larger ones, and the entire property was surrounded by a chain-link fence that was busted in multiple places. But the road to the plant was wide open.

"My uncle used to work here," Neely Kate said as we approached the abandoned site. "It used to be *the* place to work in Fenton County."

"A stinky fertilizer plant?"

"They paid well."

It may have been the place to work years ago, but now it was a real eyesore and the town had talked about tearing it down. Teens liked to come out there to party late at night, climbing around the big pipes and getting into trouble. I was worried about what we'd find. But when we followed the path where the car had turned, there were no signs that anyone besides us was currently present.

As I drove slowly down the road between two buildings, a now-familiar smell hit me. "This is it, Neely Kate. The smell I noticed on Mick and in my vision."

"A rusty, earthy smell? You're right."

"Now what?" I asked, slowing down. "Do we get out and walk around?"

"I don't know. Let's drive around first."

"Okay."

We circled the entire complex once with no sign of anything untoward.

"Let's drive around one more time," Neely Kate said. "And if we don't see anything worth investigatin', you can tell Mason and let him sort it out."

"Good idea."

I started our second sweep, driving slower, and Neely Kate gasped when I was about halfway through.

"Rose, your vision—you saw a paned window with Y-shaped crack, right?"

"Yeah."

"Like that?" She pointed to the structure on her side. A small office with paned windows on one wall jutted out from the side of the larger building. There was a Y-shaped crack in the bottom pane.

"Oh, my word," I gasped. "That's it."

"Nobody's here. Let's check it out."

I parked the car and we got out and walked slowly to the door. Neely Kate reached it first, but I pushed her back. "Neely Kate, let me go first." No need for *her* to walk headlong into possible danger.

She started to protest, but I pushed past her and tried the doorknob. I wasn't surprised to find it unlocked. The room was dark and empty, and the floor was littered with beer cans and bottles and cigarette butts. When I turned and faced the window, a chill shot down my spine.

"This is it. This is the room from my vision." I was standing in the exact same spot where I'd been in the vision.

"So…?" she asked, spinning around to take in the room. "They meet here?"

"I guess so. It makes sense. This whole area's deserted, so they'd go unnoticed."

"What do you think they do when they get together? Discuss the next place they're gonna rob?"

"I don't know." I walked around the perimeter of the room. We had found where they met, but what good did it do us? I could tell Mason, but wouldn't the police wonder how he knew? At least he could call in an anonymous tip. "I have four days to get my money back," I sighed. "And we have more questions than answers."

"At least it's something."

"But it's not enough."

Neely Kate's cell phone rang and I jumped, feeling nervous even though nothing ominous was happening at the moment.

She glanced at her phone and groaned. "Hey, Granny," she said when she answered. She looked at me and rolled her eyes. "No, Granny. I don't remember agreeing to go to Bingo tonight. I already have other plans." More silence, and then she shook her head, her mouth puckered into a frown. "Fine. Be ready at six." Another pause. "Love you too. Bye."

"Bingo night *again*?"

"She loves it, what can I say? I only wish she could get one of my cousins to take her." She gave the room one last look. "Okay, let's go. I need to at least *try* to make Ronnie dinner before I pick her up. I have yet to make it through cooking an entire meal without barfing."

"Yeah, I'm eager to get home to Mason."

"Still no call, huh?"

"No."

We started to leave the room when I noticed a folded piece of paper on the floor, partially hidden by a crushed beer can. Neely Kate made it outside before she realized I wasn't behind her. She whirled around, standing in the doorway. "Rose?" Noticing the paper in my hand, she walked back toward me. "What is that?"

I unfolded the stained and dirty sheet, surprised to see that it was some sort of chart. A table of about fifty rectangles filled the page, each filled with what appeared to be random handwritten numbers. While the paper seemed to be a copy, some of the boxes were circled with blue ink. Unable to make heads or tails of it, I handed it to my friend. "Do you have any idea what this is?"

"It kind of looks like a giant Sudoku puzzle, only the circled numbers are twenty-nine, two hundred and eighty nine, twenty-four, and one."

"I'll give it to Mason to see if he can figure it out."

We drove home in silence, as all the excitement and worry of the day had me exhausted. I was in desperate need of a nap and given Neely Kate's hormones, I suspected she was too. When we pulled down my driveway, the absence of Mason's car in front of the house was like a kick in the gut.

"Don't worry," Neely Kate said, patting my hand, then handing me my Big Bill's container. "He probably had to go to his office at the courthouse."

The thought of the food inside the Styrofoam made my stomach revolt. "Yeah. Probably."

"Are you okay out here alone?"

I turned to her in surprise. "Yeah, why wouldn't I be?"

She lifted her eyebrows. "Do you want me to actually *list* the reasons?"

I laughed. "I'm fine. Have fun at Bingo."

She leaned across the seat as I got out. "Say, you don't want to go with us, do you? Your visions might come in handy."

I groaned. "After what I saw earlier, I never want to force a vision again."

She watched me climb the porch steps and when I had the front door unlocked, I waved and pushed it open. Muffy ran through the threshold, jumping up on my legs with her tail wagging as Neely Kate drove away.

"Where's Mason, Muff? Did he go to work?"

Rather than answering, she scampered down the steps and starting racing in figure eights in the front yard. I didn't blame her. She'd been cooped up inside all day. The air was cooling off, so I put the wings in the refrigerator and grabbed a blanket to take to the porch. Muffy needed to run around and let off some energy so I knew I'd be outside for a bit. I sat in a chair and covered my front with the blanket, watching my little dog run around. I felt bad about leaving her all day, especially since Mason had left her too. Where was he? But I was too exhausted to think about it, so I closed my eyes and rested my head against the back of the chair.

Chapter Eighteen

"*Rose*?" Mason called out, alarmed.

"Mason?" I bolted out of my chair and threw my arms around his neck.

He tightened his arms around me. "You're freezing. How long have you been out here? You looked like you were sleeping. What happened?"

"I brought Muffy out, but I brought a blanket with me because it was cooling off. I was so tired I must have dozed off."

"Come on, let's get you inside. It's not safe for you to be out here like this." He opened the front door and followed me inside.

"Mason, where were you all day?" I asked as I turned on a lamp. "I kept trying to call you." I couldn't hide the panic in my voice. "I was really worried when I couldn't reach you."

"I'm sorry, sweetheart. I had to go to my office and then on to a crime scene. I didn't realize my phone was dead until I got a call about the robbery on the office phone. Then I tried calling you back, but you didn't answer your phone. I almost had a sheriff's deputy come out to check on you."

"Except you were worried which one would come."

He paused and stared into my face. "Rose, I'd call Joe Simmons myself if I thought you were in danger. I'd never put you in harm's way to save my pride. It's important you know that."

I reached for him and pulled him into a hug. "I know. And I love you for it."

"I love you too. Are you hungry? Have you eaten?"

"Not since Neely Kate stopped for ice cream."

"Judging from all your calls, I take it you had an eventful day."

"You could say that."

We went into the kitchen and I pulled the container from the fridge. "I brought you my leftover hot wings from Big Bill's Barbeque. Neely Kate and I went there for lunch."

His quirked his brow at me. "You were at Big Bill's today?"

"Yeah, Neely Kate said Ronnie Junior had a craving." When he gave me a blank stare, I added. "Don't ask."

"Rose, Big Bill's Barbeque was robbed right after closing time today."

"What?" I turned to face him, my jaw dropping.

"It was robbed late this afternoon. We're guessing it was the same guys who robbed the bank. They had those masks you described. But there were three of them this time. The third one had a Spiderman mask."

"I have some information that might help."

His eyes lit up. "Did you go see Samantha Jo?"

"Among other things." I put the container in the microwave and turned it on. "Let me start at the beginning." I fixed a plate for each of us and spent the next ten minutes telling him everything about my day—except for the forced vision—while he listened. I also gave him the chart I'd found, which seemed to confuse him as much as it had perplexed Neely Kate and me.

He was silent for a long moment after I finished, then said, "You *did* have an eventful day." He looked at my plate and the barely touched food. "Are you still feeling ill?"

I shrugged. "It comes and goes."

He watched me push my half-eaten wing to the side of the plate. "You're still not ready to take the test?" he asked, his face expressionless.

"No."

He didn't say anything for several unnerving seconds. "Okay, I'll let you take the lead on this for now."

I got up to put our plates in the sink. "Thank you."

He followed behind me. "Let's clean this up and go sit in the living room. I need to talk to you about something, and I'd rather not do it while we're hanging over the kitchen sink."

My chest constricted. "This sounds serious." A lump burned my throat. "Are you breaking up with me?"

He grabbed my arms and turned me to face him, his eyes flying open. "*What? No!* Why would you think that?"

"After the Joe situation yesterday and you sleeping in the spare room last night and not going to church with me this morning…well, my imagination ran wild."

He pulled me into a hug. "Rose, please don't worry about something like that happening. I love you, and I told you that I don't take that lightly. When I make a commitment, I stick to it." He laughed softly, his chest rumbling against mine. "You can't get rid of me that easily."

I pulled back and wiped a tear. "I'm glad to hear it."

He kissed my forehead, his expression turning serious again. "Come on. Let's go into the living room."

We sat on the sofa and he wrapped an arm around my back and pulled me close.

"You got a lot of helpful information today, but I'm most worried that Lars Jenkins thinks you have information about him doing something illegal. He is not a man to be trifled with."

"I didn't think I was doing anything dangerous, Mason. I swear. I was only goin' over to talk to Samantha Jo when I had that vision—and we were in church, for heaven's sake!"

"Hey." He looked down at me and smoothed back my hair. "You *didn't* do anything wrong, and I'm not upset with you. *Please* don't think I am. I'm so proud of the progress you've made over the last six months. You said you rarely used to do anything or go anywhere, but look at you now. You own your own business, and you have friends—good ones. But unfortunately, there's a price for venturing out into the world—you risk having visions at inopportune times. It's going to keep on happening too. The only alternative is for you to hide away from people like you did for so long, but you don't want to go back to that life…and it's not what I want for you either. You deserve much more, and the people who have yet to meet you do too."

I wiped away a tear. "Thank you, Mason."

"That being said, I'm worried you might be in danger. Especially after the robbery today. I have an uneasy feeling about all of it. Something big is about to go down, and I think you're going to get caught in the middle of it."

Mason had great instincts and I'd learned to listen to them. He'd been the only one to correctly guess that Daniel Crocker would stick around Fenton County after his jail break. "I tried my best to be careful today, Mason. I only talked to Samantha Jo because you gave me your blessing, and when we saw the Charger I only wanted to get the license plate number… We didn't even expect to see the truck. It gives me the heebie jeebies to think about it turning into our neighbor's farm the other day. For all I know, that poor man was inside." I shuddered, thinking about how close I'd been to a murderer that day. And Ashley and Mikey had been with me too.

He searched my eyes. "You need to stay out of this now, okay? It's too dangerous. Promise me."

"Okay. Do you know how much money the robbers got today?"

"About eight thousand. They don't take credit cards and it was a Sunday. Taylor said it had never been robbed before, which I find startling. He thinks there's some unspoken rule that the place is off limits."

"Maybe the robbers are from out of town and didn't know the rule?"

"Good thought. Maybe," Mason said.

"I'm sure at least one of those five people at church are involved," I said. "And I know two of them are from out of town. Lars Jenkins and Eric Davidson, although Eric seems the more unlikely of the two."

"Agreed." He grinned, pride beaming from his eyes. "I think you missed your calling, Rose. You're a natural at this."

"You're actually encouraging me?"

His smile fell slightly. "We've already established that I don't want you out there pursuing this anymore, but there's nothing wrong with you using the brain that God gave you to sort through what we know to draw some conclusions."

I stared at him in awe before continuing. "So based on my vision, they still don't have enough money for whatever it is they're planning."

"No, which means they'll hit someplace else and probably soon."

"And the fertilizer plant?"

"Unfortunately, it's within Henryetta's city limits, so the police will be in charge. I'll tell them I got an anonymous tip. I doubt they'll ask many questions. But I think you're right. Whatever group they're a part of has been meeting there."

"Too bad we didn't get the license number on the car or the truck."

"I'm glad you were wise enough to know when to stay back. I'll confess that I wish you hadn't gone to the plant with just Neely Kate. If these guys have been meeting there and you'd showed up while they were around, you could have endangered yourself."

"And what about Samantha Jo's involvement? What does your instinct tell you about that?"

"I agree with you there. She and Moose are definitely behaving in a suspicious manner. I'll see what I can dig up on them." He tipped my face up to his. "I'm sorry she was mean to you."

"I'm used to it." I shrugged, trying to lower my gaze, but he held onto my chin.

"I'm glad Neely Kate is your friend."

I smiled. "Me too."

"Speaking of mean people, what's going on with Violet? What in the world is she doing spending time with Joe? It's damn obvious Joe's only hanging around her to try to upset you and make you jealous. But what's *her* motive?"

"I honestly have no idea. Probably the same thing."

"Is she still coming for Thanksgiving?"

"We haven't discussed it, but I can't imagine she would want to after all of this."

"Is it still okay if my mother comes?"

"Of course! She's staying here, I hope?"

"I talked to her today before my phone died. She agreed to join us for Thanksgiving after I convinced her you wouldn't have it any other way. She plans to drive down and spend tomorrow night with us. Then she's going to spend Tuesday and Wednesday looking for a place for me to move into."

My back stiffened. "Oh…" I said softly.

He was silent for a moment. "That was our arrangement, and it looks like I'll finally get the insurance check in another week or so. I've overtaken your office and everything else in the meantime. I'm sorry to have imposed on you for so long." He was silent for a moment. "Mom says she'll even come back to help me furnish it."

I bit my lip to keep from crying. Why was I getting so upset? He wasn't moving far away, just back into his own place. In Henryetta. I needed to put this into perspective. "You've lived alone for a long time. I'm sure it's been a difficult adjustment living with me. You're probably eager to have your own place again."

"No, Rose. I've loved every minute of living with you. There's nothing better at the end of an awful day than coming home to see your smiling face." He kissed the top of my head. "Not to mention going to bed with you every night and waking up to your sweet smile in the morning." His hand on my waist slid higher, until it rested beneath my breast. His voice turned husky. "Along with all the things we do in your bed. And other places."

My insides warmed and I shifted so I could press myself against him more. "I like those parts too."

He lowered his mouth to mine and kissed me gently before growing bolder.

"Mason?" I asked breathlessly.

"Yes?" He lifted his head to look at me, his eyes filled with lust.

"What if I don't want you to move? What if I want you to stay?"

His hand slid up my back, pressing me closer to him. "I'd give you just about anything you want, Rose. You only have to ask."

"But what do *you* want? I'd only want you to stay if it's what *you* wanted too."

A grin tugged at his mouth. "If you're asking if I think it's too soon for us to officially live together, I confess it's faster than I would consider prudent. But I've thrown all the rules out the window with you. What we have defies any rules. I know this farmhouse is yours, and I would never presume ownership, but when I'm here with you, I feel more at home than I've ever felt before."

I smiled back at him. "Yesterday, when I was at the crime scene and I just wanted to go home, I realized part of the reason this place feels like home is because you're here. Please stay."

He gave me a long slow kiss and lifted his head to look at me. "I can't think of any place I'd rather be. I love you, Rose. I promise you that I'll always do my best to make you happy." His words were thick with emotion.

"Oh, Mason. You already do." I started to get up. "Let's go upstairs."

He held me in place, his face turning serious. "Before we do, I want to talk to you about one more thing."

I settled back against him, anxious. "Okay."

"You know I've been working on this special case and I didn't want to talk about it prematurely. But I've hit a wall, and I'm not sure how to broach it with you." He hesitated. "My special project…it involves you."

"Me?" My head jerked up. "You mean Dora's death?"

"No, something else." He paused, looking nervous, which worried me. "Ever since you told me about J.R. Simmons' blackmail attempt when we were on the run from Crocker, I've been concerned about the threats he's dangling over Joe's head to keep him in line. I've been gathering evidence to bring Joe's father down, but I'm facing a mountain of dilemmas. The first being that we live in completely different counties, which means I have no jurisdiction over him unless he does something in Fenton County. And despite all the digging I've done, I can't find any evidence directly linking him to this place."

"I wouldn't be surprised if he's never even been in Fenton County."

"You could very well be right. I could try to involve the state police, but J.R. has influential people in his pocket, people who would immediately squash any investigation I tried to hold. Not to mention my career would be on the line if he gets word of what I'm doing. That part doesn't bother me as much as the thought of tipping him off does. If he realizes I'm trying to gather ammunition to use against him, he might strike first. And I want to avoid that at all costs, obviously."

My stomach was in knots. "I don't want you to put your career on the line for me, Mason."

"I'm not even going to dignify that statement with a response except to ask you a question: Wouldn't you do the same for me?"

He had a point. I sighed. "So we're stuck."

He tipped my face up to his. "Do you really think I'd sit back and let your safety be jeopardized?"

"But your hands are tied."

"Not necessarily." He hesitated. "We can fight fire with fire. It's dirty, but that seems to be the only language J.R. Simmons understands."

I wasn't sure I liked the sound of this. "What would you do?"

"I'd find sensitive information on his family to use as a counter-threat."

My breath stuck in my chest. "How many family members does he have that are dirty enough for that to work?"

"One."

The full meaning of what he intended hit me. "You want to bring Joe down?"

He didn't answer.

I took several deep breaths. "I know he has a past, and that he's gotten himself into plenty of trouble. Joe told me so himself. That's how he dug the hole he's in now. But is there enough out there to bring him down?"

He paused. "Yes."

"What kind of threat would get J.R. to listen?"

"Joe has done enough misdeeds to face prison time, Rose."

My heart threw itself against my ribcage and I sat up straighter. "You're asking for my blessing to throw Joe in prison."

"No." His voice was firm. "I'm asking for your blessing to dig up proof to back up all the rumors floating around about him."

"You're not gathering information just to sit on it, Mason. You plan on using it."

"J.R. threatened to have you arrested for your mother's murder. Don't delude yourself into thinking you're safe. You're safe *for now* until he deems you no longer necessary. Then he'll have you arrested just to prove he can."

"But you'll protect me if it comes to that."

"You know I'd move heaven and earth to save you, but I suspect J.R. will make sure I'm stripped of power before he makes his move."

"So you're in danger too? Because of me."

He gave me a soft smile. "No, Rose. My career was in J.R. Simmons's hands long before you entered the picture. Don't forget that he's the one who had me sent here after Savannah's death."

"But you don't know that for a fact. You only have suspicions."

"My conclusion is based on circumstance and instinct, but you and I both *know* he was behind it."

I shook my head, trying to wrap my head around what he was suggesting. Gather evidence to put Joe in prison? I couldn't be a part of that. "I can't. No matter what stunts Joe pulls to try and get me back, I'd never do that to him. Ever."

"Rose. There's more."

My eyes sank closed and I pressed my back into the sofa. "Okay."

"You told me that the information he has on Violet is true. She did have an affair with Mayor Brody MacIntosh. But something else is also true."

My insides quaked. I wasn't sure how much more I could take.

"Mike *did* bribe county officials."

My eyes flew open as my anger erupted. "How can you say that, Mason? My brother-in-law would never do that."

He gave me a sad smile, keeping calm against my sea of rage. "It was when he was first starting out. He was in rough financial shape, and he faced having to redo a commercial building's plumbing. It was going to cost him thousands of dollars he didn't have. He was young and he had a brand-new baby. He was scared, so he bribed an inspector *one time*. He regrets it. Deeply."

I shook my head and whispered, "How do you know?"

"I went to see him this afternoon, Rose. I wanted to find out how J.R. had twisted the truth to use against him. That man's favorite thing to do is take a small seed of truth and transform it into a scenario that's exponentially worse."

It was too much and my stomach revolted. I jumped off the sofa and ran to the powder room, barely making it to the toilet before losing the meager contents of my stomach. I hung over the commode dry-heaving through my tears.

What was I going to do?

Mason stood in the doorway and when I was ready, he helped me to my feet. I washed out my mouth and the tears from my face before turning toward him.

He grabbed my face in both hands, his eyes burning with intensity. "I love you, Rose. And I'll do *anything* and *everything* in my power to protect you. Don't for one second think you can ask me not to."

I shook my head. "I can't condone this, Mason. I just can't."

"I know you and Violet are fighting, but would you really subject her to public ridicule? Because you know what will happen if this town gets wind of her affair. Will you stand by and watch Mike go to prison for a stupid mistake he made years ago? Do you want him to lose his business and the kids?" Tears filled his eyes. "And then there's you, Rose. J.R. could put you in prison for a long time. If you're pregnant, what about our baby? Do you expect me to stand back and risk letting all that happen without doing everything I can to take away this man's power?"

"There has to be another way. There has to be. You just said J.R. has evidence to put Mike in prison for something stupid he did in his youth. Well, you're trying to do the same thing to Joe."

"No." His mouth pressed into a thin line. "Mike made one mistake when he was twenty. Joe's still screwing up. I can give you a list from *just this year*. I've heard rumors of multiple DUIs, along with instances of obstruction of justice and misuse of power. Never mind the drunk and disorderliness and assault charges."

"No." My voice broke.

His eyes darkened with anger. "Not to mention the fact that *he killed my sister, Rose*! He may not have held the knife in his hand, but he stripped away any bit of protection she might have had by turning the police against her." Rage radiated off him.

"Is that what this is? *Revenge*?" I shouted. "Is this your way of punishing him for what he did?"

His hands shook at his sides, but his voice was deadly calm. "Do you really believe that? You think I've been waiting to strike at him, using you to get back at him?"

"Joe said you were known in Little Rock for your patience in the courtroom and that you'd lull the opposition into complacency before going in for the kill. He told me that you were only with me so you could hurt him. That you'd destroy us both to avenge your sister's death."

He took a step backward, his face ashen. "Do you really think me capable of such a thing?"

I started to cry. "No. I don't know." I shook my head. "But maybe there's some truth to some of it."

"Which part, Rose?" His voice sounded strangled. "The part about me using you or planning to destroy you?" He turned around and headed for the living room.

"That's not what I meant, Mason." I followed in his wake. "Mason, *please*."

He didn't stop until he reached the front door, his hand on the knob, his back to me. "Joe claims I have some master plan… Did it ever occur to you that maybe he has one instead?" He turned around to face me, the pain in his eyes gut-wrenching. "Congratulations to Joe Simmons and the entire Simmons family. Once again they've stolen someone I love." He opened the door and stomped down the steps.

"Mason, please don't leave. *Please*."

He stopped next to his car door and stared up at me. "You don't trust me, Rose. And if you don't trust me, we have *nothing*. There's not one damn thing left to say."

As he started to get into his car, my anger boiled over, flowing out of my mouth. "*Goddammit, Mason Deveraux*!" I shouted. "You do *not* get to make your accusations and leave! Stop being such a baby and *listen to me*!"

Both of us were frozen in shock for a moment, surprised by my outburst.

He stood behind the open car door, not getting inside but not backing away either. "I can't stay, Rose."

"God, Mason. I love you, but you can be so freaking stubborn!"

"Is *that* why you wanted me to stay?" he shouted.

"No! But it needed to be said." I walked to the top of the porch steps and ran a hand through my tangled hair. "Yesterday you told me that I couldn't walk away from the mess I made with Joe. Well, you can't leave after what we just said."

"Rose."

"No!" I stomped down the steps and pushed him against the car, slamming his door shut. "Don't you dare walk away from me like that."

"What more is there to say? You don't trust me."

"*Who the bejesus said I don't trust you*? I didn't say I didn't trust you. You fabricated that in your head."

"Don't you put this on me, Rose," he forced out. "You're the one who told me you believe what Joe said."

"Now you are deliberately skewin' my words! I *do not* believe what he said." He started to push past me, but I shoved his chest with my hands. "You're not going anywhere until we settle this!"

"You want to do this out here?"

"It's as good as any place, so yes, let's do it out here."

"Fine." He sank back into the side of his car. "If you don't believe Joe, then why would you throw his accusations at me?"

"Because I told you I think there's some truth to them."

The front porch light reflected off the hard glint in his eyes. "You want me to stand here while you accuse me of *using you*?"

"No! God, no Mason! Anyone with any sense can see that you love me. There's no way on God's green earth you would intentionally hurt me. You've proved that over and over and over again. I'd trust you with my life, Mason. I *did* trust you with my life. So stop! You're insulting me."

"Then what the hell are you saying?" he bellowed.

"I'm saying that there's no love lost between you and Joe. You think he's responsible for Savannah's death. Add on to that the fact that he's an officer of the law who's committed multiple crimes worthy of jail time."

He didn't answer, but his chest rose and fell underneath my fingertips.

"Mason, *your job* is to prosecute people for the things you say Joe has done. *Of course* you want to use this opportunity to make him pay for his crimes. You can't deny it!"

He still didn't answer.

"But as aggravating as Joe is, he's trying to change, Mason. I can see it. You of all people are a proponent of people straightening out their lives for the better."

"This is different, Rose. Joe's past isn't just Savannah." His voice broke. "He's flouted the law countless times."

I took a deep breath, worried how Mason would answer my next questions. "I know that driving drunk is irresponsible and dangerous, but did he ever do anything else really bad besides that? Like murder or…?"

"Rape?" The word was ugly, sneered from his mouth.

I held my breath and nodded.

"No. Apparently, Joe Simmons does have his limits."

I grabbed the front of Mason's shirt with both fists. "He's acting out, Mason. I've met his family. They are horrible, terrible people. I can't even imagine growing up with vile people like that. It's no wonder he's behaved the way he has in the past."

His eyes narrowed. "Do *not* make excuses for his behavior. You grew up with a hateful mother and you're not anything like him."

"All I'm saying is that he's made plenty of bad choices, but he's trying to be a better person. So please don't stoop to J.R. Simmons' level, Mason. You're a better person than that."

"Am I?" His voice was hard.

I reached my hand up to his face and rubbed his stubbled chin with my thumb. "Yes, you are. You have more integrity in your pinky toe than most people have in their whole bodies. It's one of the things I love most about you."

His shoulders slumped.

"By resorting to J.R. Simmons's playing field, you're letting him win. You're letting him take advantage of the man I love."

He shook his head. "I don't know what to do, Rose," he said, his voice little louder than a whisper. "It's like I told you, something bad is about to happen. *I can feel it*. I don't know how else to protect you. I'm scared to death."

I stood on my tiptoes, my mouth hovering under his. "We'll find another way."

He leaned his forehead against mine. "I don't think there is one."

"There is. There's *always* another way."

His arm snaked around my back, pulling me hard against his body, and he kissed me as though I was about to be taken away from him forever.

Part of me wondered how much time I actually had.

Chapter Nineteen

Monday brought more sunshine and warm weather, which was ideal because Bruce Wayne and I were hard at work trying to finish the Timberland job.

"You didn't tell me that David had a girlfriend," I said to him. Muffy was stretched out in the sunshine. Since Mason and I were both working through lunch so we could be home before his mother arrived at dinner time, I had brought Muffy with me.

"Oh, yeah. He does," he mumbled. "I guess it didn't seem important."

"You two used to spend all of your time together and he's probably gone a lot now. I bet that's hard for you."

He made a face. "It ain't nothin'. He's happy."

But I realized he'd been quieter than usual over the last two weeks. I'd been so self-absorbed with Mason I hadn't noticed. Some friend I was.

"I saw Samantha Jo with her boyfriend at Carla's trailer. I can't figure that guy out. One minute he was groveling at her feet and the next he was talking like he hated her."

"I think he does."

I looked up. "Does what?"

He shrugged. "Hates her."

I narrowed my eyes. "Then why is he with her?"

"He thinks she had something to do with that bank robbery, and he's hoping to benefit off it."

My mouth dropped. “Well, did she?”

He looked up at me and rolled his eyes. “That girl’s dumber than a dried stick in a match factory. What do you think?”

I sighed.

“Moose needs to give up the hunt. Even if Samantha Jo was part of the bank robbery, he’s not gonna get two pennies to rub together from it. It certainly wouldn’t be enough to help him raise the money to buy Crocker’s business.”

“What?” I screeched.

Bruce Wayne’s face puckered in annoyance. “There’s going to be an auction on Friday night for the territorial rights to his business.” He shrugged. “Not Weston’s Garage, but the drug part of his business as well as some equipment.”

My eyes widened. “And someone would need a lot of money for that.”

“Yep.”

“Do you know who’s interested?”

“Well…they don’t exactly go around advertising it, but it’s common knowledge that Skeeter Malcolm wants it. He and Crocker always had a rivalry. Skeeter’s trying to head off any competition at the pass.”

“Does he have enough money?”

“Who knows? Skeeter makes a lot of money, but he ain’t exactly frugal with it. And no one knows what it’s gonna go for. Could be five thousand, could be fifty.”

“But who owns it? Crocker’s dead.”

“His second-in-command, Bull Tribideau. But he don’t want it. The whole thing’s been run into the ground since Crocker’s arrest last summer. There’s been competition from Columbia County as well as some from Shreveport. Bull’s tired and ain’t got the heart for it anymore. It’s gonna take someone gunnin' to be king and that ain't Bull. So he's selling it on Friday."

"That's crazy."

Bruce Wayne shrugged.

When we took a break later, I called Jonah's cell phone.

"Hey, Rose," he answered. "You don't happen to know anything about the robbery at Big Bill's, do you?"

"No," I said in annoyance, then softened my tone. "Do you?"

He laughed. "Probably the same as what you know through Mason."

"We had a huge fight last night. After that, we spent the rest of our time making up, so I didn't get much information at all." My cheeks burned when I realized what I'd said. "In any case, all I heard was that it had been robbed and they got about eight thousand dollars. Also, they had on the same ski masks those bank robbers had on, so there's no question it was them."

"The Fenton County underworld in an uproar. Big Bill's is considered sacred. No one local would rob that place."

"Mason said that Taylor suspected that was the case. That made us wonder if whoever robbed it was from out of town."

"There's a strong likelihood of that."

"Bruce Wayne told me that Crocker's business is going up for auction on Friday."

"So it's true," Jonah muttered. "I'd heard rumors, but they seemed crazy. How do you auction off something like that?"

I told him everything Bruce Wayne had told me. "I bet Lars is going to try to buy Crocker's business. Bruce Wayne says whoever buys it will have to be hungry for success. He looks ravenous."

"I agree."

"But Moose had access to the hats, so maybe they are both part of it and the group is a lot larger than we think."

Jonah was silent for a moment. "This is getting dangerous, Rose. You need to tell Mason. Did you tell him everything you found out yesterday?"

"Yes, I told you I would. And I told him everything else too…"

"Good."

"Bruce Wayne says Skeeter Malcolm isn't frugal with his money," I said, steering us back on task. "What does he spend it on?"

"Booze. Women. Cars. The same things a lot of guys spend their money on. Skeeter just has more of it to spend."

"Do you think he'd go after Crocker's business?"

"I know for a fact he would."

"At this point, I think it's safe to assume that the bank robbers—who have now robbed Big Bill's too—are stealing the money to make a bid for Crocker's business."

"I think you're probably right. And I think there's probably enough evidence available for the police to do something about it."

"Really? The guys in my vision still don't think they have enough money to make a bid. I suspect I was having the vision from Lars' or Moose's perspective. How is it that we can't figure out who the other guys are?"

"Like you said, Rose, it could be that they live out of town. They could be from Columbia or Lafayette Counties. It's a short enough distance to drive over, rob a place, then be home before dinner's on the table."

"I wish I'd seen the license plate numbers on those cars."

"And I wish I hadn't flubbed that great line in my sermon on Sunday, but we both did the best we could, right?"

I grinned. "Yeah."

"Say, Rose, I have to go. Jessica's hollering for me."

My grin widened. "So did you ask her out yet?"

He cleared his throat. "I'm working up the courage."

"*You* need courage?"

"Everybody needs courage, Rose."

"Say, Jonah. What are your plans for Thanksgiving?"

"Uh…"

"If you don't have anything pressing, I'd like for you to come out to the farm."

"Oh." I heard the gratitude in his voice. "I don't want to put you out, Rose. It's the first Thanksgiving you're hosting."

"No, we'd love to have you, Jonah. I meant to ask you yesterday, but I got caught up in all the excitement. Bruce Wayne and David are coming. And Mason's mother."

"I'd love to join you, but I don't want to be an imposition."

"We're like family now, Jonah. Thanksgiving wouldn't be right without you, and I won't take no for an answer. Dinner will be at around five."

"Thank you, Rose."

Bruce Wayne was back to working when I hung up. I could tell he wanted to tell me something, but he was acting like it would be easier to birth a breech cow than to spit out what he wanted to say.

"Bruce Wayne," I finally said, "if you don't tell me what's buggin' you, you're gonna drive me plum crazy."

"David texted when you was talkin' to Reverend Jonah. He wants me to ask you something."

"Okay…" I said, wondering if he had some information on Samantha Jo.

"I told him you invited him and me to Thanksgiving dinner and he wants to know if Carla can come too."

"Oh." I stopped pulling a shrub out of a pot. "Of course." Especially since I doubted Violet and her kids would come. And even though we were fighting worse than ever, I was still sad that this would probably be the first Thanksgiving we'd spend apart.

He grinned. "Thanks."

"Bruce Wayne..." My voice trailed off. I was afraid to put a voice to my fears, but he needed to be prepared. I owed him that. "What would you do if you weren't working for me?"

His gaze lifted to mine, his eyes wide. "Are you not happy with my work, Miss Rose?"

"Oh! No! Of course I am. But you know I lost all that money, and Violet...well, let's just say I need to find that money or neither one of us might have a job."

"Oh. I guess your brainstorming didn't pan out."

"No. Not yet and we only have until Friday."

We worked in silence for several minutes, my mind running over everything I knew about the robbery. There had to be a way to get my money back without risking my life. "Say, Bruce Wayne. Do you think Skeeter Malcolm knows who his competition is gonna be at the auction?"

"Not all of them, but I suspect he has a pretty good idea of most of 'em."

"So Skeeter might know who committed the robberies?"

"Maybe... But you can't walk in there expecting him to just give you information if that's what you're thinkin'. He'll expect something in return."

I knew that firsthand from when I'd met him this past summer. "What if I had information to give him in exchange?"

He released a low whistle. "I don't know, Miss Rose. Making a deal with Skeeter Malcolm is kind of like makin' a deal with the devil, only at least you know you're gonna have a toasty bed when it comes to the devil."

"I only want to talk to him," I said defensively.

His eyes narrowed. "You're not gonna stop, are you?"

"Bruce Wayne. *It's our business*. You and I both put our sweat equity into this endeavor, and look at all we've done in such a short time! I'm not willing to let this go without a fight. You of all people have to understand that."

He watched me for so long I started to squirm. "I can't be lettin' you go alone. Let me call Scooter and ask him to butter up his brother before we talk to him."

"I don't want to involve you in—"

"Mason's let you ask a bunch of questions around town without puttin' up a fuss. But what do you think he's gonna say when he finds out you went to see Skeeter Malcolm on your own?"

Bruce Wayne was right. Mason would be furious.

"We'll do it my way," Bruce Wayne said, digging his shovel into the ground and spilling over a pile of dirt. "Then if we get caught or into trouble, you can blame it on me and say you were there trying to stop me."

I shook my head. "No, I can't do that."

"I think it's a smart plan. Skeeter might help you if you really have information that can help him. It's worth the risk."

"But you risk your parole if you get caught in something. And I can't guarantee Mason can get you out of it."

He pushed his shovel so deep into the ground it stood on its own then lifted his shoulders, standing more erect than I'd ever seen him. "Rose, this job has saved my life and I'm not gonna let it go without a fight. This here's war, and sometimes there's casualties. You hope to God not to be one, but you go in accepting the risk. Especially if something's worth fighting for."

I couldn't let him do this. I shook my head. "Bruce Wayne…"

"Rose, I had nothin' before this. Nothin'. For the first time in my life I feel like I know what I'm supposed to do.

Where I fit. I can't give that up without a fight. What kind of man would I be if I did that?"

"But you can find another job. I'll give you a wonderful reference."

"Not like this job and you know it, Rose. What you and I have ain't a normal job."

He was right, but it still seemed too much to ask. "You'd really risk everything for this?"

"Yes."

I swallowed the lump in my throat, willing myself not to break down. He was right. What we had wasn't a normal job. He'd proven that time and time again. "Okay." I wiped a tear from my cheek with the back of my dirty glove. "But only on one condition."

"What's that?" he asked warily.

"Violet and I…us being partners isn't gonna work anymore. We burned that bridge with a huge, roaring bonfire this weekend. So once we pay off this debt and save the Gardner Sisters Nursery, I'm gonna split it up into two businesses. Violet can have the shop and you and I can have the landscaping business. Co-owners."

His eyes widened and he shook his head. "No. I can't let you do that. You're the one puttin' up all the money."

"You work just as hard as I do, if not harder. If it weren't for you, we wouldn't be nearly as successful as we are. And now you're risking everything by coming with me to see Skeeter." I lifted my chin. "Co-owners or I let it die."

His eyes widened in dismay. "Miss Rose, you can't mean that."

"But I do."

"Shouldn't you talk to Mason first?"

"Don't you worry. I'll talk to Mason about drawing up the papers to make it official, but as far as making this decision about the business? It's mine. He has no say."

His mouth moved, but nothing came out.

I stuck out my hand toward him. "Partners?"

He stared at my hand for a moment before slowly extending his. He grasped my hand firmly and gave it a good shake, all while staring me solidly in the eyes. "Partners."

I beamed at him, thrilled with my decision but a little overwhelmed with what we had to do next to make it all work. "Why don't you call Scooter to arrange a meeting? I'll finish up here since we only have a few more shrubs."

"Okay." He walked over to his beat-up car, pulling off his gloves before grabbing his phone out of the front seat.

Muffy was giving me a look like I was crazy. "Stop staring at me like that, Muffy. It's a good plan and you know it."

"What plan are you talking about?" Joe asked from behind me.

Startled, I jumped, then spun around. Joe stood about six feet away, wearing his sheriff uniform. That look was gonna take some getting used to. "What are you doing here, Joe? And how did you know I was here?"

Muffy jumped up and ran to him.

"Violet told me." Joe squatted and rubbed my little dog's head. "I'm here looking for you."

I turned my back to him and pulled the next shrub out of its plastic container. "Well, here I am. Is this an official duty, Deputy Simmons?"

"Partially."

"Should I call my attorney?"

I could feel the anger radiating off him. "You can leave Mason out of this."

I hadn't meant Mason, but I was fine with letting him think what he would.

He stood even though a still-excited Muffy was still jumping on his legs. "Rose, will you turn around and face me?"

"Is that an official order?"

"Rose." Irritation laced his words.

Frustrated, I did as he'd asked. "What do you want, Joe?"

"I want to know what you know about the robbery at Big Bill's Barbeque."

I gave him a fake smile. "Oh? You want me to tell you who did it? Or were you hoping I'd know where they hid the money too?"

He scowled. "I'm not foolin' around, Rose."

"I don't know anything other than what I heard from Mason, so you're barking up the wrong tree."

"Why were you talking to Lars Jenkins yesterday at church?"

"I already told you. I wanted to talk to Samantha Jo. I figured it had to have been scary havin' a gun pointed at her head, so I offered her my support."

Joe snorted and turned to face the street, his gaze trailing Bruce Wayne as he moved to sit on the hood of his car. "You would know all about that, wouldn't you? How many times have you had a gun pointed at you now? Two? Three?"

"I don't know," I grumbled. "I've lost track."

He laughed, but it was a bitter sound. "You've lost track." He enunciated each word carefully. "For someone who was so determined to live her own life, you sure seem headstrong to end it."

I put my hand on my hip, starting to get really and truly pissed. "What do you *want*, Joe?"

"I told you I want—"

"I don't know anything about the robbery and that's the God's honest truth. Now, is there anything else? Because as you can see, I'm busy."

His face softened, contrition and regret flickering in his gaze. "I wanted to apologize."

"Oh." I took a half step back. I hadn't expected that.

"You were right. I thought if I kissed you, you'd see you were wrong about us."

I sighed, weary of this fight. "Joe, even if I decided to leave Mason and be with you, *it wouldn't work*. Your father still holds my life in his hands. Pretending like he's never gonna use it is folly and you know it. *He will*. It's just a matter of time. Are you really willing to do that to me? To Violet and Mike?"

He swallowed. "There has to be a way."

"To save me from your father or to be with me?"

"Both."

Profound sadness seeped into my bones. "Why does saving me from your father have to be a two-for-one special, Joe? If you cared anything about me, you'd want to save me even if you couldn't be with me. Mason would."

I started to turn around, but he grabbed my arm and spun me back around to face him, his face contorting with anger. "Don't you dare trivialize my feelings for you," he said through gritted teeth. "And don't you try and compare my love for you to his."

I tried jerking my arm out of his grasp, but his fingers dug in. "Let go of me."

"Not until you listen to me, dammit!"

"There's nothing to say! You just can't handle the truth."

Bruce Wayne sprinted toward us and stood several feet away, his hands clenched into fists. "Let her loose, Joe."

Joe turned his steely gaze on my friend. "That's *Deputy Simmons* to you, Bruce Wayne," he said, his voice full of authority. "And this is none of your concern. You can leave. *Now*."

I jerked my arm free and took several steps back. "Don't you dare talk to him like that! You're not talking to me in an official capacity and he's my friend, so don't you dare pull that deputy crap on him when all he's doin' is trying to protect me."

Anger filled his eyes. "Protect you? *From me?*" he shouted.

"Joe! Look at you! You're grabbing me and forcing me to talk to you! What do you *think* it looks like?"

His anger faded and horror replaced it.

"Joe, please." My voice shook. "Just go."

"Rose. I'm sorry." He reached for me and stopped. "You have to know that," he pleaded.

"I do, but you have to leave now."

Bruce Wayne stood next to me as we watched him walk back to his car, shaking his head like he could barely believe his own behavior. "Are you all right, Miss Rose?"

I rubbed my arm, but not because I was physically hurt. "I'm fine, and you better start dropping the 'Miss' now that we're partners."

"We're not yet," he said, watching Joe's car drive away. "Not until we get that money back. We're meeting Skeeter at four. He wants to talk to us before the evening business picks up."

"Four is good. Mason's mom is coming tonight and I'm not sure how I'd explain leaving if we had to meet him in the evening."

"Let me do this on my own, Rose. You can trust me."

I turned to face him. "I do trust you, but you're not going alone, just like I'm not. We either go together or not at all."

"United we stand, divided we fall," Bruce Wayne said softly.

"Ain't that the truth."

Still, I couldn't help wondering if Bruce Wayne was right. I was about to try making a deal with the devil.

Chapter Twenty

Bruce Wayne was sitting in his car when I pulled up to Eight Baller Billiards. He got out as I approached, my stomach threatening to expel my meager lunch.

I looked up at the sign, wondering if this was so smart after all. The last time I had come here for information, I'd given Skeeter a fake name and had gotten in over my head, drinking and playing pool with him. When I'd had a vision and told him that he was going to lose a lot of money, he'd presumed I was an undercover cop and threatened my life. But if he read the papers or listened to Henryetta gossip *at all*, that confusion would be cleared up, and I wasn't going in under false pretenses this time. I had information he might want. Hopefully, he could help me as well. Besides, I wasn't the naïve girl I once was. But I wasn't so sure I was *this* worldly either.

"You look nice, Bruce Wayne," I said as I approached him. He was dressed in a clean pair of jeans, a button-down shirt—noticeably unwrinkled—and a tan jacket. I'd never seen him look so put together. When he was on trial, he'd looked like someone sadistic had been playing dress-up with him and ill-fitting suits.

"So do you, Miss—er—so do you, Rose."

I gave him a nervous smile, giving a quick glance to my brown skirt and cream ruffled shirt. I'd decided on brown heels and a cute leather jacket at the last minute. This time, I was going for professional, not slutty. "I wasn't sure what a person should wear to a meeting like this."

A slow grin spread across his face. "You didn't ask Neely Kate?"

"Shoot, no. She would have insisted on coming. Two of us is enough, I think."

"So no one knows we're here?" he asked in an ominous tone.

I cocked an eyebrow. "I can call Deputy Simmons if you'd like."

He laughed. "Somehow, I think that's a bad idea, but so is going in with no one knowin' where we are."

I took a deep breath. "I'm starting to have second thoughts about this whole thing."

"Like I told you, Rose, I'll go alone."

"No," I pulled out my phone and started a text to Neely Kate. "Together or not at all."

Bruce Wayne and I have an appointment with Skeeter Malcolm in two minutes.

Her reply was almost instantaneous. *What???*

I'll explain later. If you don't hear from me in half an hour, text me.

I turned my phone to silent, stuffed it in my purse, and looked up, steeling my back. "Okay."

Bruce Wayne led the way and opened the glass door to the building, letting me through. The place was nearly empty, with only a couple of guys in the back playing pool and the bartender. Bruce Wayne pushed past me and walked up to the bar. "We have an appointment with Skeeter."

The bartender glanced up from wiping out a glass. He looked me up and down, then turned his gaze to Bruce Wayne. "He's expecting you. Go on back to his office."

Bruce Wayne shot me a glance and I lifted my mouth into a tight smile. When he headed for the back room, I trailed behind. The guys playing pool looked up and one catcalled. Bruce Wayne tensed, but he kept right on moving, heading through a dark doorway and down a dimly lit hall, stopping in front of a door marked *Private*. He paused a moment, then knocked.

In response to a gruff order to "Come in," he swung the door open and walked into the room, blocking my view.

"Bruce Wayne. I have to say this was a surprise," Skeeter said. "Introduce me to your friend."

He moved to the side and I saw Skeeter sitting behind a large wooden desk. He was a good-looking man with an imposing presence. Dark hair framed his face and he'd shaved off the short beard he'd sported the last time we saw each other. He wore a long sleeved T-shirt that clung to his muscles and a hint of his many tattoos peeked out from under his collar. He stood when he saw me, a slow grin spreading across his face. "And who do we have here?"

I moved closer, surprised Bruce Wayne hadn't told him I was coming. "I'm Rose Gardner."

A sly grin lifted one side of his face. "Oh, I know who you are. I was just wondering if you'd tell me the truth this time."

My face blushed and my heart raced out of control. "I intend to be completely straightforward with you, Mr. Malcolm."

"Good." He gestured to the chairs in front of his desk. "Have a seat. I'm eager to hear what you have to be straightforward *about*." As Bruce Wayne and I moved toward the chairs, he lowered into his. "And call me Skeeter. I'm nowhere near civilized enough to be a mister." He laughed and leaned an elbow on the arm of his chair while watching me settle in my seat. "Let's not mess around with all the polite nonsense of most business dealings. Why don't we cut right to the chase?"

"I agree." I took a deep breath and shot a glance to Bruce Wayne before I continued. "I was in the Henryetta Bank last week when it was robbed. They stole my deposit bag, which held a great deal of cash. My insurance refuses to cover it and the bank's insurance refuses to pay up because I didn't actually make the deposit. I *need* that money."

His eyes narrowed in confusion. "So you need a loan?"

"No. I want *my* money. I'm nearly positive the robbers still have it."

"What makes you so sure?"

"I think they robbed the bank and then Big Bill's because they want to bid on Crocker's business."

He laughed and leaned back on his chair, kicking his feet up on his desk. "Well, now. That's an interesting theory. I've heard you've been like Henryetta's very own Nancy Drew since Crocker killed your momma, though, so maybe you know something I don't."

I stayed silent, unsure how to answer.

"What makes you think your theory is correct?" He waved to Bruce Wayne. "I mean, if Bruce Wayne walked in here and told me that, I wouldn't just hand him a bunch of money." He turned back to me, his eyes turning cold. "So let's cut the bullshit and be straight about what we each want. You want your money back and I want Crocker's business. How can we make sure we both walk away from this happy?"

I took a deep breath. "If I give you useful information, will you help me get my money back?"

He chuckled. "Sweetheart, if you can help me get to these guys before they outbid me, I'll put you on my damn payroll and call it a bonus."

I gave him a nervous smile. "That's not necessary. I just want my money."

"We'll start there and leave the door open to future business dealings."

"Are you a man of your word, Skeeter Malcolm?"

He laughed. "You are a piece of work, aren't you?" He put his feet down and leaned on the desk with an elbow. "Let me give you a piece of advice, Rose Gardner, because if you're gonna get your feet dirty, a tiny piece of fluff like you needs to be prepared: *No one* is a man of his word. Not Bruce Wayne, not that sheriff's deputy you dated, and not that fancy pants assistant DA you're living with who's gunnin' to bring me down, and last but certainly not least, not me."

I tried to stifle my gasp.

"Don't look so surprised. Hell yeah, I know all about you. Scooter calls me up and tells me Bruce Wayne wants to bring his new boss by to get my help, you can bet your ass I did some digging. How do I know this isn't some big setup so your new boyfriend can get a feather in his cap?"

My pulse pounded in my head. "I'd give you my word, but apparently that's about as worthless as a three-dollar bill."

He laughed again. "I like you, Rose Gardner."

"Enough to work with me?"

"First you have to prove you're not workin' with your boyfriend. And your word doesn't count."

"Skeeter," Bruce Wayne said, sounding nervous. "She ain't. I know her and she went out of her way to hide the fact she was coming here from him."

"Why me?" he asked. "Why not just ask your boyfriend to get the money back? Or hell, I'm sure he'd give it to you."

"Even if the police or sheriff's department find my money, it may be confiscated or held as evidence. And since I didn't record serial numbers, I can't even prove it's mine. And

I won't ask Mason or anyone else to plain give me money because *this business is mine*." I was getting angry, which wasn't a smart thing to do with someone like Skeeter Malcolm, but I was tired of people expecting me to just rely on a man to solve my troubles. "Bruce Wayne and I have worked our hinies off to build this business up and I'll be damned if I'm going to let some low-life crooks take it from us. I want what's mine and I'm offering you information that will serve you. It's a win/win, Mr. Malcolm, and I'm not going to waste my time by trying to prove *diddly squat* to you. You may claim no one's word is trustworthy, but I'm telling you that mine *is*. You either take me at my word or you tell me to walk out the door."

He stared at me expressionlessly for a long moment, and I worried I'd pushed him too far. I needed his help, but I also preferred to leave this place alive and in the same shape in which I'd arrived.

Skeeter turned his gaze to Bruce Wayne. "Where'd you find her?" He sounded amused. "She's something else."

Bruce Wayne swallowed and nodded his head, his face pale. "That she is."

"Fine," Skeeter said, leaning back in his chair again. "I like you, Rose Gardner, so I'm going to take you at your word and work with you." His face hardened. "But if I find out you double-crossed me, I'll hunt you down to the ends of the earth and make you wish you were dead. Understood?"

My breath stuck in my throat and I forced out a breathless, "Yes."

"Good." He grinned again. "Now that that's settled, let's get down to business. Tell me what you know."

"I know there's at least four of them." The interest in his eyes suddenly had me worried. What would Skeeter actually do to these guys if he found them? Why hadn't I thought about that part?

"Go on."

I was already rushing headlong into this madness, and it was too late to turn back now. "The guy with the SpongeBob mask at the bank was named Mick. I saw the face of the second guy with the Batman mask, but I don't know his name. I looked at a bunch of mug shots but never found him, so there's a good chance he doesn't have a record. Then there's two more. The third guy has a brown beard and bushy eyebrows. He smokes. And the last guy—I know he's one of four guys, but I'm not sure which. Or it could even be Samantha Jo Wheaton, but I doubt it."

Skeeter pursed his lips, looking impressed. "Anything else?"

"One of them drives a gold Charger that belonged to Mr. Sullivan, the bank's loan officer, and another had a black pickup with a long scratch down the side. I'm certain that Mr. Sullivan was part of all this, but he wanted out. Mick killed him because he was worried he was goin' to talk. On the afternoon of the robbery, the black truck turned down the road where Mr. Sullivan's body was later found. Mr. Sullivan hadn't shown up to work or called in sick that day. The robbers have been meeting at the abandoned fertilizer plant and they're pooling a bunch of money for something big on Friday. I'm guessing it's the auction."

"How do you know all of this?"

I folded my hands in my lap. "I just do."

"You just do." He shifted in his seat. "That's not good enough, Rose. I need to know where you got your information." He stood and walked around the end of the desk, sitting on the edge in front of me.

I worried I was gonna throw up on his jeans. "I saw the Charger out the bank window and then I saw it again on Sunday. It turned into the fertilizer plant. The truck was there too and I'd seen it turn down the farmhouse road."

He leaned closer until his face was in front of mine, his minty breath blowing in my face. "And the rest? I know for a fact that those guys wore masks the entire time they were in the bank. I have my sources. And how do you know they're pooling money or that they killed the loan officer to keep him from talking?"

"I found Mr. Sullivan's body."

"So you overheard these men discussing the matter when you saw them kill him?"

I took a deep breath. "No, I just found his body."

He spread his hands wide. "So you found him with a note of explanation pinned to his shirt?"

"No, of course not." I swallowed, my nerves a tangled mess. "I just know things."

I let out a shriek when he grabbed my throat and gave it a slight squeeze. "I already get that you know them. What I'm interested in is the *how* of it."

I tried not to panic when my vision started to fade, not because he was cutting off my oxygen supply, but because I was about to pass out from fright. I had nothing to tell him. Why had I presumed he'd just take the information without me being able to back it up?

"She has the sight," Bruce Wayne said. "She can see things."

I would have gasped if I wasn't in a choke-hold. How did Bruce Wayne know? I'd certainly never told him.

Skeeter dropped his hold, and turned his attention to Bruce Wayne as I sank in my chair. "You're shittin' me, right?"

"No. She can see things—the future, only she has no control over it. It just hits her and she blurts out what she saw. That's how she knows. I suspect she had a vision of the robbers while she was at the bank and another one at church yesterday. She was near a group of four guys and Samantha Jo when she had it and I don't think she knows which one it was."

My eyes widened in shock.

Bruce Wayne gave me his puppy-dog eyes. "I ain't stupid, Rose. I've known since we were working on the grounds of Reverend Jonah's church. I just didn't say anything because I know it embarrasses you. And I was at church yesterday. You just didn't see me."

"Well, well, well. This *is* interesting." Skeeter sat back on his desk, looking amused. "Who else knows about your *gift?*"

"You believe Bruce Wayne?" I asked.

He crossed his arms. "I'm reserving judgment, but I'm open to the possibility. My grandmother knew an oracle in Lafayette County and swore she was legit. I wouldn't have believed it, but a few of her predictions came true."

My heart raced and I struggled to catch my breath. This whole thing was spinning out of control. "She was my grandmother."

"You don't say." He grinned, but there was something sinister underneath the expression, like he was placating me. "Now tell me who else knows you have this ability."

"Just my sister and my boyfriend." I kept Neely Kate out of it. I couldn't put her in danger.

"Both of your boyfriends?"

Why did he want to know? "I only have one at a time, thank you very much. But yes. Both of them know."

"No one in town?"

"Why do you care?" I asked, my senses returning. "What does it matter to you?"

"I want to make sure you're not telling other people things they might want or need to know."

I snorted. "I hate having visions. And if I tell someone about something I've seen, you can bet I wish I hadn't."

He studied me with new appreciation. "That night you came to the pool hall this summer and told me I was gonna lose a lot of money? That was a vision, wasn't it?"

I nodded, still in shock that this man, of all people, now knew my secret.

He grinned and propped his arms behind him on the desk, bracing himself. "Tell me if I'm gonna win the auction."

"It doesn't work that way. It's like what Bruce Wayne said; I don't have control over what I see or when I see it."

He sat up, his eyes twinkling. "You said your boyfriend doesn't know you're here. How about I keep you here until you have one?"

Oh, crappy doodles. "Then you better order out for pizza. It might be a while."

"So you don't have any control at all?"

What should I tell him? If he kept me here, Neely Kate would tell Mason, then Skeeter would think I'd set him up. He already knew this much, so I figured I might as well tell him the rest. "Sometimes I can force one, but I never know what I'm gonna see. And just because I see something, doesn't mean it will definitely come true. Sometimes the future can be changed. This summer I saw myself dead several times and as you can see, *that* hasn't happened yet."

"Obviously what you have is a rare talent that many people would kill for," he said. I had a feeling that he wasn't speaking metaphorically. "I want to buy you."

"*Excuse me?*"

He waved his hand. "Your services. I want to buy them."

"They aren't for sale."

"Then the deal's off."

I stood, squeezing my hands into fists at my sides. "You can't do that. I gave you my information. You agreed."

"And I warned you that you couldn't trust me." He laughed. "Too bad you didn't have a vision of *that*."

I spun around and headed for the door.

"Don't leave, Rose," he called after me, sounding amused. "We're not done."

"I *am*. I have neither the time nor the patience to play your games, Skeeter Malcolm."

"Rose. Stop. I was joking."

I turned around, irritated as snot. "You don't seem like a joking kind of guy."

"I'm not. That's part of the reason I like you so much. You bring out the fun-lovin' side of me."

I rolled my eyes. "Enough of this fool nonsense, Skeeter Malcolm. Are you gonna help me or not?"

He laughed. "You know I've killed men for lesser offenses than the disrespectful way you're talking to me now."

"You won't kill me. I'm too valuable."

"No?" He grinned at Bruce Wayne. "But what's to stop me from killing him to make you do what I want? Or threatening your sister? And *you know* I'd gladly have your boyfriend out of my way. Heck, either of them. What's to stop me from threatening the people you care about to get you to do what I want?"

I moved toward him, my expression cold. "Because I took you for a smart man, Skeeter Malcolm. Fear works as a motivator, but not for long. Smart men know that there are more effective ways to get what they want."

His eyes narrowed. "And what do you propose that is?"

"Mutual need. I have something you need. You have something I need. We stick to our deal, Mr. Malcolm. You can threaten me and the people I care about all you'd like, but then I'll be lookin' for the first door out. Why would either of us want to bolt if we're scratchin' each other's backs? The longevity of your asset will be more certain if you don't resort to scare tactics." Who knew those business books I was reading would come to good use with a thug? But business was business, whether it was above board or below.

"Huh. You might have a point."

"I'll try to have a vision of you as a gesture of good faith." As soon as I uttered the words, I wished I could take them back. Jonah said Skeeter spent all his money on booze, women, and cars. What if I had a vision similar to the one I had with Samantha Jo? But I usually saw whatever I intended to see when I forced a vision. With Samantha Jo, I hadn't focused on anything, which had resulted in my unfortunate encounter with Moose in all his glory.

Nevertheless, it didn't matter whether I changed my mind or not. Judging by the gleam in Skeeter's eyes, it was too late to take it back now.

"I like it."

"Then you'll help me get my money back. And if I get any new information, I promise to share it with you."

"Deal."

"Which means nothing to you, but I can assure you that I'll never purposely give you useful information or have a vision for you in the future unless you follow through with your end of the deal."

A grin spread across his face. "You're quite the firecracker, aren't you? Okay. I agree." He laughed, shaking his head. "I said I liked you, and I meant it. Hell, I'd consider proposing marriage to you to have more control of your gift, but I'm not a one-woman man. I suspect you might cut off my junk if you caught me cheatin', so we'll stick to business for now."

If he weren't serious, I would have laughed.

"How do you do this?"

"Stay where you are on the desk. I'll hold your hand, and we'll see what happens. But it might take a bit. Even a minute or more, so don't be asking how much longer it's gonna be every ten seconds."

He held out his hand, smiling from ear to ear, and I wondered again at my folly. But it was too late to change anything now. Though I could sometimes see the future, I couldn't do a darn thing to change the past.

"When I have a vision, I see it from the perspective of the person who's nearest to me. So I'll be you in the vision. I'll blurt out something that I saw when I come to. It's usually the most important part, but there's always more, and I'll tell you that part too."

He waved his hand. "Fine. Sounds good. Let's get to it."

"One more thing. If I see something bad—like, suppose I see you dead—you can't take it out on me or anyone close to me."

"Got it. Don't shoot the messenger."

I heaved out a sigh. I had a feeling that I was gonna regret this. I only hoped I saw something he found useful or he might make me try it again. I grabbed his hand and closed my eyes.

"Are you—?"

"*Shh!*" I hushed.

He laughed, then settled down. My hand began to get clammy, but he held on tight. After thirty seconds or so, I felt a vision coming on.

I was in a hazy room that looked like a warehouse. The room smelled like smoke, sweat, and stale beer. A crowd of about fifty people filled the space, mostly men, but a few sluttily dressed women hung on them like accessories. The voices echoed in the space while men were lifting paddles and shouting numbers.

"Fifteen thousand."

"Fifteen–five!"

"Eighteen!"

I didn't lift the paddle in my hand or say anything until the bidding started to slow down.

"Do I hear twenty-six?" the auctioneer called out.

I lifted my paddle. "Twenty-six."

The other bidder was silent.

"Twenty-seven," a man called out. I turned my head to see it was a guy lowering his paddle. I knew who he was. The man who'd worn the Batman ski mask.

My fists tightened with rage. I was starting to lift my paddle when someone brushed past me. I felt a prick on my leg, and within seconds my thigh muscle was burning and my head was fuzzy.

"Do I hear twenty-eight?" The auctioneer looked at me.

I wanted to lift my paddle, but I was struggling to breathe.

"Twenty-seven going once…twice…"

The men next to me were staring me in shock. "Skeeter! Make the damn bid!"

But I dropped to my knees, my vision fading, my lungs refusing to inflate. Every muscle in my body had become useless.

Everything went to black as I heard the auctioneer yell, "Sold to number fourteen."

The vision faded and my eyes flew open. "Someone's gonna kill you at the auction."

Then my knees buckled and I started to drop.

Bruce Wayne reached over and helped me back into my chair.

Skeeter's face was beet-red. "What did you see? Who did it?"

I was struggling to catch my breath.

"Rose?" Bruce Wayne asked. "Are you okay?"

I nodded, trying to keep my fear under control. "I've never died in one before. Give me a minute."

Skeeter wasn't so patient. Bending down in front of me, he growled, "What did you see?"

"What happened to don't shoot the messenger? Give me a minute! I'm a little freaked out."

"*You're freaked out?*" he shouted. "I'm the one who's gonna die!"

"Stop," I said. "You're not gonna die."

He threw his hands into the air. "You just said I was."

"And I also told you we could prevent something from happening if we knew about it in advance." I told him what I had seen. When I was finished, he looked angrier than before I'd started. "You have guys watching out for you in a situation like that, right? Just make sure they're being extra careful. But the needle hit your leg while you were bidding, so I'd bet anything one of those other three guys in Batman's team did it." Then I smacked his arm. "You cheater!"

"What did I do?" he shouted, looking confused.

"Those guys had enough money to bid on Crocker's business, which means you didn't get my cash back. *You weren't even gonna try!*" I smacked him again. "Serves you right that they killed you."

Skeeter scowled.

I stood and picked up my purse, pulling out a piece of paper on which I'd already printed my cell phone number. I slammed it on his desk with a thud, then pointed my finger at him. "When you have some information for me, text me. But Mason sees my phone sometimes, so be discreet." The last thing I needed was for Mason to know I'd made a deal with the devil.

Then, as I stomped out of the office, Bruce Wayne trailing behind, Skeeter broke out into laughter.

"I'm gonna like working with you, Rose Gardner."

Too bad I couldn't say the same.

Chapter Twenty-One

I called Neely Kate on the way home to let her know that we were safe and sound. I hadn't planned on telling her everything, but I couldn't tell Mason and I had to talk to someone.

Since I'd originally planned on being home much earlier, I'd told Mason I would cook dinner. The pickings were slim at home, so I decided to stop at the Piggly Wiggly. I still needed to shop for Thanksgiving, but I only had time to grab some pork chops and potatoes, along with a few rolls from the bakery department.

I was trying to figure out which ones were freshest when I saw a man out of the corner of my eye who looked like the Batman robber from the bank. My head jerked up and I moved down the aisle, trying to get a better look at him, but no one was there.

I was officially losing my mind.

Mason's car was parked in front of the house along with his mother's. I burst through the front door, the shopping bags hanging from my arms.

They were both in the living room, and they got to their feet as soon as they saw me.

"I'm so sorry I'm late!"

Mason's mom moved toward me and pulled me into a hug, grocery bags and all. She was a startlingly beautiful woman in her early sixties, but her warm heart was what drew me to her.

"Rose! It's so good to see you again. Thank you so much for inviting me to stay with you for the holiday."

I gave her a warm smile. "You are always welcome here, Maeve." It felt strange calling her by her first name, but she'd insisted against Mrs. Deveraux and Miss Maeve was out of the question. "You have no idea how happy it makes me that you're here."

"Mason tells me I didn't need to come to Henryetta so early. He's going to stay with you here at the farm?"

I looked for any hint of disapproval in her expression, but found none. "Yes." I set the bags down on the coffee table and hugged Mason's arm. "I've grown very fond of your son. I suspect if he moved out, we'd just take turns staying at each other's place's anyway, so why not keep living together?"

She clasped her hands together. "Well, I'm thrilled. I was just telling Mason he couldn't find a sweeter girl."

I tilted my head to look into his face. "I think I'm the lucky one," I said.

Mason leaned down to give me a kiss. "Let me help you with dinner."

I stepped away from him and grabbed the bags. "Don't be silly. You talk with your momma."

"Rose, I don't feel right not helping," Mason's mother said.

"Don't you worry! I'll put you to work on Thanksgiving. But tonight you relax and let us take care of you."

I hurried into the kitchen to get started, but Mason rounded the corner and pulled me into a hug to give me a better kiss hello.

"I missed you at lunch today," he murmured.

"I missed you too."

"You look nice." I could hear the question in his voice. "I figured you must have come home since Muffy was here when I got back."

"We didn't have anything for dinner. So I came home and showered and put on nice clothes for your momma. I don't want her thinking I'm always grungy." I laughed even though I felt bad for fibbing. "She'll figure that out soon enough."

"You sure I can't help you with dinner?"

I stood on my tiptoes and gave him a long kiss. "Go talk to your mother, who you don't call often enough. She misses you. And then after we go to bed, I'll show you how much I missed you today."

He groaned. "That's hours from now."

"Get!" I gave him a tiny push.

He grinned and my heart flooded with love.

Mason and his mother ended up helping me in the kitchen anyway. We ate at the never-used dining room table and sat talking and eating long after we finished. Mason's mother was funny and sweet, and she regaled me with stories about Mason and his sister when they were kids.

I drank it in, so grateful I nearly burst. This was what I'd spent my whole life longing for—a loving family. Was that why I was so worried it was about to be snatched away from me?

We left the dishes in the sink and Mason stood on the front porch with me while we waited for Muffy to do her business. He kissed me in the moonlight…and in that moment, I was almost happy enough to take that stupid test I'd started to carry around in my purse. I just needed to get everything settled with my business first.

"Mason, I think I'm going to split my share of the business from Violet's. It's just not a good idea for us to work together anymore."

"Rose, it's your business. It may say 'Gardner Sisters' on the sign, but you're the complete financial backer. If you want her gone, you can get rid of her."

"That doesn't seem right. She may be acting like a total witch right now, but she loves what she does. And honestly, I wouldn't be doing what I love right now if she hadn't goaded me into it."

"So maybe you split it up and you take over full ownership of the landscaping portion and you're the silent partner in the greenhouse side."

"That might actually work. Only I won't be full owner of the landscaping side."

He leaned back and studied my face. "Why not?"

"I want to be co-owners with Bruce Wayne. He feels a sense of ownership already and the work makes him so happy. I realize he didn't put any money into it, but neither did Violet and she—"

He kissed me for several long seconds, then lifted his head and gave me a grin. "If you're worried about my reaction, you needn't be. For one thing, it's your business. You can go to work wearing clown suits without it being any business of mine. And if you're worried about whether I think it's a wise business move…well, Violet didn't put any money in and she's a great co-owner, your personal arguments aside. Bruce Wayne is loyal and hardworking; he'd be thrilled to have more of a stake in the business."

"Thanks."

"What are you and Violet doing about the missing money?"

Oh, crappy doodles. "We're working on it."

He took my chin between his finger and thumb and tilted my face up to his. "If I'm going to be living here, I need to start contributing to the expenses more than I currently am.

And if you need money to help with the nursery, I can cash in part of my 401K to help."

I gasped. "Mason! I can't let you do that!"

"You love it and it makes you happy. I would gladly do it. Just tell me how much you need and I'll have my financial planner put things in motion."

Putting my pride aside, surely taking Mason's money was better than getting in any deeper with Skeeter Malcolm. While Mason wasn't as freaked out over my amateur sleuthing as Joe had always been, he would never approve of me doing business with Skeeter. "If I accepted your help, how long would it take to get the money?"

"Well, it will slow things down with Thanksgiving coming up, but I suspect we could have it by the first week of December."

I rested my cheek against his chest so he wouldn't see my disappointment. "I love you, Mason. Thank you."

"How much do you need?"

I wasn't sure what to tell him, especially since it would be too late. "I'll figure it out and let you know."

"Okay. Come on. Let's go to bed."

The next morning, Mason and I both went to work late so we could have breakfast with his mother.

"I'm not sure what I'm going to do all day," she said, carrying breakfast dishes to the sink.

"I haven't talked to Violet for a few days, but she probably needs help getting ready for the open house on Friday. I suspect she'll put you to work, though."

"Oh, that's perfect. I'd love to help."

I gave her the directions to the shop, then texted Violet. I hadn't talked to her since Friday, so I was almost sorry I'd made the suggestion, but Violet had met Mason's mother when he was in the hospital. I knew the two of them got along well.

Mason's mother is in town and would like to help you get ready for the open house. PLEASE be nice to her.

She answered back a few minutes later.

I would never consider being anything but nice to her. That's just insulting. Tell her I look forward to seeing her.

Typical Violet.

Are you still planning on coming for Thanksgiving?

There was a ten-second lapse before she answered.

Are we still welcome?

Despite everything, we're still sisters, Vi. Of course you're welcome.

There was a pause again, then: *I'll let you know.*

Bruce Wayne and I met at our new jobsite. It was a small job and would only take a few days. "We need to scrounge up some follow-up work," I said as we used a garden hose to figure out the curve of the short landscaping wall we planned to build. "The trouble is that most people think we can't work in the winter. We need to make them realize that as long as the ground's not frozen, the cooler months are the best time to plant."

"Have you got any ideas?"

I sighed. "Not a one. I guess we should worry about surviving first." I told him about Mason's offer of financial assistance. "But it's a few days late and probably several thousand dollars short. Not that I told him how much we needed."

"I suspect it's too late to get out of our deal with Skeeter anyhow. Now that he knows about your gift, he's not gonna let it go."

"Great." I sighed again.

"I'm sorry," he said. "I shouldn't have told him, but I was scared."

"No, you did the right thing. I just hope to hear something from him soon."

After we wrapped things up for the day, I stopped at the Piggly Wiggly to do my Thanksgiving shopping. The turkeys were picked over, but I found a twenty-pounder and filled the cart until it was overflowing since I was out of just about everything I would need. Just my luck, I'd gotten a cart with a sticky wheel, and the more I piled in, the harder it was to push. Realizing I couldn't fit any more groceries onto my heaping pile, I leaned over and gave the cart a good shove toward the checkout lane when a man by the bakery section caught my eye. I wouldn't have thought anything about it, except I thought I'd seen the bank robber in the same location the previous day. Stopping in the middle of the main aisle, I turned around and gasped in shock.

The Batman bank robber was standing there in the Piggly Wiggly's bakery aisle, squeezing the day-old bread.

It took me a full two seconds to overcome my shock. But by the time I'd come to my senses, he was already moving toward the back of the store.

"Excuse me," a grumpy woman snarled.

My cart was currently angled diagonally across the main aisle, blocking customers coming from both directions.

"I'm sorry," I muttered, leaning into the cart and putting all my weight into it to change directions.

I finally got the buggy turned around and headed down the cereal aisle toward the possible robber, hoping to intercept him. But as I reached the end of the aisle, a cart came barreling out of nowhere and slammed into mine, sending it toppling onto its side with a loud bang. The contents of my cart spilled out, the turkey sliding across the floor and slamming into a stack of canned sweet potatoes, which toppled over like pins in a bowling alley.

Several customers screamed and jumped out of the way of rolling cans.

"You tried to kill me!" A man's irate voice filled my now-aching head.

I glanced up to see Officer Ernie with his half-empty cart. He was dressed in skin-tight acid-washed jeans, a Def Leppard T-shirt, and a puffy, sleeveless powder-blue ski vest.

I put my hands on my hips. "You're the one who slammed into me!"

"I shoulda known." The police officer shook his head with a disgusted look. "If there's trouble, I can bet you're a part of it."

"I need to—"

"You need to clean up this mess."

"But I think I saw one of the bank robbers!" Oh, Lordy. Why did I tell him that?

He snorted. "And I saw the Easter Bunny on aisle four. Start cleanin'. Now."

The Henryetta police would never listen to me and I needed to track down that bank robber since that liar Skeeter Malcolm wasn't going to come through on our agreement. I jumped to my feet and took off running toward the back corner of the store, but Officer Ernie caught up with me and grabbed my arm. I shook him loose, but he tumbled sideways into a giant cereal box display arranged into the shape of a giant turkey.

The tower of boxes fell, a few of them bursting open to send tiny cereal letters flying everywhere. I gaped at the angry police officer climbing to his feet in front of me.

He grabbed my arm before I had the sense to take off running. "Rose Gardner! You're under arrest."

As he handcuffed me, pushing me out the front doors, I wondered what else could possibly go wrong.

I should have learned long ago to never ask that question.

Chapter Twenty-Two

I stared at the holding cell walls, not surprised by how familiar they looked. I'd been in this same jail cell several months before for contempt of court.

I flopped down on the small cot, which wasn't any more comfortable than it had been last time. "I wonder if they'll give me a bologna sandwich this time too," I muttered to myself.

Mason's voice drifted down the hall. "Only if I leave you in here for long enough to find out." He stopped at the front of my cell, hanging onto one of the bars. "I'm feeling a bit of déjà vu."

I gave him a regretful smile. "Hey."

"Hey yourself. I hear you had an eventful afternoon."

"You could say that."

A slow grin spread across his face. "For this to truly be déjà vu, you'd need to come over here and talk to me through the bars."

I shook my head, smiling. "And I was hoping you were here to spring me loose."

"Come on over here and work out your plea bargain."

I got to my feet and walked over to the bars. "What are the charges, Mr. Deveraux?"

"Destruction of property, willful vandalism. Evading a police officer." He tried to look serious, but a smile tugged at his lips. "You've been a very bad girl, Ms. Gardner. How do you plead?"

"Not guilty." I turned serious. "Mason, I saw the bank robber from my visions. He was at the Piggly Wiggly. I saw him yesterday too, but only from the corner of my eye. But this time I got a good look at him and I'm positive it was him. I started to run after him, but Officer Ernie slammed his cart into mine, spilling my food everywhere. And when I ran after the robber, Ernie hunted me down. He fell into a cereal display and the bank robber got away."

"So I heard, but with a slightly different spin."

"Are you mad?"

"Why would I be mad? Every assistant DA loves to hear that his girlfriend has been arrested."

I cringed. "I'm sorry."

His hand covered mine over the bars. "Don't be. This town needs shaking up. Kind of like my life before you barged into it on that fateful day in July. I knew immediately that you were a whirlwind of trouble. It's one of the many reasons I love you."

I rested my forehead on the bars. "Thank you…I think."

"Let me go finish up some paperwork to get you out of here."

"I still don't have a turkey, Mason. It slid across the floor of the Piggly Wiggly and knocked over a tower of canned sweet potatoes."

He grinned. "I'm really wishing I was there to see this display of destruction and vandalism."

"It's not funny. What are we gonna do about Thanksgiving dinner?"

"There's still time to get a turkey, although you've been indefinitely banned from the Piggly Wiggly. I guess that means I'll be doing all the shopping. Which also means we're gonna starve unless we drive over to the Brookshires's in Columbia County."

"Mason."

"Sweetheart, we'll get it sorted out so you can go back to the grocery store. In the meantime, revel in the fact I have to do the shopping. Most women would love for their boyfriends to do the grocery shopping for them."

"You obviously don't know most women."

He laughed. "Sit tight and I'll have you out in a bit."

"I've heard that before."

He started down the hallway and looked over his shoulder. "So you know I'll get you out."

True to his word, I was out in less than thirty minutes, but by then it was close to five o'clock. When Mason realized the time he released a groan, then said, "It's too late to go back to work, so why don't we just head on home?"

"What are we gonna tell your mother?"

"The truth. Trust me. She'll love it."

"What about my truck? It's still in the Piggly Wiggly parking lot."

"We'll leave it and just ride into town together in the morning."

"Okay. But what are we gonna do for dinner? All my food's lying on the grocery store floor."

"Stop worrying. We'll pick up Chinese take-out."

He called in the order and we picked it up on our way home.

Mason was right about his mother. I told them the sordid details of my encounter with Officer Ernie as we ate at the kitchen table, both of them bursting out into laughter. Maeve said she found my predicament amusing and she promised to shop for our Thanksgiving dinner.

"Oh, by the way, Rose," she said, as she broke her fortune cookie in half. "When I was at the shop this afternoon, Violet said she's planning on bringing her chestnut stuffing."

I shot a glance at Mason. "So she *is* still coming. She told me she was gonna think about it."

Maeve read her fortune. "It says 'Great things are in your future.'" She glanced up and smiled at me. "I'd have to agree with that. What's yours say, Rose?"

I grabbed one of the two leftover cookies and broke it in half, almost afraid. "An unexpected amount of cash will appear soon," I read out loud. Mercy, I hoped that was true, but so far Skeeter wasn't telling me a blessed thing.

"Rose," Maeve said. "It might make it easier for me to get all the supplies for Thanksgiving if you make me a shopping list. And I forgot to mention that Violet said she's going to bringing a marshmallow salad and a pecan pie."

I made a mental tally of who was attending, and something else occurred to me. "I can only imagine what Violet's gonna say when she discovers I've invited Bruce Wayne, David and David's girlfriend." I had forgotten to tell her.

Mason drew in a breath and shot me an ornery grin. "It's going to be a Thanksgiving to remember."

That was an understatement.

Maeve and I came up with a menu and a shopping list before I went to bed, the excitement of the afternoon having exhausted me. I watched from the bed as Mason emerged from the bathroom in his pajamas and headed for the bedroom door. He'd slept in a spare bedroom the night before, though he'd hid it from his mother.

"Mason, please don't sleep in the other room. I miss you."

He stopped with his hand on the doorknob. "We've already discussed this, Rose."

"No, Mason. *You've* discussed it. Did you talk to Jonah this afternoon?"

He kept his back to me. "Yes."

"Don't you think sleeping in the other room is running away from your problems?"

He sighed. "You know it's not that."

"Then come back to bed, Mason. If you have a nightmare, I won't wake you up."

He moved away from the door and sat on the edge of the bed. "I can't promise I won't hurt you."

I grabbed his hand. "I'd rather take my chances than sleep without you." I reached behind his head and pulled his mouth to mine, convincing him that staying in bed with me was the best idea since the invention of the wheel.

I was in a deep sleep, my back pressed against Mason's front, when I heard a phone ringing. Mason reached over and grabbed my cell off my nightstand while I struggled to wake up.

"This is Mason Deveraux." He sounded so serious and professional that my grogginess cleared and I lifted my head.

"Yes," he said. "We'll be right there." He held onto my phone after hanging up.

"What happened?" I asked, looking up at him.

"That was Officer Sprout. Your nursery was broken into."

"What?" I bolted upright.

"The alarm was going off, so he went by to see if it was a false alarm. It wasn't." He started to get out of bed. "I'm going down there to check it out. You stay here and get some rest."

I got out of bed on the other side. "I'm going too."

"There's no reason for you to go, Rose. I can take care of it."

"It's *my business*, Mason."

"I know. My offer wasn't meant as an insult."

"I know, but I'll never be able to sleep." I opened my dresser drawer to pull out a pair of sweatpants. "I'm going."

He relented, and I called Violet on the way into town.

"Vi, did the police call you?"

"Yeah." Her voice was shaky. "Mike's on his way over to watch the kids and Joe's going to bring me."

"Do you seriously think Joe bringing you is a good idea, Violet?" My voice was cold.

"I'm sure you'll have Mason there for you to look after your best interests. And I'll have Joe looking out for mine. If your boyfriend has a problem with it, tough."

"Joe's coming?" Mason asked after I hung up.

"I'm sorry."

"It's fine. The two of us are going to have to see each other sooner rather than later. I only wish you weren't part of it."

I couldn't say I didn't feel the same way.

Two police cars were parked in the nursery parking lot, and Detective Taylor met us at the front door. "I need to warn you. It's quite a mess."

My stomach in knots, I started through the front door, sucking in my breath when I saw the destruction. The entire place had been vandalized. The display shelves were empty and tipped over and everything that had been on them was smashed. All the artificial Christmas trees that Violet had spent so much time decorating were strewn in pieces around the store. Broken ornaments crunched beneath our feet as we walked. All the wreaths and decorations on the walls had been pulled down and tossed in a pile. The room was cluttered with so much crap I could hardly make my way though. A giant *Stay Away From* was painted in red across the wall behind the cash register, the warning clearly unfinished. We had started to pick our way through the mess to the back room when Violet and Joe showed up.

I slipped my hand into Mason's to reassure both of us.

"Damn," Joe muttered as he crossed the threshold. "This isn't a robbery. This is a personal vendetta." He glared toward me. "Who have you pissed off now?"

"Excuse me?" I shouted.

Mason's hand tightened around mine. "Chief Deputy Simmons, I'll ask you to speak to Rose respectfully or not at all."

Violet started crying. "I've spent weeks on this. Weeks. And now it's completely ruined." She turned to face me. "This is all your fault, Rose!"

"*My fault?*"

"You're trying to find out who robbed that bank." Her eyes narrowed. "Yeah, I know. Joe's told me *all* about it."

"This has nothing to do with me."

"The giant graffiti on the wall says otherwise," Joe bit out.

Mason wrapped an arm around my shoulders and tugged me against him. "Before we start making accusations, perhaps you should conduct an actual investigation, *Simmons*."

"This falls under the jurisdiction of the Henryetta police."

Mason released a sound that started as a rumble, then grew into a roar. "For the love of all that is holy, Joe. If you care *anything* about either one of these two women, will you *please* conduct an investigation? Their business has just been destroyed."

I closed my eyes and sank against him, his words sinking in.

There was nothing left to save.

"I want to go home, Mason."

He lowered his mouth to my ear. "You don't want to look around more?"

"There's nothing left to look at."

"Oh, God," Violet said, hurrying across the room, picking her way through the debris. She rounded the corner and searched the shelves and the floor.

"Violet." Joe made his way over to her. "What are you looking for?"

"The deposit bag. I had to pick up the kids and I didn't have time to get to the bank, so I put it under the counter to keep it safe." She started to cry.

I was grateful I hadn't given her the check I'd been paid the previous day for the Timberland job. I brushed back my hair. "Most of our sales are usually by credit or debit card, right? We'll be fine."

"That's just it. I haven't gone to the bank for several days. We had several thousand in cash."

I started to laugh and all three of them looked at me like I was a two-headed cow. "That's how this all started—because Violet didn't go to the bank and we lost thousands of dollars. It seems fitting for it to end this way too."

"With all due respect, Rose," Violet said in tightly controlled voice. "Losing cash is one thing, but we've just lost almost everything in the store. All the preparations for the Christmas Open House have been ruined. So not only do we not have the money to pay off our debt, we have no income to keep us going. All thanks to you."

"Violet." Mason's voice was harsh. "Your insurance will cover this loss."

"But not in time. We're sunk."

Mason groaned and looked up at the ceiling. "It's three o'clock in the morning and we're all tired and upset. Let's not start making accusations that we'll regret in the light of day. We'll let the police and sheriff conduct their investigation and go from there."

We left soon after, while Joe and Violet stayed. Despite our animosity, I grieved for my sister. My money may have been tied to the store, but my heart wasn't. My heart belonged to the dirt and the plants of the outdoor jobs I'd been handling with Bruce Wayne.

"I know it looks bad, Rose, but insurance will cover this."

"It won't be the same, but it's all just stuff. Violet and I, though… Well, this will only make things worse. I'm not sure we can fix them."

"I know Violet's done some incredibly hurtful things to you, but don't give up on her. I suspect you're right in thinking you'd be better off splitting up your business, but… Well, I'd give anything to have Savannah back, imperfections and all. Violet is your family. That means something."

He squeezed my hand, and I found myself wishing someone would give the same speech to Violet because it sure felt like she'd given up on me months ago.

Chapter Twenty-Three

I couldn't go back to sleep after we got home. Every time I closed my eyes, I saw the destruction of everything Violet and I had put so much work into, destroyed. Even if Skeeter got our money back at this point, it wouldn't be enough.

Instead, I went to the kitchen and tried to scrounge up enough ingredients to make a pumpkin pie. After I made enough dough for four pies, I sat at the kitchen table and nursed a cup of coffee, trying to figure out how to pick up the pieces of the Gardner Sisters Nursery and move on.

"Good morning," Maeve said, standing in the kitchen doorway in her bathrobe and slippers. "You're up early."

I offered her a weak smile. "We had an eventful night."

"You seem to have a lot of those, I hear," she said as she poured herself a cup of coffee. My back bristled, but I couldn't hear any hint of accusation in her words. She padded to the table and sat in the chair across from me. "Mason needs a bit of shaking up. You've brought some much-needed excitement into his life."

My mouth parted in surprise.

"Didn't expect that, did you?"

I released a nervous laugh. "No."

"He hasn't always been this serious. He's got a heart of gold, and before his father died he used to be so light-hearted." She took a sip of her coffee and cradled the cup in front of her.

"Van's death was hard on all of us. Everyone loved Van, and Mason was just like him. But for all of Van's great character traits, it turned out that he was exceptionally bad at financial planning. We struggled after his death."

"I'm sorry," I murmured.

A soft smile lit up her face and she patted my hand. "That was a decade ago. We struggled through it, but Mason changed. He thought he had to step up and be the man of the family, and he took that role seriously. So when Savannah began to act out, Mason took it hard. He tried to help her—we both did—but you can only help someone who wants to be helped, and no matter how much we loved Savannah, she didn't want to change."

I turned my hand over and covered her fingers with mine. "I can only imagine how difficult it was for you both."

She pressed her lips together. "Mason felt like he failed her and he didn't handle it well. He'd succeeded at everything in his life, yet he felt like he'd failed at the one thing that mattered. He smiled even less after that."

"You're right. He *does* have a big heart. He's so accepting of all of my friends when other people in my life have been judgmental of them. So I can only imagine how hard it was for him when Savannah refused to get help."

"Then you can guess at the rage and the sorrow he experienced after her death. He felt like he'd failed her all over again. And when he hurt that man and lost his job…" She took a deep breath and her voice broke when she spoke again. "I thought I'd lost him too."

I squeezed her hand, not knowing what else to do. Words seemed so inadequate.

"Then he moved here and he hated this place. He could have found another job—a better one—someplace else. But I think he considered working here as his penance." She paused and smiled. "Until he met you. He told me about your first meeting soon after it happened. Did he mention that to you?"

"He told me a couple of months later."

"Every time he talked about you, something in his voice changed. He changed. The hardness started slipping away."

"He just needed a friend."

"You underestimate your influence, dear. He needed *you.*"

I blushed.

"So don't apologize for the excitement that seems to follow you around like the Pied Piper. He loves it and he loves you. I'm very happy for you both."

Mason appeared in the doorway while his mother and I were smiling at each other like a couple of fools. He froze in his tracks. "Why do I get the impression I should run for safety?"

I turned and gave him a wicked grin. "Shouldn't a man appreciate the fact that his girlfriend loves his mother?"

He grinned as he headed for the coffee maker. "While I *do* appreciate that more than you can possibly know—" he poured coffee into his cup "—I also know that the two of you will be an unstoppable force of nature if you team up together."

"Get used to it, Mason," she said. "In fact, I'd like to talk to you about something important if you have a moment. I would have mentioned it last night, but we got distracted."

Worry flickered in his eyes as he sat in the chair at the head of the table. "Of course, Mom."

I started to get up. "I'll leave you two to talk."

Mason's mother grabbed my hand. "No, I'd like you to stay, Rose. This involves you too."

"Okay." I sat down, my stomach a bundle of nerves.

"You both know that I came down here with the purpose of finding a new home for Mason. I had already set up the appointments, so you can imagine my surprise when I found out about the change in plans."

Mason cringed. "It wasn't like we purposely didn't tell you, Mom. We just decided—"

"Mason," she laughed. "I'm not angry. But I'd already made the appointments, so I kept them."

We both watched her as understanding began to dawn on me.

"One of the houses was darling. And you know that I've been thinking about selling my house in Little Rock, so…" She looked sheepish. "I'm considering moving here to Henryetta. Now, you two don't have to say anything, but think about it—"

"Mom, I would love that," Mason interrupted.

I swallowed the lump in my throat. "I'd be so happy. Honestly. This is perfect."

She beamed. "Well, okay. I'll put in an offer."

"This calls for a celebration dinner tonight," Mason said, standing. "We'll go out to dinner at the Little Italy restaurant."

I went upstairs to get ready for the day, wondering if it was time to take the pregnancy test. Mason and I had smoothed out. His mother was moving closer to us. But my business was even more of a mess than it had been yesterday. Maybe it would always be a mess. Maybe there was no perfect time.

Bruce Wayne met me at the store and we walked through the wreckage. His gaze shifted to the wall. "I'm gonna call Skeeter. If you're gonna be helping him, he needs to be helping you."

Just what I needed—protection for my business from Henryetta's probably soon-to-be top-ranking criminal.

"Have you heard anything from him?"

"No," I scowled.

"What do you want to do about this mess? Start cleaning?"

"I don't know," I said, completely overwhelmed. "I suppose the insurance adjustor needs to come see it first. Violet's in charge of that stuff." The Christmas trees were supposed to be delivered today but we didn't have the money to pay for them. Violet had placed the order and was supposed to meet with the delivery guy. I decided to let her deal with telling him to take his shipment back. "The fact is we lost more money last night. Money we couldn't afford to lose. We're up crap creek without a paddle."

A grin tugged at his mouth. "Then we better get some nose plugs."

That was one of the many reasons I liked working with Bruce Wayne. I bumped my arm into his and grinned up at him. "Let's go finish our landscaping job. It may very well be our last."

He sobered. "Then let's make it a good one."

We'd just gotten to the job site when I got a text from an unknown number. After I read it, I knew it had to be from Skeeter.

I heard about your bad luck. I've declared you as my own and plan to make it right.

"What does that mean?" I asked Bruce Wayne after I read him the text, afraid to hear his answer.

"It means that Skeeter is making it known that you fall under his protection and anyone who messes with you will meet his wrath."

"Oh, crap."

He sucked in a deep breath. "It could be a good thing." Only he didn't sound so sure.

"What's the flip side to that, Bruce Wayne?"

"Everyone and their brother is gonna be curious as to why he's got an interest in you. Skeeter rarely claims things, so they'll be even more curious. Especially when they add in the fact that you're with the assistant DA."

"What can I do?" I asked, panicked. "What if this hurts Mason somehow?"

Bruce Wayne put his hand on my arm. "Deep breath, Rose. It's not gonna get back to him. Maybe Jonah will hear about it, but not Mason."

"How did I fall into this hole?"

"I dug it for you. I'm sorry."

"No." I waved my hand. "What's done is done. We can't go changing it now."

We worked in silence for several minutes and I could tell Bruce Wayne was beating himself up over Skeeter. I needed to get his mind off it.

"Can you believe Violet's still planning on coming to Thanksgiving dinner tomorrow?" But then again, maybe she'd changed her mind after our middle-of-the-night argument.

"That should be interesting."

A new thought struck me. "You're still coming, right? I know you hate conflict and you might be worried we'll argue."

"I'm still comin'. I wouldn't miss it. Do I need to bring something?"

"Nope. Just yourself."

We had things wrapped up by three and I hurried home, feeling a rush of gratitude that Mason's mom had offered to do the shopping. When I got home, I found her in the kitchen, with the turkey in the sink.

"Nothing like giving a turkey a pre-Thanksgiving bath," she said when I walked in.

"I'm sorry. I should have bought it last week, but with the bank robbery and everything else…"

"Not to worry. We'll just force him to warm up. Did you have a good day?"

"As good as can be expected when you're staring into the face of your business's demise."

Her eyes widened. "What?"

I waved my hand. I was sick of worrying about it. "Just me being dramatic about the break-in at the shop. What I want to know is how your day went. Did you sign the paperwork on the house?"

"I did, and I get possession on the fifteenth. Things are working out perfectly."

And that's exactly when nausea started to churn in my stomach. Nothing in my life stayed perfect.

Chapter Twenty-Three

I woke up on Thanksgiving morning feeling more thankful than ever. I had a house I loved, a loyal dog—except when she was kissing up to Joe, of course—and a loving man whose mother was a wonderful asset to our lives. I had so much to be thankful for I decided to ignore my troubles and revel in the positives.

Mason was still dozing and I snuggled against him, almost wishing we could stay in bed half the day. My phone dinged with a text message and I leaned over to grab it, figuring it was Violet telling me that she wasn't coming after all. I wasn't expecting the message on the screen.

It's all going down today. Your presence is required. Time TBD

They had moved the auction. Why? And I'd never agreed to go in the first place. What was I going to do? But even as I asked myself the question, I knew I had to go. The real question was what would I tell Mason?

He rolled over and pulled me against his chest. "Who was that?"

"It doesn't matter." I set the phone down on my nightstand. "I can think of a much better use of my time."

His lips found mine and his hand skimmed along my neck before he lifted his head. "Rose, your heart is racing at a million miles per minute."

"It doesn't take much for you to get me worked up."

His eyes pierced mine. "Are you sure that's it?"

"What else could it be?" Then I thoroughly distracted him, so that he never thought to ask me again.

After we got up and got ready for the day, I texted Neely Kate.

I have to go into town later, but I can't tell M why. Will you cover for me?

She answered within seconds.

What are you up to?

I took a deep breath, trying to figure out what to tell her. But before I could answer she sent:

It's about Skeeter, isn't it?

Yes

She didn't answer me for ten minutes and I worried that I'd pushed her too far.

Promise me you'll be careful

Pinky promise

When?

I'll text you when I know. I'll tell M I'm helping you make pies.

But I'm not making pies.

Even better

I was a nervous wreck for the rest of the morning, and I did a really bad job of hiding it. Mason's mother and I were in the kitchen making multiple dishes for the dinner later that afternoon and I kept dropping things.

"Are you okay, Rose?" she asked after I dropped a bag of potatoes that spilled all over the floor.

"Yeah, fine," I murmured. It was past eleven and I still hadn't heard anything more from Skeeter.

"It's normal to be nervous while hosting your first Thanksgiving," she said, squatting next to me and helping me pick them up. "It's going to be lovely. Don't worry. It's the company that matters. The food comes second."

I leaned over and gave her an awkward hug. "Thank you." This woman was as kind and understanding as I'd always wished my own mother would be.

My cell phone buzzed with a text in my sweater pocket. I finished scooping up the vegetables and set them on the counter. "I need to go to the restroom. I'll be right back."

Mason's mother put her hand on mine. "Deep breath. Everything's going to be just fine."

Too bad she didn't have the sight.

Running into the powder room, I fought a fresh wave of nausea. I dug the phone out of my pocket with shaky fingers, both relieved and strangely disappointed to see it was from Bruce Wayne…until I read the message.

Skeeter wants us to meet him at the pool hall at 12:15

I wasn't sure I could do this. I wasn't sure I *should* do this.

It was time to pull out my excuse.

When I found Mason, he was in his office talking on the phone. He gave me a sheepish grin and held up a finger. "Thanks, I'll see you in a bit," he said before hanging up.

"You're going somewhere?"

"Only for a little while. We have a strong lead on your store's break-in."

"You do?" I asked in surprise. If they arrested the robbers, I might be able to cancel my meeting with Skeeter. "What is it?"

"I can't give you too many specifics since it's an ongoing investigation, but all evidence is pointing to Brody MacIntosh's wife."

"*What?*" I felt vindicated—after all, Joe and Violet had blamed *me* for the destruction of the store—but this also meant

I was nowhere close to getting out of my date with a hardened criminal.

"Looks like she figured out that Brody and Violet were sneaking around again, meeting at a motel outside of town."

I sank into the doorjamb. *Oh, Violet*. What had she done?

"Joe is going to tell Violet the news. They seem to have gotten closer. It will probably be easier for her to hear from him than from Detective Taylor. Taylor agreed to make the arrangements at my suggestion."

I nodded, feeling numb. "Good idea."

"You okay?"

I took a deep breath and forced a smile. "I will be. I'm just sad for Violet." I paused. "What would drive her to this? This isn't the behavior of the sister I know."

"People change, Rose. And not always for the better."

Or sometimes they didn't change at all.

I took several steps into the room, my eyes landing on the papers on the desk.

Mason lifted his hands in defense. "I know I promised not to work today, but I figured you and Mom were busy in the kitchen, and that if I knocked out some work now, I'd free up time for this weekend."

"It's a great plan."

"I need to run into the office, though. I might be gone for a bit."

"Oh." I hoped they weren't planning to arrest Brody's wife on Thanksgiving Day. Although rumor had it she liked to shop, so arresting her on Black Friday might even be worse. She may have destroyed our business, but part of me understood why. Her husband had cheated on her, and his status as mayor made that transgression all the more embarrassing. But I decided to take Mason's errand as a blessing in disguise. It would make it easier for me to slip away.

He stood and moved toward me. "I hope you're not too disappointed in me."

"Mason, it's fine. Do what you need to do and we'll plan something fun with your mom for Saturday. Maybe we can drive down to Shreveport and do some early Christmas shopping."

A smile lit up his eyes. "That sounds perfect. It's a date."

I pulled him into a hug. "When this is all done, let's try to have more of those."

"When what's all done?"

Oh, crap. "You know. The bank robbery nonsense and the mess with the nursery."

He gave me a kiss, amusement written across his face. "Is there ever a dull moment with you, Rose Gardner?"

"I used to be dull as dirt. Now…"

He kissed me again. "Sweetheart, I wouldn't want you any other way. So put away whatever thought's putting that worry on your face. I'll run into town and hopefully this won't take too long."

"You take as long as you need." It meant I didn't have to come up with an excuse he might not believe.

He left soon after and I gave his mother my excuse about Neely Kate needing my help.

"Go help your friend, Rose. We've got everything covered here."

She was so nice that I felt bad about deceiving her. But no matter how nice she was, I couldn't very well tell her I was going into Henryetta so I could attend an underground auction.

I ran upstairs to change, unsure what the appropriate attire would be for such an event. I decided on jeans with my leather boots, a cream-colored turtleneck sweater, and my brown leather jacket.

I had almost made it into town when a sheriff's car headed in the opposite direction turned on its lights and did a U-turn on the highway, pulling up behind me. Groaning, I steered my car over to the shoulder and stopped, the sheriff's car stopping too. I hadn't been speeding, so I had no idea why I was being pulled over. Or at least I didn't until I saw who was sidling up to my car.

Joe.

I rolled down my window, my irritation growing. He was gonna make me late for my meeting with Skeeter.

"What do you want, Joe?" I asked as he reached my door.

He was wearing his sheriff's uniform. The sun made his copper highlights stand out more than usual and damned if he didn't look good. He had to have every single girl in the county after him. Why was he wasting his time on me?

Joe ignored my question. "License and registration."

My mouth dropped. "You've got to be kidding me."

"License and registration." His voice was firmer this time.

Shaking my head, I reached for my purse on the passenger seat and plopped it on the console.

"Where are you headed?" he asked.

"Neely Kate's, not that it's any of your business," I grumbled as I opened my purse, digging around for my wallet. Something tumbled out of my bag, but I kept right on searching. "We're makin' pies," I added to bolster my alibi.

"You need to be careful today. The roads are—" His words cut off abruptly.

Gasping, I realized what fell out of my purse and looked down at the pregnancy test in my lap for confirmation. I hastily picked up the box and stuffed it back in my purse, but it was too late. Joe had already seen it.

"What was that?" he asked gruffly.

I looked up at him, feeling faint. "Joe…"

"Was that a pregnancy test?"

I opened the truck door, expecting him to protest. Instead, he took a step back as I got out.

"Was that a pregnancy test?" he repeated.

I nodded, tears burning my eyes.

He looked like he was going to be sick, but then a wave of hope washed over his face. "Is it *mine?*" His voice broke.

I took a step toward him as a car passed us on the highway, swerving into the other lane to avoid hitting us on the shoulder. "Joe." I was breaking his heart all over again and it was killing me.

"Is it *his?*" His words sounded strangled.

I closed the distance between us so that we stood between my truck and his car. "I don't even know if I *am* pregnant. That's why I have the tests."

"But it's his?"

I swallowed. "Yes."

He ran a hand through his hair and spun away from me. "Oh, God."

I watched him, unsure of what to say. I wanted to apologize, but I hadn't done anything that necessitated an apology. Still, it ripped my heart out to see him in so much pain.

He turned around to face me, close to breaking down. "I wanted to be the one to have babies with you." He took a deep breath and blew it out. "When I was in Little Rock, missing you, sometimes I'd imagine what it would be like when we were finally together all the time. You and me married with kids of our own. It was what got me through the loneliness of being without you." His face twisted in agony. "Especially the last two months." He choked on a sob, then swallowed. "We're not going to get back together, are we?"

I knew I had to tell him no, but I couldn't make myself say it.

"So I've really lost you."

"I'm sorry," I said, fighting my tears.

He turned his back on me and walked to his car.

"Joe."

But he ignored me as he opened his car door and started to climb inside. Before he shut it behind him, he stopped and turned back to face me. "I still love you, Rose. I'll always love you. If you change your mind or you and him don't work out, I still want you." He took another breath. "And if you *are* having his baby, I want you to know I'd love it as my own if you decided to take me back. I swear."

"I know," I forced out past the lump in my throat. I had no doubt that he would, if for no other reason than because the baby would be mine.

He ducked inside his cruiser and pulled back onto the highway, heading into town.

I got back into my car and held the steering wheel for nearly a minute, taking deep breaths before I was ready to start driving. I was about to face Skeeter Malcolm. I couldn't afford to be distracted by Joe.

I drove through town, passing the nursery to remind myself why I was going through this. What I saw made me slow down and pull my truck into the parking lot.

The grass beside the building was covered in evergreen trees.

How in the world had Violet paid for them? It was just one more distraction I had to set aside so I could concentrate on what needed to be done.

I reached the pool hall at twelve-ten, my stomach a mess and my nerves even worse. Especially after my encounter with Joe. Maybe Skeeter didn't want me to attend the auction. Maybe he just wanted me to have another vision of him to see if his fate had changed.

And monkeys were gonna start flying out of my butt.

Bruce Wayne was waiting for me when I pulled into the parking lot. I studied him as he walked over to me. Something about him seemed different, though I couldn't put my finger on it. After a moment the reason for the change struck me—he was more confident. His shoulders were less hunched, his head was held a little higher. When I met Bruce Wayne in the Fenton County Courthouse months ago, he had been a man who was afraid of life and everything in it. Now he seemed like a man who had something to live for.

"We can figure out a way to get you out of this," he said.

"I've been trying to come up with one for days without any luck. I think it's better to just get it over with. Besides, you're not doing this without me. Not even if Skeeter allowed it."

"This won't be the end of it, Rose. You have to know that goin' into this."

I stared at the front door. He was right, only I wasn't sure what to do about it. "Let's do it. Then we can go eat some turkey."

He nodded, a grim look on his face. Walking side by side, we entered the dimly lit hall and headed back to the office. I knocked on the door and Skeeter called out, "It's open."

He was at his desk, and the two men who'd been playing pool the last time we were here were sitting on the sofa against the wall.

"Rose. Bruce Wayne." He lifted his glass, which contained an amber liquid. "Welcome to the party."

The scene was set up to intimidate and the way Bruce Wayne's footsteps faltered slightly told me it had worked with him. But I was done with the theatrics.

"I never agreed to go to this thing, Skeeter. I'm supposed to be cooking Thanksgiving dinner."

"I need you, Rose. We still haven't found the men who robbed the bank."

"And our agreement was that you'd get my money back for me. So far you haven't come through."

"I can get you the money." He shook his head. "That's nothing. But this means those guys are still coming today. I need you. If you keep me safe, I'll make sure you get everything you lost, with a generous bonus besides."

"I don't want your money. I want my own."

Confusion washed over his face. "Money's money. What difference does it make where it comes from?"

"It makes a difference to *me*."

He leaned forward. "All the more reason for you to come. If they show up, they'll have your money and then some. You can have it all. As a thank-you gift."

"I only want what's mine. The rest belongs to the bank and the barbeque."

"And the Piggly Wiggly," one of the guys on the sofa added. "It got robbed last night."

Skeeter shot him a look that said *shut up* in no uncertain terms.

I blinked in shock. "The Piggly Wiggly got robbed? Then they probably got a buttload of money from all the Thanksgiving shopping."

"And they knew just when to rob it too," the other guy said. "Right before they made their night deposit."

Excitement washed through me. "They must have had an inside guy, just like they had Mr. Sullivan at the bank."

No one said anything.

I put my hand to my temple. How could I have been so stupid? "I saw the guy in the Batman mask at the Piggly Wiggly twice. He works there." I looked up at Skeeter. "Actually, I'm pretty sure he's the assistant manager." My excitement over finally piecing things together spurred me on. I turned to Bruce Wayne as I continued with my explanation. "This guy fired David because he took the ski masks home instead of throwing them away. The ones used in the robbery. He probably thought it couldn't be tied back to him if they were all gone. Anyone could have taken them out of the trash, but he used a Piggly Wiggly bag in the robbery."

All four men in the room watched me with a mixture of amusement and shock.

"Oh!" I exclaimed as something else hit me. "The guy, I think his name is Merrill, used to be David's friend until he moved away. He recently came back and is in dire need of money after a divorce. He needs the money and he's been out of town, so he wouldn't know that Big Bill's is off limits."

"She figured out in less than a minute what we couldn't figure out in three days," the guy who'd volunteered the Piggly Wiggly information said.

The look on Skeeter's face was murderous, but whether it was for his minion or Merrill, I couldn't be sure.

Oh, crappy doodles. What if I had inadvertently just gotten Merrill killed?

"You can have all the money we recover, Rose. If you help me stop them, you can keep every penny."

I could see how a lesser person would be tempted, but I'd be putting those other businesses that had been robbed in the exact same position I was in now. "I told you I don't want it. I want what's mine, and then I want you to give the rest back to the places that earned it."

Skeeter laughed. "Someone with integrity. That's cute."

I was so in over my head. Instead of figuring out how to get out of this, I needed to switch to self-preservation tactics. "I don't want anyone to know I'm helping you."

He looked amused. "I already claimed you, Rose. What difference does it make?"

"*Claimed me?* I'm not some discarded item to be picked up and owned, Skeeter Malcolm!"

"You're a valuable asset and I need to make sure you're protected."

"All you've done is taken a nobody who no one paid any mind to and painted a bull's-eye on her back. Everyone with half a brain is going to figure out that I'm special for some reason."

"Oh, Rose Gardner. I can assure you that people in my circles have taken notice of you, if for no other reason than that you bested Daniel Crocker *twice*. If you're worried about the secret of your ability getting out, put your fears to rest. It's in my own best interest to keep it quiet. People will assume I'm making a claim on you to protect my own personal safety—the saying keep your enemies close comes to mind. But as long as I'm top-dog in Henryetta, you'll be safe."

The full implication of his words settled in. "So it's in my best interest to make sure you not only remain alive but as top-dog." I sighed. I'd always known he was smart, but I hadn't planned on him being so calculating. He'd set me up, and I'd walked right into it.

"I'm happy you catch on quick."

"What do you want?"

"I want you to see my future again."

"That's it?"

"For now."

I groaned. "Fine. Let's do it. I have a turkey I need to get into the oven." Maeve was taking care of it, but no need for him to know that.

He laughed and walked around to the front of the desk. "You want to do this like last time?"

I nodded as he settled against the edge. He held his hand out to me. I took it and closed my eyes, surprised when a vision hit me within seconds. I was also surprised that it was the exact same vision I'd experienced two days earlier. That had never happened to me before.

"Someone's gonna kill you at the auction," I blurted out when it was done.

"*Again?*" he shouted, standing.

"You haven't done diddly-squat to find those guys!"

"I've been doing things."

"Your guy just said I gave you more information than you've dredged up in three days!" I shouted in disgust. "I'm beginning to wonder whether you're as good as everyone says you are."

"*What did you just say?*" he bellowed, hurting my ears from our close proximity.

Bruce Wayne, who had been standing quietly behind me, took a step forward. "She didn't mean anything by it, Skeeter."

I put my hands on my hips. "The hell I didn't. A man like you should have been able to dig up *something* by now!"

Skeeter's eyes narrowed. "I have information, but not enough. Not until you filled in some pieces."

"*Filled in some pieces?*" I shouted. "I just gift-wrapped it for you and handed it to you with a bow on top! If you expect me to help you, then you have to live up to your end of the bargain," I said, irritated as all get-out. I was tired of all the half-truths. "They have my money. Tell me what you know. If you know anything at all, that is," I snorted in contempt.

A low rumble came from Skeeter's chest and the other men in the room froze. "Fine," he growled, pushing away from the desk. "The word is they aren't your normal bidders."

"What does *that* mean?"

He looked up at me. "It means these guys have watched one too many episodes of *Breaking Bad*. They think they can be king if they have enough money to buy Crocker's business. They're nobodies with no experience. These amateurs don't know shit. Which your information supports. A loan officer and a grocery store manager." His face contorted in disgust.

"Seems to me they're more capable than you give them credit for," I threw back at him. "Or if they're as dumb as you insinuate, what does that say about *you?*"

Bruce Wayne's eyes bugged out of his head.

Skeeter's body tensed and his cold eyes landed on me. "Do you know how many people have talked to me that way and gotten away with it?"

The tension in the room was so thick, if someone lit a match, the entire place would have exploded.

I knew I should back down, grovel even, but I was good and ticked off. I'd had enough. This arrangement wasn't working out in my favor at all. I was the one supplying all the information and getting nothing in return. "I have no idea, but maybe it's time someone *did*."

Skeeter watched me for several long seconds, looking like he was trying to figure out the best way to dispose of my body, then he burst out laughing.

"What's so funny?" I asked, getting madder.

"You," he pushed out while catching his breath. "Good God. Where have you been all my life, Rose Gardner, and how did I not know about you before now?" He shook his head while regaining control. "Good thing I've claimed you before someone else discovered you. And I feel a hell of a lot better bringin' you with me to the auction now. Especially after all of this."

He may have been trying to appease me, but he was just making me madder. "You may have *claimed* me, Mr. Malcolm, but there's no way on God's green earth I'm walking into that auction with you. It's one thing to be marked, but it's another for me to be seen actively helping you. I'm living with the assistant DA, for heaven's sake. Even you can't be arrogant enough to believe someone won't use this against me. Not to mention the risk to you if someone decides you're with an informant."

"You're the only person who's seen these guys. I need you to come with me so you can point them out to Jed and Merv. They'll have your money on them to bid for Crocker's business. So if we stop them, you'll get *your* money returned today."

I groaned. "Damn you." I was good and stuck.

He laughed and glanced over at his goons. "So she *does* use cuss words."

"I can't be seen there, Skeeter. I *can't*."

"It's worth the risk."

"To you!" I shouted.

"She can wear a hat," Bruce Wayne said. "You know, one of those old-fashioned kind with a veil. It'll cover her face and no one will know it's her."

Skeeter held out his hands. "Well, there you go. You can wear a hat."

"I don't own a hat like that!" Only I knew someone who did. She had a spare bedroom closet full of them. "I have to make a call."

Skeeter stood, his eyes turning cold. "I don't think so."

"Will you calm down?" I asked, not caring that I sounded snotty. "I need to ask my friend to bring me a hat."

I spun around and stomped out into the hall, not waiting for permission before I dialed Neely Kate on my phone. "I have a bizarre request."

"Coming from you, that's sayin' something."

"You know that black hat you got last month? The one with the veil?"

"Oh. Yeah! I'm telling you, hats like that will be back in vogue before you know it. That's why I'm stockpilin' them. So I'll be ready."

"It's hard to see through that thing, right?"

"Yeah. Remember? I wore it to Bingo night with Granny and nearly broke my neck tripping because I couldn't see a doggone thing."

"I need to borrow it."

"Sure. I'll bring it to you tomorrow."

"No. I need it *now*." When she didn't answer, I continued. "I have to help Skeeter with this thing and I don't want people to know it's me."

"Where are you, Rose?" she asked, sounding worried. "And what are you doin' that you need a disguise?"

"I don't have much time, Neely Kate. Can you bring it to the pool hall like five minutes ago?"

She didn't even hesitate. "I'll call you when I'm almost there."

I hung up and walked back into the room. "Fine. I'll go, but I'm wearing a disguise."

Skeeter shot me a cocky grin. "Okay, but we're leaving in fifteen minutes."

Neely Kate called me twelve minutes later. "I'm pulling into the parking lot now."

I was already waiting for her by the door, so I ran outside as her car rolled up. "Are you sure about this, Rose?" she asked as she handed me a brown bag through the open window.

I nodded. There was no point in telling her I didn't have a choice.

She eyed me up and down. "My hat will *not* go with that outfit. I put my new black dress and a pair of heels in there too. Good thing we wear the same size."

"Thank you, Neely Kate."

She grabbed my hand and squeezed. "Just be careful, okay? And call me when you're done so I know that you're safe."

"I will."

The clock was ticking, so I ran inside and quickly changed, pleased with what I saw in the mirror. The reflection showed a woman in a figure-hugging black dress, a V cutting low in the front to reveal what little cleavage she had. I'd found a handful of bobby pins at the bottom of my purse, so I put my hair up into a French roll that would conceal its length and color. I couldn't see the lower half of me, but the hat alone would mask my identity. No one I knew would recognize me if they saw me dressed this way.

Skeeter banged on the door. "Come on! Let's go!"

I swung the door open and his mouth parted in surprise before he quickly recovered and offered me his arm, a grin spreading across his face. "This arrangement keeps getting better and better. I'm beginning to rethink that marriage proposal, but I value the family jewels too much to take the risk." He chuckled. "And after watching you this afternoon, Rose Gardner, I'm more than sure you'd be a jewel thief."

I narrowed my eyes, not that he could probably see through the veil. "If I help you and you renege on me, Skeeter Malcolm, you'll find out how true that statement is."

He and his men burst into laughter as we headed out the back door. Too bad for him, I hadn't meant it as a joke.

Chapter Twenty-Five

I mused about the absurdity of it all as I rode in the back of a black sedan on the way to the warehouse. Previously mousy, socially inept Rose Anne Gardner was dressed as a wanton woman and riding in the back of a car with Henryetta's current criminal mastermind. All while her assistant district attorney boyfriend waited for her to come home and her chief deputy sheriff ex-boyfriend searched for reasons to tie her to a criminal investigation.

This was straight out of a made-for-TV movie.

Skeeter sat next to me while Jed—the guy who'd told me about the Piggly Wiggly robbery—drove and the other guy, Merv, rode shotgun. Bruce Wayne was following us in his car after Skeeter had snarled that there wasn't room for him in the back. I didn't understand Skeeter's insistence until his hand landed on my knee when we were two minutes out of the parking lot.

I shoved his paw aside. "Hands off, Skeeter."

"Just admiring what I've claimed," he said with a shit-eating grin.

"You may have claimed my *gift*, not that it's yours to claim in the first place, but you most definitely *cannot* claim *me*. So keep your hands to yourself or the whole deal's off, chips fall where they may."

"You have to act like my girlfriend inside."

"I will do *no* such thing," I said firmly.

"Rose," he groaned. "If I bring you in there—"

"For all they know, I'm an investor you've brought with you."

"That makes me look weak." His voice was harsh.

"It will make you look strong. Like your reach stretches outside of this godforsaken town."

"Huh," he said, thinking it over. "That's actually a good idea."

"So it's agreed. *Hands off*. Everyone knows you like the ladies. The fact that you're not touching me will catch them off guard, which will in turn throw them off their game." I had no idea if they would or not, but it sounded good and Skeeter looked impressed.

We drove south of town, toward Pickle Junction. They'd been sympathetic to Crocker in this area, so geographically, it made sense. But it also meant I was on Joe's turf, not the Henryetta PD's. Whether or not that was a good thing remained to be seen.

Jed stopped the car in front of a large barn, like he was dropping us off at the red carpet at the Academy Awards. Skeeter opened his door and slid out, holding his hand out to me and pretending to be a gentleman. I nearly snorted, but I took his hand anyway, hoping my tight dress wouldn't slide up and flash my underwear to the world. Granted they were black lace and sexy, but those were for Mason's eyes only. Not the riff-raff of Fenton County.

When I was out, Skeeter shut the door and Jed drove off to park with the other twenty-some odd cars that were parked behind the barn, blocked from view of the road. Skeeter lifted his bent arm and bowed his head with a playful grin. "Shall we?"

Releasing a sigh, I let him escort me to the entrance. The barn's double doors were open, but the entrance was sectioned off with folding screens that blocked the view inside. A table with two men sat to the right, just inside the doors. One of the men had a metal box in front to him and the other had a leather ledger; together, they were signing people in and collecting money. Two more guys were patting down the entrants before they were allowed inside. Several men and a few women were in line ahead of us.

"You have to pay up front?" I whispered in surprise. "How do you know how much to pay?"

"It's a deposit. Five thousand dollars to show you're an actual contender, plus a thousand-dollar fee to take part. And the winner is expected to pay up the balance once they've won."

"What happens if you win and don't have the money with you?"

He waggled his eyebrows. "You don't want to know."

I swallowed, trying to stave off another fit of nausea. "What's to keep someone from stealing the money?"

"Them." He gestured to two men who were standing in the shadows behind the table, both carrying machine guns.

"Oh."

He chuckled and leaned close to my ear. "You're very curious. I think I've underestimated you again."

"*Again?*"

He didn't answer. Instead, the guy with the ledger waved to Skeeter, and we bypassed the ten people in front of us and approached the table. Skeeter handed them a wad of hundred-dollar bills. They counted them and placed them in the metal box, then wrote Skeeter's name in the ledger. The guy looked up at me. "And your guest's name?"

"That's none of your damn business." Skeeter's eyes narrowed and the burly man at the table actually looked intimidated.

"I'm sorry, Mr. Malcolm, but they're Bull's orders. To make sure no informants show up. Every person who enters has to have someone vouch for them."

"Do you think I'm stupid enough to bring in someone who would set us up?" His voice rose and his eyes widened. "Do I look like an idiot to you?"

"No, sir. But I still need a name."

Skeeter looked like he was about to reach over and snap the man's neck. Literally, not figuratively.

The guy hunched over his ledger. "How about Lady in Black?"

Skeeter's back straightened. "Good. And I have three more guests coming."

"Each person who's bidding is allowed only three guests, Mr. Malcolm. No exceptions," he said as he handed Skeeter an auction paddle.

Skeeter seemed less concerned with this rule. "Fine. Jed and Merv." He turned to me. "Your man will have to wait outside."

I was thankful he didn't name Bruce Wayne, and the more I thought about it, the more it seemed like a good idea. Bruce Wayne was walking across the parking lot toward us, although I didn't see his car anywhere. Where had he parked? I pulled out my phone and texted him.

You're waiting outside.

He looked at his phone and then up at me, shaking his head then texting: *Together or nothing*

He was throwing my words back at me.

We're still together, but it's better if you don't come in... People might link you to me and Skeeter. And they're patting people down and making them leave their weapons outside. If there's trouble it will be outside.

Besides, we don't have a choice, I added for good measure.

He watched me for several seconds.

Okay, he finally wrote.

One of the men started to pat Skeeter down and the other told me to turn around.

Skeeter pointed his finger at the guard next to me. "If you touch her in any way that would be considered inappropriate, I will personally cut off your fingers."

The man gulped. "Yes, sir."

I stared at Skeeter, my jaw dropping in shock. What was that all about?

It would have been easy for me to creatively smuggle in a weapon considering the quick appraisal I was given. The guy barely touched me before declaring that I was good to go.

Whether I wanted to be here or not, what I saw fascinated me. I'd mistaken it for a warehouse in my vision, but I realized now it was because the space was larger than a typical barn. There were more people here than I'd expected, but assuming everyone had brought their plus-threes, I estimated there were only about ten bidders. Skeeter moved to the back of the crowd, making it easier for me to see everyone.

"What's your number?" I asked, wondering how I could have been so stupid.

Skeeter held up his paddle. "Nine."

"I saw the number of the guy who outbid you. His number was fourteen. It may have changed from my vision—it happens—but everything else is as I remember it."

Skeeter snapped his fingers. "Merv, go find out who logged in as number fourteen and keep an eye out for that paddle."

Merv walked off and Jed stood next to us, his arms at his sides.

I shifted my weight and kept my eyes on the crowd. "I thought this was supposed to go down tomorrow."

"Let's just say the wrong ears were perking up," Skeeter said. "It was safer this way."

"You don't think I had anything to do with that, do you?"

He turned his gaze to the front of the room, his face expressionless. "You wouldn't be here if I thought you did. And you sure as hell wouldn't be at home cookin' that turkey you're so set on gettin' back to."

What the hell had I gotten myself involved in?

"Why did you threaten that guy who patted me down?" Skeeter had answered all my other questions and curiosity was getting the best of me.

He turned to face me and lifted his eyebrows. "Your suggestion was genius. Look at all these idiots with their bimbos. They're a dime a dozen. But you're dressed sexy as hell yet still classy and not only are you acting like the freaking Queen of England, but I'm treating you that way and making sure everyone else does too. They're dying to know who you are and it makes me look important. And it's all about appearances, R—" He grinned. "You need a name I can use in public."

I blinked, not that he could see me very well. "That's not necessary, seeing as how this is a one-time venture."

He grinned. "Lady in Black. Lady for short."

"That's the stupidest name on the planet."

"You got a better one?"

"No." I looked around, getting impatient. "When does this thing start and how long will it last? I've got a—"

"I know, you've got a dinner to get back to. But think bigger than your family dinner," he leaned close and whispered in my ear. "This here's poetic justice when you think about it. You ended the Crocker empire and you're here to see it reborn from the ashes."

I hadn't considered it that way, but I had to admit he was right.

Merv sauntered back, wearing a scowl, which I took to mean that he had bad news. "No dice, Skeeter. They say the list is confidential. They have a new page for each bidder so I couldn't even look over his shoulder."

Skeeter frowned as he surveyed the room. "Merv, take Lady here around the room to seek the guys out."

He wrinkled his nose. "Who?"

Skeeter shook his head. "This is Lady. That, and only that, is how you will address her. Got it?"

He nodded. "Yeah."

I didn't wait for Merv. My only purpose here was to find the robbers and point them out to Skeeter. He would have to handle the rest. At this point, I'd be happy to swing by the pool hall later tonight to collect my money. My first problem popped up when I didn't see any of them. My next problem occurred when my phone vibrated in my hand with a call. I glanced at the screen and cringed. Mason. He would expect me to answer it if I was at Neely Kate's. If I didn't, he'd start to get worried.

I had to move this show along.

I made another pass through the crowd and saw two of the guys from church—Lars Jenkins and Eric Davidson. Lars had a paddle with the number six on it and Eric was hanging back at the edge of the crowd, looking like he wanted to blend in with the shadows.

I made a beeline to Skeeter, Merv trailing behind me like an abandoned puppy.

I turned to face Skeeter and leaned in toward his ear. "Lars Jenkins is here. When I had my vision at church, he was one of the four men near me. He fits the profile and he's pretty rough. I wouldn't put it past him to kill someone to get what he wants." I took a breath. "Lars had a paddle, but the number on it is six, not fourteen. And he wasn't the bidder in my vision."

"And the other guy?"

"Eric Davidson. He works at the Burger Shack. He's hanging at the edge of the crowd. He doesn't even *have* a paddle."

"And the guy who was bidding in your vision?"

"He was the guy from the grocery store. The one who wore the Batman mask in my vision. I don't see him here. But it could have changed. I'm sure there are four of them. Maybe Lars is going to do the bidding instead."

His face hardened and he held out his hand to me. "Make yourself have another vision."

"Here? *Now?*"

"I need to know what I'm facing and your job is to help me do it."

I shook my head and grumbled. "This is a terrible idea. You know I'm going to blurt out what I see. And there's no guarantee I'll even see anything related to the auction. I could see you sittin' on the toilet for your morning constitutional."

"*Do it.*"

Sighing, I reached for his hand and closed my eyes. I was anxious and nothing happened for nearly half a minute.

"What's takin' so long? They're about to start."

"You are making me nervous," I hissed. "Apparently, I have to be relaxed to force one."

"Then calm down."

"You *calm down*. You're making it worse."

I could see Jed over Skeeter's shoulder, his eyes widened in shock. I supposed not many people spoke to Skeeter that way and got away with it. "Okay, I'm going to try again, but don't tense up."

"How the hell am I not supposed to tense up when there's a good chance someone is still gonna try to kill me?"

"Skeeter," I hissed. "Jed's got your back, quite literally. Now let me do this."

He took a deep breath, then looked at my veil.

I closed my eyes, forcing myself to settle down. The vision appeared within seconds, playing out identically to the first two.

"Someone's gonna kill you while you're bidding."

He jerked his hand from mine. "Again?" He shook his shoulders. "*Son of a bitch!*"

Several people turned around to stare at us.

"Skeeter," I said in a low voice. "Maybe you should leave and let Jed or Merv bid for you."

He shook his head, his face red with anger. "That's not how this works. I want the power. I have to bid. I told you that it's all about appearances."

"And you're making a fine impression throwing a fit like a five-year-old."

His eyes narrowed and I knew I'd gone too far. But he forced his shoulders down and took a deep breath. "You're right."

Jed's mouth dropped open like a trap door.

The auctioneer climbed a small stage and banged a gavel on the podium. "Attention. We're about to start the bidding. The rules are simple. We accept bids until there's a winner. The winner will come immediately to the stage and pay with cash. If he doesn't have enough, he forfeits and the second-highest bidder will be the winner." He cleared his throat. "The winner procures all territorial rights previously belonging to

Daniel Crocker along with his land and greenhouse. This does not include Weston's Garage. Are there any questions?"

No one spoke, but the room filled with nervous tension.

"If there are no questions, we'll let the bidding begin."

Skeeter leaned in close to me. "Do you see him yet?"

My stomach twisted with anxiety. "No." I glanced at my phone to check the time and saw Bruce Wayne had sent me a text.

Merrill, the PW asst manager is hanging around outside.

I gasped and Skeeter turned toward me. "What?"

Bids were being made, but they were still low, lingering around five thousand dollars.

"Bruce Wayne says the Piggly Wiggly assistant manager is hanging around outside."

Skeeter flicked his finger to Merv. "Take care of it."

I grabbed Skeeter's arm. "What's he going to do?"

Skeeter rolled his eyes. "Take care of it."

I couldn't shake the thought of what Merv might be doing to *take care of it*. What if I was wrong? "I'm not giving you another piece of information unless you promise me you won't kill any of the men I tell you about." I couldn't live with that on my conscience.

"It's a dog-eat-dog world, Lady. And if you step into this ring, you have to accept that. Besides, I already told you that you can't trust my word."

I moved close enough to him so that he could see my face. "Skeeter Malcolm, I won't help you with another blessed thing unless you promise me right now that you won't kill these men. And if you don't hold true to your word, I'll find your great-grandmother, Idabelle, and tell her you lied to me."

His mouth gaped. "*Grandma Idabelle*?"

"You may be a malcontent, but I hear your great-grandmother has quite the temper, so I bet she can still cut a switch to tan your hide. Didn't she start the family business with moonshine during Prohibition, back when all business deals were made with handshakes?" I knew the first part was true. I was counting on the second.

His face darkened. "Times have changed."

"Maybe so, but we need to be able to trust each other, and if I find out you haven't lived up to your word, I'll tell Idabelle."

"Fine," he growled, looking over his shoulder at Jed. "Call Merv and tell him the new rules."

Jed looked like Skeeter had told him go cuddle puppies.

Skeeter's gaze turned back to the podium. "You don't see anyone else who could be involved?"

This wasn't going well. "No."

"Keep searching. The bid is at twelve thousand, and we have until twenty-one or so."

He didn't have to tell me that, but it obviously made him feel better to say it.

"They might not all be here," I said. "It would only take two of them to do this. One to bid and the other…"

"To kill me," he finished. "You said there's two possible guys here. Jenkins and Davidson. If Jenkins is bidding, that leaves Davidson." He glanced at the place where we'd last seen Eric. "Where is he?"

Sure enough, he was gone. "I don't know." But the more I thought about Merrill and Mr. Sullivan being part of this mess, the more it made sense that Eric Davidson was likely involved too. He must have been the guy whose vision I'd experienced at church. That only left Mick and the man from the fertilizer plant unaccounted for.

"I sent Merv to take care of the grocery store manager, but I can't send Jed away." He sounded worried.

"Surely Big Bad Jed can take care of a scrawny thing like Eric Davidson."

"He can, but…"

"Twenty thousand!" the auctioneer shouted. "Do I hear twenty-one?"

No one responded.

"Do I hear twenty-one?" the auctioneer repeated. "Going once—"

Skeeter growled, then lifted his paddle and shouted, "Twenty-one."

"Do I hear twenty-two?"

"Twenty-two!" the last bidder called out.

"Twenty-three!" Skeeter shouted without being prompted.

"Do I hear twenty-four?"

No one answered.

Jed stood almost directly behind Skeeter, scanning the crowd.

"Do I hear twenty-four?" the auctioneer shouted. "Going once."

I tensed, my nerves pinging with anxiety. This was going differently than my vision, but I couldn't shake the feeling that something bad was about to happen.

"Going twice!"

I held my breath.

"Twenty-four!" a quiet voice rang out from a corner.

All eyes in the room turned toward it. Skeeter and I gasped simultaneously.

"He was in my vision at the fertilizer plant," I hissed.

"That's my goddamned dentist!" Skeeter growled. "You said it was the grocery store manager who was bidding!"

I shook my head, trying to figure out what was going on. "Merv must have stopped him. So your dentist took his place."

"Do I hear twenty-five?" the auctioneer called out.

"Twenty-*six!*" Skeeter hollered, lifting his paddle. Then he lowered his voice, shooting a glance back to Jed. "Do either of you see the Burger Shack guy?"

"No," we both said.

"Twenty-seven?" The man at the podium looked toward Skeeter's dentist.

"How much money do you think they got from the Piggly Wiggly?" Skeeter asked Jed.

His minion looked scared. "It's hard to say, Skeeter."

"Take a goddamned *guess!*"

"Maybe ten thousand or so."

"So they have at least thirty K," Skeeter muttered. "Where's the damn fast food guy? How hard can it be to find a scrawny kid?"

"I don't know," Jed answered.

Skeeter lifted his paddle. "*Thirty thousand*!"

A man was slowly inching his way toward us, hanging at the periphery of the crowd. I knew I'd seen him somewhere, but I couldn't place him.

Skeeter's dentist cast a glance in our direction, then stood straighter and called out with more confidence, "Thirty-one!"

"Thirty-three!" Skeeter rumbled out, flexing and unflexing his hand.

"Thirty-four!" the dentist practically shouted.

"Jed." I glanced back at him. "Over there. The man standing by the guy with the blue shirt. He's making a beeline toward us and I know him somehow."

"That's Doc Gentry," Jed said. "The big-animal vet."

"Oh, my word," I exhaled. In my vision, Skeeter had been killed with a syringe of something. Doc Gentry had access to powerful tranquilizers that could down a man in an instant. It made sense that he would smell of fertilizer.

He was about six feet away when someone bumped into the vet and he shouted, "Get out of my way."

I recognized his voice. "Dr. Gentry is Mick. The bank robber."

"My dentist. The vet. The damn grocery store manager. *What the hell is going on here?*" Skeeter hissed. "Stop him, Jed."

"You're the one who said they'd watched too many episodes of *Breaking Bad*."

"I didn't actually *believe* it!"

Jed took off after Mick. Mick saw him coming and turned around, heading for the exit.

"Going once," the auctioneer called out. "Going twice…"

Skeeter lifted his paddle, watching Jed grab the veterinarian. "Thirty-five!"

"Do I hear thirty-six?"

All eyes turned to the dentist, who was watching Jed lead Dr. Gentry to a back corner. His face paled.

"Thirty-six?" the auctioneer asked again. "Going once… going twice…"

Skeeter's body was so stiff I could have done laundry on it.

"Sold! To paddle nine!"

A big grin broke out on Skeeter's face right before I heard Joe's voice shouted through a speaker, "Fenton County Sheriff's Department! Everybody drop to your knees with your hands on your head."

Oh, shit.

Chapter Twenty-Six

I could *not* let Joe find me here.

Skeeter snarled like a wild animal. "Jed!"

Jed was already on his way back, Mick nowhere to be seen. Jed threw something on the ground behind him, and a huge plume of smoke billowed into the air. Shouts and screams filled the room.

Skeeter grabbed my arm. "Come on."

I couldn't see where he was leading me with all the smoke around us, and a small part of me considered staying put, but I figured Skeeter had as strong a sense of self-preservation as I had, maybe more. Sticking with him and Jed seemed the best plan.

Skeeter and Jed must have already planned out an escape route. Skeeter trapped my wrist in a firm grip, and it occurred to me that even if I *wanted* to stay behind, he wouldn't have any part of it. I had trouble keeping up in my four-inch heels, but after several seconds of running, Skeeter stopped. I slammed into him and he grabbed my shoulders to keep me upright.

I could barely make out Jed bending over and lifting something up. I wanted to ask questions, but I could hear a huge commotion at the other end of the barn, and I knew we needed stealth to get away.

Skeeter tugged me around Jed and dropped his grip. “Me first, then Lady,” he whispered before he turned around and disappeared down a pitch-black hole.

Jed had found a trapdoor.

When Skeeter was halfway down, Jed turned me around and guided me to the opening. I struggled to find my way in the darkness. My feet found wooden boards, but the pointy toes of my shoes didn’t cooperate, slowing my progress. I’d made it down several steps when I felt hands grab my waist and haul me the rest of the way. I squelched a shriek of surprise.

Skeeter set me on the ground and pushed me against a damp stone wall, his hand covering my mouth. “Shh!” It was pitch dark all around us.

Jed jumped down next to us and the darkness gave way when a flashlight beam flickered on. Moments later, Skeeter’s smiling face came into view. “Always have an escape plan, Lady.”

“My name is *Rose*,” I said angrily, but I was scared to death and anger was the easiest emotion to latch onto.

“Not anymore.”

Jed pushed past us and took the lead, Skeeter following behind. I took up the rear.

“How did this happen?” Skeeter asked.

“When I went after Doc Gentry, I passed a guy who said he thought he might have been tailed here” Jed answered. “I was about to warn you.”

Thank goodness he wasn’t blaming me.

We walked through the narrow stone tunnel for several minutes before we stopped at a dead end in front of another poorly constructed board ladder attached to the wall.

Jed climbed up first and lifted the trapdoor, looking around in all directions before declaring it safe.

Skeeter leered at me, gesturing toward the ladder. "Lady first."

It was a terrible pun, but I refused to acknowledge it. "There's no way on God's green earth I'm going up before you and letting you look up my dress."

He laughed. "I wouldn't have thought of it if you hadn't brought it up."

"Liar," I said, taking a step back and crossing my arms. "I know your reputation."

His grin fell. "In all seriousness, Rose, you're going up first. Now."

There was a time and place for picking your battles and now didn't seem to be the time *or* place, especially since the sheriff's department might be hot on our heels.

"Fine, but keep your gaze averted."

Skeeter laughed and turned to face the side wall. "I'm giving you five seconds before I look up."

He actually started counting "One Mississippi, two Mississippi," while I scrambled up the makeshift ladder. He reached five by the time Jed reached under my armpits and lifted me out, setting me gently on the ground.

"Where are we?" I asked, looking around and seeing nothing but trees. I suddenly realized what a precarious position I was in—alone in the woods with two men of very questionable character. But taking advantage of me seemed to be the very last thing on their minds as they coordinated with one of their buddies to pick us up.

"What about Merv?" I asked, though the person I was really worried about was Bruce Wayne.

Skeeter shrugged. "I'm sure Merv is fine. He knew the getaway plans."

When I took my phone out to call Bruce Wayne, I saw that he'd already tried to call *me*. He'd also sent multiple warning texts after seeing the sheriff's cars pull into the lot behind the barn. The rest of his messages asked where I was and if I was okay.

He answered on the first ring. "Rose? Are you safe?"

"I'm fine. I got out with Skeeter and Jed. I take it you are too since you're answering your phone."

"I'm fine. I parked down the road on a county road and I heard 'em comin'. I hid in the woods, but was worried about you. Joe's there."

"Yeah, I heard his voice."

"And Mason's there too. I saw him getting out of his car as I was sneakin' away."

"Mason?" My heart raced. "Is he okay? Did the people inside put up a fight?"

"I don't know, Rose. I'm sure he's fine."

"Okay," I said, my voice shaky. "You go on home, Bruce Wayne. I'll have Skeeter take me back to my car and I'll see you at five for Thanksgiving dinner."

"Okay." I could tell he didn't like my plan, but there wasn't a better alternative.

We started hiking through the woods, which proved a challenge with Neely Kate's heels sinking in to the soft ground. Skeeter reached over to help me, but I shrugged out of his reach, which brought on a new round of chuckles.

"How can you act so nonchalant?" I asked, just barely starting to calm down from all the excitement. "We were almost arrested!"

"This ain't our first rodeo," Jed laughed.

I didn't even want to consider all the other misadventures those two had experienced together.

A car was waiting for us when we reached the road. Skeeter opened the back door and waited for me to climb in before sliding in next to me. Jed rode shotgun. The men discussed how the sheriff's office could have figured out where to find the location.

"Bull had the perfect code," Skeeter mused. "The way he put together that numbered chart to communicate the place, time, and date was brilliant. I don't know how anyone not in the know could have made heads or tails of it."

I bit my tongue. Lord only knew what Skeeter would do if he found out I'd played a role in the bust, even if it was inadvertent. I kept quiet the entire ride to the parking lot of the pool hall. As soon as we parked, I got out of the car without saying a word.

"Rose," Skeeter called after me.

I stopped next to my truck door.

"I owe you." He walked toward me, stopping several feet away. "And I don't say that to many people."

"That very well may be, Skeeter Malcolm, but you didn't follow through on your end of the deal," I said, my voice firm, but most of my fight was gone. I'd resigned myself to the demise of the nursery. I had put everything on the line…and failed. "You're still alive and now king of Fenton County, but I'm still out my nine thousand dollars and losing my business tomorrow."

He started to say something, but I ignored him and got in the truck, pulling out of the parking lot as he watched me in silence.

I drove home, worried how I'd explain wearing Neely Kate's black dress when I got home. But Mason's car was still missing from the front of the house. I slipped in through the front door, thankful when I heard Maeve in the kitchen talking to Muffy, which explained why my dog wasn't barking at my entrance. I was halfway up the stairs when a tread squeaked, eliciting a round of barking from Muffy.

"Rose?" Mason's mother called out. "Is that you?"

"Yeah," I hurried up the rest of the stairs and called down. "I got flour all over me at Neely Kate's and I have to change clothes."

"Okay."

I groaned as I realized my original clothes were still at the pool hall. I stripped off the black dress and put on a sweater and skirt. As I stuffed Neely Kate's things in the back of my closet, I reflected on how I'd gotten here. I may have lost my business, but I reminded myself of the gratitude I felt for the people in my life. Mason, my friends. Mason's mother, and Violet, despite all her meanness lately. I was even grateful for Joe and the part he'd played in helping me become the woman I was today. I could replace my business, but I couldn't replace a single one of the people I cared about. I rested my hand on my stomach. If I found out I was having a baby, I'd accept it with a heart full of love and acceptance.

It was time to stop delaying the inevitable. I was ready to know the truth.

I found my cell phone and called Mason.

"Rose," he answered, sounding concerned. "I tried to reach you earlier. I was worried, especially after I called Mom and she said you were at Neely Kate's and Neely Kate didn't answer her phone either."

"I was tied up. When will you be home?"

He sighed. "Soon, I think. I got called to go on a big raid, but there's not much more I can do here."

My stomach tensed. What would he do if he found out I'd been inside that barn? "Hurry home because there's something we have to do together."

His voice went husky and I could hear the hint of a grin behind it. "Does it involve a bed? I'm not sure how we'll explain it to my mother, but we can come up with something creative."

I laughed. "No. It's not that. It involves peeing on a stick."

He was silent for a moment. "You're ready to take the test?"

"Yeah. I've been waiting for the perfect moment, because if you and I are having a baby together, I don't want there to be one ounce of sadness when we find out. But I realize there *is* no perfect moment. And we'll love the baby, surprise or not."

"Sometimes the best things in life are surprises, Rose."

"I know," I said, biting back tears. "Look how I found you."

"I'll be home as soon as I can."

"I know. I love you."

"I love you too."

I went downstairs to help Mason's mother in the kitchen, but she seemed to have everything under control.

"I'm so sorry I wasn't here to help. I feel terrible."

She waved off my concerns. "I loved doing it." Her voice cracked. "I miss cooking for Mason, Savannah, and Van. I'm just grateful to be here helping."

I pulled her into a hug. "I'm so glad you're here too."

She stepped away, swiping at her eyes. "The potatoes are boiling. The green beans are simmering. The sweet potatoes, dressing, and turkey are all in the oven," she said, surveying the kitchen. "And we'll start the gravy after we pull the turkey out. Then we'll have what Violet brings, of course."

I sighed. "If she comes."

Maeve winked. "She will."

We were setting the table an hour later when Mason came home. He found us in the dining room and pulled me into a hug, kissing me like he hadn't seen me for days instead of a few hours.

"Mason!" I protested through my laughter. "Your mother is watching."

"Don't mind me," she sing-songed as she disappeared into the dining room. "I've got everything under control if you two need a few minutes alone."

Mason smiled down at me and whispered, "Let's go find out if we're having a baby."

I grabbed my purse and we took it upstairs. I pulled the multiple boxes out and laid them on the bed, trying to decide which one to use.

"Whoa," Mason said, lifting his hands.

"Neely Kate got them for me. She said she got multiple tests… just in case."

"Just in case what?"

I shrugged. "I have no idea. But I also have no idea which one to use."

Mason grabbed a box with a name brand and handed it to me. "Try this one."

I made him sit on the bed while I peed on the stick. After I put the test on the comforter and set the timer on my phone for two minutes, we sat on the bed holding hands and looked at the nursery through the sheers.

"If we're having a baby," I whispered, "do you want a boy or a girl?"

"I honestly don't care, Rose. As long you and the baby are happy and healthy, that's all I care about." He took my hand in his and cradled it gently. "How about you?"

I looked up at him and gave him a soft smile. "A girl, I think. So I can give her all the love I always wanted when I was little." A tear slipped down my cheek. "What if I'm a terrible mother, Mason? What if my little girl or boy feels unloved?"

He shook his head, fierce determination in his eyes. "That will never happen, Rose. How could it?"

"I don't know."

"Rose, you bless everyone you meet with love. I can only imagine the love you'll give our children."

He kissed me gently, then pulled back to look in my eyes. The love shining through his gaze was almost overwhelming.

"Your mother thinks we're up here having sex."

His grin was wicked. "Maybe we should after we find out."

"Let's wait and see what it says first."

As if on cue, the timer dinged and my hands started to shake.

"I love you, Rose Gardner, no matter what that test shows."

I gave him a quick kiss and picked up the stick off the bed and turned it over.

"One pink line," Mason said. "What does that mean?"

"It means there's no baby," I said quietly.

He wrapped an arm around my shoulders and pulled me snug against him. "How do you feel about that?"

I looked up at him. "The timing would have been terrible. But while part of me is relieved, there's a part of me that wants a baby with you and is kind of disappointed. Isn't that stupid?"

"No," he said, kissing me gently. "That's exactly how I feel."

"So what do we do?" I asked.

He grabbed my hand and held it between both of his. "We haven't even talked about marriage and I'm not sure either of us are ready for that yet. So having a baby right now would kind of feel like putting the cart before the horse." He chuckled. "Call me old-fashioned."

"I agree."

"Whew." He looked relieved. "But I do want to marry you someday, Rose. I want to stand at the altar while you walk down the aisle in a beautiful dress. I'll take you to Italy on our honeymoon, and then we'll come home and make love every chance we get until you're pregnant." He smiled. "And we'll fill our house with children—as many as you want—and I will be the most blessed man who ever lived. All because you're mine."

Tears slid down my cheeks. "I want that too."

He kissed me and wiped my cheeks. "And we'll have it all when we're ready, because I'm not going anywhere, Rose. I'm yours."

Then we didn't go downstairs for quite some time.

Chapter Twenty-Seven

We went back downstairs shortly before our guests started to arrive. Maeve had pulled the turkey out of the oven and started the gravy. She was crouched down, feeding scraps of turkey to Muffy, who had made a new best friend.

She smiled when Mason and I entered the kitchen and my cheeks burned with embarrassment.

"We had something we had to take care of." Mason wrapped an arm around my waist and pulled me close. "What can we do to help, Mom?"

She beamed at us. "I've got it under control."

The doorbell rang and I ran to get it. Bruce Wayne, David, Carla, and Jonah all arrived within a matter of minutes, but Violet and the kids still hadn't shown up by five-twenty when we were ready to sit down for dinner.

I had mixed feelings about her absence. I dreaded seeing her, but I was more upset about her not coming than I'd expected.

Maeve and I were setting the last of the food on the table when the front door burst open and Ashley and Mikey ran through, Ashley carrying a pie.

"Aunt Rose!" they called out. I ran into the living room and dropped to my knees, scooping them into a hug as Maeve retrieved the dessert.

I looked up over Ashley's shoulder at Violet's nervous face.

"I wasn't sure if we were still invited," she said, juggling two dishes in her arms.

Maeve hurried into the room and grabbed one of the containers from Violet and pulled her into a side hug. "Rose is very happy you're here, aren't you, Rose?"

Nodding, I stood. "It wouldn't be the same without you." I wanted to ask her about the Christmas trees on the nursery lot, but now didn't seem like the right time.

Violet was more reserved than usual for most of the evening, but everyone sat around the table eating and laughing. Mason and I exchanged glances several times throughout the dinner, reminding me once again of how blessed I was.

Several hours later everyone left and Mason carried a sleeping Mikey out to Violet's car, Ashley and Muffy in tow. Violet stopped in the front door, hesitating.

"Rose, we need to talk."

I took a deep breath. "I agree."

"Can you come by the shop tomorrow? Say around eleven?"

Now would be a good time to ask about the trees, but I wasn't up for a fight. One night wouldn't make a difference. "Sure. I'll drop by. We need to figure out what to do about the mess anyway."

She gave me a long look, deep sadness in her eyes. "Thanks for letting us come for dinner. If the roles had been reversed, I'm not sure I would have welcomed you."

I bit my lip. "I know."

"And you still let us come?"

"We're sisters, Violet. Till death do us part. The last few months can't change that." I paused. "But we're not the same."

"I know. Can we talk about this tomorrow?"

I nodded. "Yeah."

I was watching her walk to her car when I noticed an envelope sitting in the wicker chair on the porch, labeled with my name. I picked it up and opened the seal, gasping when I saw the bills inside. I pulled out a small piece of paper and read the note.

Rose,

Only with you am I a man of my word,

S

"What's that?" Mason asked from behind me.

I crumpled the note in my hand and showed him the envelope. "My money seems to have just dropped out of the sky."

Mason gave me a long look. "Imagine that."

Imagine that indeed.

***

The next morning, I called Neely Kate on the way to the nursery.

"Uh…" I hedged.

"And what do you know about the Lady in Black?"

"*What?*" I asked in a panic. "Where did you hear about that?"

"It doesn't matter who told me, Rose. What matters is how it all happened."

I groaned. "It's a long story."

"I expect full details."

"Okay, soon, but I have to tell you something else first."

"Okay…"

"I took the pregnancy test. I'm not pregnant."

"Are you sure? It might be too soon to tell."

"I'm sure. Once we found out I wasn't pregnant, Mason hounded me into calling the doctor to find out why I haven't been feeling well. When they said they couldn't fit me in until next week, he grabbed the phone and convinced them to see me sooner."

She laughed. "He can be pretty persuasive when he wants to be. What did the doctor say?"

"It's a combination of stress and my hormones trying to get back to normal. I'm fine."

"Well, thank goodness for that, although I confess it would have been fun to have babies together."

I grinned. "Well, maybe with the next one. But wait a couple of years, okay?"

"Deal."

I was pulling up to the nursery parking lot and my stomach was in a knot when I saw two cars there—Violet's and a sheriff's car. "Neely Kate, I have to go. Violet asked me to meet her at the nursery at eleven. I'm pulling up now and I think Joe is here."

"Uh-oh," she said. "Maybe I should take off and come down there."

"No, don't do that. I'm fine, but I'll call you after I find out what this is all about."

"Good luck."

There was no sign of Violet and Joe outside, but a teenage boy was standing next to the Christmas trees. He was wearing a black apron bearing our logo.

What in the world?

"Rose," Violet called from the doorway. "In here."

I walked through the hole that used to be the front door and I suddenly wondered how Violet had gotten word out that the open house was cancelled. But then again, the way the town liked to gossip, everyone probably knew within twenty-four hours that we'd been vandalized. The place was still trashed but a small area had been cleared and three folding chairs were set up in a circle. Joe stood behind two of them, wearing his uniform.

I took a step back. "What's going on? Are you here in an official capacity, Joe?"

"No." He shook his head. "I'm on break to be here. Violet and I have something to talk to you about. Why don't you come sit down?"

I didn't want to sit with them, but I was so nervous, and I was afraid my legs would give out. I took a seat while they sat in the opposite chairs. Violet was pale and looked like she was about to throw up.

"Why is there a kid out there wearing our logo? And how did we pay for the trees it looks like he's selling?" I asked.

"That's what I need to talk to you about." Violet took a deep breath. "I figured out how to solve our problems."

"You and me?" I asked. "Or our business problems?"

She swallowed. "Business."

I nodded and my gaze swung from one of them to the other. "Okay, but first I need to tell you that I got our nine thousand dollars back. As soon as we're done here, I'm going to the bank to catch up on our loan payments. At least we don't need to worry about that anymore."

Joe's eyes hardened. "How did you get your money back?"

I shrugged. "I don't know. It just showed up on my front porch last night."

"And does this have anything to do with the stolen money being returned to Big Bill's, the Piggly Wiggly, and the bank this morning?"

"It was?" I was stunned. Skeeter was full of surprises.

Violet looked even more nervous. "We don't need it now."

I gave my head a shake. "How can we not need it now? Did they already foreclose?"

"No. I paid off the loan entirely on Wednesday."

"But...how..."

Then I knew. And I knew why Joe was there.

My anger surged. "*How could you?*"

"I was trying to help, Rose," Violet pleaded. "You have to believe me."

I tried to catch my breath. "Why didn't you discuss it with me first? This involves me too, Violet!"

"Rose," Joe said, leaning over his legs and clasping his hands together. "It's okay. Violet was trying to save your business, and I'm not sure why you didn't come to me in the first place. You had to know I'd want to help."

I shook my head. How had this happened? "I didn't come to you because we're not together, Joe! I'm with Mason now! I don't want you to have a stake in our business!

"Damn it," Joe said, sitting up straighter. "I put as much effort into getting this place up and running as you both did. You have to know I want it to succeed. Why would you lose your business over your stubborn *pride?*"

Violet reached a hand toward me, then stopped. "Rose, it's not as bad as it seems."

"No, it's worse!" I stood. "I quit."

"What do you mean you quit?" she asked, jumping out of her seat. "You can't quit. You own this place!"

"Apparently, not anymore!" I tried to get control of my anger. "You can't do this. I'm not even sure it's legal."

"Rose." Joe stood and moved closer to me. "Just look at this calmly and rationally. Your business was in trouble and I had the money to help. Nothing illegal happened. I'm the chief deputy sheriff for God's sake."

"When are you going to get it through your head that we're *done?*" I asked. "I don't want to be with you, Joe McAllister!"

"Well, I should hope not," a woman drawled behind me in a genteel Southern accent. "Especially if you don't even know his name."

Joe and Violet stared at the doorway, horror painted on their faces. Even before I turned around to see a beautiful redheaded woman in the doorway, I knew who was standing behind me.

Hilary.

"What the hell are you doing here, Hilary?" Joe barked, walking halfway across the room toward her.

"Joe," she pouted. "Is that any way to treat me after you haven't seen me for a couple of weeks?"

Joe cast a glance toward me and I could see the wheels turning in his head. He'd spent the last week trying to convince me they were done, yet here she was.

"I told you we're done, Hilary," Joe said, gruffly. "Now will you do us all a favor and just leave? You're not wanted here."

She took several steps into the room and gave him a seductive smile. "I think you might change your mind after I tell you our good news."

He shook his head in confusion. "What are you talking about?"

"Joe, darling." She closed the distance and placed her well-manicured hand on his chest. "Congratulations are in order. You're going to be a daddy."

I sank down in my chair in shock.

Oh, crappy doodles.

***

Thirty-Three and a Half Shenanigans
coming November 4, 2014

About the Author

New York Times* and *USA Today* bestselling author Denise Grover Swank was born in Kansas City, Missouri and lived in the area until she was nineteen. Then she became a nomadic gypsy, living in five cities, four states and ten houses over the course of ten years before she moved back to her roots. She speaks English and smattering of Spanish and Chinese which she learned through an intensive Nick Jr. immersion period. Her hobbies include witty Facebook comments (in own her mind) and dancing in her kitchen with her children. (Quite badly if you believe her offspring.) Hidden talents include the gift of justification and the ability to drink massive amounts of caffeine and still fall asleep within two minutes. Her lack of the sense of smell allows her to perform many unspeakable tasks. She has six children and hasn't lost her sanity. Or so she leads you to believe.

You can find out more about Denise and her other books at:
www.denisegroverswank.com
or email her at denisegroverswank@gmail.com